TRACE AND
ELIMINATE

A Novel from the Inspector Stark Series

KEITH WRIGHT

Book 2
Copyright @Keith Wright 2019 – revised edition

Keith Wright

For Jackie

Contains realistic and graphic descriptions of death
and includes issues which some readers
may find upsetting or offensive.
The language and terminology is of the period and may be offensive to some.
It is intended for adults only

1

James was smiling as he leaned out of the car window to wave to his wife and child. Sarah stood on the porch, clutching their little girl's hand, and waving back enthusiastically. 'Bye, James. Love you!'

'Love you too.' He began to close the electric window, diminishing the sound of Sarah's request: 'Bring some milk back if you can.' He gave a thumbs up sign, indicating he had heard, although it was a pain in the arse.

He wasn't to know this was the last goodbye. That he would never again feel the softness of her cheek against his, or the squeeze of little Katy's all-giving hug. Maybe he should have known. If he had been more aware, and had his wits about him, he might have seen, but he wasn't.

He glanced over towards the door, as he reversed the car, and saw them troop back inside, into the warmth.

Sarah's good-bye, although distant, had alerted the hidden figure into a state of taut expectation, stomach churning, and mouth dry. There was no going back now.

The route was a familiar one to James, or Jim, as he was sometimes called, or if you were his parent's; Jack. His Mum and Dad had been the only ones who ever called him Jack. When Sarah first heard of this anomaly, she used her skewed logic: 'If they wanted to call you Jack, they should have called you John'.

That was why he loved her.

James drove the same roads every weekday, from home to the office. Despite the bitter chill, and depressingly overcast sky of an Autumn morning, the inside of the car was beginning to cosy-up, and his tape of Pavarotti warmed the cockles of his heart. He liked a good old blast of a tenor or two, to get the blood pumping. His blood would be pumping soon enough, but he did not know that, because he didn't pay attention.

Although it was eight o'clock, the roads were not as bad as they could be; and James felt he was making good progress. He lowered his foot on the accelerator and let the music flood over him, his deep, slightly off-key voice endeavouring to match the great singer's. Things were looking up. He considered himself to be one of the 'new breed' of solicitors. At Johnson & Brown he was the blue-eyed boy, and at twenty-five the future was looking distinctly rosy.

He slowed down, as a solitary cyclist pushed his bike across the road, who waved and smiled in acknowledgement, and James reciprocated. All the efforts he had made, and the years of College then University, and the law exam; all that drudgery were paying off. James had it all. A nice house, a decent car, and a beautiful family. Katy was three, the best age, and that innocence, and dependency was what he thrived on. What else was there? Maybe two holidays a year instead of the one, but he was working on that. He needed a decent case; maybe a high-profile murder case to get his teeth into. He just needed to bide his time and one would come his way.

He slowed down as he approached the rail-track junction, sensing danger, there was something of a commotion. Some guy was farting around in the road, surely, he can't be drunk at this time of the bloody morning. He indicated to turn left, once he had figured out what this idiot was going to do. Was he waving him down? No. All was well. The crazy guy had decided to stagger off back onto the pavement and away down the side street. Maybe it was drugs, or something? His car was almost at a stand-still. James reached to turn the music down a little.

His head smashed into the side-window with the force of the blow to his neck. The large carving-knife slid easily through his carotid artery, severing both his trachea and oesophagus and chipping the glass of the window as it exited the other side. The killer held the force of the blow and twisted the knife savagely, grunting with the exertion. Steel could be heard grinding on bone and gristle. The bastard withdrew the knife in preparation for a second blow, but it quickly became apparent that another would not be necessary. James slumped in his seat and instinctively raised his hand to his throat, but it hovered in mid-air, his dying brain not really fathoming what was happening. His body worked hard to pump blood and adrenaline to the source of the trouble, but this was a bad move, as it pumped out of his artery at an alarming rate, like a geyser in Yellowstone park. With each heartbeat, the spray of blood diminished until it became a mere trickle. The killer had waited, and watched, with growing excitement, as James' demise played out, before opening the rear nearside door and fleeing, only a second before the car, still rolling, slewed into a telegraph pole. The impact caused little Katy's daddy, to flop around like her favourite ragdoll. A whistling sound was emitted from the gaping hole in his neck, which was making his mouth redundant, desperately trying to suck in air, on its behalf, and failing. The whistling subsided like a boiled kettle, and the trickle of blood halted as Pavarotti's final tremulous diminuendo top C faded. 'Vincero!'

*

For several minutes the car remained undiscovered, the cassette player, having moved on to the next track, delivering a strident operatic melody.

Outside the vehicle, and a full thirty yards away, a repetitive squeaking could be heard. A young newspaper delivery boy cycled towards death. His heavily laden bag tilted him slightly, and his front wheel was weaving as he puffed and panted up the slight incline and over the brow towards the static vehicle.

He was still half asleep, as he faced the challenge of delivering the morning newspapers to the neighbourhood to get his two pounds and twenty pence. He cycled past the car, his mind miles away, until it slowly dawned on him. He applied the brake. 'That's weird.' He got off the cycle and looked back towards the vehicle. It was at an angle and appeared to have hit the telegraph pole, it wasn't on fire or anything, so it was probably okay. He could see someone inside, though; the bloke had a funny look on his face, but he couldn't see properly, with the light shearing across the windscreen. Instinctively he felt that something wasn't right. The paper boy was a boy scout and he had sworn an oath to 'do his best' and 'to help others.' In his innocent mind, he felt he should investigate, and started to tentatively walk towards the car, wheeling his bicycle. As he reached the driver's side window, his eyes met those of James Deely, grotesquely frozen in death. Unseeing eyes, glazed and soulless seared into the memory of the young boy, imprinting the image onto his brain as surely as a branding iron on a cow's backside. He stared at the face trying to comprehend what the image was. He took in the sightless eyes, the copious amounts of blood, the displaced swollen tongue, and the gaping hole in the side of his neck. The boy-scout made an assessment. 'Fuck me!'

*

Detective Inspector David Stark sat in the heavy traffic. His dark hair had slivers of grey at the temple, and his handsome tanned face frowned at the delay. The frustrating thing was that he could see the side road ahead of him, which he knew to be a short-cut, to avoid whatever the hell was holding them up miles ahead. 'I bet it's an accident.' He muttered to himself.

David was currently second in command at Nottingham Divisional CID. It was only a temporary role: 'Acting Detective Chief Inspector', whilst Bill Rawson was away on yet another course at Bramshill Police Training College. Bill was only passing through the CID on his route to higher things, Stark was there to stay. He wasn't entirely sure he wanted promotion anyway, as it would take him further away from doing the job he loved.

Still, the constant flow of traffic coming the other way blocked his opportunity to break away from the queue. He wanted a quiet day today, he had a ton of paperwork to do, which he had been putting off for far too long.

'Finally!'

He swung the black Cavalier to the left and travelled along for fifty yards on the wrong side of the road, before he turned up the side road towards freedom and Nottingham Police Station.

Nobby Clarke greeted him at the nick. 'Morning, boss.' Nobby had been Stark's Detective Sergeant for several years. He was a tough, unyielding character, if not the brightest star in the sky.

'Morning Nobby, all quiet?'

Nobby followed Stark into his office, trying to contain the cumbersome array of lever-arch files and prevent them falling from his arms. It was Nobby's job to prepare the briefing for Stark each morning. 'Yes, I've got the briefing pads.' They included, the night crime report, missing from homes of note, newly reported crime, teleprinter messages from other forces; that sort of thing. Nobby placed them on the floor in a heap. 'Oh, I nearly forgot, there's a report of a fatal RTA, car v lamppost, some kid found it on Papplewick Lane, it's only just come in. Traffic are attending apparently.'

'That's nothing to do with us, let Traffic deal with it. That's probably what held me up this morning. Inconsiderate bastard, having the gall to die on my route in to work. What's wrong with people, Nobby?'

'I don't know boss, it's all self, self, self.' He laughed. 'I thought you were a bit later than normal.'

'Is that why I can't see a cup of coffee on my desk?'

'Sir, with respect, bollocks!'

Nobby got up to put the kettle on, chuntering to himself.

*

Police Constable Paul Wood was the traffic officer attending the report of a fatal 'RTA'; Road Traffic Accident. He was experienced, and well qualified to deal with 'fatal's. Not all traffic officers were. He had seen plenty of them in his time; the horror, the gore, and the never ending, and usually, avoidable deaths of men, women and, the worst of all abominations, children.

His eyes were wide and alert as he skilfully raced through the peak-hour traffic; sirens blazing and lights flashing. On hearing the siren, some drivers would immediately slam on their brakes, instead of easing into the side. 'Get out of the fucking way, you stupid old fart!' Paul cursed, as the umpteenth well-intentioned driver, stopped in the middle of the bleeding road as he appeared behind them at great speed. It was with relief that he hit the country roads leading towards Papplewick, and the scene of the reported accident. As he approached the junction, he saw an elderly man waving both arms in the air to attract his attention. He was relieved to see that an ambulance was already at the scene, but the relative inactivity of the paramedics had daunting implications. Paul quickly took stock of the situation and parked his car in the most suitable spot to warn oncoming vehicles. Safety first. He had to make do with a 'Police Accident' sign on the other side of the road.

'Morning.' Paul greeted the paramedic.

'Morning, Paul, all right?'

'I'm good, thanks, you?'

'All right, thanks, there's nothing for us on this one, Paul, I'm afraid, he's been dead a while, by the looks of it – blood loss.'

'Okay,'

'We've got another shout, Paul, are we okay to shoot off?'

'Erm, okay, sure, I suppose you better had, just send me the report through the post, will you?'

'Will do – enjoy.' He slapped the officer on the back.

'Thanks.'

This meant that the ambulance wouldn't remove the body, and it was another thing Paul needed to arrange. Dead bodies can begat dead bodies, because of drivers passing by, 'rubber necking', and veering into the vehicle in front, or worse one that is oncoming. Paul walked up to the blue Volvo and looked through the window of the driver's door. The sight briefly took him aback. Pavarotti singing 'funiculi funicula, funiculi funiculaaa!' was something of a distraction. He noticed the seatbelt holding the body in place as he turned off the engine, which was still running, and it thankfully silenced the din. Despite Paul's lack of medical qualifications, it was fair to say the driver was dead. He checked to make sure there was no-one else in the vehicle, in the foot-well, at the back, and as he could see the rear nearside door was wide open, that no passengers had been thrown out into undergrowth. Nothing. 'Looks like he was on his tod'. He assumed the door was ajar because the Paramedics had done a similar check. Paul opened the front passenger door, to clamber on the seat and have a proper close-up look at the body. He had to settle for leaning in as the blood was all over the seat. The vast amount of the substance was obvious, but there were no easily recognisable trauma injuries to his head, chest or lower legs that he could see. These were the usual points of injury. Paul could see the huge wound to the side of the neck, but what had caused it? He looked at the front of the vehicle and the telegraph pole. Hardly a scratch was evident. He started to get a strange feeling rise in his belly. He returned to look back inside the vehicle. This didn't make sense. The old man tapped Paul on the shoulder.

'I can see you're busy, officer, but do you need me to wait, or can I go home?'

'Did you find them, or did you witness the accident?'

'Neither, I rang in to report it. I reckon the young paperboy might have seen it. He was the one who told us, like. I only live across the road, and he ran over and knocked on our door. He was worried about finishing his round, so he's buggered off.'

'What is your name please?'

'Jenkins, Derek. We live at twenty-five, it's the one with the red door and azaleas.'

Paul had no idea what azalea's looked like, but he could cope with a red door. 'I'll come over later and get a statement from you. What shop does the boy work at? Did he say?'

'It's the one at the top of Victoria Street.'

'Excellent. Sorry you had to see all this.'

'Don't worry about that, lad, I worked down the pit for thirty years, I've seen worse.'

Paul smiled. 'Thanks again, I will see you shortly.'

Two other cars had stopped, either out of curiosity or public-spiritedness but none of the occupants had witnessed anything. There had simply been no-one about when it happened.

Paul again returned to the car and leaned inside to see what the dead man could have possibly snagged his neck on. Nothing.

There was no way that the 'accident' could have caused the death of the man. So, what had? Could it be some sort of an embolism? Surely not. He wished the paramedic was still there. He shouldn't have let them rush off like that. He pushed his traffic officers peaked cap on to the back of his head and scratched his head. He yet again peered at the wound. It looked as though he had been stabbed. He wanted to be as certain as he could, because he did not want to call the cavalry and end up looking like a chump.

Paul returned to his traffic car and displaced the black radio phone. He radioed through to the control room at Nottingham Headquarters, known on the radio as 'NH'.

'Alpha Quebec Two Five to NH.'

'Go ahead, NH over.'

'I am ten-twelve at the scene of the RTA on Papplewick Lane. I can confirm it is a one oblique one, but can you request CID to attend as it looks suspicious.'

There was a pause. 'Confirm request CID to attend?'

'Confirmed.'

'Ten Four, stand-by.'

His radio message would send shock waves throughout the force both now and for the weeks ahead.

*

Stark tapped his fingers irritably on the steering wheel. The stitching, abrasive to his fingertips. The queue of traffic spanned a good 400 yards in front of him, as the road curved to the left, and out of sight. DC Ashley Stevens sat in the front passenger seat, his black hair quaffed back, his solid gold watch and bracelet an indication of the private income that he was party to.

Ashley's father had used his redundancy money all those years ago, to invest in a little video shop, hoping that it would give him an interest and enough money to live on. Within five years he had twelve similar shops throughout the Midlands and was a millionaire. Today he had over two hundred stores. His only son, however, refused to join his business, and remained a detective, albeit a financially secure one. It was an odd quirk that at twenty-eight, Ashley had a better house and car than the Head of CID.

Ash turned in his seat and strained to see through the rear window of Stark's car. He could see the red CID vehicle several places back in the queue. He smiled at the ruddy face, seemingly hewn out of granite, of Detective Sergeant John 'Nobby' Clarke, who had his head poking out of the driver's side window. Nobby was agitatedly pointing forwards, in thrusting motions. He looked annoyed and was shouting something incomprehensible.

Ashley, however got the message.

'I think Nobby wants us to make progress, sir,'

Stark turned and saw Nobby gesticulating wildly. He wound down the window and gave him the thumbs up. Stark's foot became heavy on the accelerator pedal, the rev counter straying into the red. He pulled out onto the wrong side of the road, switched his lights on and pressed his horn. A glimpse in the mirror saw Nobby follow suit. The sudden increase in speed jolted Ashley, and he clung to the dashboard. A few seconds later several cars appeared, heading straight for them, but they moved over just in time, and motioned their discontent with various movements of their fingers and fists.

'Piss off! We're the Queens' men!' Stark reciprocated.

After a hair-raising drive, the two cars arrived at the scene of the reported 'accident'. By this time there were three traffic patrol vehicles present. The young patrolman had done everything: Scenes of Crime officers had just attended, and a uniformed Inspector was strutting around, barking orders to his underlings. Stark hated this initial stage, with everyone running around like headless chickens. He knew the importance of haste, since any suspects could be in the vicinity, but he was not prepared to sacrifice evidence by poking around too early, before Scenes of Crime had finished. Stark's first job was to extinguish the infectious mania the uniformed Inspector was creating amongst the troops, by his excited behaviour, and he approached him with a smile.

'Morning, Mark. What are we looking at?'

The red-faced Inspector was young in service and scarcely hid the relief he felt on seeing Stark arrive. He used his long black stick with its glistening silver top to point at the car.

'I think the Traffic officer has done the right thing, Dave, by asking you to attend, it looks a funny one. The one oblique one is the driver, no passengers are in the vehicle, but the rear nearside door was wide open when the Traffic officer arrived. Obviously, you will see for yourself, but it looks to me, like the driver has been stabbed in the neck.'

'Okay. What have you done so far?'

The Inspector swallowed. 'Well, erm, we've preserved the scene. As you can see, Scenes of Crime are here, and now you are. I've started a couple of my lads doing some house-to-house enquiries up the road. I've asked for CID support. That's as far as we have got.'

'So basically, you have waited until we got here. I'm kidding.'

Mark grinned nervously. 'There is nothing else we could do, David, there are no witnesses and hence no descriptions to circulate of possible offenders.'

'Can you get traffic to erect a tarpaulin to prevent a view of the body, please, Mark?'

'Of course.'

Nobby had been party to the conversation, hands in pockets, head bowed. He had little time for the new-style 'college inspectors. Nobby, as an ex paratrooper hated the 'hairy-fairy' way the Inspector conducted his business. Nobby could be a belligerent detective. He didn't understand, nor did he *want* to understand, the modern management techniques, which he felt were much too cautious and naïve. They were okay in their place, if you like that sort of thing, but he felt the police service was not that place.

'Do you want me to do the biz then, sir?' he asked Stark.

'Please, Nobby. You've heard the set-up, haven't you?'

Nobby returned to his vehicle, grabbing the radio handset.

'Juliet Quebec two nine to NH.'

The female voice answered promptly. 'Juliet Quebec two nine, go ahead, NH over.'

'Yes, we are at the scene at Papplewick, Juliet Quebec zero two is with me. Still no update on descriptions, no witnesses are evident yet. Compliments of DCI Stark; request mounted section, Dog Patrol, and gain authority for police helicopter to search surrounding fields and woodland, plus a unit of SOU for searching. Also set up a snatch plan immediately. Over.'

'Ten four, NH out.' The young lady had a lot to organise.

Stark joined him at the car. 'Did I hear you ask for a snatch-plan to be put in place?'

'Yes, boss, all the major junctions will have a traffic car on them within minutes.'

'I know what a snatch-plan is, mate, but there is no description or vehicle, what are they looking for?'

'Anything suspicious?' Nobby said with his confidence waning a little.

'I wouldn't have bothered with that just yet, Nobby, but leave it for now, the Control room Inspector might query it, though.' Just as he spoke the radio sounded.

'NH to Juliet Quebec two nine.'

'There you go!' Stark said. 'Just ignore it, let's have a look at the motor.'

Stark peered through the open driver's door. 'I think we can safely say he's dead!' He walked around the vehicle, careful not to collide with SOCO who were putting on their white overalls. He looked through the window, focussing on the severe neck wound, glancing at the minimal damage to the front of the vehicle. Mark, the uniformed Inspector hovered around behind him. Stark spoke to Nobby. 'Any observations, Sergeant?'

'It's a suspicious death all right; someone's bleeding throated him!'

Stark turned to the uniformed Inspector: 'There you have the voice of an expert!'

2

'It's such a secret place – the land of tears.'

Antoine de Saint-Exupery (1900-1944)

Within half an hour, the circus was in full swing. All heads arched backwards, as the police helicopter roared deafeningly overhead and away into the surrounding countryside, momentarily killing all conversation. Some officers instinctively ducked their heads.

Detective Superintendent Wagstaff had arrived. He looked more like a Wing Commander in the RAF than a Police Superintendent; with a neat handlebar moustache and dated suit. He was known to be a decent enough man, but he had the capacity to turn, if he took umbrage, or felt that someone was taking advantage, and it had been known for a detective to be 'wearing a big hat' by the Monday morning. This was the 'Sword of Damocles' threat that hung over all CID officers: the big hat!

Stark informed Wagstaff of the state of play. The dog man had picked up a couple of tracks but was complaining that it was 'bloody impossible!' with the amount of police who had been milling around the scene. Two mounted officers had been sent out into the fields and nearby forestry, to follow up any potential sightings from the helicopter. They were careful to keep away from any potential tracks for the dog man, taking a circuitous route.

Scenes of Crime had taken their photographs, and the dark-suited undertakers had 'bagged the stiff' with a deftness born of experience. This allowed the forensic experts full access, blood samples were swabbed, fingerprint marks taken from inside and outside the car, fibres and human hair removed from the upholstery with strips of Cellophane, and soil and debris removed from the floor with a dustpan and brush. All items were logged, and times noted and then labelled. Eventually the appointed Exhibits Officer could search the vehicle, take out all personal possessions and similarly bag them up and label them. The car would be taken apart later in a sealed garage at the Forensics Bay and the tow lorry was on its way. The Exhibits officer recorded the following items:

- One red and blue woollen blanket – taken from rear floor of car.

- Seven miscellaneous cassette tapes – taken from centre console of car.

- One 'Pavarotti' cassette tape taken from car radio/cassette machine.

- One opened bag of Fox's glacier mints – taken from driver's door pocket.

- One Volvo owner's manual – taken from glove compartment.

- Eleven 'Johnson & Brown Solicitor's' business cards entitled 'James Deely'- taken from glove compartment.

- Two 'Bic' Biro pens – taken from glove compartment.

- One windscreen scraper – taken from glove compartment.

- One de-icer spray taken from glove compartment.

- Two photographs, one of woman, holding small girl; one of red-brick house, ranch style, with SOLITUDE written on back – taken from glove compartment.

- One ornate teardrop clasp earring – taken from underneath front passenger seat.

- One car jack and tool bag – taken from boot of car.

- One briefcase containing miscellaneous legal documents and a note pad – taken from boot of car.

Other CID officers – Starks officers – had arrived at the scene. Detective Policewoman Stephanie Dawson; 'moaning' Jim McIntyre, his pock-marked face as miserable as sin; ginger haired Steve Aston, and the new young 'Aide to CID', Cynthia Walker. Cynthia was a mixed-race young woman, tall, thin and elegant with long painted nails.

Stark had not requested they come to the scene, there was little they could do. This was what Mark, the uniformed Inspector had meant, when he said he had summoned CID support. This irritated Stark. He sent Ashley and Steph to trace the newspaper boy. Nobby was to return and start setting up the Incident Room, along with the others, so that they could get organised and sort out the priority actions. Just as they were breaking free, the radio in Nobby's car resounded.

'Juliet Quebec zero two from NH. Quebec zero two, over.'

There was a sense of urgency in the Control Room operator's voice. Nobby turned towards Stark who was in heavy conversation with Wagstaff. 'Sir, they are shouting you on VHF.' Stark walked quickly over, and picked up the handset, through the open car window, its curled wire stretched tight as he leaned against the roof of the car, the coolness of the metal penetrating his suit jacket.

'Quebec zero two, go ahead.'

'Sir, the helicopter crew have a sighting: a white male, approximately twenty years, walking close to a copse, two miles south-west of your location.'

Stark quickly despatched the Mounted Section as the distant

whirring of the helicopter carried hope of an early conclusion.

As soon as he heard the message, the mounted officer, clad in black gear, cracked his crop against the muscular backside of Garth, the thumping of his heart coinciding with the accelerating pounding of hoof beats. Terrance Sheridan had won many prizes for show jumping and was the most experienced horseman in the Nottinghamshire Constabulary stables. The motion of his body was graceful; at one with the galloping horse. as he jumped the field boundary walls and moved with great speed, negotiating obstacles with ease. Before long Terry could see the copse ahead. He slowed Garth to a trot as he approached the glade. He could see the figure of a man within the shade of the trees and wondered if he should call for back up. An officer on a horse is less vulnerable to a knife attack so long as he keeps his distance, but if Garth got cut. . . His decision was made for him when Mounted Officer Samantha Hackett arrived alongside him on her horse. Terry signalled the location of the man, who appeared to be lying flat. He whispered to Sam.

'I think he's seen us.'

The two walked their horses up to the edge of the wood increasing the gap between them as they did. Steam billowed from the beasts' nostrils, matched to a lesser extent by their riders. A male voice shouted out to the officers from the trees.

'What d'you want?'

Terry shouted a reply. *'Police! We want a word, please, show yourself. Come on out from the treeline. Do it now!'*

The repeater radio crackled confirmation that the copse had been sealed off from the far roadside by traffic officers, who had drawn their truncheons and fanned out in a line. Whoever was in there wasn't escaping. A young man of around twenty, with long hair appeared from the shadows. He wore only his shirt. He held a pair of denim jeans in his hand covering his private parts. He shouted to the officer:

'Leave it out, mate, I've got a bird in here, what's going off?'

Terry shouted beyond the youth to the trees. 'Show yourself then love, don't be shy.'

A woman of about thirty-five appeared. She negotiated the bracken and fallen twigs, carefully clutching a pile of clothes in front of her naked breasts. A short white skirt, still unzipped, hung loosely on her hips. Two unlikely lovers, who had been in the wrong place at the wrong time. Terry stated the obvious. 'You must be bloody freezing, you soft buggers. I suggest you get your clothes on.'

PW Samantha Hackett's eyes widened as the youth brazenly put his jeans back on. As the denim reached his nether regions, his semi-erect penis flopped into display before he tucked it into his trousers. She was not unimpressed and shifted in her saddle as the young youth cheekily winked at her.

Terry reported back to Stark that all was in order and the Traffic Officers could put their truncheons back in their trousers.

*

The owners of the newspaper shop on the corner of Victoria Street in Hucknall had broadened their horizons in recent times. To stave off competition from the new, multi-branch giants, they had started to sell a variety of foodstuffs to supplement their moribund trade, attempting to hold on to the 'corner shop' image of personal, friendly service. Most customers were known by their first names and had been going there for years, mainly because they couldn't be bothered to walk that bit further to the bigger shops.

Close to the shop doorway, at the corner of the building, an elderly man sat on the wooden slatted bench, watching the world go by. He wore a cloth cap, grey decaying sports jacket and a red piece of cloth tied loosely around his neck in the style of a cravat. His left hand rested on the gnarled handle of a walking-stick, which he affectionately referred to as his 'bike'. At eighty-two years of age, George had lived a hard life; his dingy skin and calloused hands bore witness to thirty-seven years down the pit. He passed many an hour sitting on 'his' bench and over the years had attracted the attention from school children who passed by.

Children and the very old, share an affinity in their thinking, an honesty of expression born of innocence or the acceptance of forthcoming demise. No self-image to portray, no games to play, only forthright observation of life.

George had quickly sensed young Jason's terror as he had run into the shop, recklessly abandoning his beloved bicycle in the gutter. He had been alarmed by the helpless expression on the paper-boy's face. It was obviously no trivial matter, but much as he wanted to enquire, his instincts told him to bide his time. He had been trying to support the lad recently with all his troubles. Just using words of encouragement and a bit of accumulated wisdom about how to deal with life's problems. Adults were too stupid to listen to the older folks', but children had a bit more about them and took it all in.

As the white Ford Escort pulled up in front of him, George pretended to toy with a piece of rubbish on the pavement with his stick. His peripheral vision took in the shapely stockinged leg of Detective Constable Stephanie Dawson as it preceded the statuesque blonde out of the car. Her beige raincoat, tied tightly at the middle, accentuated her slim waist. Stephanie caught sight of the elderly gent, whilst Ashley increased his step to catch up with her. She remembered the man from her days on the beat and smiled warmly in recognition. George tapped the peak of his flat cap and nodded in reply. It was serious. They were detectives. His trembling hand fished in his jacket pocket for nicotine relief from the nub-end he had saved for later. He lit it and struggled to his feet, pivoting on his stick, successful at the second attempt. His deformed, bow-legs, shuffled into reluctant movement. His back was slightly more hunched than usual, and he retched into a coughing bout as he struggled towards the solitude of his nearby flat. He realised that whatever had happened was too great for a curious old man to interfere with. He could only hope young Jason would tell him in his own good time. The poor lad had enough troubles at home.

Steph could hear the distant sound of a boy crying as the chiming of the shop bell faded and the door slowly closed behind the two detectives. The shop was small and drab and had a smell of stale tobacco about it. The crying was coming from a room behind the counter. The doorway to the adjoining living-room was filled by the portly newsagent, a balding middle-aged man with black-rimmed glasses. He wore a dark-red, round-necked pullover that highlighted small flecks of dandruff on his shoulders. He spoke with a slight West Country accent.

'Morning.'

'Good morning. We're from the local CID. I understand you have a young paper-boy who works here, who may have seen an incident earlier. ' Steph said.

'He's in the back. You'd better come through.'

The three walked into the undersized living-room. There were two large, somewhat bedraggled settees, cardboard boxes spilled over with various brands of cigarettes, cluttering the dusty old carpet. A small boy with ginger hair and freckles and wearing school uniform was hunched at the far end of one of the settees. His head was buried in the crook of his elbow, which rested on the arm of the furniture. He had cried enough; now he was aware of strangers present in the room and embarrassment encroached upon his misery. He glanced briefly at the newcomers. Steph sat down next to him. She put her hand on his knee and the smell of her perfume and the warmth of her gesture comforted him a little. He struggled to catch his breath; he gulped, and took longer, more deliberate inhalations. Stephanie was sympathetic as she patted his leg.

'Eh, come on, it's all right, there's nothing to fear, darling. Try and calm down, there's a good lad.'

The boy gulped again. He took his head away from his arm and stared ahead vacantly; he did not acknowledge the others. Steph continued.

'What's your name?'

The boy continued to stare straight ahead, his eyes red, his bottom lip trembling uncontrollably. 'Jason.'

'Listen Jason, we're detectives. There's nothing to worry about at all, we're going to help. Where's your mum and dad?'

Jason whimpered. 'They're both at work, don't tell me mam about it, will you?'

Stephanie would do the talking. The two men looked on.

'Why don't you want us to tell your mum?'

'She'll kill me.'

'No, she won't – don't be daft. You've not done anything wrong. You've done everything right. We've come to thank you for doing so well.'

'She won't think that; you don't know her.'

'Jason.'

'What?'

The shop doorbell rang, and the newsagent rose in response, somewhat pleased that the charged atmosphere was broken by the arrival of a customer. Ashley asked the man to close the living-room door, afraid that more distractions would impair the boy's concentration. This the man did. Stephanie continued.

'Are you feeling a bit better now?'

'A bit, yeah.' Jason wiped his nose on his sleeve.

'Is your Mum at work?'

'Yes, but don't tell her, *please.*' he whimpered, his voice trembling.

'Whereabouts does she work, Jason?'

The boy reluctantly told Steph that she worked at the local hosiery factory. Ashley did not need any prompting. He left the room and went in search of her. Steph continued talking to the boy, aware that he might have information needing an urgent response. Somewhere there was a murderer walking loose. Eventually Steph broached the subject.

'Did you see anybody near the car, Jason?'

'No, I didn't. Is the man all right? I didn't know what to do, I've never seen a car crash before.'

'Did you see the car go into the telegraph pole, then?'

'No, it was already there when I saw it. He's dead, isn't he?'

'I don't know yet, they have taken him to hospital,' Steph lied. 'It doesn't look good, though. He wouldn't have felt anything, if he has passed away.' Steph lied again. 'Did you see anybody at all,

Jason?'

'Don't lie! I've seen him, he's fucking dead!'

'Woah! Okay.'

The boy sobbed through the rest of his reply. 'I didn't see anything, and it wasn't me that caused the accident!'

'Is that what you think, Jason? That we reckon you caused it?'

'Me mam says not to trust you coppers. You will set me up, she says. She's always on about it.'

'Jason, whatever your Mum says, let me assure you that we know you did not cause any accident. I've already told you how well you did, running across the road to get help. That was a great idea.'

Steph talked Jason through the entire scenario, trying to understand everything he did, everything he touched. He eventually calmed down and explained that he hadn't done much but look through the window and run for help.

'Just close your eyes and think back to when you were cycling towards the car. Listen for all the sounds you heard and what you were thinking.'

Steph waited patiently.

'Thinking about it, I do remember hearing a car starting up a couple of minutes before I reached the man, my gears are bust on me bike so it's not very quick apart from downhill.'

'Where was the car that you heard, do you remember?'

'It was somewhere up the top hill, near Selby's Farm. That's what it sounded like anyway.'

'I know it. Did you see this car, Jason?'

'No, I didn't see it, but I definitely heard it start up.'

'Brilliant work! Well done Jason, I think you could be a detective one day!'

The boy stifled a smile which turned to horror when the door burst open.

'Come on, get up you little bastard! How many times have I told you? You don't talk to these lot. Wait till I get you home, you little twat!'

The woman was small, heavily made-up with bleached blonde

hair, and a star tattoo on her cheek, she looked what she was – a hag.

Steph stood up quickly. 'There's no need for that! The lad's done nothing wrong. He's trying to help us. He's upset.'

'There's no wonder he's upset with you interrogating him, is there? I should be here before you speak to him. I know my rights. Anyway, he'll get over it, whatever the fuck it is. Dragging me out of work for nowt. This is costing me money, you know, you little shit – and it is coming out of your paper-round money! Every bloody penny! Come on. *Home! Now!*'

Jason began to cry again as his mother forcibly ushered him out. The detectives looked on, feeling helpless. There was nothing they could do, in truth. Steph wanted to follow the woman, to take the child away from her, but for what?

'I tried to calm her down in the car, Steph, but she wasn't having any of it.' Ashley said almost apologetically.

Steph shook her head. 'What a cow. What chance has that poor little sod got in life? Come on, let's get out of here.'

*

The identity of the dead man had been traced by the Police National Computer: by the DVLA details of the owner of the car. There were also the business cards in the glove compartment and the driving licence and credit cards in the dead man's wallet, retrieved at the mortuary. A surreptitious telephone call to Johnson & Brown solicitors had revealed that James had not yet arrived to work and was late for an appointment.

Stark had felt it appropriate to collect young Detective Constable Steve Aston from the station and take him to James Deely's house to break the news to his family. Steve might learn from the experience. Steve, was a junior CID officer with only a year's experience as a detective. He was not the stereo-typical DC, but a seemingly sensitive man, and a vegetarian. He had a sickly white pallor to his face which contrasted with his ginger hair. Nevertheless, he was, whether by luck or judgement, a successful 'thief–taker': even with the most hardened of criminals, his polite nature would disarm them and enable him to be successful where others were not. Now he stood at the door of Deely's home, next to the solid, taller figure of David Stark. 'Solitude' was the house name according to the plaque adorning the wall at the side of the door – a bizarre name for a house.

The door was answered by a little girl with auburn hair, who peered at them suspiciously as she swung on the door handle.

'My mum says that if you are selling something, we don't want any, but thank you.'

Deely's wife, Sarah, appeared at the door, flustered. 'I'm sorry about that. What can I do for you?' She smiled warmly. She looked quite chic, spoke well and was dressed in casual but expensive clothes.

Stark produced his warrant card. 'We're from the CID, love. Can we come in and have a word with you please?'

'Yes, of course. Is there something wrong?'

Stark didn't answer but smiled at her. The living-room was elegant. The furniture was expensive, and everywhere was spotlessly clean. Stark sat in an armchair. Sarah sat next to the Inspector, her slim figure leaning forward slightly, and she brushed her auburn hair back from her face. She was alert and interested.

'I suppose you are used to people asking you if there is something wrong every time you knock on their door. People always look on the dark side, don't they? I guess you know that more than anybody. Would you like a cup of tea?'

Stark was the spokesman. 'Perhaps in a minute. . .'

The little girl ran full force at Stark, she was clutching a train. Katy caught his stomach causing him to expel air rapidly. Sarah interjected.

'Katy, now stop that. Go into the playroom, there's a good girl.'

'Aw! Mummy!'

'Go on, there's a good girl, do as you are told please. We want to talk; you're not missing anything. Off you go.'

Katy left the room reluctantly. Sarah closed the door behind her. She sensed something was wrong; her heart started thumping. 'Do you know she's like that all day. She never stops. She's forever playing with boy's toys. Give her a doll and she doesn't want to know. A right little tom-boy she is. Anyway, I'm sure you don't want to know all this. Did you say you would like a cup of tea?'

Stark sat on the edge of the armchair, with Steve looking on from the settee with a concerned expression. 'Perhaps in a minute, Mrs Deely-'

'Please, call me Sarah, so what is it I can do for you, Mr . . .?

'I'm David Stark, Detective Inspector, and this is Steve Aston, from Nottingham CID.' He paused. 'Listen, Sarah, I'm afraid I have some bad news for you.'

Sarah stood up sharply. 'I think we will have a cup of tea. Do you take milk and sugar?'

She didn't wait for an answer but went into the spacious, wood-panelled kitchen and began filling the kettle. She was humming a tune to herself. Stark had no option but to follow her in there. 'Mrs Deely, there is a reason we are-'

'I've told you, call me Sarah.' Her voice had irritation in it as she plugged in the kettle. Stark took her arm. 'Just stop a minute, Sarah. Look at me, love.'

Sarah stared down at the work top. 'This is silly – I'm very busy you know. I'm just making a drink, there's nothing wrong with that is there? It's not against the law in my own home is it?'

Stark's face was solemn. 'Sarah, its James. Something terrible has happened. Its bad news, I'm afraid.'

Sarah wrenched her arm free and opened a cupboard. She began taking out cups and saucers.

'Would you prefer mugs; I know most men do. You don't have to stand on ceremony here you know.'

'Sarah, listen to me. It's James, he's been involved in something terrible, it's very bad news. I'm sorry.'

Sarah's eyes began filling with tears. 'My husband has not been involved in anything, I'll have you know, and so don't start making accusations you can't back up, Inspector. I have been more than civil with you- '

'Sarah, I'm sorry to have to tell you this, but your husband has been killed. I'm so sorry, come and sit down.' He put his hand on her shoulder which she immediately shrugged off, responding aggressively.

'If this is someone's idea of a juvenile prank, then I don't think it's funny. My husband has *not* been killed, which I know for a fact because I waved him off only a couple of hours ago, for God's sake! So, if you are going to be silly you can leave, now, please, thank you very much. I have some shopping to do.' Sarah rested her hands on her hips and stared at him challengingly. Stark's heart sank.

'Sarah, it's the truth, I'm afraid. No-one would joke about something as awful as this.' She turned and leaned on the kitchen top. She screwed her eyelids shut, forcing a tear to trickle down her cheek.

'I am so sorry, but it *is* the truth, Sarah. James has sadly been killed. It's a lot to take in. Come and sit down.'

'Has he? Has he really? So, who has identified him, then?'

'Nobody has, but it's his car, his identity documents, his business cards in the car. He hasn't arrived at work.'

Sarah flounced to the far side of the kitchen and dialled a number on the wall-phone. 'Kath? It's Sarah. Can you nip round and have Katy for an hour? I've got to go out, only it's important. No. Nothing to worry about, it's a misunderstanding that's all. Sorry? Yes, that would be great. Thanks.'

She walked past Stark and got hold of her coat. 'Come on then, let's go and see who this man is. Let me go and do the "identification", because I'll tell you what, mister, you are in deep trouble. James is not without connections, and when he hears about this-'

Her neighbour, Kath, arrived at the back door and let herself in. Sarah shouted to her, 'Thanks Kath,' then turned and went to open the front door. She placed her hand on the Yale lock and her head rested on her hand. She froze. Stark could hear nothing, but suddenly a loud wail rose from within her. Sobs racked her body.

'I can't do it. Tell me it's all a mistake. *Please!*'

Her pent-up emotions erupted, and she fell into the arms of Stark, who held her against his shoulder, helplessly. No words were enough to relieve the enormity of her grief.

Kath ran over. 'Come on, love. Whatever's happened? Come and sit down.' The two helped Sarah into the living-room. Stark noticed little Katy in the doorway of the playroom, sullen, wide-eyed, a finger in her mouth.

'Steve, can you get the little girl, please?'

Steve went and grabbed Sarah's daughter who also began to cry in her confusion. Steve tried to comfort her, but Sarah opened her arms and little Katy ran into them, and they hugged and sobbed together.

Twenty minutes passed; Steve Aston made a pot of tea. The two men looked on awkwardly as Kath held the distraught Sarah and rocked her on the settee. Kath was crying too. Sarah instinctively held on to Katy, who was frightened. A heart-wrenching scene.

Stark went into the hallway and surreptitiously radioed for a policewoman to attend and there was a brief debate with the uniformed Inspector, who was reluctant to grant the policewoman overtime for the task, as it would undoubtedly take her beyond the end of her shift. Stark was succinct. 'You aren't paying for it out your own pocket, Mark, are you? Get her down here. Pronto!'

Once the policewoman arrived, Stark met her at the door and explained the situation. She was to console Sarah, and when the time was right, try to get as much information out of her, about James, and try to discover any motive a killer might have. Stark would arrange for a Detective Policewoman to come and assist if he had the capacity to supply one.

As Stark left with Steve Aston, he waved to the policewoman to come over to the hallway. He took the policewoman's arm and whispered to her, 'Just check her alibi, and make sure all the carving knives are here. Do you understand what I mean?'

'Of course, sir.'

'Stranger things have happened.'

'Also, when you get chance ask her if she owns a tear drop gold earring. Be careful in case it isn't hers. Maybe say it was found at the side of the car on the road or something like that, rather than it being in the car itself. She's got enough on her plate right now.'

'Yes, of course, sir, leave it with me.'

Steve Aston sneezed as they stepped out on to the drive. He fished out a handkerchief and blew hard on his nose. 'Bloody hell, Steve, are you, all right?'

'No, sir, I've got a bloody cold. I can't seem to shake it off.'

'You want to get some meat down you. All this rabbit food is weakening your resistance.'

'There's more vitamin C in vegetables than there is in meat, actually. Anyway, I refuse to be drawn. I know you're only taking the mickey, sir.'

The two men got into the CID car. Stark paused.

'What's the matter, sir?'

'Nothing, I'm just wondering who is going to do the formal identification of the body?'

'Could Sarah do it once she's calmed down a bit?'

'Maybe, but I want it doing now, if possible. I want the post-mortem doing as quick as we can.'

There was a silence.

'Fuck it. It will have to be one of James' work colleagues. I haven't got time to mess about.'

Steve sniffed. 'I bloody hate mortuaries. It's the stench I hate, the smell that sticks in the back of your throat and to your clothes and those weird buggers that work in there.'

'You'll be all right, Steve, you can't smell anything with your cold. Are you on about the morticians, those fucking weirdo's?'

'Who wants to work in a room with thirty bodies all around you? That is seriously weird.' Steve said.

'Somebody has got to do it, I suppose.' Stark said pragmatically. 'You know, there's a woman who works in there, one of the morticians, and I kid you not, I went in on a Sunday afternoon, with a body, and she had got her fucking motorbike stripped down in there, doing some sort of repair. She said it was ideal on a Sunday, while it was quiet.'

'Jeez.'

'They are a special breed.' Stark pulled out of the drive. 'She wouldn't have it, would she? Mrs Deely, I mean.'

'No, it was heart breaking listening to it, poor soul.'

'When they are in denial like that, you've just got to tell them straight, Steve.'

'I guess so. What's next on the agenda then, sir?'

'We need to get sorted, young Steve. We will have a briefing back at the nick, now we've done the death message, it took a bit longer than I had hoped. It didn't quite go to plan, did it?'

Steve laughed. 'No, not really.'

'You never know, they might have arrested the offender by the time we get back there.' Stark said his optimism flying in the face of likelihood.

'That would be good.'

'Wouldn't it just?'

*

Nobby Clarke parked the CID car in the space marked 'Police' at the front of the Queens Medical Centre; Accident and Emergency Department. He muttered to himself as he approached the electronic entrance doors. 'First, he wants me to set up the Incident Room, then he says just nip to the QMC to do the ID. I wish he'd make his bloody mind up!'

He joined the queue of three people in front of him, waiting for them to describe their ailments, and be given a ticket. He glanced at his watch and was fidgeting, peering over shoulders.

After one severe headache, a stubbed toe and a suspected fractured wrist, the middle-aged woman at the reception smiled at him. 'Name and address please.'

'No, you're all right, love, I'm not a patient. I'm from the CID. I'm trying to arrange an identification of a James Deely.'

'Identification? Is he a patient?'

He leaned closer and spoke quietly. 'Sort of. He was found dead this morning.'

'Oh, I see. So, who do you need to speak to?'

'I was hoping you might tell me. The mortuary might be a good place to start. I don't know if he has been taken down yet, but usually the undertakers take them straight there.'

The woman dialled a number. 'It's ringing.'

'Pass it here, I'll speak to them.'

'Hello, mortuary.' It was the voice of a young woman.

'Hello, love, I'm Detective Sergeant Clarke. I'm in Casualty reception at the moment, and I'm meeting a man here shortly, to do a formal identification of James Deely. Is he down there?'

'Yes, he's the throat guy, yes, he's here.'

'What condition is he in for an ID?'

'He doesn't look very well, I mean-'

Nobby laughed. 'Very funny. You know what I mean. Does he look good enough to do an ID with a member of the public?'

'Sure. If you give me ten minutes, I'll put him a bit of make-up on and something round his neck to cover up the wound, and he'll look like a million dollars.'

'I'm okay with you putting a bandage round the neck, but no make-up. There will be a P.M. and the Pathologist will hit the roof if it has been touched.'

'Oh, OK, Of course, they don't tell us anything in here. I'll get him to the C.O.R. and see you there.'

'The what?'

'The Chapel of Rest. Not that *I'm* going to get any by the looks of it.'

Nobby shook his head and laughed. 'Okay, see you in a bit.'

Nobby handed the phone back to the receptionist. 'I'll be outside if a bloke called Alan Johnson comes to reception. I'll keep an eye out for him outside while I'm waiting.'

C.O.R. he thought. Why not call it the bloody Chapel of Rest, for Christ's sake? Nobby, sat on the wooden bench beside the main door of the massive hospital complex. He lit up a cigarette, glancing at the people arriving, seeing if he could spot someone looking like a partner at Johnson & Brown solicitors. After a few minutes a serious-looking man, in his mid-fifties walked past him. His hair was receding, and he wore a dark suit and tie. He was painfully thin and gaunt. Nobby looked through the glass doors and saw the receptionist indicating to the man that Nobby was outside. He stood up and went to meet him. They shook hands at the entrance. Nobby led the morose gentleman through the maze of corridors towards the Chapel of Rest. Alan Johnson said very little.

The two met the green-smocked figure of Jenny Smith, the happy-go-lucky mortician to whom Nobby had spoken on the phone. She behaved more demurely for Alan Johnson's benefit. Nobby explained the procedure to Mr Johnson and they all stepped inside the small room. Only the sign outside the door made it a 'chapel of rest'. The body lay on its back, covered by a purple silk blanket with a cross embroidered on it. The deceased's face was exposed, and a bandage was wrapped round his neck. The dead man's eyes were shut, but, as often happens, they were not fully closed, and as they stepped into the room his unseeing eyeballs glistened a welcome. Alan Johnson let out a sigh and bravely marched towards the exposed face of the man. Nobby was quick to ask: 'Is this James Deely, your employee?'

Alan croaked out a reply, 'Yes, that is James Deely, God love him.'

'Thank you, Mr Johnson.' Nobby ushered the dazed man outside the room and went back inside, just in time to see the mortician throw back the blanket and reveal the naked corpse.

'Thanks a lot, love. I'll be down in a minute, put the kettle on, will you?'

'Seeing as it's you.'

'Oh, and one other thing.'

'What's that?'

'Wash your hands first, will you!'

She walked towards Nobby with her hands in front of her as if she was going to touch him. 'Oooh' she said, laughing.

'Piss off, you weirdo!'

3

'Two social workers walk past a man bleeding in
a ditch. One says to the other, "We must find
the man who did this, he needs help!"'

Anon.

Stark sat in his office, alone. It was happening again. He was in a flop-sweat. The pain in his chest was muscular, caused by the tightness of his anxiety. He stood and paced around his office trying to shake it off. This was not the way to do it, his breathing was too quick; the answer lay in the breathing. He sat back down at his desk, and started to slow his breathing down, but his heart grew thunderous. He persisted, his eyes closed, his head spinning. He kept hearing shouts and noises from outside and would occasionally open one eye to check no-one was coming in the door. The prospect of addressing a crowd of people was the only time he was triggered like this. He would much sooner face a knife wielding thug, than go in front of a crowd of people.

This had only started in the last eighteen months or so, and he couldn't shake it off. It was his little secret for now. His strategy was to hope that it would eventually go away. Not much of a strategy but he was wary of discussing it with anyone, in case he was thought to be 'flaky'.

If he could just get his breathing right and lose the sweat, he would go for it. He put the fan on in his office. Bliss. After a few minutes he was ready, or at least as ready as he was going to be.

A mixture of detectives and uniformed personnel were gathered in the Briefing Room of Nottingham Police Station, seated round an array of tables, each crowned by a large tin ashtray sporting individual brewer's names.

The detectives spoke between themselves, as did the uniformed officers drafted in from the Special Operations Unit – experts trained to cope with diverse situations; from firearms sieges, to searching premises, to policing football matches. The detectives sat closest to the whiteboard at the far end of the room, smoke wafting from their cigars and cigarettes. There was a high level of chatter, as each group speculated on how long the enquiry would run, and various weird and wonderful theories on the case were expounded upon.

Jim McIntyre interspersed his brash, throaty comments with the occasional passing of wind, which he synchronised with the raising of buttocks to emphasise the action. It was all posturing and a bit pathetic.

The nattering hushed as Stark and Detective Superintendent Wagstaff, entered the room. Stark's black hair looked a little unkempt, which was unusual. Stark remained on his feet as Wagstaff sat down on a chair placed at the front, facing towards the crowd.

Stark wiped his forehead and waited. Eventually a silence fell before he spoke. 'James Deely is dead. Murdered. Anybody know who killed him?'

The silence continued with a couple of glances at each other. Stark would sometimes throw in a wild card like this to keep them on their toes.

'Well, in that case, we've got a long way to go. Here's what we know, and it ain't a lot. James Deely is a solicitor for Johnson & Brown solicitors in the High Street. He was driving to work at about twenty past eight, or thereabouts, this morning, happy as Larry, when someone decided to stick a knife through his neck.'

There was a buzz of excited mutterings. Stark's chest was growing tight again and he rubbed his hand up his forehead as if to style his hair. 'I'm going to keep it simple for you, I know you are all chomping at the bit to get out there. The Post-mortem revealed no great surprises. The man was stabbed in the left side of his neck. The thrust severed his carotid artery, his trachea and oesophagus, causing him to die from blood loss and clinical shock. The thrust of the knife was done with such force that it exited the other side and chipped the glass of the side window. One blow was sufficient to kill him outright.' There were various intakes of breath at the news. 'So, it's a big bloody knife, around eight inches long and two inches wide.' He took a deep breath and then another. 'OK, from the direction of the blow, it seems highly likely that the killer was secreted in the well of the car, behind the front passenger, or more likely the driver's seat. The car was not forced to gain access. It is, of course, possible that someone ran to the car whilst stationary and opened the door and attacked him, and whilst we are not ruling that out, it seems random, albeit definitely still on the table as a hypothesis. Maybe a local looney tune.'

Stark took a sip from the mug of tea left thoughtfully on the desk, by Steve Aston. 'There was a gold tear-drop earring found in the car underneath the seat, so we are trying to understand whether this is his wife's or somebody else's.' There were various 'ooh's' and 'naughty boy' type comments at the news. Stark continued. 'Also, for what it is worth, Deely was due to visit an old friend today, a social worker called Roy Prentice. He will have to be traced and eliminated from the enquiry. The murder took place near the junction with Papplewick Lane and Station Road. The body was found by a paper-boy on his round and the alarm was raised. The vehicle is a light blue Volvo C453 FDP. That is the crux of the enquiry, as it is at the moment. All the forensics have been done. The knife was taken away from the scene by the offender and so it is outstanding. I am expecting some fibres from the foot well where the offender lay in wait, but let's see. There will need to be some house-to-house in the vicinity of the scene, but also importantly around Deely's home address. Could the offender have got into the vehicle and laid in wait? When did they get in the vehicle? How did they get there? Any sightings of suspicious behaviour? The normal stuff. We have absolutely no description of the perpetrator, so keep an open mind, please.'

Stark wanted to wind it up, his shirt was wet through with sweat, underneath his suit jacket, and the faces of those staring at him were becoming blurry. He fought his way through it, trying not to think about dropping to the floor in a dead faint, as he knew this just accelerated his anxiety and could mean he indeed may drop to the floor in a dead faint. 'If the uniformed lads and lasses liaise with their sergeants and get your actions, remember we are looking for witnesses, not just the offender. DS Clarke and I will have a word with the CID lads and give them their actions. Please be vigilant, people, we are as strong as our weakest link.'

Jim McIntyre muttered. 'Don't let it be you.'

'Don't let it be you.' Stark said. 'Thank you for your time, and good luck!'

A low hum returned to the room, interspersed with laughter; several officers stood up and stretched, looking for their sergeants.

Stark went to sit with the CID group. He dabbed at his forehead and neck. 'I think I've caught your bloody cold, Steve, thanks for that.'

'Sorry, sir.' Steve said.

'Charlie, if you and Nobby work together and follow-up on the house-to-house leads when they surface. Steph, will you carry on with Ashley and see where you get at Selby's Farm? Your paper-boy heard a car start up there just after the killing, didn't he?'

'He sure did, sir.' Steph confirmed.

The new aide to CID, Cynthia Walker's face dropped when Stark instructed her to partner up with 'miserable' Jim McIntyre and do some background at Deely's work-place. She had the feeling that Jim did not take too kindly to 'ethnics' as he called them.

Steve Aston felt a bit out of it, while Stark arranged an office manager. He hadn't been allocated anything yet, and he felt a something of a spare part. Wagstaff, had already told Stark he would monitor events from the Incident Room, and Stark should be out and about marshalling the team and keeping his 'finger on the pulse'. This suited Stark down to the ground. He was already feeling much better, as his tenseness, caused by the briefing was subsiding. Steve did not have to wait too long. 'You and I will go and see Deely's mate, Roy Prentice, young Steve. Get your coat, kiddo.'

Suddenly the room grew cold as Detective Inspector Lee Mole walked in with his side-kick DS Carl Davidson.

'Goodness me, if the devil should cast his net!'

Wagstaff smiled. 'Hey, Lee. How are you my friend?'

'All the better for seeing you, sir.' Mole said. 'How is the murder going?'

'Early days, Lee, early days.' Wagstaff said.

'You're quiet David?'

'Am I?'

'Are you all right? You look a bit tired, a bit clammy, in fact.'

'He's busy, Lee, he's the main man now.' Wagstaff said.

Mole grimaced. 'Is he really?'

'The top guy.'

'I thought that was me, sir.' Mole seemed genuinely hurt by the comment.

'Really, sir, you flatter me.' Stark said.

Wagstaff left the office, smiling. 'See you gentleman later.'

'Cheers, boss.'

'Is the murder all a bit much for you, David?' Mole jibed.

'You feel brave enough to start sniping now Wagstaff is out the office, do you?' Stark said.

DS Davidson found his voice. 'Mr Mole and Mr Wagstaff go back many years, sir. They're old friends.'

'True, Carl, true.' Lee nodded, seemingly pleased with himself.

'To what do we owe this pleasure?' Stark asked.

'Just in the area, and we wondered if we could assist in anything. What's the story with the murder, then, David?'

'There will be a comms going out later, and a press release.'

'Well, you can share the info, now can't you. We might be able to turn something up for you.'

'Lee, we are keeping it tight, I'm sure you will get the news soon enough. Anyway, I do not want people doing activities that are not directed from the Incident room, its poor investigative protocol. I want to know who is doing what, and when. You should know this, Lee.'

'OK, just trying to be helpful, David.'

'Lee, everyone in the room, knows what you are trying to do, so back off, there is no pot of gold at the end of this rainbow, for you. I'm leading the hunt, and I don't want any rogue elements traipsing through it unmonitored, thanks anyway.'

'Please yourself.'

Lee and Carl left from their fishing expedition. There had long since been acrimony between the two teams; mainly because Mole and Davidson would undermine Stark and his crew at any given opportunity. He was a glory hunter, but dangerous, and Stark wanted him at arms-length.

*

Ashley grimaced as he drove his nice clean Porsche 924 on to the muddy wasteland, adjacent to the cottage at Selby's Farm. The farm buildings consisted of a cowshed, a large barn for hay, several oversized garages, a pigsty and two or three decrepit buildings, whose use was not easy to determine for city folks, such as Ashley. Past the buildings was a big old house, covered in Ivy, its plaster peeling. Both he and Steph approached the small wooden door. Despite repeated knocking there was no reply. Steph peered through the dirty windows and was alarmed by a deep male voice suddenly expressing concern at their presence.

'What d'you want?'

The two detectives turned sharply. Behind them stood a man in his thirties. He was wearing a scruffy green quilted gun jacket, wellington boots, and exuded an aroma of the finest pig shit.

Ashley spoke. 'Hello there, we're from the CID. Can we have a word?'

'What d'you want with me?'

'It's not you particularly, it's anybody on the farm really. You see there's been a murder, just across the field, at the bottom there. The young boy who found the body says that he-'

'Is this going to take long, 'cos I'm a busy man and I got a stack of jobs to do.'

'OK, it shouldn't take too long. As I was saying, there was this lad who heard the noise of a car starting up from the direction of your farm. I wonder if you could enlighten us as to where it might have come from.' Ashley intentionally withheld the time of day; he was referring to.

'I've no idea. There are cars coming and going all the time here. I've got two tractor vehicles, a van, and a flat-bed lorry on the farm. Cars starting up don't mean nothing, does it? What does that prove? Now can I get some work done?'

Steph had heard enough, what with the hag at the newsagents and now this idiot. 'Look, can I just explain something to you, Mr . . .?'

'Tennant.'

'Mr Tennant. Some poor sod has been killed this morning. You may or may not know that a murder enquiry means that every tiny bit of potential evidence is followed up, and that is what we are doing right now. You see, this maniac may still be in the vicinity, for all we know, and when you and Mrs Tennant, and your kids are tucked up in bed, he may just decide to swing an axe through your skulls, do you understand? We're not here for our health, or because we have a fascination for your bleeding tractor units, or to piss you off, we're trying to solve a murder, so the sooner you co-operate, the sooner we can leave you in peace. That's not being unreasonable now is it, Mr Tennant?'

'No need to be like that. Anyway, I ain't got no kids, and if he did come around here, he would be looking down the business end of a shotgun, make no mistake!'

Steph sighed. Ashley took over. 'Is your wife around?'

'Yes, she is.' He yelled. *'Mary!'*

The front window opened, and a small insipid-looking woman poked her head out. Her voice was timid, and the detectives struggled to hear her. 'What is it, dear?'

'These people reckon they are detectives. They want to know if there was a car starting up round here this morning.'

The woman looked through Steph, towards Ashley. 'What time this morning?'

'Some time around twenty past eight.'

'Oh, that would be me with the tractor. Why what's wrong?

'Somebody's been killed near Papplewick and we're just checking out any activity in the area at the time of the crime.'

'It wasn't no car, I don't reckon. It would be me, taking the pig feed out on the tractor, it's too heavy to carry all that on my own, dear.'

They had found their source of an engine starting, mission accomplished. Steph was curious as to why it was called Selby's Farm. Mrs Tennant explained that it was the former owner, John Selby, who had since died. Mr Tennant did not wait to bid goodbye and the two detectives returned to Ashley's Porsche and got inside. He paused before turning on the ignition.

'What's that smell?' he asked.

Steph screwed up her face. 'I'm no expert but it smells like shit to me, origin unknown.'

Ashley looked underneath his shoe within the confines of the vehicle. 'Oh, for fuck's sake!'

Ash got out and used a stick to scrape at the soul of his shoe, his face red with embarrassment as he hopped on one leg. An Alsatian dog came up to him and started sniffing his leg, as he hopped and scraped, and Ash tried a swing at the unwelcome dog. 'Piss off! You flea ridden, stinking, fucking, mangy, mutt! Go on, bugger off!'

Steph struggled in vain to withhold her laughter, which she eventually stifled. Ash drove off in a huff; the smell still permeating through the inside of the car.

'I don't see what's funny!' He said.

'Oh, Ash, you can be such a Prima Donna.'

'It's not that Steph, I'm wearing £200 aftershave and now all you can smell is 'Eau de pig shit!'

*

Dave answered his phone promptly. 'Stark.'

'Sir, it's Kelly Harper, the policewoman at Sarah Deely's house.'

'Hello, Kelly.' He grabbed at the cord of the phone, which was pulling too tight, so he leaned in a bit towards the phone, to slacken it.

'I thought I would give you a quick call, while Sarah is upstairs with her daughter. She said I could use the phone.'

Stark laughed. 'OK, fine. It would be tricky, if she'd said no, wouldn't it?'

'Just a bit. I've asked her about the earring.'

'Oh, yes. What did she say?'

'It's not hers.'

'I thought as much. OK that's helpful, Kelly. How is she doing?'

'She's just in a daze, which is normal. She's on autopilot. To be honest, it's good that she has a kiddy to look after, it keeps her distracted, and she hasn't really had time to dwell on anything, I suppose.'

'Has she said anything of note?'

'Not really, I might have a chat with her when she has put the baby to bed. It's not really the right environment at the moment.'

'Good thinking, Kelly. It sounds like you are approaching it in the right way. If there is anything of any great significance, give me a call or shout me up on the radio. Yes?'

'Yes, no problem, sir. Oh, there is one thing that is probably worth mentioning.'

'What's that?'

'She said she was always nagging James about leaving his car unlocked on the drive, so anyone could have snuck inside, by the sounds of it.'

'Interesting. Thanks, Kelly, I'm grateful.'

*

The afternoon was ending. A thin layer of smog wrapped its

arms around Nottingham city centre, heralding the encroaching dusk. In close-by Trinity Square, busy office workers darted from place to place, like bees returning to the hive, whilst others, tired from shopping, queued at a bus stop wearing the vacant stare of a battle-weary soldier. A policeman strolled through the square. There was sound all around, yet no sound, just background noise; the roaring of buses, the wind rustling through awnings, an audible canvas to the penetrative and repetitive intrusion of the newspaper seller shouting: *'Heebin Po!'* Deciphered by those in the know as *'Evening Post.'*

A beanpole of a man, prematurely balding, and wearing a shiny suit, turned from the news vendor and hurried away to escape the anticipated blare of his next cry. Jim McIntyre and Cynthia Walker looked on from the CID car, as the man disappeared down an alley, past a dry cleaner's, to the side stairs. There was a sign on the wall with *'Johnson & Brown Solicitors'* emblazoned on it.

Cheryl's suspicions of Jim's attitude towards black people had been vindicated immediately, in her eyes, as he had raised the subject as soon as they had left the station. She really did not want to go there, she just wanted to be a detective, not a black detective, or a green one, or any other damned colour. She was determined not to be distracted by this all too visible badge and just be good at her job. The problem was, it wasn't her decision. However, she really did not like Jim McIntyre, that was a given, but she would be professional. The two detectives walked up the handful of steps to the reception. The receptionist showed them through to the senior partner, Alan Johnson. As they entered the room, Alan was finishing a conversation with a younger man, with wavy hair and a spotty complexion. He seemed quite upset. It was Alan whom they had seen buy the newspaper; and the pages were now spread across the table. The pages relating to the article about the suspicious death of a local solicitor were exposed. The young man rose and made towards the door.

'Don't go.' Cynthia said. 'We're from the CID, we're here about James. If you could spare a few minutes, it would be helpful.'

'Of course.' Alan shook their hands. 'This is Phillip Bond, one of our rising stars here at the company.' Phillip also greeted the two detectives.

'Didn't you identify James earlier, at the hospital, Alan? DS Clarke was there with you, wasn't he?' Jim asked.

'I did. Not a nice thing to do, but at least it saved Sarah the trauma. I shall not forget the experience in a hurry, that's for certain.'

'It's a pretty awful thing to go through, we are grateful.' Cynthia said.

'It is a necessary part of the procedure, so I guess it's just part of life. Something you would never dream of, but there you are. Phillip and James were quite close, weren't you Phillip?' He nodded. 'I suppose as the senior partner, my relationship with him was a little bit more, at arms-length, shall we say, a different dynamic than perhaps, Phillip's was.'

'No doubt.' The young solicitor agreed.

'That's why I thought it would be useful for you to stay.' Cynthia said.

They all took a seat around a coffee table, just as the tea and coffee were brought in by the receptionist. She appeared flustered and was puffing and panting like a St Bernard dog in an avalanche.

Cynthia took the lead. 'We would just like to understand a bit more about James if possible, just some general questions, if you don't mind?'

'Of course,' Alan said, 'In fact Phillip, if you would like to answer, and I can chip in where appropriate.'

'Yes, no problem, Alan. It's still a bit raw for me, so I am a little emotional, strangely.'

'There's nothing strange about that.' Cynthia said. You wouldn't be human if it didn't affect you.'

'What sort of man was he?' Jim asked.

'That's a hell of a question.' Phillip scratched his head. 'He's a good friend, sorry, it still hasn't sunk in properly yet, *was* a good friend. Oh dear, he was always jovial and ready to have a laugh with anyone. He was a bloody good solicitor. One of those guys who was good at everything, was friends with everyone; he had it all and for it to end like this is just, so…so unfair.'

'I know it's a cliché, but it is true, that he had his whole life in front of him, and a wonderful life it would have been, I'm sure.' Alan said.

'It has come as a shock to everyone, it really has.' Phillip said.

Jim sounded insincere. 'Yes, I'm sure. Who did he associate with? In his spare time, I mean.'

'Quite a few people really. I would have the odd game of squash with him. There were a few people he'd met along the way, as we all have, friends from school, college, that sort of thing.'

Jim was blunt. 'So, who would want to murder him?'

'Nobody, that's the whole point, it is so ridiculous, everybody loved the guy. Nobody can quite believe it. It's Sarah and Katy who I feel for. How are they bearing up?'

Cynthia tried to reassure him. 'As well as can be expected, I think Sarah can't quite take it all in, just yet. It's understandable, of course.'

'Poor thing.'

'Do you know anything about his past?'

'I know he was a local lad, went to Nottingham Polytechnic, took a law degree and ended up staying here. That's as much as I know, really.'

'He had top marks in his year for the region, on the law exam. Very bright young man' Alan said.

'We all knew he was going places.' Phillip added.

'What about problems with clients?' Cynthia asked.

'Nothing extraordinary. We all get the odd one or two, who don't like the end result, and blame us, but he never mentioned anything of note.'

'Would he have mentioned it, or would he have kept it to himself?'

'I think he would have mentioned it, yes, he was very open.'

Alan nodded in agreement.

'Do you keep any records of problem clients or concerns?'

Alan answered. 'No, we don't. It doesn't warrant it, to be honest. It's quite a rarity.'

Jim jumped in with both feet. 'What about women? Was he putting it about a bit, any mistresses?' Cynthia cringed at the indiscreet way Jim was asking such sensitive questions.

'Truthfully?' Phillip glanced at Alan, who nodded. 'Truthfully, possibly, he was quite a magnet for the ladies, and if he was made an offer, he was probably the sort who couldn't refuse. I don't know of anyone, before you ask.'

Cynthia spoke. 'Normally we would ask to look at James' personal record and his diary, that sort of thing. Is that a problem with his line of work, legal privilege and so on?'

'That's a good question,' Alan said. 'I suppose I had better seek advice on that one. It might be that we have to check there are no legal issues first.'

Jim jumped in again. 'This is a murder enquiry; I will remind you.'

'I know officer, and believe you me, we want the killer caught just as much, if not more, than you do. But we still have a duty under the Solicitor regulations, and indeed the law, to protect our client's confidentiality. Trust me, if we can help, we absolutely will.'

'Will you find out and let us know, please? We understand that there may be issues, but it could help.' Cynthia said.

'I should have an answer first thing in the morning.' Alan smiled at her.

'That's most helpful, thank you. I think that is about it, for now. If you think of anything in the meantime, please don't hesitate to call, even if you think it is insignificant.'

'Yes, of course. We want to help.'

*

The killer had not finished. Far from it. In fact, this was only just the beginning. It was a shock to see so much blood gush out from that pathetic bastard's neck. It was a surprise how easy it had been. How smoothly the knife blade pierced through his neck, leaving a slow gurgling death, which the killer was determined to watch. It was enjoyable. He had it coming. There was no remorse. Why would there be? With every squirt of blood, a thrill. He had died in terror, doubt and confusion, which was just how it should be. It was pay-back time.

Getting in the car had been easy, he never did lock it, the gullible fool. Hearing Sarah shout 'I love you', only fuelled the hatred, drove the desire to destroy James and everything he had done. He had done more than enough, caused too much suffering for one human being to endure, he had to pay. Justice had to be served, and there would be no clever lawyer to bail him out. The clever lawyer was dead. *He* was dead. That made sense. That gave balance.

There was more work to do, but now with a renewed confidence; the next one was less of a risk. The next one would be easier. It was just a case of making sure that they were dead, squashed, eliminated from God's green earth. All that was necessary was to trace his movements, track him down, and finish the job. Trace and eliminate; that felt good.

*

'Trace and eliminate Roy Prentice – due to meet James Deely on the day of his demise,' was the action allocated to Steve Aston by Stark. The DI wanted to do some work with Steve, he was due a final appraisal and the decision as to whether he stayed on CID would be Stark's and he had not seen much of him in action.

Arnold Lodge Community Home was a large converted house which accommodated twelve boys between the ages of fourteen and sixteen. These boys were either in 'voluntary care' – put there by disinterested or incapable parents – or were the subject of care orders directed by the courts. The reason they were there, ranged from them being persistent criminal offenders, to being the victim of child abuse by a parent. It usually became a 'Lord of the Flies' existence, unfortunately.

There were two living-rooms; one had a pool table in it, the other a row of chairs and a television. Next to the TV room was a compact office where staff could go to write their reports or to escape the kids.

Roy Prentice was a small, podgy, white man, with a large bushy black beard. He wore ragged jeans and a baggy, plain white T shirt with Bob Marley's face printed on it, along with an African National Congress badge. Roy Prentice was well known to the police: he was a militant. He would regularly attend gay rights and anti-poll tax marches, not in quiet protest to support his well-meaning beliefs, but as an agitator, whipping up the younger more vulnerable element to fever pitch, and then disappear into the background while they took all the flak. He was vehemently anti-police and was a member of a political group who employed him to make videos of police activities at marches and demonstrations, which could later be edited, or stills taken for propaganda material. Roy's colleague at the home was a total contrast. Derek Brook was a quiet, caring man, more concerned to instil common sense and values into those in his care, than use his position to ram political doctrine down their throats. He spent long hours using his vast knowledge of psychology and child-care to get the most out of those entrusted to him. It was a thankless task, but none the less gave him much satisfaction. The kids in their care sought a sense of belonging. Some chose gangs, some chose Roy's 'family'.

Prentice sat in the office, reading a newspaper, his feet resting on a swivel desk chair. Derek was writing in the daily diary, reporting on the day's events. One of the residents ran into the office excitedly. 'Coppers are here, Roy.'

Roy stood up, but Derek beat him to the door. 'It's all right, Roy, I'll go.'

Derek opened the front door and was met by Stark and Steve Aston. Derek smiled in recognition at Steve. 'Hiya, Steve, how are you?'

'I'm fine, thanks, Derek. Yourself?'

'Steady. What's happening?'

Steve introduced Stark and explained they had come to see Roy Prentice. 'Oh, right.'

By this time four of the resident children had appeared at the foot of the stairs, and were hanging off the bannister, staring at the men as if they were from out of space.

'Who have you lot come for?' One of them asked.

Derek ushered the kids away. 'All right, anybody would think you'd never seen a policeman before. They've not come for anybody, as far as I know. Now get back upstairs, out of the way. Come on. Offski.'

Derek led the detectives towards the office to distant cries of 'Pigs' and 'Filth' from the youngsters. Prentice met them at the office door. Stark put out a hand.

'Hello there, I'm Detective Inspector Stark. I wonder if I could have a word with you, please.'

Prentice ignored the outstretched hand and looked questioningly. 'Yeah.'

The boys from the stairs had re-joined the detectives and were smiling, arms folded.

'Well, can we go into the office or what?'

It was Prentices turn to fold his arms. 'You can say anything you like in front of my boys. We don't have secrets here, Inspector Bark.'

The kids giggled at the juvenile comment. 'Woof!' One of them mocked.

Stark corrected Prentice's 'mistake'. 'Detective Inspector *Stark*, actually. I know it's a lot to remember, but I'm sure you'll manage.' Stark had met his ilk before.

Derek barged past Roy and opened the office door. 'Come on in guys. I'll make you a cuppa in a minute.' Prentice leaned on the doorjamb. Stark invaded his private space and they stood nose-to-nose. 'Excuse me, Roy.' Stark smiled as Prentice removed his arm. 'Thank you so much.'

Derek switched on the kettle in the corner of the room and the three men sat down. Stark had had enough of Prentice already. Steve tried to make conversation with Roy.

'What time are you on till tonight then, Roy?'

Roy put his feet on the desk and placed his hands behind his head. 'I don't know if I should answer that, am I under caution?'

Stark recoiled. 'Have you got some sort of a problem, Roy, you know, because if you have, well, I'm all for getting it out into the open.'

'Me? Problem? Nah, I'm fine me, I've got a roof over my head, a steady job, three square meals a day, my freedom, I'm not oppressed by fascists. I'm one of the lucky ones, me.'

Stark shrugged a laugh. 'Well, I'm glad to hear it. Do you know a James Deely?'

'I might do, why do you ask?'

Derek passed the round of coffees out, and there was a deathly silence in the room as Stark sipped at his cup. He was in no hurry; he could sense Prentices curiosity burning away. Still silence. Stark smiled at Derek.

Prentice couldn't control himself any longer. 'I said, why do you ask?'

'He's dead.'

'Yeah, right, not funny. Seriously why do you want to know?'

'I've just told you, haven't I? He's dead, and somebody mentioned that James Deely, God rest his soul, was due to see you later today, so instead of him, you've got us, and he's got the morgue.'

Prentice rose from his seat, mouth open, his face aghast.

'You're joking. What? How is this possible?'

Stark sipped at his coffee. 'It's possible, all right. Do you know him, then? Sorry, *did* you know him?'

'Don't be clever, you bloody well know I do . . . did.'

'Well, I wasn't sure, you seemed to be being a bit cagey about your relationship, any reason for that, Roy?'

'No, you're just being typically arsey.'

'Roy, the only person with a chip on his shoulder is you, my friend, now are we going to talk like grown-ups?'

'We are, well I am, at least.'

'How did you know James Deely?'

'I've used him as a solicitor a couple of times and one of the kids here, told me yesterday he had stolen a car, and so I wanted to meet him today to bring the lad in to the station. As you know, we have to bring them in if they tell us stuff like that, but I always make sure they have proper representation, before I take them to the station.'

'That's very considerate of you, I take it that it wasn't your car he stole?'

'Er, no they wouldn't steal my car.'

'Why James, in particular? Any reason?'

'I know him from college, we went to the same Poly at Nottingham.'

'Did you socialise?'

'Other than the odd pint after a shift or when I'd seen him at the police station, no. We would have had a pint tonight for example. Anyway, how did he die?'

'Is there anything else, you can tell us about him, Roy?'

'I don't think it's right to tell you anything else, that's for his family, not me. So, how did he die?'

'I don't think I should divulge those details, Roy, do you? I mean, it wouldn't be right now, would it?'

'Oh, I see what you mean, I guess not.'

'It's only right, isn't it?'

Talking to Roy was like pulling teeth, long and painful. Stark gleaned that he lived at Bulwell, and that he drove a blue Vauxhall Cavalier. As they left, Derek saw them out.

'Sorry about . . . you know.'

'It's not for you to apologise, Derek, there are lots of Roy's in the world. Did he get to work on time?'

'Yes he did. Twenty minutes early in fact.'

'Not agitated?'

'No more than normal.' They laughed.

'And nothing unusual in his behaviours, or anything we should know about? It's the sort of thing we would be interested in with anybody, it's purely a routine question. We aren't "oppressing" him.'

'I know, you don't need to tell me that, Inspector. No, nothing out of the ordinary; I would tell you if there was.'

One of the kids appeared in the hall. 'Stop being a fucking grass, Derek.'

'Thanks for the coffee, Derek. We'll leave it with you. Incidentally, I don't know how you do it.'

Derek sighed. 'Because somebody's got to.'

*

It was 9 p.m. before Stark got back to Nottingham Police Station. He spoke in private with Detective Superintendent Wagstaff, in his office.

Wagstaff was reminiscing. 'You know David, I had a case like this; I think it was 1971. A tramp had slept overnight in the victim's car and panicked when she left early in the morning. Something to bear in mind, there isn't always some big motive behind a murder.'

'True.'

Stark never underestimated Wagstaff, he was sometimes the subject of ridicule because of his upright bearing, moustache twiddling, and the idiosyncratic way he would speak over your head or look at the window when he spoke. Yes, he was old-school, but he had an amazing memory and could quote precise conversations you'd had a year ago and sometimes he would come out with a little gem. One thing David had learned in managing investigations, is that it is no good having a team who all think alike, that was a recipe for narrow thinking. You needed different mind-sets and an understanding that everyone had a voice.

'What have you got in mind, David? I fear this could be a runner, with no obvious motive jumping out at us.'

'Could be, but its early days yet, sir. We need to sort the press release out – '

'I will sort that out, David.'

'Okay, that's good, thanks. Investigation wise, I want to expand the house-to-house out towards Linby village and search the victim's home whilst the policewoman is still there.'

'Tippy-toes, David.'

'Tippy-toes, it is, sir. We will be tactful, don't worry. HOLMES will be set-up tomorrow so the database will start throwing out actions from there.'

HOLMES was the clumsy acronym for Home Office Large Major Enquiry System. All results of activities on the murder enquiry, or 'actions' were inputted, and it would throw out further enquiries, and you could search the database to find matches of all enquiries where, say a 'red car' is mentioned. The idea was that nothing was missed once the enquiry became unwieldy. It saved a lot of time and cut down massively on errors, and key issues being missed by tired analysts.

'That's all well and good but don't forget you are running the case, not that whirly-gig thingamajig.' Wagstaff said.

'I know, HOLMES is a big help, but if I prioritise the actions in the right order, then that tends to steer the investigation the right way.'

Wagstaff was moustache twirling. 'I think it would be an idea to get Force Support to widen their search parameters, David, it would be good to get the knife. Keep using the dog-section and mounted.'

'You know sir, I always wanted to answer the phone in their department and say; "Inspector Stark, Dogs Mounted!"'

'Why? Oh, I see, a joke, yes very good, David. Ahem!'

Stark wished he'd never bothered. 'Fingers crossed for the forensics; they should have something for us imminently.' He said.

'Yes, finger's crossed. Until we have something more solid, it's family, friends and background. Yes?' Wagstaff said.

'That's it, sir.'

'I'll update the Chief, shortly.'

'Fine. Give him my regards.' David had only seen him twice in the three years he had been Chief Constable, and one of those was for a bollocking.

'Yes. We will do a press conference in the morning. De-brief the lads for me, and I'll probably see you later.'

Stark caught sight of the gangly, Detective Sergeant Stuart Bradshaw at the far end of the corridor as he was returning to his office.

'How's it going, Stuart?'

'All right, sir, I was just looking for you. We have pretty much done on the car, and so will await whatever Forensics come up with. I've done you a list of all the items recovered, and obviously we've got to work closely with Forensics to see where the information is going to take us. I've got a copy of the list here, if you want it?'

'Of course, thanks. Have you got time to go through it with me now?'

'Sure.'

Starks office was halfway down the corridor, a smallish room with just a desk, two chairs and a metal filing cabinet. On the wall was a photograph of Stark's CID Initial Course, class of 1972: a group of apprehensive young men in kipper ties and flared trousers, smiling inanely. On his desk was a photograph of his wife, Carol, and their children, Laura and Christopher. Someone had thrown a rubber plant in the corner of the room, but it looked a bit tired and lonely. Maybe that was why Stark liked it, so did he sometimes.

Stark took a seat behind his desk and encouraged Stuart to draw up a chair next to him. He stared down at the list.

Thirty-six fibres recovered from rear seat of vehicle.

Nine hundred millilitres (two pints approx.) of (congealed) blood recovered from within car.

Thirty-one fingerprints found on or inside the vehicle.

One ounce of debris (believed soil) removed from floor of vehicle.

Forty-nine human hairs found inside the vehicle.

No footprints of any note found at scene.

Twenty-seven fibres on front offside seat of vehicle.

'Thirty-six fibres from rear seat?'

Stuart explained. 'Yes, but they could be anybody's; friends, family and of course they could be years old.'

'Still, we can get a list of everyone who had lawful access to that car. If it is only a handful, we may be able to eliminate some of the fibres and get the list down to the suspect's only.'

Stuart grimaced. 'I think the list is fine, but I also think you will find the scientists at Huntingdon lab would prefer the one suspect to compare with, it will be much easier.'

'You're right, I'm just thinking aloud, here. There is the potential, of course, that the authorised passenger also happened to be the killer.'

'That is true.'

'Now then, let's see, 900 milli what? Oh, two pints of blood, right, well until it is analysed, we assume that is the deceased's for now. That is just the congealed blood, I take it. He will have lost a lot more.'

'That's it.'

'Thirty-one fingerprints found on inside and outside of the vehicle. Okay, well, we will be taking elimination prints from everyone, where exactly were they?'

'Normal places a passenger would leave them, windows, dashboard, glove compartment, mainly windows and outside of doors. In my opinion, they don't look recent but who knows? Maybe I'm wrong. I hope so.'

'Let's see what comes of it on the database, but if the killer has no form, or has been in the armed services, we are buggered.'

'That is even if any of the prints are the killers. There is no guarantee, it seems pre-meditated so surely they would have gloves on.' Stuart observed.

'You would think so, wouldn't you? What else is on your list? Soil, well, yes.'

'We've taken a control from the garden of the dead man's house to see if they can get a match.'

'I can't see that taking us anywhere. I don't know; we'll have to see. They could still have soil on their shoes or trousers, I suppose. It's a bit of something, I guess. "Forty-nine human hairs found inside the vehicle" That's great. That is more like it, if it is a stranger who's done it; all we need to know is who the bloody hell they are!'

Nobby Clarke came into the office tapping on the open door with his knuckles, out of courtesy, as he did so. He sat down, nodding to Stuart who was in mid flow.

'That is always the tricky part.' Stuart laughed.

'Just a bit.'

'It's not a bad trawl to go at, sir, there will be the post-mortem stuff to work on, fingernail scrapings and the like.'

'You've done a cracking job, Stuart, well done, mate.'

Nobby piped up. 'Sorry, to interrupt, boss, but we are ready for the de-brief, whenever you are.'

'No problem, we've done here. Thanks again, Stuart, keep me posted, won't you?'

'Of course.'

Stark and Nobby joined the others for an informal de-brief, it was pretty obvious that they had not got very far, and it quickly ran dry, as did Nobby. 'Can I suggest something, boss?'

'What's that Nobby?'

'Can we adjourn to the bar? I'm bleeding gagging for a drink.'

Cries of 'Great idea, Nobby,' and 'Best thing you've said all day,' made the decision easy for Stark.

*

Nottingham Police station bar was on the top floor, away from the everyday goings-on, next to the administration offices. The bar area was not overly large, but it had concertina doors running the length of the room, which could be opened to reveal a dancefloor for bigger functions that were periodically held there. The bar committee had to keep it solvent after all. It was quite tastefully decorated and despite its location felt very much like any other bar. The only difference was that there was nobody trying to listen to what was being said, apart from when the public were admitted for 'do's.

Stark was surprised to see Wagstaff there, who immediately latched on to him, with Jim McIntyre hanging on. Stark would have preferred to have been stood with his team, but endured Wagstaff's enforced separation, for now.

'So, the chief said, "While ever Waggy's got his spoke in, the wheel won't come off!"' Jim McIntyre broke into uproarious laughter at the unfunny anecdote. He really was a git at times. Stark smiled politely.

DI Lee Mole walked in and joined them at the bar.

'Look at this, a murderer on the loose and the team are on the lash! Not bad is it?'

Wagstaff laughed. No-one else did.

'They've only just finished, Lee, be fair.' Wagstaff said.

'Crime doesn't sleep, sir. I must be too old-school, too well-disciplined.'

'Mind you, I'm old school myself.' Wagstaff commented.

'Are you, sir? A man after my own heart. We need to stick together.' He winked at Stark.

Stark was trying not to be drawn but couldn't resist responding to the snipe. 'Well, Lee, everyone needs some down-time. If they work through the night, they will be dead on their feet in three days and then what?'

'I'm just saying, that's all. Chill out, dude.'

'It's called management, there's a book on it in the library.' Stark said.

'I don't' get time to go in the library Dave, I'm too busy cracking heads!'

'You've got all on cracking a smile, Lee, never mind heads.'

Lee ignored the comment. 'Do you want a drink, sir?' Lee asked

Wagstaff.

'That's very kind, Lee, I'll have a pint, please.'

Jim wandered off towards the team, who were at the far end of the bar, deep in conversation.

Charlie was quizzing Cynthia. 'So, have you had any problems since being in the force, Cynthia? Being a person of colour, I mean?'

'Let's not go there, Charlie.' Ash said.

Jim jumped in with both feet, as usual. 'I'm interested too, I know a lot of blacks who always seem to think they are bad done to.'

Ashley interjected. 'Do we have to? We are having a drink, it's a bit heavy, after a long day.'

Cynthia put her hand on his arm. 'It's OK, Ash, I think that a black officer changes people's attitudes when he or she arrives at a station.'

'D'you think?' Jim waded in. 'Or do you think he just makes people talk in hushed tones, and look around the room before they make comments?'

'Rome wasn't built in a day.' Cynthia said.

'When in Rome...' Jim said.

Charlie joined in. 'I worry that it is divisive. We all police ourselves, don't we? If someone picks on the Aide too much, or bullies them, one of us old farts will tell them to cut it out.'

'So, I'm reliant on your moral compass am I, and when *you* think I've had enough you will step in. Is that good enough, do you think?' Cynthia said.

'I take your point.' Charlie was pragmatic.

Ashley chimed in. 'So, what do we think about James Deely, then?'

It didn't work.

Cynthia continued. 'The problem is, you don't know what it is like to walk into a police station for the first time and be welcomed by 'here comes the nigger!'

Jim laughed.

'Have you really had that?' Charlie asked.

'We all have.'

'That's not right, is it? That's just bang out-of-order!' Charlie shook his head.

'It's not right is it Jim?' she asked.

'People are so damned sensitive nowadays; Christ knows what it will be like in twenty years' time. People call me Jock all the time, who gives a fuck?'

'But Jock isn't a derogatory term is it?'

'Is that your view or mine? Put it this way, love, if I turned up at the Afro Caribbean Club, would I be welcome?'

'Maybe.'

'Och, come on, hen, you know I wouldn't. What if I wanted to set up a White British Club on the tax-payers money, would I be allowed?'

Ashley tried to get some common ground. 'It amazes me that the police and the black community clash so often.'

'How do you mean, Ash?' Cynthia asked.

'Well, we're a minority group within the community; we're stereotyped by the media. Members of the public judge us as a group and not as individuals, they have pre-conceived ideas about us, special derogatory terms for us, 'pigs' and 'filth' and all that shit, do you know what I mean?'

Cynthia smiled. 'Interesting.'

Nobby had cornered Steph at the far end of the bar, as soon as they all started talking about race. The two were speaking in hushed tones.

'Come off it, Steph, an attractive woman like you, must have scores of men after you.'

'I do until they find out I'm a detective and it changes the dynamic. I want a man, not a wimp, and those that think they can take me on are all mouth and trousers. They've got nothing to back it up.'

'Maybe you are talking to the wrong men.'

She played her tongue across her white teeth, the fullness of her mouth accentuated by blood red lipstick. 'Nobby, you're so transparent, you really are.'

'You can't blame me for trying, now can you? I'm serious, though.'

'I don't go for cops, Nobby, and certainly not someone senior to me. Anyway, you shouldn't flirt with officers who are underneath you on the greasy pole.'

'But that's the whole point.'

'What is?'

'To get you underneath me!'

They laughed.

'And as for the greasy pole!'

4

*'If a man is going to be a villain,
in Heaven's name let him remain a fool.'*
William Temple

Arrangements had been made for the press conference to be held at Sherwood Lodge that morning and Stark stood in the station kitchen to watch the TV. Wagstaff was front and centre as Stark watched the dying embers of the broadcast.

'Have you any leads at the moment?' A journalist asked Wagstaff.

'There are several avenues of enquiry being investigated. We are always ready to hear from members of the public with any information; even if they consider it to be trivial, it may be of use to us.'

'How was Mr Deely killed?' One press member shouted. 'What was the cause of death?' asked another.

The police press officer toyed with her collar surreptitiously giving a 'cut-it' sign across her throat.

'I'm sorry, no comment at this stage. That's all for now, we will keep you updated with any developments. Copies of the press statement are at the front. Thank you.'

The director sent the shot back to the news studio and Stark sat at the police station kitchen table. He began studying the witness statement of the Home Office pathologist who had performed the post-mortem. He had taken it in to read while he had a sandwich. It was nearly lunchtime. The statement started with the details of Professor Hargreaves, he marvelled at the list of qualifications that heralded the statement: 'I am a Home

Office pathologist, a consultant pathologist and a Professor of Forensic Medicine at the Queens Medical Centre, Nottingham. I am a Doctor of Medicine, a Bachelor of Surgery, a Member of the Royal College of Surgeons, a Licentiate of the Royal College of Physicians, a Fellow of the Royal College of Pathologists and I hold the Diploma in Medical Jurisprudence.'

'Strange, nothing about him passing his cycling proficiency test.' Stark chuckled to himself.

The statement continued with the detail about them cataloguing all marks and blemishes to the exterior of the body before the highlighted sections of the internal examination: Mouth, neck structures, Larynx and Pharynx, Thyroid Gland, Cervical Vertebrae, Chest wall, Pleural Cavities, Bronchial Tree.

As he came to the vital organs, Professor Hargreaves included the weight of each one, measured out as is on the scales as if in a butcher's shop.

Lungs, Heart, Thymus Gland, Oesophagus, Abdomen, Stomach, Intestines, Liver, Spleen, Kidneys, Adrenal Glands, pancreas, Gall Bladder, Ureters.

Having been to countless post-mortems, Stark could envisage the funk as each organ was removed, a clinging stench that haunted you for days. He read on.

Bladder, Aorta, Inferior Vena Cava, 'I think I met her at a club, once, she's a flamenco dancer.' Varying lengths of observations relating to different body parts were written out beneath each heading. Head, Skull, Meninges, Brain, Cerebral Arteries, Skeletal System.

Hargreaves went on to list some twenty-two main exhibits he had taken, including hair (head and pubic), various swabs (penile, anal, nose, mouth), blood, liver tissue and stomach contents. The learned pathologist then did a resume of the events that in his opinion had caused the relevant injuries or peculiarities to the individual body parts. The statement terminated with several pages of pre-printed line drawings of the human outline, front and back, with the areas of evidential interest marked on them in pen. An idiot's guide to the endless medical terms used throughout the statement. Stark had a feeling they were for his benefit as much as anyone else's. He finished his sandwich and strode back toward his office. He saw Cynthia coming out of it.

'Are you all right, Cynthia, did you want me?'

'Have you seen Nobby anywhere, sir?'

'No, I haven't, oh I tell a lie, he was in the kitchen about twenty minutes ago, he left when Wagstaff came on the telly. He won't be far away; I wouldn't have thought.'

'Is that the pathologist's statement, you mentioned this morning?'

'It is, you ought to read it when you get chance, it's amazing, the complexity of it.'

'What does it say?'

'Well, thinking about it, it basically says he was stabbed in the neck!'

'Wow! That is complex, sir.'

'Go on, bugger off Cynth, you cheeky sod.' She laughed her way back to the general office.

Stark followed her path. He could hear, Jim McIntyre complaining as usual. 'I was office manager for the Marriott murders. Bloody marvellous, you do a good job and what thanks do you get? Bugger all, apart from freezing your bollocks off chasing shadows half-way round Nottingham with a bloody- oh hello, Cynthia.'

Stark walked in. 'Will you shut the hell up? You are constantly moaning all the time, Jim.'

'I'm only kidding on, Boss.'

'Are you? Well get your coat on and take Cynthia to do house-to-house follow ups, and if there aren't any coming in, have a look at the local dosshouses and Sally Army hostels, to follow up on Wagstaff's "tramp in the car" theory.'

He then instructed, Nobby, Charlie, Steph and Ashley to throw up any local prison releases of note and check them out.

*

Cedar Tree Probation Hostel was on the outskirts of Nottingham and in its time had been the subject of various protests from neighbouring estates, usually via the local newspaper. Ex-offenders all put in one place, often created a nervousness, perhaps understandably, by people living nearby. Whenever one of its residents had re-offended, there were pleas to have the place shut down.

Simon Leivers had been in charge of the hostel for almost seven years and was totally dedicated to the rehabilitation of the prisoners who were sent there as a half-way house; from prison, back into the community. All the residents were men, and many were sex offenders, but they did not discriminate, some armed blagger's and GBH merchants also frequented its halls, and subsequently strolled around the centre of town, with the public oblivious to the dangerous criminals walking amongst them. Simon was quick to defend those in his charge, but in fairness he was, by contrast, very strict about rule-keeping. There were clear rules to the place and while ever they were adhered to, he was fine; but once they were broken, he turned, he would come down hard. He was a firm believer that trust works both ways. He wouldn't let them down, but if *they* let him down, if they were consistently late after curfew, or worse, re-offended; Simon would be on the phone to the police and they would be back in the clink. With less important rule breaking, they had a 'three strikes and you're out', policy.

Simon had most success with the young sex offenders.' Some of these were just young men who had never been taught how to respect barriers, and had got themselves into a situation with a young girl that was later regretted, and the girl would tell mummy or daddy and the youth turned from suitor, to sex offender in the blink of an eye. These lads were the easiest to deal with, many from reasonable backgrounds, once they knew that rules were there for a reason, many did not re-offend. Almost all the others, in truth, were a waste of time, they had no remorse, and were just learning more and more from fellow inmates, on how to commit crime, and broaden their horizons in doing so. Simon had known DC Charlie Carter since he first came to the hostel. He liked him and trusted him to be fair whenever he dealt with those on probation. A slight man, he stood wiping his spectacles as he warmly greeted Charlie, and Nobby.

As they settled down in the office for tea and biscuits, Simon asked the question: 'Is it a social call, chaps, or do we have business to attend to?'

Charlie took the lead. 'I suppose its business, Simon. I don't know if you've read in the paper about the murder of the young solicitor in Papplewick?'

'I have. Ah, I see. I heard it on Radio Nottingham. I hope there's nothing concrete that brings you to our door?'

'We are doing the rounds, Simon, for prospective candidates, more checking movements than anything.' Charlie said.

'I'm with you, let me guess, Gerry Sanders? Released on parole after a four year stretch for wounding a young man in a totally unprovoked attack?'

Charlie grinned as he replied. 'Got it in one, Simon. Is he in?'

'He should be yes, what are you intending doing with him?'

'Well, firstly does he have an alibi?'

'When was it?'

'Yesterday at, let's say 8 a.m. onwards.'

'That's early. Unfortunately for Gerry I can't alibi him, as he leaves for work at 7.45.'

'What does he do?' Nobby asked.

'Just a bit of labouring, most of them are only capable of humping stuff about, but they earn a few quid, and it gives them a sense of worth.'

'Where does he work?'

'Er, I can't remember the name, he works there a couple of mornings a week, it's the top farm at Linby.'

'Selby's Farm.' The two detectives said in unison.

'That's it.'

'Does he share?'

'He's shares with a bloke called Pete Brown, who's in for

burglary of dwelling houses.'

'Sanders is in solely for the wounding, isn't he?' Charlie asked.

'Yes. He hasn't really settled in that well, though he's been here about a month. I must admit that I get the feeling that he's unhappy about something; he hasn't opened up to any of us yet. Hopefully he will.'

Simon led the detectives upstairs and into the second bedroom on the right. Gerry lay on his bed, fully clothed, as did Pete. The room was compact, and it was as if the two occupants had drawn an imaginary line down the middle, each half, the mirror image of the other. Each had a single bed, a bedside cabinet, a wardrobe and a sink; which they both urinated in when they couldn't be bothered to go to the communal loo. The room was clouded by smoke as the two puffed on cigarettes. The two glanced at each other at the unexpected intrusion.

Simon introduced his guests. 'This is Gerry on this bed, and Pete over here. Guys, these two gentlemen are from the-'

'CID. We know, Simon,' Gerry interrupted. He was a slim man, heavily tattooed, with long hair and a leather string bracelet on his wrist. He was in his late twenties but had the mind of a teenager.

Pete, was a fresh-faced youth, who looked as if butter wouldn't melt in his mouth, until he spoke: 'What are we supposed to have fucking done, now?'

Gerry raised a hand to his mate. 'Cool it Pete. What can we do for you guys?'

Pete ignored the advice. 'Fucking pigs! I'm sick of this bullshit!'

'All right, Pete. Let's have less, please.' Simon didn't want a scene.

Nobby ignored the callow youth and spoke directly to Gerry. 'We want to talk to you, Gerry. Nothing to get your knickers in a twist about, we just want to know your movements, so we can eliminate you from a job yesterday.'

'Here we go. I knew it. Are you arresting me?' Gerry grew agitated for a moment.

'That shouldn't be necessary.' Charlie answered.

Gerry lay back on his bed and put his hands behind his head. 'OK, shoot.'

'Eight o'clock, yesterday.'

'I was down the pub, two pint limit, that's cool, Simon, yeah?'

'Not last *night* Gerry, we mean eight o'clock in the *morning*.'

He sat up on the bed. 'Fuck off, you're here about that murder, no fucking way, dude.'

'How do you know about the murder?' Nobby asked.

Pete interrupted. 'This is all kinds of bullshit, man.'

'They let us listen to the radio, you know, and, shock, horror we have a television.' Gerry answered, sarcastically.

'All right, Gerry, so, where were you?' Nobby asked a second time.

'Exactly where I am right now, only my little peepers were closed. I was in the land of nod, am I right, Pete?'

Pete nodded, unconvincingly. 'Yep.'

'So, you don't mind giving us a witness statement to that effect then, down at the nick?' Charlie said, sensing deceit.

Gerry jumped of the bed and stood up. 'That's cool by me, dude. Go for it. Come on let's do it, man.'

'Let's have a look round first.' Nobby said. He began opening drawers. It wouldn't take long.

'I've given permission for the search, it's the house rules; you know that. OK?' Simon clarified with Gerry.

'I thought you were at work yesterday?' Charlie asked.

'I overslept, man.'

'Where do you work?'

'Selby's farm two days a week. He's a miserable old cunt, a right fucking slave driver, you should be investigating him not me.'

'What do you know about the murder then, Gerry?' Charlie asked.

'Only what I heard on the radio, dude, some solicitor got killed, or what's-a-name, er thingy, a suspicious death, that's it, but everyone knows that shit means murder.'

'How long have you been at the hostel?'

'About three months.'

'Enjoying it?'

'It's like, dead cool man, it's like prison with its pants down, man.' Pete started giggling.

Simon smiled. 'That's not a bad way of describing it, in truth.'

'Cheers dude.' Gerry gave Simon a high-five.

'Do you want a brief to represent you when we get to the station? We are just going to get a statement off you, that's all, but it's up to you, it could take a few hours waiting.'

'No, I'm cool, as long as you ain't snowing me.'

'Who are your solicitors?' Nobby asked.

'Fenwick and Blythe, in the city centre, same crew my old man had, passed down through the generations.'

'That is beautiful, a lovely heritage.' Charlie said, tongue-in-cheek.

Nobby lifted the mattress; there was a small slip of paper.

'What's this?'

'That's nothing, man, just some rubbish. Give it me, if you like, I'll bin it.' The room seemed to go down a couple of degrees.

Nobby picked it up and read it aloud. 'Bernie Squires Turf Accountants, a series of bets by the look of it. Timed at, let's see, here we are, twelve minutes past eight, yesterday morning.'

Simon put his hand to his face.

'So why lie, Gerry?' Nobby asked.

'It's against the house rules, dude, no gambling. Sorry, Simon, it's the first time, man, honest.'

Simon was not best pleased. 'It will be a formal warning, Gerry, three strikes and you're out and that is number two.'

'Man, that stings.'

This changed things. It could be someone else's betting slip, of course, but it seemed unlikely. It would have been more damaging to Gerry as a murder suspect, if he was at work yesterday at Selby's Farm, close to the scene, rather than his initial thinly alibied explanation of being in bed. This was now a reasonable alibi at the betting shop; across town from the murder scene, at the relevant time. The statement would be checked out. He would be in the system for checks if forensic came back with anything. They weren't going to nick him, anyway, so...

'I'll tell you what I'm going to do, Gerry.' Nobby said.

'I'm going to give you a break, and take a witness statement in Simon's office, seeing as you have been co-operative, well, sort of.'

'That's cool, man, appreciate it.' He shook Nobby's hand.

'Are you cool, I mean, are you OK with that, Simon?' Nobby said.

'Absolutely fine by me. If it suits your purposes.'

'It does.' The detectives said in unison.

*

Stark and Steve Aston noticed the change in Sarah Deely, just in one day. The dark rings beneath her eyes, underlying the nightmare her life had become. She was chain-smoking and drinking too many Martini's, any time, any place, anywhere. She was a mere shell of her former self- no more 'airs and graces'. The hushed conversation included a rather plump detective policewoman, from the Family Support Unit who had replaced Kelly.

Sarah was much more accepting of the situation, but still felt like she had been hit by a steam train.

Stark was trying to negotiate around the delicate act of asking pertinent questions without being too insensitive.

'I know how difficult this must be for you, but it is so important to help us find the person who has done this. Do you mind telling us who James' family are, please, Sarah?' Steve Aston scribbled down the information in his notepad as they went along.

'There is us of course, and then his father, Cyril, who lives miles away, in Torquay, his Mum has passed away. That's about it really, no siblings, and then there is my side of the family who we only see on high days and holidays.' Her voice was nasal, her nose and mouth bunged up, because of all the crying.

'Does his Dad know what has happened?'

'Yes, I rang him. He's distraught, he's not a well man as it is.'

'What about James' friends?' Stark subconsciously rubbed his fingertips along the leather arm of the chair as he formulated the questions.

'We aren't big socialisers, to be honest. He has his work friends. I know he plays squash with a couple of them. There is a guy called Roy, who works at a kid's home, but that is just an occasional pint. James can't stand him really. Sorry, *couldn't* stand him, I can't get used to talking about my husband in the past tense.'

'Talk in the present tense, if it is easier, it's perfectly fine.' Stark said.

'I'll do that, if you don't mind, just for now. We are both too knackered at the end of the day, to want to be bothered to go out on the town. Katy takes it out of me. Occasionally he will go to the Horse and Groom – he knows a couple of the regulars there, they do a quiz night.'

'Is that it, Sarah? Anybody else?'

She stared ahead vacantly; her mind moved away from the question. 'I still can't believe this is happening, nobody would want to do this to us.' She sipped at her drink.

'Is there anybody else who could tell us about him, Sarah?'

'No, um, well there is his old gang of friends from college, they meet up every year, sometimes more than that.'

'Who are they, Sarah?'

'I doubt they can help you, they all went to Nottingham Polytechnic together a few years ago. In fact that Roy, from the kid's home, he went there as well, I think.'

'Are there a lot of them?'

'Not really, just a handful, Stuart, Jonathan, Caroline – There's a few more, maybe half a dozen all told. As I say, they only meet two or three times a year, if that.'

'Do you know their surnames?'

'Blimey. Stuart, I'm not sure about. Jonathan Stacey, Caroline, um, she got married to one of the group – they were all in the same year at college. Roy Prentice was one of them, did I say that? Have you seen him? Surely he told you?'

'Roy isn't the most helpful, I'm afraid. I'm sure we can trace who they are in the fullness of time. What about James' habits? What did he do on his days off, for example?'

'Days off? He used to sit at the table catching up on paperwork, most of the time. It was a bone of contention between us, you know, the fact that he never stopped working. He just said it would be worth it in the end. What a load of crap that turned out to be.'

'Anything else?'

'No, just playing squash, did I mention that? He even saw that as networking. Occasionally I managed to get him to take us to the park or the castle, normal, family stuff, you know.'

'Would you say he was a solitary sort of person?'

'Solitary? Why do you say that?'

'Just the name of your house – Solitude.'

'Oh, no, that was just a silly joke of his. He was a solicitor. The house is at a high altitude. Solitude was a combination of the two words – solicitor and altitude.'

'I get it. Quite clever, really. What sort of an upbringing did he have, Sarah?'

'Very good, from what he told me. He never wanted for anything. Spoilt, I suppose you might say. His parents doted on him. His mother died when he was only sixteen; I don't think he ever fully got over it. Maybe they are re-united now.' She began to sob and was comforted by the policewoman.

Stark gave her time to recover, before continuing with the questions. Steve made a cup of tea for everyone, with Sarah's permission. The policewoman was trying to sooth her when she broke down in one of her intermittent outpourings. Eventually there was no avoiding 'awkward question' time.

'It's a horrible thing to have to ask, Sarah, but you are probably aware that I've got to ask it. Think carefully before you answer; it may be crucial to the enquiry.' He paused to give added weight to the importance of the question. 'I am not suggesting anything by the question at all. It is a question we always ask. Do you know, or did you have, the slightest suspicion, that James was seeing someone else?' He scrutinised Sarah as she answered.

She took a deep breath, the intake was jagged, and it made her shudder. 'It had crossed my mind occasionally. What woman doesn't think about it, when she's alone and her husband is late home every night?'

'Was he seeing somebody, do you think?'

'I don't think so, but who really ever knows?'

'Was there anything else, apart from him being late home, which made you have those thoughts?'

'No, nothing, it was just insecurity on my part, I suppose.'

'Anything from his past which you think might be serious enough to mention?'

'Not that he told me, I can't see it, no.'

'Sarah, were *you*, are *you*, seeing anybody else?'

She shrugged out a laugh. 'Me? No way, I am . . . was . . . very happy!'

'Was James happy?'

'Yes. I think so. Overworked, but happy, in his own way, yes.' Her voice was still choked with emotion.

Stark glanced at the DPW as he asked the most awkward question of all. 'Did you have a good sex life, Sarah? Pardon me for having to ask this, it is part of the overall picture.'

'It's okay, I get it. Did we have a good sex life? Truthfully? No, not really. But in my opinion, that's only a small part of a marriage. We were both pretty exhausted by the time we got to bed, and with a kiddie running around the house, there is little opportunity to swing from the chandelier.'

Stark smiled. 'I think we can all relate to that. Just finally, on the same subject. Did James have any strange, not strange necessarily, but unusual sexual proclivities? I guess I'm talking about BDSM, swinging, that sort of stuff? Again, sorry to have to ask such a personal question.'

'No, neither of us were into any of that stuff, we were just a normal, regular family.'

Stark thanked her for her time and complimented her on the

admirable way she had coped with his questions. She didn't have the energy to see them outside, which was OK. She lit a cigarette, and when the policewoman put the television back on, faded back to her private thoughts, clouded by the contents of her Martini glass.

*

For the next couple of days, with desperation never far away, Stark and Wagstaff struggled to find a motive. Could it be totally random? Their team struggled to get any clue, all the routine stuff was done, James' diaries were examined, his personal record at work reviewed, his clients; all of it came to nothing. No secret lover was found, no dark secret, no great enemies, and no motive. The enquiries were getting further and further away from James Deely. There was his college friends to consider, but it all seemed a bit of a long shot. It was baffling and frustrating, but just as Stark thought he was starting to make progress, as is often the case, something happens which changes everything.

*

It was dark. Cold for autumn, and the rooves of the houses threatened a sheen of frost. Stuart Millichip slammed the front door of his mother's house behind him and clambered onto his Harley Davidson motorcycle. He was coughing and spluttering again; he had been trying to shake the cold off for weeks, but he couldn't shift it. Coughs and sneezes in a motorcycle helmet were never a good thing. Despite his scruffy appearance – dirty jeans, wrinkled Def Leppard T shirt, and his long black greasy hair, with the dubious Freddy Mercury moustache – his bike was immaculate. 'If you paid as much attention to yourself as you do that bloody bike, you might get yourself a job and a decent young lady,' was a regular gripe his mother would throw at him from the doorstep. Stu zipped up his leather jacket and set off towards the Fox and Grapes public House, his bike roaring, giving him the attention, his personality never could.

As he pulled onto the street, he didn't notice the Ford Granada coming around the corner, and the car followed him as he turned left at the top of the road. The Granada tailed three cars behind the motor cycle; along the main street and out into the less densely populated area of the town. Stu was oblivious; he was looking forward to his game of pool and a pint. When he turned right into the pub car park, the Granada continued past, but turned around in the mouth of the next junction and parked in the entrance to a quarry, with a full view of the pub car park. Now wasn't the time. The driver was prepared to wait, it would be easier when he had consumed a few beers.

5

'Prejudice: A vagrant opinion
without visible means of support.'
Ambrose Bierce

Stark sat in his office, toying with Steve Aston's note pad: 'James Deely, by Sarah Deely'. He was deflated. He felt they were getting nowhere. He didn't seem able to get a grip on the enquiry. What do you do? You have a man, apparently of good character, who is killed. There appears to be no reason to kill him. Is it a maniac? A psychopath, who kills for the sake of it? 'Christ, I hope not,' He muttered under his breath. His desk phone rang.

'Stark.'

'Hello.'

Stark smiled. It was Carol. 'Hello beautiful.' He pictured her smiling eyes, framed by the short wispy haircut that gave her that 'pixie' look.

'I'm bored.' She said in an affected, pathetic voice that sought sympathy and attention.

'Why are you bored, my little pixie?'

'I've got nothing to do. I'm on my own. There's nothing on telly, four bloody channels, and still nothing worth watching!'

'Get out and go and see somebody then. Laura can watch Chris for you.'

'See who?'

'I don't know, - your mum, my mum, any of the family. What about your friends, what are they doing?'

'Wendy's out with Bill; it's his day off. And Rebecca's been at the park with the kids, they will be tired having been out all day.'

'Sandra?'

'She never goes out, she just likes to gossip on the phone, anyway she might be seeing someone.'

'Really?'

'Don't say anything, I don't know for definite, she's fed up with her husband being away.'

'That's not good, you don't do that, it's not on. The blokes just trying to pay the bills.' Stark glanced at his watch, then at the notepad. Thoughts were crowding for attention in his mind. Who would want to kill James Deely, what is it about him?

'I can see the appeal of taking a lover.' She teased.

'Mmm. Yes.'

'You're not even listening to me, are you?'

'Yes, I am. Go into town. I don't know, I can't run your life as well as my own, Carol, bloody hell, you don't need me to tell you what to do with yourself, surely?'

'When are you coming home?'

'Probably late, I can't come home and leave the lads to do it all.'

'Why not? You're supposed to be the boss, aren't you?'

'Carol, we've been through this a thousand times, for God's sake.'

'All right I knew I shouldn't have called; I know your precious police work is more important than me.'

Stark sighed. 'Of course, it's not, Carol, I'm busy, love, I haven't got a clue where this murder enquiry is going and everybody is on my back, Wagstaff, that arsehole Lee Mole keeps shit stirring every verse end. They all want to know why we aren't progressing, yet nobody can come up with anything we haven't done, or suggest anything of use themselves. I'm in the stocks here, with everybody throwing rotten tomatoes at me.'

'Oh, can I join in? That sounds like fun.'

He laughed. 'You would, as well.'

'Haven't you got any further with it, I'd hoped we would have got back to normal by now?' She said, without thinking.

'Don't you bloody start! It's one of those without any motive, I don't know if it's a maniac, a tramp sleeping rough in the car, or what? I don't know, I just get the feeling that it was planned, that there is more to this guy than meets the eye.'

'What is it you used to say when you were training the aides, years back, what did you used to tell them, the young detectives who were fresh out of the box? The advice you gave them when they were stuck with a case.'

He smiled. 'Go on what you know.'

'There you are then.'

'It's that simple is it?' He smiled.

'I don't know, but what else is there?'

'Thanks, pixie.'

'My pleasure. I thought it was *me* ringing *you* up for some sympathy!'

'I'm going to have to go, love.' Stark was yet again torn by wanting to be with his family, and his duty to the force. Carol uttered the words that were said too frequently between them recently. 'OK then, see you when I see you.'

'See you when I see you.'

'Love you, Mr Stark.'

'Love you, Mrs Stark.'

'Bye.'

Stark replaced the receiver. He shrugged out a laugh and mocked Carol's voice. 'I'm bored,' then he sighed, 'Go on what you know.'

He looked at Steve's notepad.

*

Jim McIntyre scoured the area looking for somewhere to park. There was an atmosphere in the car. Cynthia did not have much she wanted to say to Jim, and vice versa. It was a little strained. It had started to spit with rain, and the view was limited by the haze created by the streetlamps, the droplets of rain on the windscreen and the inadequate wipers of the CID car.

'There's a space over there, Jim.' Cynthia pointed.

He parked the car and they both scurried over to the

large Victorian building that was the Salvation Army hostel for 'down-and-outs'. A flea ridden old vagrant was sitting precariously on the stone steps, his long beard was shades of white and nicotine brown. He greeted them in a drunken drawl that was barely coherent.

'What you fucking bastards, doing with, what. . .' His torso rocked back and forth and side to side as he spoke, like a seaside puppet clown activated on the insertion of a twenty pence piece.

The detectives ignored him and entered the dimly lit, seedy world of despair that only few are forced to behold. There was a large foyer, with a tiled floor, which made it easier to clean vomit and other involuntary bodily fluids. A television room was to the left, crowded with derelicts, all focusing in on the comic quiz host, who, to most of the poor sods watching, in their inebriated state, may as well have been speaking in Swahili. To the right was a reception booth, with a young, not-so-down-and-out man, standing behind the counter.

Cynthia extended an elegant hand, which he shook. 'Hello, we are from the CID. Who's in charge?' She placed her hand on the chipboard, improvised counter, feeling it's rough surface on her soft hands.

'Hang on a sec and I'll get him for you.'

'Thanks.'

The young man sauntered down a corridor, leaving the two detectives feeling slightly uncomfortable in the madhouse. In the distance, shouts and swearing could be heard echoing through the rafters. A semi-brawl had started in the television room. Someone threw a chair.

'Ignore it.' Jim whispered to Cynthia out of the corner of his mouth. 'They'll be kissing each other in a minute.'

The youth returned with a small, balding, bespectacled man, wearing a grey shirt with the Salvation Army motto emblazoned on it. The Salvation Army superintendent had a soft but reassuring voice and he exuded an air of complete calm. 'Hello, how can I help you?'

Cynthia spoke. 'I don't know if he mentioned, we are from the police.' The man nodded. 'We're working on a murder enquiry and one of our tasks is to check all night shelters, to see if any of the occupants were out at the relevant time.'

'I think you have been to a couple of other shelters in Nottingham, haven't you? Or so I hear.'

'We sure have.' Jim confirmed.

'So, what is the relevant time?' The man smiled.

'Between half-seven and nine, last Monday morning.'

The superintendent took them into the reception booth and began thumbing through a jotter. He perused the entries for the relevant time and date.

'Let me see, it's a good time to check, actually, pretty early. There were only two missing from the hostel.'

'How many are here, in total?' She asked.

'Sad to say, there are about 112 with us at present.'

'How can you be so precise?'

'They are all logged in and out, and we do a physical check on them every two hours.'

'Why so regularly?' Cynthia asked.

'We have a lot of deaths, unfortunately; some give up the ghost, others are disease ridden, and refuse treatment, or have cancer, others drink themselves to death and get alcoholic poisoning, others commit suicide, of course.'

'That is awful.' Cynthia shook her head despairingly.

'Isn't it. We usually lose around one a week, two in winter.'

'How do you check them?' Jim asked.

'Each resident has his own cubicle, and we have a look in it. You see, if they don't sleep here for three nights, then their cubicle is swilled down and offered to someone else. We turn a lot away.'

Jim asked the obvious: 'Who are the two residents who weren't here then?'

'Jock Pulton and Barry Weir.'

'Are they here now?'

The superintendent glanced through the glass at the TV room; the fighting had ceased. 'Jock, was in the TV room about half an hour ago, but I think he has gone up to his cubicle now. His is number 102. I'll take you up.'

'What about Barry Weir?' Cynthia asked.

'He's not been back since Monday night, but that is not unusual for Barry, he's very much a street vagrant.'

Cynthia scribbled down the details of the two men from the jotter: both were in their late fifties. Quite old for vagrants; they don't tend to live beyond their sixties; if they are lucky. The superintendent led them up the stone staircase. The relentless wails and hacking of phlegm becoming increasingly louder with each step. He led them to the landing of the second floor. The lighting seemed barely adequate, but the heat was almost overwhelming and unfortunately seemed to emphasise the smell of sick and urine coming from the cubicles. It was a lengthy corridor, the cubicles coloured light blue with small numbers stuck on the doors, often with punch holes in them.

'This is it.'

Cynthia knocked on the door. There was no reply. She tried again, with the same result. Jim pushed at the door, and it swung open gently. A giant of a man was lying on the metal-framed bed. Apart from the off-white shirt and multi-coloured tank-top, he was naked. His legs were heavily ulcerated. The cubicle might have been better described as a cell, there was just enough room for the two detectives to step inside. When Cynthia saw the state of the man's undress, she stepped back outside.

Jim spoke as he shook at the man's shoulder. *'Come on, Jock, wake up pal, it's the police. Wake up, Jock.'*

Jock eventually opened his bulbous, bloodshot eyes, and queried the presence of his guests, in a broad Glaswegian accent.

'What dyee fackin want?'

He rose from the bed and struggled into his drab trousers, which stank of excrement and God knows what else. As he pulled them on, he fell back on to the bed and sat there, his face blank. He blew through his lips making a noise like a horse neighing. As Jock attempted to fight off his befuddled state, the intoxicants flooded his brain, causing him to close his eyes, head bowed forward. He shook his head from side to side sharply, his jowls flopping loosely as he did so. It was like a walrus landing on dry land after escaping the sea. Suddenly, he stopped his waking routine, sat bolt upright and stared at Jim.

'Who the hell are you?'

Cynthia asked. 'Is he decent?'

'Yes, you can come in.' Jim said. 'We're from the CID, are you awake yet, Jock?'

'Oh, it's the rozzers, is it? Shit! What in Christ's name have I been up to now, lad?'

Naively, Cynthia sat on the edge of the bed. 'We just want to know where you were on Monday morning, Jock, that's all.' She said.

Jock did not acknowledge her, addressing Jim.

'All I'll say to you is this, lad. If that chickaboo doesna take her fat black arse off ma bed, we're fighting, dyee understand me?' Jock stared at Jim. Jim looked at Cynthia. She reverted to the stance she had shown many times in the police. She smiled, stood up and retired to the door. She could have made a big issue of the vagrant's poisonous attitude, but really, what was the point? He was non compos mentis. She put the needs of a murder enquiry ahead of squabbling with a man, who had no chance of understanding what she was saying. Jim sat in her place, and then moved back slightly, unable to bear the halitosis.

'About half-seven in the morning, Jock, last Monday. What about it?'

Cynthia felt a pang that Jim had not reprimanded the man for his racism, but she was not surprised.

'You're a Scotsman, are you not? Jock said.

'I am and proud.' Jim said.

'Where dyee hail from?'

'From Coates, just outside Edinburgh.'

'Beautiful city, Edinburgh. Coates you say. I had a cousin used to live on Glencairn Crescent, Willy Brown, dya know him?'

'I don't, Jock. What about Monday morning, where were you my friend?' Jim had sprung back into a full Scottish dialect when in the presence of a fellow Scot, it was automatic.

'Oh Christ, man, ma heed hurts.' Jock rubbed a dirty hand through his lank hair.

'I can see that but try and remember for us and we can leave you in peace.'

'I canna remember that, lad.'

'You're gonna have to try, Jock.'

Jock scratched at his rat's nest hair as the lice too, were waking. 'All I can remember, and don't hold me to this, is walking up Mansfield Road, aboot two in the morning, and Christ, I remember waking up in some bloody coal shed, in Sneinton. I think it was Monday, but ma heed's puddled half the time.'

Jim looked at Cynthia. 'I think that's going to be as good as it gets.'

*

The noise in the Fox and Grapes was incredible. Heavy rock blared out from the jukebox, the customers had to shout to be heard, and there were loud cries and cheers from the group watching the pool match in the alcove at the end of the room. Most pubs have a layer of smoke hanging in the air; this pub had a layer of air hanging in the smoke. The smoke was mixed, mainly tobacco, but the piquant smell of cannabis joints was all too evident. It was a 'spit and sawdust' pub which a couple of years earlier had been ready for closure, before it became a regular for the bikers. Since then it had the best takings in the area. This meant the clientele were able to take more liberties than others might, and do whatever they liked, pretty much; with the landlord forced to turn a blind eye. The pool table and dartboard were the focal points. Apart from these there was little else in the pub other than the wooden tables and chairs. The police were aware of accusations from various quarters that drugs were a feature of the activity inside the place, but it was contained, and any trouble was sorted out by themselves, so it was not a priority. Out of all the niche groups of society, bikers were the least problematical.

Stu Millichip had lost his pool match but sat close to the table and watched his mate's progress. He was puffing on a particularly strong joint which didn't help his sore throat, but he kept easing it with pints of ale. He needed to skin up but he was running short of cash and so he would have to make do with skunk until he could afford something more hallucinogenic. Things were getting desperate. The mixture of his pints of mild and the dope had warmed his mind into a relaxed state: he was at one with himself, and every muscle in his body tingled as he sat sprawled on the wooden chair. Despite being chatty with everyone at the start of the evening, he was now beyond intelligent conversation; he would laugh into his pint when he heard others around him laugh; the reason behind the amusement a mystery to him. He had got to the state where the ale seemed to brim in his throat, and he decided it was time to leave. There would be no 'lock-in' for him tonight, he had had his quota. All he had to do was guide his machine towards home and collapse on the settee, or his bed, if he could manage the stairs. It was a dangerous proposition with the roads being so wet and his mind so befuddled.

As he struggled to his feet, he grunted his farewells, and his wave to the crowd was prolonged and exaggerated, causing some amusement.

'I bid you all a good night.' He performed a theatrical bow which created a loud, throaty burp. 'Bollocks!'

The freshness of the cold air brought a shiver and some relief to his smoke-filled lungs as he began to walk across the car park towards his beloved Harley Davidson motorcycle. He did not see the Ford Granada now pulling into the far entrance. Stu's mind was cloudy; he felt a little sick and swallowed hard to combat it. He paid scant attention to the blurred headlights in front of him. The Granada slowed momentarily. Within seconds its rev counter was in red. The great noise made by the powerful engine stopped Stuart in his tracks, and he attempted to focus on the cause of the din. The driver watched as Stu stopped and turn to face the headlights. Contempt coursed through taut veins, malevolence tightening into concentration. No mistakes.

Stu's puzzled expression turned into a smile. 'Who's pissing about?'

The driver revved hard and the engine strained to unleash the power. The car covered the thirty yards in two and a half seconds. Stu had no time to even take his hands out of his pockets as the vehicle hit him with almighty force: Stu's legs going backwards and his upper body forwards within a split second; his head striking the windscreen surround, and crashing to the tarmac face first, hands still in pockets. The force being the equivalent of his legs, and then head, being hit with a full swing of a sledgehammer. He was out for the count, but still alive. His unconscious body emitted a groan and his eyes flickered in spasm. The groan turned into a gurgle as vomit raced up his throat and into his mouth, as the body disposed of stomach contents to divert the energy towards staying alive. The driver could not be certain that he was dead and circled the vehicle around. Stuart felt no pain this time as the front tyre crashed into his face, initially scraping it along the road, until it rolled onto his head and crushed the skull, followed by the rear tyre which did it all over again. His brain had been compressed and tore through the meninges membrane as it squashed into a pulp. His left eye popped out the socket and dangled across his face, hanging in front of his other unseeing eye. Brain pulp settled in the vacant eye hole. Stuart's heart continued to beat of its own accord, the brain failing in its duty. It managed to splutter for a few seconds and then stopped. The slaughter was complete.

The screeching of tyres had drawn the attention of a young couple who were just leaving the pub. They witnessed the latter part of the macabre incident. The Ford Granada left the car park on the far side, its lights now turned off. The couple froze in abject horror. The girl screamed, and the man ran towards the corpse, stopping some yards away as he saw the awful sight. He grimaced and turned, running as fast as he could back towards the pub. The girls scream had alerted the bikers inside who came pouring out, expecting a fight of some sort. There was a telephone kiosk in the foyer. The young man shouted to his girlfriend. *'Don't go near him!'*

He was breathing heavily as he tapped out the three digits.

'Which service do you require, Police, Fire, or Ambulance?' The female voice was calm and aloof.

'Ambulance, no, Police! Both the fuckers, you silly cow!' he gasped.

'Thank you. Putting you through.'

6

'A fellow who is always declaring he is no fool,
usually has his suspicions.'

Wilson Mizner.

A thousand thoughts clouded David Stark's mind as he approached the turning into the Fox and Grapes' car park. He had been passed the call only minutes ago. Surely there was no way he could deal with two murders at once, it would have to be another DI. He turned the corner and parked his car on the road, both entrances to the car park were being cordoned off. Despite popular myth, there were no blue lights flashing at the scene; those were to get vehicles somewhere quickly or warn drivers of a hazard in the road not to flatten the battery once they had arrived. The entire scene was lit by floodlights drafted in by the Traffic Department. Policemen were milling around, and all heads turned towards the approaching Detective Inspector Stark. He spoke with a traffic sergeant; his inspector was elsewhere, dealing with another 'fatal'. Stuart's body had been removed by the ambulance to the Queens Medical Centre, where he had been declared 'Dead on Arrival'. A considerable number of Stu's friends were gathered close to the entrance of the pub, sitting on a wall. Stark spoke to the grey-haired traffic sergeant.

'Please tell me it's an accident.'

'Sorry, sir, it appears to be a deliberate act. According to a couple over there, the car turned around and went over him a second time, to finish the job.'

Stark rubbed his chin and stared at the sticky, congealed lump of blood and brain on the tarmac, which used to hold Stuart's thoughts and emotions. It pin-pointed where Stuarts head had been. The ambulance had taken Stuart to the hospital, even though there were no vital signs.

'What have you done so far?'

'I've got everybody's details, even the voyeurs who've arrived late for the show. We are putting the tape up, getting the floodlights finished and waiting for SOCO. I grabbed a couple of pics of the body in situ, from the camera in the "fatal" traffic car, but we haven't done a search of the scene, or taken the different angles of the photos or even started the fatal RTA process yet. I wanted to wait for you to check you were happy with what we were doing.'

A car came screeching around the corner, causing one of the girls in the biker crowd to scream. 'What the hell?' Stark said.

Detective Inspector Lee Mole and his side-kick DS Carl Davidson got out of the car.

'Fuck me.' Stark muttered.

Mole spoke as he approached them, 'It's OK, the cavalry has arrived. We can take it from here.'

'What do you mean you can take it from here?' Stark asked. The sergeant, left them to it, sensing conflict.

'Waggy's orders, he said there is no way you can deal with two murders at the same time, unless it's something to do with the one you are already dealing with, which it clearly isn't, and so he wanted the elite team to take this one. Its "sus" isn't?'

'Fair enough, if that is what Wagstaff has said. Its suspicious all right, Lee, the car has turned around and gone back over the poor sod while he was lying on the floor.'

'Yes! Happy days! We're in here, Carl.' The DS smiled and nodded, and he gave his boss a high-five.

Stark was embarrassed on their behalf.

'Let's just have a quick word with the couple who saw it.' Stark suggested and they walked over to the biker crowd.

The girl with long blonde hair and studded leather jacket was crying. The guy comforting her seemed older, probably mid-thirties, with black hair and stubble. He seemed close to tears himself. Stark took the couple back into the pub with Mole and Davidson, in tow. They all sat in the corner of the now deserted bar.

'So, what's happened?' Mole said impetuously.

'Hold, on Lee, they should be spoken to separately, they could influence each other's recall.' Stark said.

'Woah, hold on, David, I'm not stupid you know. I'm grateful for your interest, but it is my case now, and it will be much quicker doing it this way.'

Stark shrugged, but it was a schoolboy error. He lit a cigar and sat back, as Mole started to speak.

The girl was still tearful, and the man spoke. 'We aren't being split up; she needs me.'

'There you go.' Mole said, with Davidson chuckling.

'Tell it to the judge.' Stark said dismissively.

The man spoke again, his thoughts spilling out. 'I've never seen anything like it, I tell you. Jesus, man, the poor geezer didn't stand a chance. That was out of order, big–time.'

'What exactly did you see?' Mole asked.

'The guy, Stuart, we know him as Stu, don't we, Helen?' She nodded. 'He was just lying there, and the car just turned around and ran over him again, right over the poor guy's head. Man, that sucker popped – big time, I've never seen anything like that. Shocking, man.'

'Did you see how Stu happened to be lying on the floor in the first place?' Mole asked.

'He must have been run over, but I didn't see that, he was groaning slightly, I think. The driver of the car knew exactly what he was doing, he waited, he watched and then he killed him, right in front of our eyes. I'm telling you it was deliberate, man. That fucker knew what he was doing, I'm telling you.'

'Did you see the driver?'

'No, it was too dark in the car, but we were just bothered about Stu.'

'Any reg number?'

'No, I didn't see one.' Helen spoke for the first time. 'He turned his lights off, so you couldn't see it.'

The biker squeezed her hand. 'There you go, deliberate, he turned his lights off. There, see, told you.'

'What sort of car was it?'

Stark was thinking about going and leaving it with the 'elite'. There was nothing here for him. He was busy enough.

'A Ford Granada, new style. I'm not sure what colour though.'

'Tell him what Stu was saying earlier in the pub.' Helen urged him.

'What?' Mole asked.

'Oh, he was banging on about all sorts of shit, but he was telling us he went to College with that guy who got killed the other day, the solicitor. Do you think it could be something to do with that?'

Stark leaned forward. 'He what?'

'Him and the solicitor that got killed. They went to college together. They were mates, big time.'

Mole's head dropped. He was gutted.

'Oh dear, looks like you'd better leave it with me, Lee.' Stark said, trying not to smile.

Mole and Davidson rose sharply and left the table. 'It's bullshit!' Mole said.

As the two got outside, Mole was marching aggressively towards his car with Davidson moving his little legs to keep up. As Mole got to the driver's door, he trod on something and looked down. He noticed a piece of glass on the floor. It looked like glass from a headlight. He used his foot to usher it down a grate behind the car.

*

Stark, Wagstaff, and Nobby Clarke sat in the Detective Superintendent's office, sipping mugs of coffee in the dead of night. Wagstaff spoke.

'Well we have two murders in a matter of a few days that have a common link. We know Stuart Millichip and James Deely used to hang around in the same gang of friends at college. The question is why are they being killed?'

Stark was quick to offer his view. 'We have to treat them as linked; it is just too coincidental. When you think we only have six or seven non-domestic murders a year, in the whole of the County. I mean, it's not just that they went to the same college – they were in the same year, the same tutorial group and in the same group of friends. The "why" question is the key. That is where the priority lies. Find the motivation and we find the killer.'

Wagstaff was stroking his moustache. 'True, David. I think we need to have focus teams, one for the fundamentals, for each murder and the third being the bridging team, looking for any constants or connections between the two, notably the old college friends, wherever they may be.'

'They seem to have had very different outcomes since they left college, you couldn't get two more different people than Stuart Millichip and James Deely.' Stark sipped at his mug. 'I think its best that my team look at the bridge between the two, get to work on the college connections.'

'That's no problem.' Wagstaff agreed.

'There is a potential problem we need to think seriously about.' Nobby offered.

'What's that?' Stark asked.

'Well, it's obvious, I suppose; who the hell is next?'

'Shit, yes, we can't assume that it ends here, but we can't give them twenty-four-hour protection either.' Stark said.

Nobby agreed. 'Sure, but it is starting to look like one of them will be the next victim, and one of them is the killer.'

'Quite possible, Sergeant. It is still supposition, however.' Wagstaff said. 'We must target these friends, it could be two separate events, but as you say, David, and I agree, it seems too much of a coincidence.'

There was a lull caused by tiredness, and the reality of the situation as it slowly began to sink in.

'We need profiles of both victims, detailed, looking in all the nooks and crannies. We need to get out to the remainder of the group and try to get to the bottom of this. Somebody else in the group must know, or at least suspect, what this is all about?' Stark said.

'Post-hast, David, Post-haste.' Wagstaff said.

'It will be interesting to see who is least bothered about being protected.' Nobby added.

'Possibly so.' Wagstaff agreed.

Stark looked at his watch, it was twenty past two in the morning. 'Is that everything done for tonight?'

'Yes, I think so.' Wagstaff said. 'The post-mortem will be around 11 a.m., and we've got a team of five detectives, under the supervision of the incident room DI, starting us off overnight. The investigation proper will start in the morning. The snatch plan has brought nothing, which is a shame. Traffic are doing a mobile sweep for the Granada, I would have thought it would be abandoned, yet there is no report of one being stolen. Maybe they haven't discovered it yet, who knows? I suggest we try to grab some sleep and start back at eight o'clock tomorrow morning.'

'You mean today, sir,' Stark smiled.

*

Dave's mind was awash with waves of sound, which faded into the voice of a Radio Two Disc Jockey. He rolled over and peeped from beneath the covers at the digital read-out – 7.00 a.m. He closed his eyes again and buried his head into the soft, accommodating pillow, languishing in the warmth of the quilt. 7.00 a.m. 'Bloody Hell!' He turned on the light. He felt hot and sticky. His tiredness had not been chased away by the four hours' sleep, and his head throbbed as he staggered out of bed and put on his dressing gown. He flopped down onto the toilet and closed his eyes; he just couldn't wake up. He clumsily navigated his way downstairs, slipping on the second to last stair; the momentum causing him to burst into the living-room.

'My God, the creature from the lost lagoon,' Carol Smiled.

'Why didn't you wake me up?' The creature asked.

'You've got plenty of time, what's the matter with you? You didn't get in until the early hours, Dave. You have worker's rights, you know.'

'Darling, I'm the Detective Inspector on a double murder case, we don't have rights.'

'They will always flog a willing horse.'

'It's not like that . . . it's too early, Carol, let me grab a bite and try to wake up first. Oh, and good morning.'

'Good morning.' She pecked him on the lips.

Christopher and Laura sat transfixed at the television, as it pumped out some soporific trivia. David lurched into the kitchen in a trance, facial muscles in a state of collapse. He teased two strands of bacon out of the sizzling pan and slapped them between two slices of bread and returned upstairs, the thought of using a plate had not entered his mind.

Carol stood, hands on hips, at the bathroom door.

'Well, I've seen it all now!'

David had placed the bacon sandwich on the lavatory cistern and had begun to shave, intermittently biting into the bread. Some shaving foam had stuck to the sandwich. Dave, his mouth full of bacon, barked out a garbled reply that Carol interpreted as 'Shut the fuck up, I'm late.'

He didn't have time for a full shower, but quickly brushed his teeth, washed, and rinsed his head under the shower handset. He checked that Carol wasn't around and quickly ran a tap and dropped his cock and balls into the sink and gave them a bit of a soap up. He dressed hurriedly and shouted his farewells as he left via the front door. Carol shouted him back.

'*Dave!*'

He returned to the door.

'Don't I get a kiss?'

He kissed her on the lips, his own lips tight with irritation, and clambered into the car. He took potluck as he reversed out of the drive, condensation on the windscreens hindering his all-round vision. His heart sank as he heard a dull scraping noise; he had caught the offside wheel arch on his perimeter wall. He glanced at the clock: 7.32 a.m.

'Sod it.'

He crashed the gears and sped off, spinning his tyres in temper.

Once at the police station car park, he examined the damage to the car. Dints and scratches. 'Bollocks!'

Throughout the morning briefing, Stark was sullen. He was in a bad mood, he had been a minute late and he had damaged his car –what else could go wrong? The night shift detectives had passed on their actions and were asked to explain their individual results before Stark would allow them to go home. The Incident Room Detective Inspector had been Phil Dowty, a balding, wiry man who for some inexplicable reason spoke with a cockney accent, despite never having lived outside Nottingham. Some said he was drafted to London for a few weeks, years ago to support rioting and he came back like it. He explained how he had visited Mrs Millichip' 'gaff' and broken the news to her. He confirmed that both Deely and Millichip had not only attended the same college – Nottingham Polytechnic – but had associated closely together within the same group of friends at the time. Phil listed the college cadre of friends on the whiteboard.

Jonathon Stacey
Tracey Sewell
Caroline Winner
Mark Winner
David Seaton
Roy Prentice
~~Stuart Millichip~~
~~James Deely~~

He put a line ominously through the bottom two names of Stu Millichip and James Deely.

Stark read through the list and recalled the uncomfortable

meeting he had had with Roy Prentice at the care home. As the briefing closed, Charlie shouted to Stark, 'Phone call for you, boss.'

'Cheers Charlie. Stark speaking.'

'Roy Prentice here. I shall be at Arnold Lodge Community Home, all morning, and I won't go out until two of your detectives get here.'

'Morning Roy, what are you talking about?'

'What am I talking about? Well, that's really reassuring. I am talking about my life, Inspector, that's all, and I demand protection until this psychopath is behind bars.'

'Obviously you're talking about the murder of Stu Millichip.'

'There's no wonder you're a police inspector, is there? Well? What about it?'

'What about what?'

'Police protection. It could be any one of us next! This murderer is obviously something to do with the college, with our gang. He's got it in for us, any fool can see that.'

Stark sighed. 'Look, Roy, there are more people than you, impacted by this. I will get someone to come around to see you and give you some advice. We can fit a Home Office alarm at your house. We will review what else might be needed in due course.'

'In due course? I am not a bloody fool, Inspector, I know when I am being fobbed off, and I am entitled to a bit more than that.'

'Roy, you are entitled to the same treatment that everybody else in your position will get, and we don't have the resources to give 24/7 protection for six people, unless there is a direct and substantiated threat.'

'Yes, but there is. . .'

'Good day to you.'

Stark slammed down the phone. 'What a prat. First to complain about the police, first to demand criminals are released, and first to want help from the police if the nasty man might be coming his way. Well, fuck him, he can wait!' He spotted Cynthia walking in the far door. 'Hey! Cynthia. Did you trace that vagrant, what's his name? Barry, something?'

'Barry Weir.' She walked over gracefully, like a lynx, taking her time, hypnotic. 'Yes, we traced him, but we have not spoken to him, yet, though.'

'Why not?'

'I don't think we need to, sir. The day before the murder he was a resident in the cells at Central Police Station – overnight and well into the afternoon the following day. He'd been arrested for being drunk and incapable, and criminal damage. It can't be him.'

'Have we double-checked?'

'Of course. I've spoken personally to the officer who dealt with him, and viewed the custody record myself.'

'Well done, Cynth. No need to talk to him, have you marked the action off?'

'Just about to.'

'Nice one,' He smiled at her and thought he noticed a lingering smile and knowing look in return.

The phone at his side rang.

'Stark.'

'Your attitude is typical of the entire police force! It's pure fascism. I have my rights, and I am going to ensure that I get them. My basic human right is that my life must be protected by the police, when it's in imminent danger!'

'Roy, I've told you that somebody is coming to see you, when they can, and you telephoning me every verse end is merely delaying me sorting it out. Goodbye!' He replaced the receiver on the cradle harshly, raising his fists and roaring loudly. Ashley looked puzzled. 'Are you all right, sir?'

'Never been better, Ash, I'm late for work, I prang my car, and Roy Prentice gives me GBH to the ear, apart from that everything in the garden is rosy. Thank you so much for asking.'

Cynthia covered the phone as she whispered: 'Mr Stark, phone call for you, it's a Roy Prentice?'

'Inform him I have a brilliant solution to all his problems. Tell him to go upstairs, open a window, and throw his pathetic, whiny little body out of it, preferably on to something extremely hard or pointy!'

'I'm sorry Mr Prentice, but DI stark has gone out. Can I take a message?'

*

Wagstaff looked silly. His portly build and heavy moustache did not suit the tight-fitting paper overalls he now sported. He sat in a small annexed room at Nottingham City Hospital mortuary with two Scenes of Crime officers and an Exhibits officer; Detective Constable Brian Canley. Brian had done several post-mortems as Exhibits officer. He had nineteen years' service mapped out on his weathered face. They all wore the ridiculous white overalls and plastic disposable shoe coverings –it was like an 'Andy Pandy' convention for the underwhelmed.

Eventually the shout came to go through the clear plastic doors into the postmortem room. It was a large room, big enough to accommodate five slabs and a viewing gallery. Stuart's naked body was on the first slab. In front of the slab was a wooden table, upon which lay a large, twelve-inch knife. This would be used to dissect all the organs once they were out of the body and on the 'chopping board'. Underneath the table was a sink, and a flexible tap for rinsing away excess blood and offal, whenever necessary. The rats in the underground sewerage system would have a field day when the postmortem detritus eventually reaches them. Behind the first table, on the far wall, was a blackboard with body parts printed on the left and blank spaces to be filled in, with the weight of heart, brain, spleen, etc.

Professor Hargreaves entered the room somewhat theatrically; the headline act. He was dressed in a green cotton V-necked T-shirt, green trousers, ankle-length rubber boots, a white full-length plastic apron and surgical gloves. He was a remarkably cheerful man, considering his line of work; he was in his fifties, with short brown/greying hair and gold rimmed spectacles. He was ex-public school and spoke with a plum in his mouth. Hargreaves always commented on proceedings, consulting regularly with the senior officer in the case at points of interest.

Various photographs were taken of the body at the direction of Prof Hargreaves, and Wagstaff, including the devastating trauma to the man's head and the dangling eyeball, which Hargreaves took a pair of scissors to, and snipped off. Placing it in a kidney shaped bowl, where it rolled until it settled. It seemed to be looking at them.

Thereafter he wasted no time and made a large cut to the chest in a V-shape, exposing the sternum and ribcage. The mortician then proceeded to use a surgical hacksaw to saw through the sternum, pull open the ribcage, revealing the organs beneath, swimming in their ocean of slowly putrefying blood. Hargreaves took out the heart and lungs as a whole and slapped them on to the table. He then separated them, and weighed them individually, before he began to dissect them with his big knife. He would repeat this with every organ. Wagstaff had never liked post-mortems and had suppressed his nerves by lighting up a cigar. Brian whispered, 'You can't smoke in here, sir.'

'Can't I? What do you think I'm doing now then? The Prof doesn't mind. It helps ease the stench! My old boss used to flick ash into the carcass!'

The mortician assisted the pathologist with the more strenuous activities, like sawing off the top of the skull with a trepan to get the brain out, and folding the face down, away from the skull. The eyeball watched it all.

Occasionally the Scenes of Crime man would photograph various parts of the dismantled body, with Hargreaves thrusting a ruler against the part for scale. As the pathologist examined the area of Stuart's throat, he became rather interested: the back of it was quite decayed and swollen, extending down the oesophagus and the lymph nodes were also inflamed. He had seen this before. It was the first sign and quite a distinctive pattern of swelling, and there was no doubt that the lab would have to confirm it, but it was worth commenting on.

'Mr Wagstaff. Your man could well have acquired immune deficiency syndrome.'

'What does that mean? Oh AIDS. Seriously?'

'I can assure you it's not a joke. Most likely drug abuse as a cause, I notice pin-pricks on veins in his feet. I think he's a user.' Hargreaves scraped at the section of gullet he now held in his hand. 'Could be a dirty needle. I say AIDS, let me correct myself, I suspect it to be HIV and the throat problems to be a symptom of a seroconversion illness.'

'What's that, Professor?' Wagstaff enquired.

'The onset of HIV usually has a seroconversion illness; flu-like symptoms and most notably for us, this terrible sore throat. I can see on closer inspection a rash on his left side. These are all indicators that his immune system is not reacting as it should be and looking at it, they are consistent with HIV from my experience. It needs to be confirmed, but a drug user, using or sharing needles is high-risk. I will be surprised if it isn't.'

'That's a turn up for the books.' Brian said.

Brian hadn't seen this before. 'Do we need to quarantine the area, are we safe, here, Professor?'

Hargreaves looked over his glasses. 'Perfectly safe, so long as his blood or fluids don't enter your body. The danger would be if you have any exposed cuts or anything like that. No more contagious than any other disease, just dire consequences.'

Brian was seemingly unnerved. 'I've heard bad things about this AIDS stuff, some bloke shagging a monkey started it in Africa, now all the queers have got it.'

'I don't think the origin has been confirmed, Officer. For your information, whilst it *was* passed to humans by apes, probably in the 1920's, it's more likely it was by humans in the African Congo eating chimpanzees' meat which was not properly cooked. Shall we move on?'

'Yes, sir, sorry sir.'

*

PC Cox was well respected in the Traffic Department. There wasn't much, if anything, that Vernon 'Dick' Cox hadn't dealt with in his time, and because of this experience and know-how, he was an accident investigation officer. He was brought in specially to deal with any major Road Traffic Accidents and Fatal's. Dick telephoned Dave Stark's extension.

'Stark.'

'Hello, sir, it's Dick Cox from traffic. How are you?'

'I'm fine, Dick, how's Jackie.'

'As I always say, sir, Jackie loves Dick.'

Stark laughed even though he had heard it a dozen times before.

'How's Carol?'

'She's OK, still setting me impossible goals, but that's marriage for you.'

'You're not on your own. I've rung because I've worked out the minimum speed the vehicle was travelling at the time the deceased was hit, you know your murder – Millichip was the chaps' name.'

'Great. What was it, Dick?'

'Thirty-seven miles an hour.'

Stark was scribbling on his pad. 'What are your views on that?'

'Nothing really. Well. I can tell you that a collision at only twenty miles an hour can kill. The car park of the Fox and Grapes is pretty large, but even so, to get up to that speed you would have to be giving it a lot of welly.'

'Fair enough, anything else, mate?'

'I would say the car was *accelerating* at the time of the impact with the deceased, not braking, which could be significant for your murder investigation, I would have thought.'

'How do you know that, Dick?'

'I know we haven't got the offending vehicle, but by looking at the initial impact injuries to his legs and measuring the height of a Granada bumper – which obviously is the first point of contact – we reckon the bumper was slightly higher than its normal height. If the car had been braking, the bumper would have been lower to the ground.'

Stark smiled. He didn't have to query Dick, but the Accident Investigation experts always fascinated him, all pure physics of course. 'Lovely work, mate. There's not much forensic on the body or scene, such as glass and all that, which I find surprising.'

'I would have thought there would have been some debris, even a bit of glass, but it does happen, Scenes of Crime will come back with his clothing, which might have something under the microscope. As he's been hit, his legs have gone back and he's gone forwards and unfortunately his head has hit the windscreen surround, which is par for the course with pedestrian collisions. The corner of the windscreen is one of the hardest parts of a car, something has to give, and it is usually the skull, rather than the car.'

'What about it turning around?'

'Yep. It turned around and went at him again, slower speed this time at 32 mph, the tyres hit him full on and scraped and squashed his head, pretty much to a pulp. Not pretty.'

'What about car tread?'

'Difficult to say. If pushed I would say Michelin; it will need some forensic work though. I've done you a statement, I just thought I would call, in case you wanted to ask any questions, and you won't get the statement for a couple of days if I put it through the internal.'

'No, get a car to bring it over.'

'Are you sure?'

'Yes, I'm sure, I don't want it floating through the internal mail.'

'No problem, I get it.'

'You've done a brilliant job, there, Dick as ever, it amazes me how you can tell all this stuff?'

'We had skid marks left at the scene by the offending vehicle, so basically you would drive a similar car at thirty miles an hour and apply brakes, leaving a skid mark, which could then be comparable in length to the one at the scene. We did two tests to put into the formula. There is another test, a pedestrian test which I think is less reliable, although they tell me it isn't, but dependent on whether it is an adult or a child, if you know the point of impact and where the body finishes, it should tell you the speed of the vehicle.'

'That sounds a bit spurious, Dick, I can see us getting a bit of grief about it at Court.'

'Not really, it's a physics thing, they tend to accept it. Cleverer people than you and I, say it works, scientists, mathematicians, so who are we to argue?'

'It is the precision that amazes me, what sort of a formula is it for Heaven's sake?'

'Well, if you're asking me, Dave?'

'Yes, go on; just out of curiosity.'

'Let me get my card... Here you are. The basis of it is: D squared equals U squared; minus V squared over 2x5. That should give you the acceleration rate-'

Stark was grinning to himself. 'All right, I get the picture. You lost me at the first minus sign.'

'You did ask! Then by making V squared which equals U squared plus 2 a s. This will give the speed in metres per second of the actual braking speed of the offending vehicle, so from there-'

'Dick, stop it, stop it, mate, I get the picture. Great work. I'll be in touch. Love to Jackie, make sure she keeps loving Dick.'

'Will do, sir, cheers.'

'Cheers.'

Stark scribbled next to his figures the most important piece of information that Dick had given him – INTENTIONAL!

7

'A cynic is a man who, when he smells flowers,
looks around for a coffin.'

H.L. Mencken

Jim drove, as Charlie sat almost regally in the passenger seat of
the battered old CID car. 'Two old stages in an old stage.' Charlie
had said. Jim appeared to be in high spirits, commenting on
a variety of scantily clad young ladies braving the cold in the
name of fashion, He spoke again testing Charlie.

'What do you make of Cynthia Walker, then, Charlie?'

'Bloody hell! Are you obsessed with the girl or what, Jim?'

'No, but I've been put with her a lot on this enquiry, and I keep
having to bite my tongue.'

Charlie laughed. 'Yes, I know what you mean. Times they are a-
changing.'

Jim gave Charlie a sideways look, and licked his lips, like a
python flicking its tongue. Like the snake he was. 'There's a
rumour going around that she is keeping written notes on
everybody, about all the racist comments.'

'You're fucked, then Jim, you're the only one, I've heard saying
them.'

'No joke, seriously it could mean a load of trouble.'

'Well, nothing would surprise me nowadays, Jim. Surely not
Cynthia, though, she seems a lovely girl, to me.'

'If you like that sort of thing. I'm not saying it's true, just to be
a bit wary around her, that's all. I heard it from a bloke that used
to work with her.'

Charlie had to check himself. He'd known Jim for years, knew what a troublemaker he was, and how venomous he could be. He was always first to jump on the gossip and allow himself to get carried away by it all. Jim would often instigate the gossip himself, which Charlie felt was probably the case in this instance. Jim was seeking to recruit him into this toxic nonsense and Charlie was not going to have it. He was aware of the CID sub-culture that can make a man's life hell should they take a dislike to him or distrust him. He had seen a Detective Sergeant hounded out by his detectives turning against him and hunting in packs, never mind an aide to CID, and he did not want this happening to Cynthia.

'Just hold your horses, Jim. Cynthia is a nice young woman; the signs are she could make a decent detective in time. She's done nothing against us and tried to settle in with everyone. She's friendly and helpful and she deserves a fair crack of the whip.'

'She's a fucking nigger, Charlie, and she's thick as pig shit, her reports have got a lot of spelling mistakes in them, and they are often arse about face,'

'Listen, Jim, take a tip from me, you've got to move with the times and stop this type of talk; you are going to get yourself in a world of shit, if you're not careful. Let's not get into the rumours bullshit – her reports are a bit wayward, granted, but I'll let you into a little secret, shall I? So, were mine when I first went on CID, and guess what?'

'What?'

'So were your fuckers, for that matter. Who do you think you are fucking Einstein?'

'I'm not saying that she isn't any good. I'm just being a mate to you that's all. All I'm saying is that I don't trust these bloody spooks. They're troublemakers, paranoid, they should concentrate on their work instead of sagging under the weight of the chips on their shoulders. They want to make the rules up as they go along. You wait and see, there'll be civil war in this country, blacks against whites, and guess who's going to have to sort it out? That's right. Us.'

'Bloody hell, Jim, take a deep breath will you, for God's sake.

Let's just take people on face value, I've got bigger things to worry about?'

'You're going soft in your old age. Anyway, what you got to worry about?

'These bloody piles are killing me for a start. I can't get right.' He shifted in his seat.

'Piles, Jeez! Not good.'

'Exactly, you're being a bloody arsehole, and I've got a bloody arsehole!'

They both laughed.

Charlie pointed ahead, 'Here it is Jim, that semi on the left with the white door, look.'

They pulled into the kerb. As the two ambled over, towards the house Charlie noticed ultra-violet light coming from an upstairs window. It took a while for the door to be answered. A lady with long brown hair cascading over her shoulders, stood before them, draped in a towel and little else. She was tanned, very tall and athletic looking.

'Sorry, I was on the sunbed, thankfully it finished as you were knocking, or I wouldn't have heard. How can I help?'

'Caroline Winner?'

'Yes, it is.' She rubbed her hand through her hair and shook her head. She fancied herself a bit by the looks of it.

Charlie produced his warrant card. 'Good morning, we're from the CID. I wonder if we could have a word with you. It is rather important.'

'Er, well, yes, I suppose so. As I said, I have been under the sunbed, so you will have to excuse me for a moment while I make myself decent.' Charlie thought she looked pretty decent as she was. Caroline ushered the two detectives inside, and sat them down in a sparsely furnished room of pastel shades. As Charlie sat down a little too hard, he uttered 'Ouch, you bugger?'

'Sorry?' Caroline asked.

'Apologies, it's my knee, playing up.' He rubbed the bogus injury.

'Excuse me a second.' She ran upstairs to get dressed.

Jim looked puzzled. 'Knee?'

'Well. I can't say it's my bloody piles, can I?'

They sat in silence for a couple of minutes looking around the room. Charlie pointed at the bookcase.

'What?' Jim asked.

'Look at the book on the shelf, Jim: One hundred sexual positions.' Charlie whispered.

'I can't hear you, one hundred?'

Charlie raised his voice. 'You deaf bugger, one hundred sexual positions, that was quick, Caroline.' He said, as she breezed back into the room with a figure hugging, linen, short dress on.

'I just threw this on, what can I do for you gentlemen?' She threw her hair back again.

Charlie was relieved he had got away with it. 'Have you time for a chat about a couple of people you knew at college?'

'Yes, of course, but first I should offer tea, or coffee?'

Jim's eyes lit up. 'Never let it be said that we would refuse such an offer. Tea, one sugar each, please.'

'Milk?'

'Yes, please.' They both said.

As she walked into the adjacent kitchen she spoke. 'I see you were admiring my book collection.'

'Shit!' Charlie whispered, as Jim was giggling like a schoolgirl.

'Yes, very nice, Caroline, an interesting assortment.' He shouted.

He could hear cups and kettle being shifted around before Caroline returned. 'It won't be a minute. I'm afraid Mark's not in now, he won't be back until late tonight. He's got housewives' aerobics at the leisure centre. We like to try to keep fit.'

Jim spoke. 'Oh, you're fit all right. Nobody could argue with that, my love.' He forced a smile with his nicotine-stained teeth. The comment flew past Caroline, simply because never in her wildest nightmares had she contemplated romantic innuendos from a pock-marked, pot-bellied, middle-aged Detective.

'I'll pour the tea.' She said.

Charlie spoke when she returned with the drinks. 'Have you

read in the papers about James Deely and Stuart Millichip?'

'Who?'

'James Deely and Stuart-'

'Oh, from college. Sorry I wasn't thinking. No, I've not heard from them. Let me see, it must be over three months ago now. Why, what's happened? Nothing bad I hope.'

Charlie glanced at Jim. 'Surely you've seen the papers or the news on the telly lately?' Jim said.

'No, we never do. It's so depressing isn't it? Our lives are too full to bother about such things. We like to live in our own little bubble. What have they done?'

Charlie broke the news. 'They've not done anything, but I'm afraid to say, I do have some bad news for you; prepare yourself for a shock, Caroline.' He paused a moment. 'They've both been killed.'

Caroline rested her forehead in her hand. 'Oh my God, those poor, poor men – and their wives, well, Stuart wasn't married, but you know what I mean, his poor mother!'

'You have some tea there, Caroline.' Jim reminded her.

'Of course, I have silly me.' She took hold of her cup momentarily before spilling some of the contents onto the table. She covered her eyes and spoke to herself. 'For God's sake, Caroline, pull yourself together. I'm sorry gents, I'm usually fine in a crisis, but it's such a shock. What happened? Were they together? I can't believe no-one has been in touch.'

Charlie felt like Caroline was being a little over the top, but everyone reacts differently. He was curious about her reaction. 'Whilst I appreciate it is upsetting it's not a crisis, as such, if you only see each other once a year.' Charlie said.

'You misunderstand me, Inspector.' Charlie ignored the mistake in his rank. '. . . but James used to call me at least once a month, though as I say, it must be three months now. You see we were pretty close, but not too close, you understand – I am a married woman.' She rubbed her hand through her hair yet again. 'We were all close, we kind of grew up together, we were the gang – "The Magnificent Seven," we called ourselves, ready to take on all comers. We changed it to the "Magnificent Eight" when Stu became part of the group.'

'Wasn't Stuart part of the group at first, then?'

'No. He was a year younger than us, that's all, but he was friends with David and he became part of our scene, I guess.'

Caroline stared into space. Charlie found it slightly irritating that she had this habit of frequently shaking her hair back over her head, then stroking it with her manicured hand. Again she exaggerated herself as she snapped back to the present: 'Sorry, I was just thinking about the good times, halcyon days, I think you might call them. So, were they together then, when they were killed?'

Charlie glanced at Jim. 'No, they were separate killings. James was stabbed, and Stuart was run over by a car.'

'I can't believe it, why ever has all this happened do you think?' Charlie continued to do all the talking but looked a little uncomfortable in his chair, and he seemed to be adjusting the position of his buttocks as he spoke. 'Well, we were kind of hoping you could tell us the answer to that question?'

'Why me? I mean. . .'

'Obviously we view it as something of a coincidence that two relatively close college friends, are murdered ,within a couple of days, and being one of the "Magnificent Eight", we thought you may have some idea what could have prompted someone to do it.'

'Are you sure Stuart was murdered? People are getting killed every day on the roads. He was crazy on that motor bike at times, you know.' She said.

Jim nodded. 'We are sure, Caroline, what can you tell us about the two men?'

'I take it you will be talking to all the other members of the gang, then? Surely it can't relate to us. It's years since we were at college together.'

'We will be talking to everyone, rest assured on that one, my love. What were Stuart and James like?' Jim asked.

'Um, I knew James fairly well, Stuart not so well. James was a charming, clever man, everybody loved James. Every so often we have a bit of a reunion, you know, no spouses allowed, apart from mine of course – shame.' She laughed and became slightly distant as she spoke. 'I must admit, and the others will probably tell you the same, I had a bit of a soft spot for James, but that was all a long time ago, and I think you'll find that Tracey – Tracey Sewell – had the hots for him at one time too. In fact, I'm sure they had a bit of a fling with each other, back in the day, if you know what I mean. But that's all so long ago now. She still dresses the same as she did then, poor cow. Have you met her?'

They shook their heads.

'Very tight skirts, heavy make-up, attractive still – in her own way, of course. Not what I would call classy. But it doesn't do for us all to be the same does it?' She threw her hair back again.

Charlie stood up from his chair. 'Ouch you bugger! Sorry, Caroline, I'll have to stand up for a few minutes, if you don't mind, my . . . knee, is really giving me some gip.'

'Of course, that's fine. I've got some deep heat if you want me to spray it on the source of the pain.'

Jim laughed. 'Hah!'

'No. Thanks, anyway, Caroline.' Charlie said.

'Go on Charlie, I'd love to see that.' Jim said.

'Get on with it, Jim, I'm fine, thank you very much.'

Jim was still grinning as he spoke. 'I take it you don't get on well with Tracey, then?'

'Oh yes. Don't take me the wrong way. *She* slags *me* off when I'm not around, there's nothing malicious or anything. Just us girls being a bit bitchy, I suppose. Although, she has been really tense, lately, certainly in the last couple of years, maybe eighteen months.' Caroline whispered, unnecessarily. 'I think she's got problems at home. He's a very bland sort of person, her husband, I mean, a bit dull I would say.'

'What about Stuart, what was he like? Did you or Tracey have a crush on him?'

'Good Heavens, no! He was a year younger than us, but he was always at the do's we had. A nice lad really, a bit quiet, but a bit of a sportsman at college, you wouldn't think so now. A couple of the girls around college used to like him, but there was always something a little different about him. He was a very quiet and shy boy really. I can't put my finger on it, to be honest with you. He's really gone downhill now, you know. Occasionally, I bump into him in town. He speaks, but I've heard he's on drugs and he's always in a group, a right set of yobbos' they are, too. They give me the willies, they do.'

Jim glanced down at his list of names. Charlie was hovering around, standing, shifting his weight from one buttock to the other, making it all a bit strange. 'Can't you sit back down yet, Charlie, you're putting *me* on edge never mind, Caroline.'

'Okay, fine.' He sat down gingerly on the edge of the seat. 'Ouch, you bugger.' He said again without realising it.

Caroline looked bewildered by his antics.

Jim continued. 'What about David Seaton?'

'What about him? He's quite a nice, respectable bloke, an intellect certainly, perhaps even a little eccentric for a young man, but he wouldn't hurt a fly. I always used to feel a little bit sorry for David. I don't think he had the best of childhoods; his father was a bully; overbearing, as David called it. Sometimes he would confide in me and Tracey. Are we all under suspicion then? Is that why you're asking me all these questions?'

'I think suspicion is a bit of a strong word. You are the only people who can give us detailed background about the group and the dynamic and those college days, that's all.' Charlie explained.

'Hang on, are we . . . I mean, is there a fear that one of us could be the next victim. Could we be in some sort of danger?'

Jim smiled his yellow smile. 'I doubt it very much, don't start worrying about that.'

Charlie jumped in. 'There is nothing to suggest that, Caroline, but by all means remain vigilant, just as a precaution.'

'Well, I hope we aren't, because if someone comes and murders me after all this, I shall come back and haunt you.' She let out a nervous laugh, she seemed quite relaxed about it all.

'What about Roy Prentice?' Charlie asked.

'Now then, you can definitely lock him up! He's an obnoxious little sod at times, pardon my French. I don't get on with Roy at all. He's always moaning about the police, the government, everybody apart from himself, of course. He always takes the contrary view; you know, one of those type of people. Strange, he was a good friend of James, and they weren't alike, at all. I don't know why James felt he had to socialise with him. You'll have to judge for yourselves when you meet them. You did say you were going to speak to everyone, didn't you?'

'Yes, we did. I suppose it's pointless asking you about Mark because you'll only be biased, being his wife.' Jim smiled.

'No, I won't be biased. Mark doesn't like lingering on the past. He comes with me to the get-togethers we have. Usually, anyway. I think he's a bit jealous of James, but don't tell him I told you that! Still, he won't have to be now, will he? Thinking about it he is jealous of Jonathon as well, I don't know why, when you look at Mark, you'll see why all the wrinkly housewives fancy him; he's a cracker.' She whispered again. 'Not the brightest star in the sky, but a cracker all the same. Go and see him at the leisure centre. That's where he works; did I say?'

'Is there anyone else, Jim?' Charlie asked.

Caroline answered. 'There's Jonathan Stacey, who I've just mentioned. You've not asked me about him.'

'I was just about to.' Jim said.

'He's a medical student, soon to take his finals. He's a dish as well. We get on very well together. Tracey always thought we should be the ones who got married, not Mark and I,' she laughed. 'If you're looking for your killer amongst that lot, you can forget it straight away. Everyone will be upset about the news. I'm surprised nobody's rung me about it.' She said again.

'You won't be the only one we ask, Caroline, but can you tell us where you were between eight and nine o'clock in the morning last Monday?'

'In bed.'

'That was quick.'

'I'm a programmer and I can work flexi-hours, so I don't have to be at work on a Monday until around half-ten. I can have a lie-in. Mark was at the leisure centre.'

'You can't say that Caroline, all you can say is that you know he wasn't at home.' Jim corrected her.

'I don't even know that to be honest, I was zonked out until ten, and was ten minutes late, believe it or not.'

'Can anybody alibi you for that time?' Charlie asked, still buttock juggling.

'No, sorry, I was on my own. Apart from the milkman. I'm joking.'

'What about last night, around eleven at night?'

'I do have an alibi for that: Mark. He had just come in, it might have been just after then, I wasn't keeping track. He was late because he sometimes stops for an orange juice at the club, but he got in around that time. We sat up watching sport on the telly, but he must have had a busy day as he dozed off on the settee, which isn't like him, really.'

'It sounds like you are busy people, do you get much time for each other?'

'It suits us. We are both very independent people. I mean, I haven't seen Mark, all day today, for example.'

'Have you got a Ford Granada motor vehicle, or do you have access to one?'

'No.'

'That's pretty succinct, that's good.'

'Oh, I tell a lie, Mark's sister's husband, has one, but we haven't seen her all week, so I suppose we have access to that in theory, although we have never had to use it.'

Charlie took a witness statement from Caroline, committing her to paper regarding general background and her movements as well as the issue with the Ford Granada, and the details of the owner, which was a slight concern. He also took down her details on a PDF – a Personal Description Form, describing her own physical appearance. Eventually Charlie and Jim left the house, slightly intrigued by her.

*

Detective Policewoman Stephanie Dawson and Detective Sergeant John 'Nobby' Clarke were made for each other really. Nobby was an ex para, a hard man, but Steph knew just how to handle him. She enjoyed his endless attempts to bed her and led him on, in truth, just enough to keep the game alive. No way would she ever let it go beyond that. It wasn't good practice to sleep with your Detective Sergeant. Anyway, Steph enjoyed their friendship; she didn't want to jeopardise that. Steph was wearing a well-tailored, clinging dress, which was blood red; her blonde hair stroked her back with every sway of her hips. When she leaned forward, Nobby could see her bare breasts almost down to the nipples, the outlines of which were also apparent through the material.

Nobby spoke. 'You know you handle that gear stick extremely sensually, Steph.'

She didn't look at him but began to massage the top of the stick as she sped along, purely for Nobby's benefit, and put on an American accent, from the deep- south, when she chose to reply.

'Why thank y'all for saying so, sir.'

Nobby played along. 'They're a mighty fine pair of legs you're displayin', little lady.'

Steph giggled and stroked his knee. 'You really are too kind, saying all those things to a little old country girl, who ain't never bin with a real man 'afore.'

'Pleasure's all mine, missy.'

Steph threw a glance at Nobby. 'Has anybody ever told you, you're mental, DS Clarke?'

'No, they haven't DC Dawson, anyway you started it. How come you never let me finish it though?'

'Because it wouldn't do. I've told you a hundred times, Nobby, we can't go to bed together, it just wouldn't do; we work together. Never mix business with pleasure.'

'Let's just stick to business then, we could become sleeping partners?'

'You never give in do you?'

'Maybe I could resign?'

'Yes, absolutely, you do that, pack your career in for three minutes in the sack with me.'

'Three minutes. Rubbish! I reckon I could make at least four.'

Steph had heard different from some of his former conquests, they were begging for him to stop, not for more. He had a legendary reputation. Still he pressed her.

'There's absolutely no reason why anyone would have to know. I'd carry on as normal. I'd still shout at you, if you were naughty.'

'I like to do a bit of shouting myself, usually when there's something hot and stiff being rammed between my legs.'

'You're a dirty, bleeder, Steph.'

'It's not a crime to like a bit of cock is it? Or is it only men who can enjoy sex?'

'Of course not. You know I like it when you talk dirty, anyway.'

'I know, you do, my darling.'

'I don't want us to hook up anyway.' Nobby lied.

'Yes, you do.'

'Well I do, but what I mean is I want you to want it, as much as me, not just to catch you in a weak moment. I don't want it to be a one off.'

'I bet you say that to all the girls.'

'No, I don't, well, yes I do, but I mean it with you.'

'Nobby, just accept that much as I love you to bits, it ain't never gonna happen, cowboy.'

'We'll see, one of these old days I might just grow on you.'

'That's no good. I want you to grow in me, not on me.' She was shameless, was Steph.

'Oh, I will; one of these days, I will.'

*

Tracey Sewell was just how Caroline Winner had described her: wearing a very tight short dress, and heavy make-up that paradoxically made her face look considerably older. Her bobbed brown hair was like the rest of her at this precise moment – a mess. She never had time to make herself look attractive and the heavy make-up was merely her lack of self-confidence, an ingrained insecurity that she had never been able to shake off since she acquired it in childhood.

In contrast, her husband, looked what he was, a bit of a non-entity: the sort of man who wore woolly jumpers to parties, sipped half-pints and bought Cliff Richard CD's. But his appearance belied his real personality: he was someone without pretentions, someone who always had time for other people, and was an all-round solid guy. Maybe that was what attracted Tracey to him in the first place. She leaned on his strength of character whenever there were problems. She lacked the inner strength that only Gary could give her. They were both so different; their strengths and weaknesses cancelled each other out. Recently it had been a testing time for the two of them, but they were struggling on admirably, taking a day at a time. They loved each other dearly, despite the strain they were under, but that love sometimes manifested itself as hate, when the stress she couldn't contain, exploded from her. They had been arguing heatedly for some time.

Tracey had her back to him and was staring blankly out of the rear patio windows. She turned quickly, swivelling at the hip, arm outstretched, striking Gary fully in the face. The force of the blow rocked his head to one side. He clenched his teeth and slowly turned his head to face her. 'You bitch, what is the matter with you?'

Tracey's anger was at boiling point, her face contorted with hatred, tears welling up in her eyes. She pointed a finger right into his face. 'Don't you ever throw Sally in my face again, you bastard! What do you know about it? Eh? Fuck all, and you never will know what it's like, will you?'

Gary shook his head, tears were in his eyes also, tight lipped, he spoke: 'So we've finally come to this. This is who we have become is it? This is the extent of our relationship, is it? People come through worse, but there are no half-measures with you, are there? You've really lost it, Tracey, and that makes me sad. All of this has got to stop.'

Gary caught her hand, in mid-swipe, close to the wrist, and bent it back, causing just enough pain for her to squeal. 'Stop it, Gary, you're hurting me.'

'Stop hitting me then!'

She grabbed at his hair with her other hand, and yanked harshly.

'Ouch. Get off my fucking hair!'

He grabbed her wrist and used his body weight to drop them both to the floor, forcing her to release her grip. Tracey started thrashing at Gary with her palms slapping him repeatedly as he tried to block her blows, trying desperately to think how he could make this stop without hitting her.

He kicked out at Tracey, as they writhed on the floor, and her slaps turned into scratches as she stuck her nails into the side of his face, and clenched her fingers, drawing blood.

''For fuck's sake, pack it in, Tracey you're fucking mental, woman!'

'I'll show you what fucking mental is!'

Her eyes were wild as she went for his privates and his panic grew. He managed to push her off, but she was on his hair again with both hands. He grabbed at her throat.

The sudden ringing of the doorbell startled them, and they froze, highlighting the ridiculousness of their situation. After a moment they broke free of each other.

'Shut up! Ignore it,' Tracey whispered, as she bent at the waist and peered round the living-room door, along the hall, towards the front door. Both their hearts were pounding, and they were gasping for breath, with the exertion of the fight. She could see the outline of a man and woman behind the frosted double-glazing. Gary felt his cheek, blood appeared on his fingertips. He shook his head in despair. The man knocked this time; loudly. They could hear the two strangers laughing about something.

'It's probably Jehovah's Witnesses. They'll go in a minute.'

Gary whispered. 'This is crazy, go and see who they are?'

The silence was interrupted by a police radio. Gary whispered again. 'Bloody hell, it's the police. We're going to have to answer it, Tracey.'

'It could be the neighbours reporting us. Leave it.' Tracey said.

'It could be important, they're in plain clothes, I'm going to answer it.'

'Gary, don't! Don't you dare! Gary!'

He ignored her and strolled down the hall and opened the door. 'Hello.'

Nobby showed his warrant card. 'CID. Nothing to worry about. I wonder if I could have a word with you. Is your wife in? Oh, are you, all right?'

Gary laughed. 'I'm fine, thanks. I hope you're from the RSPCA, because I want to report my cat assaulting me.'

Nobby laughed. 'Oh dear, will it attack strangers?'

'It's fine, I've thrown the bloody thing out the kitchen window.'

Steph spoke. 'We thought we could hear a commotion going on in there. Is your wife in?'

Gary shrugged his shoulders. 'Sure. You'd better come in.'

Tracey disappeared into the kitchen to make cups of tea for everyone. Once she returned, Nobby explained the reason for their visit and James and Stuart's demise. She took it all in her stride. Tracey spoke freely about her college days and seemed to reminisce with conviction and clarity as if they had only finished yesterday. Gary interrupted her. 'Tell them about James and the row with Jonathon.' Tracey glared at Gary.

'They don't want to hear about silly arguments.'

'No, we do, anything, even if it seems innocuous.' Steph encouraged her. There was a strange atmosphere in the room as if the couple had been arguing or they were hiding something.

'There isn't a deal to tell, really. Of course, as Gary says, James and Jonathon Stacey didn't get on at all. It was all so petty.'

Tracey crossed her tanned, muscular legs.

'OK. So why didn't they get on, Tracey?' Nobby asked.

'It was nothing really, we were only kids, and fifty quid was a lot of money, when you are a poor student.'

'What was the issue with fifty pounds?' Steph asked.

Tracey sighed. 'If you don't hear it off me, I suppose the others will tell you about it. Jonathon accused James of stealing fifty quid, from his jacket pocket, when we were at college one day.'

Gary butted in. 'Tell them about the fight. That's relevant.'

'You didn't even go to the damned college, Gary! Will you stop sticking your oar in, I'm quite capable of telling them myself.'

Gary shook his head and went to the kitchen. 'Okay, I'll leave it with you. Just trying to help.'

'What fight?' Nobby asked.

'There was an almighty row, ages ago, which ended in Jonathon getting a bit of a good hiding from James. Jonathon never broached the subject again in James' presence, but he often commented about him when he wasn't there – "No wonder he defends criminals; it takes one to know one!" That sort of thing, silly really, but it obviously was burning away in the background.'

'How long ago was it that he made comments like that?' Nobby asked.

Tracey reached over for the ashtray, which she placed on the settee arm, and lit up a cigarette, her hands noticeably shaking as she endeavoured to match flame with tobacco. She took a deep inhalation of smoke, and then blew it out as a long sigh. She leaned forward on her seat, resting her elbows on her knees.

'Sorry, what did you say? I was miles away then.'

'I said who – no sorry, you've got me at it now. When, did Jonathon last make such a derogatory comment about James?'

'I actually stopped smoking for five years until . . . until a few weeks ago. I know it's a filthy habit, but it gets me through the day. Sorry, I've done it again, what did you ask me?'

Nobby glanced at Steph. 'That's OK. When did Jonathon last slag James off, basically?'

'Oh, the last time I saw him, not at a get-together, he gave me a lift home, a couple of months ago. You see, if he saw me in town, he would give me a lift home, the same with Caroline too. They're good like that.'

'What did he actually say? Can you remember?'

'I'm afraid I can't. It was something about James, nothing to write home about, just a bit "sarky", you know.'

'Was it a quip about James as a college student, or about him as a person now?'

She flicked some ash into the ashtray at her side. 'I'm sorry, Sergeant, I honestly don't recall.'

Steph asked, 'What about Stuart Millichip, did Jonathon get on well with him?'

'As far as I know, yes. Stu was just wallpaper most of the time, I don't mean to be unkind, but he rarely got into anything too deep with anyone. He would just show up. He was a decent enough guy, just very quiet.'

Steph lowered her voice. 'Caroline seems to think that you had a bit of a soft spot for James, is that right?'

Tracey laughed. 'She stands need to talk! It was all a long time ago. He did cut a dashing figure, back then, I mean, so yes, I did find him attractive, although I am a happily married woman now, so it's ancient history, really.'

Steph glanced at Nobby, who spoke. 'What about Stuart Millichip, what can you tell us about him, beyond being a bit quiet?'

'As I said, he's quiet, I actually liked Stuart. Shame he never quite got anywhere in life. He was no dummy, mind you. He just dropped out. Perhaps he's right and we are the mugs, who knows? The others got on well with him. He still lives with his Mum, and has got into the wrong crowd, I think. I guess it doesn't matter now, but rumour was that he was into drugs, including some of the hard stuff. He was that quiet we wouldn't know the difference I don't think.'

'So, he didn't divulge anything to you? He wasn't worried about anything?'

'No, not that he said to me, anyway.'

There was a brief lull, as Tracey went into another one of her trances, staring at the carpet. After a few seconds she snapped out of it. 'You're better off talking to David Seaton, than me; they were good friends, Stu and David. Now, David really *is* a weirdo.'

'David Seaton?'

'Yes, he gives me the creeps. I mean, he was never the most popular member of the gang, but he looks scruffy now, for a teacher. I think he's gone a bit funny.'

'What do you mean funny?' Steph asked.

'You know, *funny*. Um eccentric then, if you like. I don't think hygiene is high on his list of priorities. When you think about it, we are all a bit strange in our own way. When we were at college together, we all seemed alike, but as we have got older, I can see now, that maybe we are all very different people.'

'What about Tracey Sewell?' Nobby asked.

'That's me.'

He laughed. 'I know that, what sort of a girl were you? How do you think the others perceived you?'

'Oh God. Um. All right, I think. I enjoyed being with the gang. It gave me a sense of security. If you don't have friends to meet up with in a large college, it can be quite overwhelming. I enjoyed the night life particularly. If I could ever drag them to a disco, I would do. I loved to dance, still do as a matter of fact.'

'I like a bit of a boogie as well,' Steph said. 'What about, Mark Winner, Caroline's husband?'

'He was just a fitness guy, pretty tasty body, but dull as ditch water. I think he was too busy looking in the mirror than bothering with anybody else. I'm not sure how Caroline ended up with him, he's well-hung apparently, which is a big draw for Caroline. BBBC Caroline would say?'

'Do you mean BBC?' Steph smiled.

'No BBBC. Boring, But Big Cock. She told me about it, well she couldn't *wait* to tell me about it after she first slept with him. I won't go into details but apparently it's a real wanger.'

'Nice.' Steph said.

Tracey laughed, which turned into a cough. 'I don't know what sort of a problem he would have with Stuart. He might have been a bit jealous of James, but not Stuart.'

'Can you think of any reason why anybody would want to kill

James or Stuart?'

She stared straight ahead as if deep in thought and pursed her lips. She had a drag on her cigarette. 'No, I can't. It's all a bit of a mystery, to be honest with you. I hope you'll sort us out with protection, will you? We could be next.'

'We will fit you up with some police alarms and panic buttons, just as a precaution.' Steph smiled reassuringly.

'That's good, thank you. Are you any closer to knowing who it is, or will we have to have them fitted for a long period of time do you think? The whole thing just makes me a bit uncomfortable, it's not the best time for us to have all this.'

Before they answered, the telephone rang, and Gary re-emerged from the kitchen and answered it, in the hallway. 'It's for you, Tracey.'

'Excuse me a second.' she said and went to the hallway.

Nobby and Steph could hear Tracey and Gary's muffled voices.

'Who is it?' Tracey asked Gary.

'Work, some kids have got into the compound again apparently, and damaged the cars.'

'Fancy ringing me at home for that.' She tutted.

Gary mocked her boss's voice, seemingly similar to bugs bunny – 'Anything in or immediately outside the compound is your responsibility.'

'You're a sarcastic bastard, you are.' She said as she snatched the phone from him. 'Shaun, hi, problems I understand?'

Whilst Tracey was on the phone, Gary spoke candidly to the two detectives. 'I'm sorry if Tracey seems a little sharp, but we've got quite a bit on our plate at the moment. We've had a recent death in the family.'

Steph made all the right noises. 'Oh dear, I'm sorry to hear that.'

'It's some weeks ago, but these things take time, as I'm sure you'll appreciate. We're both under a lot of strain, that's all.'

Nobby, as ever, was to the point. 'Who is it that's died, if you don't mind me asking?'

'No, I don't mind at all. Our little girl, Sally. She wasn't even two yet. A cot death. Change the subject for God's sake. Don't mention it to her, she'll go up the wall, if she knows I've mentioned anything; she's in denial, I think, at the moment. We're trying to get our lives back together but it's tough. To say the least.'

They fell silent after such a revelation, waiting for Tracey to finish on the phone.

'What's the cat's name?' Steph asked.

'Cat?'

'The one that scratched you.'

'Oh, our cat, sorry I was miles away. It's called Ginger, not very original I know.'

Nobby and Steph were somewhat relieved when they left the strange ambience of the Sewell household. As they walked down the drive, Nobby gave her a tap on the back side.

'Oi!' She said. 'No hanky-panky, or even hanky-spanky, Sergeant Clarke.'

She got into the car and refused to let Nobby in for some time.

'Sorry, I thought it was open.' She lied.

'Very funny. What did you make of that pair then?' Nobby asked.

'I just think there is some domestic strife. I think she scratched him, there's no bloody cat. I suppose it's hardly surprising if they've lost a child. I don't believe the cat story, do you?'

'Not really. She looked a bit flushed when we walked in. I think we interrupted them, but as you say, it's all part of the madness that is grieving for a child.'

'Did you hear them in the hallway? She sounded quite nasty towards him.' Steph said.

'Yes, but as I say, you might be a bit tense if your child was found dead, which, incidentally, is what you will be if you spank my backside again in public.'

'Is it all right to do it in private, then?'

'I saw you ogling her in that short skirt, DS Clarke.'

'Jealous, are we?'

'You wish.' She turned the ignition.

*

PC Bill Saint was a cynic. He had been in the Control Room for twelve years; he had only another four to go, before his back or knee- he hadn't yet decided which – would go and then so would he, with the equivalent of a twenty six-years' service, a big fat medical pension and no more hassle. The Chief Constable would have no objections. For the incrementally enhanced wages they were paying Bill, the Chief could have two keen probationary PC's out on the streets.

There were six lines available for use on the internal telephone system and all were ringing. Bill opened a packet of chewing gum, not the best habit, for a person employed to talk on the phone and the radio all day. The switchboard operator had gone to lunch, thereby diverting all calls through to the Control Room and Bill. The civilian operator was ensconced in the tele-printer room gathering up all the messages from around the UK and categorising them. The other policeman had a snooker challenge going during his 'snap-time'. Bill was on his own. He had just completed a computer check for an officer, and was slowly filling out the details on the log, his ears long since desensitized to the buzzing and ringing going on all around him. Once he had finished, he stared at the array of lights on the external line; these were regular calls, not 999 referrals; they went through the Force control room. Nine times out of ten such a call would be delegated to a patrolman and the Control Room operator would have very little to do, other than mark who it had been allocated to. The eventual reply would mark off the outcome of the message, or if it was ambiguous, put on a pile for the Sergeant to review and decide whether to agree its closure or otherwise.

'Nottingham Police.'

It was a female voice, she sounded pleasant. 'Oh, hello. I wonder if you could help me. My name is Monica Kendall.' Bill started to fill in her details on the message pad. 'I work for Green

Acres Care Home and I have an elderly lady here, who is obsessed with the thought that she can help you with your murder investigation.'

'What murder investigation? Oh, yes, I'm with you. I'll put you through to the Incident Room.'

'No, don't bother doing that. All I want is to get it out of her mind, so that she thinks she has at least told the police about it. I don't for one-minute think that it is any use whatsoever, but once she's told someone in uniform that should put her mind at rest.'

Bill lit up a cigarette and raised his eyes towards the wall clock. It would soon be two o'clock – off duty and next door for a quick pint. 'I haven't got any men to send round, so the best thing for you to do is pop into the station. Is she mobile?'

'Oh, yes. She most certainly is. She has all her faculties, but she keeps going on about messages in the Evening Post personal column, which she thinks are connected to the killings. We just want somebody to humour her, that's all. Is there anybody we should ask for?'

'No just come to the front desk and somebody will be there, and they can sort it out for you, if you explain the circumstances to them. OK love?'

'Yes. Thank you very much indeed. Bye.'

Bill screwed up the partly completed message paper and threw it expertly into the waste-paper bin across the room. It landed dead centre. He had done it before.

8

Cynthia Walker felt far more at ease in the company of Steve Aston than she did with Jim McIntyre. Cynthia was driving the blue Fiesta to the home of David Seaton, in the Bulwell area of Nottingham.

It was with some disappointment that they discovered that David Seaton was not at home. They spoke to the woman next door, who turned out to be the epitome of the nosy neighbour and seemed to know more about David than he probably did himself. She was one of those women who had a sense of scandal about everything, and it showed in her voice when she spoke of the most normal of events, as though it should be on the front page of the newspaper. She lived her own life vicariously through others and her over-active imagination filled in the missing pieces. She was a big woman, in her late fifties, wearing a smock-type dress. She had thin straggly hair. She stood with her loose-skinned arms folded, relishing the prospect of telling the detectives everything she knew about one David Seaton.

'Oh, I'd got him weighed up - don't you worry about that - as soon as I first clapped eyes on him.'

Cynthia looked puzzled. 'What do you mean?'

She looked around, as if someone might be listening in on them. 'Pervert!'

'A pervert? OK, what makes you say that?' She asked.

'Listen young lady, I've got fifty-seven years of experience and one thing that experience qualifies me for, is knowing a pervert when I see one.'

Cynthia looked briefly at Steve. Her face was deadly serious, she obviously believed every word she was saying.

'So, what is it that makes you actually think that? I take on board you are an experienced lady, but what is it particularly that leads you to make this claim?' Steve asked.

'It's not a claim young man, I'm not *claiming* anything. I've got proof!'

Steve raised his eyebrows. 'OK. Great can we see this proof?'

'You can't see it, as such.'

'Ah.'

'I'm not one to cast aspirations about people. I can back it up all right, don't you worry about that.'

Cynthia was getting a little irritated but ignored the word misappropriation. 'Can I just assure you Mrs?'

'Mrs Roberts.'

'Mrs Robert, that we are not *worrying* about anything, we are just trying to make sense of what you are saying.'

'So, come on then, what's this proof, Mrs Roberts?' Steve asked.

She did her looking around routine again, before dropping the bombshell: 'Binocals!'

'Binocals?' Steve repeated, confused.

'Binocals, is that what you call them? Those telescope things, but there is two of them.'

'Binoculars?'

'That's it binocals, I've seen him at the windows, upstairs, peering out, usually late at night when the courting couples are outside. They all come up here you know.'

'How do you know the couples come up here? Cynthia asked.

'Well, I sometimes peep out through the curtains, but only to make sure they are not up to no good, it's unnerving, for all I know I could be ravaged when I take my bin out.'

The two stifled a grin.

'You've seen him looking out the window with binoculars and

that makes him a pervert does it?' Cynthia asked.

'It does in my book. Our Glenis put two fingers up to him one night – he just stepped back into the room. He didn't know he could be seen; you see. That showed him all right. She's not backwards at coming forwards, isn't our Glenis. How's that for proof.'

The two of them were dumbstruck. Eventually Cynthia said. 'Listen, Mrs Roberts, you've been very helpful, thank you very much.'

'I've got a list as long as your arm. Curtains drawn morning, noon and night, mysterious bicycle rides with one of those kernapsack thingies on his back, and sometimes he doesn't return at all. He's a strange one – I've seen his ilk afore.'

'OK, we get the picture, Mrs Roberts, thank you.'

'Do you need to see our Glenis?'

Steve raised a palm. 'No! No thank you, you've been really helpful.'

'She'd make ever such a good detective, our Glenis would, you ought to get her on your books, she'd soon sort 'em out for you. She's a big girl an all, she can look after herself can our Glenis.'

'I bet she can.' Steve said.

'Are you going to arrest him?'

'Just leave it with us, Mrs Roberts.' Cynthia said.

'Are you off to the school then?'

'Which school does he work at?' Steve asked.

'Alderman Derbyshire School. However he's not been ripped to shreds there I do not know. It's a rough school, you know. He's about three stone wet through!'

Cynthia nodded. 'I know it's quite rough. I used to go there.'

'Oh, I wouldn't have said that about you.' Mrs Roberts looked her up and down. 'You've done all right for yourself ain't ya gel?'

'Thanks.'

'No duck, no offence, you just look, like you, I don't know. . .'

'It's OK, Mrs Roberts, I understand what you mean. It's been said before.'

'So, did *he* teach you then?'

'No, I'd left before he arrived.'

'Lucky for you, I say. If you need a statement or owt let me know, ducky.'

Cynthia smiled. 'We will. You've been very helpful.' Cynthia tugged at Steve's suit jacket to hint they should go.

'You drop by any time; you'll get a lovely cuppa. Our Glenis might be in next time. You wait till you see her, young man, you'll be back then, mark my words. Are you married?'

'Erm. No.'

'Eh cheeky!' She laughed uproariously.

'Sorry?'

Cynthia tugged at his suit jacket even harder. 'Thanks again Mrs Roberts.'

She waggled her Bingo wings at them, in a wave, as they left.

They were giggling as they walked.

'Oh my God!' Cynthia said.

'Bless her.' Steve said.

'Oh, you are such a big softy, Steve.'

As they reached the car they paused. Steve asked. 'Where next?'

'Let's do Roy Prentice and get it over with. I'm just in the mood for him.'

*

Cynthia sat in the comfortable armchair of the staff room of Arnold Lodge children's home. She was very upright, straight-back, legs crossed precisely; really quite demure. She didn't feel demure, she was knackered. The office had a funny smell to it, a bit like stale chip fat, for some reason, and she could hear hi-jinks and banging around on the floor above their heads. She was trying to let the excited voice of Roy Prentice wash over her. Steve Aston was perched on the edge of his seat, a concerned look on his face. He had been hooked and now Prentice was playing with him before trying to land him.

'It's taken you two hours to get to see me. Where the bloody hell have you been?'

Steve stammered through an answer only to be interrupted.

'Well, we had to see other people and-'

'Fine. That's great. Ring up the *Evening Post.* Tell them to write that in my obituary: "Sorry to announce the death of Roy Prentice, but unfortunately, the police had to see other people". I could have been killed. Anyway, you're here now, so I can rest. Are you armed?'

Cynthia spoke. 'I'm a bit confused, Mr Prentice, what are you talking about?'

'You're here as my police protection, aren't you?'

'No, we are not. We are here investigating a murder.'

'Inspector Stark promised me that I would have proper protection.'

'I can't see that, there will be a man from Crime Prevention coming around later, to fit some alarms at your place of work and at home. They are special alarms that repeat directly over police radios and all officers drop everything to respond immediately.'

'You what! So, who is protecting me *away* from work and home? Was Stu at home when he was killed? No. Was James at home? No! This is because of who I am isn't it? My political views should be irrelevant to the police. You're supposed to be impartial.'

Steve empathised. 'Listen, Mr Prentice, I'm sorry that you're upset. We can't offer twenty-four-hour protection-'

'You're sorry!' He laughed mockingly. 'You're *sorry*! That's rich, that is, I've heard it all now.'

'It isn't definite that the two murders are connected, don't forget.'

'What are you doing here, then investigating your murder if they aren't connected?'

Steve continued his previous answer ignoring his jibe. 'All the uniformed patrols are informed of the situation, and whenever they are available, they will perform high-profile policing in the designated target areas.'

'What a load of shit!'

Steve was offended. 'No, it isn't. It's far better to have a visible presence, than a surreptitious one, I assure you. It's a greater deterrent.'

Prentice sighed. 'Sure. Listen, you might be able to fob off the general public with this sort of crap, but I know exactly what's happening here, and I assure you that you will regret it.'

Cynthia chipped in. 'I understand your frustration, and in an *ideal* world, you would have constant protection, but in the *real* world, that is not practicable. How long do you want it for? A week? A month? A year?'

'Today would be nice.'

'To do that we would have to take officers off the street dealing with *known,* immediate danger. Should we abandon that response to the public and ignore women being beaten, gang fights, rapes, and the like, to protect you, just on the off-chance?'

'I don't' care about those other things, they are your problems to sort out. I am exposed to danger and being refused help by the police, that is all I know.'

'I get that. Look, do you know how many officers are covering this area?'

'*I don't care!*' His voice was raised, he was panicky.

'Two. Two officers on shifts of eight hours are available to respond. How can we protect six of you twenty-four seven?'

Spittle was forming around his lips as he almost screamed. '*I don't care!* Choc ice!'

Steve looked puzzled. 'Calm down, Roy, we are just explaining the situation to you. What do you mean "Choc ice"? What's that all about?'

Cynthia interrupted. 'Black on the outside and white on the inside, that's right, isn't it, Roy?'

'You said it, sister.'

'And what do you know about being black? Don't you consider that a racist comment?'

'I do more to help the black community than your sort ever will, constable. How can you turn your Babylon back on your brothers and sisters? They have rights you destroy. You are the worst of the worst. You make me sick. You're just another pawn, a puppet of the Establishment, the State police.'

'The same state police you are begging for help from?' She said.

'If you expect me to co-operate you can go whistle. What about the proletariat? We're just forgotten, are we? Trodden over by the jackboot of fascism, of which, like it or not, you sister, are a lap-dog.'

Cynthia shook her head. They were supposed to be here to conduct a murder enquiry. There was a lull. Prentice fished around in his desk drawer, carelessly leaving it open. He spoke, his attitude apparently changed.

'So, what can I do for you officers?'

Steve glanced at Cynthia who shrugged. 'We want to know what you can tell us about James Deely and Stuart Millichip.'

'Stuart is a bit of a mystery to me, I haven't seen him, really since college, he turns up at reunions, but we don't tend to speak. He was a bit of a loner then and he is now. Very quiet. He was ineffectual. He came from a working-class background. He was OK.'

'What about James Deely?' Steve asked, glad that they would be able to go back to the Incident Room with some information, and not be criticised for messing up. Cynthia was still seething from Roy's abuse.

'I came across James in my professional capacity, as well as knowing him of old. If any of the boys were in trouble with the law, we would use James as their solicitor. Occasionally, we'd have a drink and a chat over lunch – on him, of course. He was a good man, who fought for real justice. He was genuinely interested in why the boys had gone off the rails.'

'Would you say you knew James well?' Steve asked.

'Fairly well. And in answer to your next question, no, I can't think of anybody who want to kill him.'

'What about at college?'

'It's well known that James and Jonathon Stacey weren't the best of friends. Don't ask me what it was about, because I don't know, but I hardly think it can be anything to do with his death.'

'What about his love life at college?' Cynthia asked, scarcely able to speak, with the anger wrestling with her professionalism, inside her guts.

Prentice didn't look at her but answered to Steve. 'How long have you got? Let's say he enjoyed female company.'

'Anybody in your group of friends?' She asked with a dry mouth.

Again, Roy blanked her and spoke to Steve. 'Tracey Sewell was one of his conquests, and although he would never admit it, I thought he had a thing with Caroline, I think Jonathon thought that too, but don't quote me on it. That's why there was no real love lost between them, they were love rivals.'

'What about Stuart? Was he involved with any of the women?' Steve asked.

'No. He'd just started getting involved with motorbikes; they were his love. If he did have any flings, I didn't know about them, let's put it that way. He pretty much kept himself to himself.'

Prentice had become far more affable, inexplicably, and answered all the questions readily and with conviction, but Cynthia was suspicious and angry. What had caused his change of tack? Perhaps the accusation of racism? Maybe it had sunk in how bigoted he was being? Anyway, other than James' alleged assignations with both Tracey and Caroline, there was little he told them that they hadn't already known.

As the detectives stood to leave, Prentice was most polite.

'If there is anything else you want from me, don't hesitate to ask. I shall be in for the rest of the day – although it's going to be a warm one – I might nip across the road to get a choc ice.' He was grinning, one arm across his chest, the other displaying an erect middle finger at Cynthia. She had had enough and went nose-to-nose with him.

'The only thing I want to say to you, you pretentious, misguided, fucking idiot, is that, sure, you have rights, but so do I, and one of them is not to be spoken to like a piece of shit, purely because I am trying to make a difference. You slag the police off, and come crying to us at the first whiff of trouble. You have no clue about what we do, or how we do it, and if it was left to the likes of you, you'd run a fucking mile-'

'Cynthia, don't bother.' Steve said.

She continued her onslaught to Roy. 'You make me want to vomit, you pathetic, whiny, little man. Why don't you lock up all your doors and hide under your bed, sucking your thumb, and if you need the nice policeman's help give us a call.'

Cynthia stormed out the office. Roy spoke. 'What the hell? That is out of order talking to me like that, I've done my utmost to help you.'

Steve shook his head and walked out, after Cynthia.

After they left, Prentice walked over to the open desk drawer and turned off the miniature tape recorder. 'Gotcha!'

*

Ashley Stevens and DI Stark had been hanging around the Accident and Emergency Room at the Queens Medical Centre for rather too long, when a buxom nurse appeared from nowhere. 'Dr Stacey will be with you shortly. He is due to go off duty in the next ten minutes.'

Stark nodded. 'OK. Thanks, we'll wait out here then.'

Ash whispered. 'I wouldn't want to tangle with her on a dark night, boss.'

'She'd teach you a thing or two, I bet.'

Stark looked around the waiting room: coughs and splutters; a couple of drunks. Heads lolled back, their gaping mouths rasping; the walking wounded displaying an array of cuts and crude self-made bandages. The regulars, aware of the long wait, had bought sandwiches and newspaper to pass the time. Aggressive shouts could be heard, emanating from a room somewhere beyond the Casualty area. Stark craned his neck to see where the idiot was, but he could see nothing.

DI Lee Mole and DS Carl Davidson swaggered into the A&E waiting room as if they owned the place. Carl Davidson had an unlit cigarette in his mouth as if he was smoking it, but then he was a complete dick.

'This is all I need.' Stark said.

'Hey, look who's here, Carl. The homicide squad. Not like the rest of us, these guys, they only deal with murder, don't you David?'

'What brings you here, Lee, late for your lobotomy pre-op?' Stark said.

Ash laughed.

'I don't know what you mean. What does he mean, Carl?'

Carl shrugged and drew out the cigarette and held it at the side of his face. 'Too complicated for us, boss.'

'Yes, we're not clever enough to understand it, not being murder cops and all.'

'Well, you clearly don't understand it do you?' Stark pointed out.

Ashley strolled over to the drink dispenser to get out of the way of the sniping, and studied its operating instructions. As he did, he felt a nip on his backside. He turned around sharply. Deep-blue eyes, matching the colour of her nurse's uniform, gazed at him.

Ashley's face lit-up. 'Hello there, fancy seeing you here.'

'I did tell you I was a nurse, so it's hardly surprising, is it?'

He smiled. 'No, I suppose it isn't really.'

'You're a policeman, aren't you?'

'Detective, yes. However, did you guess?'

'It's pretty obvious, even if you did tell me you were an insurance broker.'

'I did not!'

'Oh yes you did. Three weeks ago, at Ritzy's night club.'

'I know. You don't have to remind me. How could I forget?'

'We all know it's like a CID convention in there. Why did you tell me porkies?'

'I don't know. I suppose it's because it saves a lot of endless questions about the job, that's all.'

They were joined by Carl Davidson. 'What have we here? Rather attractive lady, Ashley. Not trying to keep her all to yourself, are you?'

The nurse curled her lip at the skinny little man in a jacket that was three sizes too big. 'Do you know this person, Ash?' She asked.

'Never seen him before in my life.' Ash said.

'Yes, he does. We are the real detectives. These guys are just playing at it.'

Ash looked to the heavens and groaned.

'Is that right?' The nurse replied. 'Mind you, I can see that just by looking at you.' She winked at Ash.

'There you go, Ashley, a lady who can recognise a real man when she sees one.'

'I don't think she actually said that, Carl, she just said you look more of a dick than I do.'

'Funny. I don't get it.'

'It's what the yanks call detectives, oh, forget it.'

There was a lull and Carl just stood there grinning at the nurse. Eventually Ashley spoke. 'Carl, can you give us a minute please, this is a private conversation.'

'That's up to the lady.' He was twirling the cigarette in his fingers.

'What he said.'

'See ya later. If you're lucky.' He made a strange clucking noise and winked at the nurse, before ambling back towards Stark and Mole.

'Get me a sick bucket, quick! Who is that prat?' She said.

'Oh, he's nobody. Just an idiot. Every village has one.'

'Anyway, as I was saying, before we were so rudely interrupted by whoever that man was. Why didn't you give me a call? You said you would.' She asked

'I lost your number, what is it, again?'

'It's 274718.'

Ashley scribbled it into his diary, his gold bracelet jangling as he did. He looked a little sheepish as he asked, 'I'm sorry, what was your name again?'

'Sharon, God, you weren't that drunk. I know for a fact you

weren't that drunk.' She gave him a smile. 'And if you were, I hope you're that drunk again next time we meet.'

Ashley smiled. 'I will definitely give you a call. I was kicking myself for losing your number, but like an idiot, I just couldn't remember your name.'

'Keep digging, why don't you?'

The doors opened and a doctor shouted to Ashley. 'Someone waiting for Dr Stacey?'

Ashley glanced over at Stark. Ash responded. 'Hello, yes, it's us.' He turned to Sharon. 'I'm going to have to go, Sharon, I'll give you a bell, I promise.'

'You make sure you do.' She wagged a finger.

Young Doctor Stacey wore a white, waist-length cotton-jacket with too many cheap pens sticking out of the breast pocket. He was dark haired and had an affable smile. Stark produced his identification and explained the reason for their visit. Stacey's manner was relaxed, and he was easy to talk to.

'I've just finished my shift. We'll go down to the annexe room, shall we?'

Stark was relieved he didn't have to spend another second in Mole's company. Jonathon strode ahead, leading them down endless corridors. He was fairly tall, not quite six foot. Twenty-six years old, with such a promising career in front of him. Perhaps this was the reason for his cheery persona? The NHS had not yet stripped away at the layers of optimism.

At an open door he paused. 'This'll do.' He winked at Ashley. 'Nice girl, young Sharon, isn't she?'

Ash laughed. 'Very nice. Good stamina.'

'Really?'

'To work such long hours in a large hospital like this, I mean.'

'Oh, yes of course, absolutely.' Dr Stacey said.

They both chuckled like schoolboys.

Dr Stacey addressed Stark. 'I have been expecting a call to be honest, you said you wanted to talk about the murders. Tragic, isn't it?'

'Yes, it is.'

'I saw James Deely in the mortuary, you know. I nearly fell over when they wheeled him in. I'd just nipped in for some toxicology bags and there he was. Quite horrendous when it's a mate of yours. Quite a shock.'

'Oh God, that's not best is it?' Stark sympathised and asked Stacey where he was at the relevant times and dates.

'When James was killed, on the Monday, I must have been at the hospital, if I remember correctly. Although to be truthful, I was on call, so I would probably have been skiving somewhere.' He smiled a broad toothy smile. Stark matched him.

'Can anybody corroborate that, Jonathon?' Stark asked.

'Um, I don't know to be honest. Various people saw me, but whether they can put a time on it, I don't know. I hope so.'

At Dr Stacey's dictation, Ashley wrote down a handful of people who may have seen him on the morning in question.

'What about when Stuart Millichip was murdered?' Stark asked.

'I was in the postgraduate library, on campus.'

'Who with?'

'Nobody. I was on my own, and before you ask, no I can't remember who else was there. In fact, I don't think anyone was in at that time of night.'

'Who was at the desk? Surely they have someone looking after the place?'

'I think it would have been June, one of the student casual workers. Yes, it would have been June's turn to be on afternoons in there.'

'Is she on duty now?'

'Let's see. . .' He glanced at his watch. 'She'll be on afternoons today, so yes. That's fortunate.'

'Times must be changing, Jonathon. I thought young doctors would be out boogying at ten-thirty at night not studying in the library,' Stark observed.

Jonathon thought for a moment. 'Now then Inspector, you mustn't generalise. OK. You're right, I would normally be out, but I have a lot of catching up to do for that very reason, so I'm trying to be a good boy.'

'Have you any theories on what this is all about, you know, why James, and why Stuart?'

'Not really, it's all very strange. I've been racking my brains trying to see a connection, other than the fact that we were all mates, particularly since one of us could be next. I'm trying to work it out, in case it might be me!'

'It's a worry.' Ash said.

'It is, one has been knifed in his car, one killed by car at a pub, what's next, me in the library with the candlestick!'

They all laughed.

'You don't know anyone called Colonel Mustard, do you?' Ash laughed.

'Now, you come to mention it.'

'I'm sure you'll be fine.' Stark said. 'Can you tell us what you can remember about your college days, Jonathon? The things that seemed to matter at the time; that have stuck in your mind.'

'Crikey! I suppose the people themselves, really. David Seaton was a bit of a loner, I can't see him having it in him. David was a mate of Stu, although they must have just sat looking at each other, because you could never get two words out of either of them. Stuart was getting into his motorbikes, and eventually just dropped out. Roy Prentice, was big into politics, he was a militant socialist; still is. James Deely and his bonking exploits. He was a bit of competition for me, young James was, and of course there were Caroline and Tracey, both attractive women. James had a bit of a play with the two of them, I think. Mark Winner eventually came from nowhere and ended up marrying Caroline, lucky guy.'

'Did you sample the delights of Tracey and Caroline?' Ashley asked, genuinely interested.

'I'd be a liar if I said no. One or two of us did at one time or another, even Roy Prentice had a bit of a look at Caroline, believe it or not, but we were young horny kids, for Christ's sake. It's to be expected.'

Stark pondered. It was strange that Jonathon hadn't

mentioned the rift over the alleged stolen £50 and the resultant fight. It wasn't something you forgot. He would put that on hold for now. He asked Jonathon a question he had been mulling over himself. 'Why now, do you think? What has happened after all this time that could relate to college?'

Jonathon's brow furrowed and a broad grin emerged. 'Don't ask me. That's one for the experts, in other words; you guys. You do have my hearty good wishes, though, in your quest. Drop by anytime, if you need to ask me anything else, of course.'

Ashley took his personal descriptive details and quickly got his fingerprints on the convenient plastic pliable ink strips, for elimination. After scrubbing the ink off with disposable wipes, Jonathon shook both their hands and bade them farewell.

Stark and Ashley took a stroll over towards the postgraduate library. It was a dry night.

'What do you make of the good Doctor Stacey?' Ashley asked his boss.

'He's still as much in the frame as anyone, as far as I'm concerned. Interesting that he never mentioned the £50 allegation and the fight that Tracey Sewell, told Nobby about.'

'I thought that, sir. I wasn't sure whether to ask him. But I was worried that you wanted to hold it back and let him volunteer it.'

'I did.'

'The £50 thing doesn't help us with Stuart, though, does it? I mean it's no motive to kill Stuart. The £50 thing is scarcely a viable reason anyway.'

'No. We aren't there yet, are we?'

'No, boss. He seemed an affable enough person, though. Very accommodating, nice guy, at first glance, anyway.'

'I thought you were going to ask him out on a date, at one stage.' Stark smiled.

'I did think about it, boss.' Ash joked.

Once at the library Stark introduced himself, and Ashley, to June Clifford, the library attendant. June had wide-rimmed, ornate spectacles, and frizzy hair. In her turquoise woollen top and 1950's style bra; her breasts looked pointed. A fashion victim you might say. Retro style.

Stark explained the reason for their visit. June was positive. 'I know for definite that Jonathon Stacey was here, because funnily enough, he and I were talking about it only last night.' She fingered her gold chain as she spoke and adjusted her spectacles.

'So, you're definite that Jonathon was in here?' Stark wanted it underlining.

'Yes, I am. One hundred percent.'

'Why were you talking about it?' he asked.

'Oh, I don't know, now. It just came up.'

'Who mentioned it, you or Jonathon?'

'Blimey, Jonathon I think, why?'

'I just wondered that's all.'

'Anybody else around at the time he was in the library?'

'No, it was deserted apart from me and him.'

*

Stark had told the lads to go to the bar and he would catch them up, he just wanted to ring his Mrs to tell her he would be a little late.

'It's so sad though.' Carol Stark said in her pathetic voice.

'Why are you even looking at the obituaries column in the bloody Evening Post?'

'Haven't you seen them?'

'Seen what?' Dave leaned across the table and picked up that evening's edition from his side-table. He thumbed through the pages as Carol spoke.

'Stuart Millichip, from his mother. It's very touching.'

Stark found the page and read down it until he saw the message:

> *'Millichip, Stuart.*
> *A mother's heart is broken.*
> *Memories are all that's left.*
> *I was always proud of you, son.*

Now I'm just bereft.
Your loving Mother.'

Dave agreed. 'Yes, it is sad, isn't it? And a bit funny.' He began doodling on his blotting-paper as he listened to his wife.

'Dave! Don't be so bloody horrible! It's sad.'

'It's the rhyming thing I can never get, with an obituary, it always has a hint of parody about it.'

'What are you talking about? You've got no soul, that's your problem.'

'Just saying that's all.'

'Well, don't. There aren't any messages from his friends, I notice.'

'They probably don't even read the Evening Post, and anyway, blood's thicker than water. She is his mother after all.'

'I meant his college friends.'

'Oh, I thought you meant his biker mates. True, you would have thought there would have been something, even if as a collective.'

'Did you meet her?'

'Meet who?'

'His mother.'

'No, she was seen by another DI from the incident room on the night itself. Why the interest suddenly?'

'Dunno. Bored, I suppose.'

'Not again, Carol. What have you been up to today?'

'Nothing really. The usual. I think Chris had a fight last night.'

'Why?'

'I saw Mrs Alladice in town, and apparently her neighbour's son came in with his face all bruised and grazed. He told his mum that our Chris had done it.'

'That's not like him. I'll talk to him when I get chance.'

'It will be all too late by then, Dave.' She sighed.

'If she comes around, tell her I'll give her a ring and sort it out, but I would have thought if she was going to come around, she would have done so by now.'

'I guess so, you don't think she'd have reported it to the police, do you?'

'Christ, I hope not! I'll check. I doubt if she has. Someone would have told me. It's just a kid thing. It's a bit of gossip from Mrs Alladice, probably. I will speak to Chris though.'

'That would be good.'

'Unless you want to.'

'Dave!'

'OK. I'll talk to him. I'm on my way shortly. I'm just going to have a bit of a de-brief in the bar and I'll be home.'

She sighed. 'Can't you come now, Dave?'

'Once I've finished work, I will be home, don't worry.'

'It's not work though is it? It's the bar.'

'It's a de-brief. Honestly love, the location is irrelevant, it's in the police station bar, because I'm thinking of you, my love.'

'Bullshit.'

'I am! It saves having to have a de-brief and then go to the bar afterwards. It saves time.'

'I believe you, thousands wouldn't. OK. Look forward to seeing you later.'

'You too.'

'Bye.'

'Bye.'

Stark threw the Evening Post in the bin in the corner of his office. He didn't see the personal column adjacent to the obituaries, which was a shame.

*

The swing doors of the police station bar burst open, and Stark's men marched to the counter, in quick time. Nobby muscled his way to the front, shouting over his shoulder. 'The gaffer's on the love-phone, but he's given me a tenner to get you all a drink.' Cries of 'Excellent,' and 'Cheers gaffer,' filled the air. They were easily pleased. Nobby distributed the drinks and the men formed two circles of conversation.

Nobby raised his whiskey glass. 'Sip ahoy.'

There were groans. They raised their glasses and joined in 'Sip ahoy.'

Ashley looked drawn. 'I'm knackered. How about you, Cynthia?'

'Not too bad, it's been a long day, though. That twat Roy Prentice doesn't help. Are you going down the place of no return, tonight?'

'Ritzy's? I don't know. As I say, I'm a bit cream-crackered. I might get my second wind.'

Cynthia smiled. 'You will.'

Nobby spoke. 'Chief Inspector Turley came into the office today.'

'Oh yes. What did he want?' Charlie asked.

Nobby laughed. 'Very important job. Checking the offices were clean and tidy.' He mocked Turley's mousey voice. 'Oh, these chairs should be pushed under the desks, look at all the ashtrays – filthy!'

Charlie shook his head. 'Bloody hell, how does he cope with all the pressure? Hasn't he got anything better to do?'

'Yes, collect his bloody enormous wages.' Jim grunted.

'You know, when I was in the army-' Nobby started.

'Here we go,' said Ash.

'No, hear me out. When I was in the army, you were given a job to do as a private, at which time you couldn't be a corporal. But by working hard, you eventually developed the nous to become a corporal. You couldn't do the job of Sergeant, but, again, after so long, you learned the ways, and, yes, you could do that job, so you got promoted to the rank of Sergeant, and so on and so forth. But in this bloody job, you look at blokes like Turley and you think to yourselves, could I do his job right now? And the answer must be, yes! I could!'

Ashley started:

'Yes, you're saying. . .'

'No, hang on Ash, let me finish '. . . but the burning question is, could Turley do my job, or your lads' jobs? And we all know what the answer to that is, don't we, kiddiewinks?'

Charlie spoke. 'That is true with Turley, but all of them aren't like that. Turley is an *admin* Chief Inspector; what the hell does he do all day?'

'Christ knows,' said Nobby. 'But I know one thing: it ain't the crap we have to deal with.'

'Has Turley ever been on CID?' Ashley enquired.

Charlie shook his head. 'No chance. He did an aide many years ago, I can remember him; he was bleeding useless. He didn't stop on CID.'

Nobby chipped in again on the verbal assassination. 'He was moaning to DI Stark the other week that every time he walked past the CID office, we were sat around drinking tea, doing nothing.'

Ashley sipped at his pint, oblivious to the irony. 'You're joking!'

'No. Honestly!'

'What a prick.' Ashley said.

Nobby clearly had a bee in his bonnet. 'It doesn't half annoy me. What does he know about being on CID? Does he see us at midnight when we've been on since eight in the morning? Where the bloody hell is he? Tucked up in bed with his night shirt and cap on, after getting home at four o'clock in the afternoon! What a prat.'

'What did Stark say to him?' Ash asked.

Nobby explained to the men the way Stark had used the intricacies of managerial nuanced debate.

'He told him to fuck off and count some paper clips!'

They laughed. 'Good old Stark.'

Stark came into the bar with his men's laughter ringing in his ears. Nobby grunted. 'Here's Stark, keep shtum.' He shouted over to his DI. 'Your pints on the bar, boss.'

Stark picked his pint of lager and joined Steve Aston, who was engaged in conversation with Steph. Jim McIntyre was listening in.

'Yes, but as police officers we're never going to be made redundant, are we?'

'You never know Steve; the way inventions and technology are going.'

Stark changed tack, as the others gathered round him. 'Charlie, who would you put your money on for our murders?'

'Bloody hell, boss. It's too early to say. But if we are having a guessing game, I'll have a tenner on David Seaton.'

Jim laughed. 'My God, Sherlock lives! He's not even been spoken to yet!'

'I know, but it's got to be a weirdo, and so far, everyone says he fits the bill. It's always a weirdo with non-domestic murders.'

Steph commented. 'Talking of weirdo's, I think Tracey Sewell seems a bit strange to me. There's definitely something wrong there.'

Cynthia had her turn. 'I hope to God its Roy Prentice, because I want to be the one who nicks him if it is!' The memory prompted her to ask, 'Eh, Steve did you do a full pocketbook entry about his aggressive attitude, and the choc ice thing?'

'Yes, but I don't see the point, to be honest with you.' Steve said

'As long as you have, that's all. I've met his sort before. I don't trust the pillock.'

Nobby took a turn. 'I'll put my money on Jonathon Stacey. He sounds a bit too clever for me, and he's the only one with an actual grudge against James Deely.'

Steve didn't agree. 'Do you really think, a Doctor, would kill someone for fifty quid?'

Nobby bristled. 'I've known people kill for a fiver, son, never mind fifty quid! As for him being a Doctor, everyone is the same with their pants down.'

Steph nudged him. 'You speak for yourself!'

They all laughed.

'What about Stu Millichip? Where does he come into it?' Steve asked.

Nobby shrugged. 'No, it's definitely not him, Steve.'

They all laughed as Steve went bright claret.

'I didn't mean that, I meant generally.'

'I know, Steve, I'm only kidding, pal.'

Jim offered his pearl of wisdom. 'I don't think it's any of them. I think it's a fluke, unconnected. More importantly though, boss, what do *you* think?'

'I'm keeping my powder dry, for now. We don't know, do we? As Nobby says, it's early days, and as you've each suggested someone different, it shows the amount of work we have to do.'

'Cop out!' Charlie said.

'No, it's not that, we still have to see David Seaton and Mark Winner. Let's see where that takes us. I'm not sure we know enough about the cross–shagging going on between them all. That's my gut instinct at the moment. Let's just keep an open mind for now.'

'Is that going to be on the press conference boss?' Charlie asked.

'What?'

'We are considering all aspects of the case but focussing on the cross-shagging!'

They laughed along with Stark. 'Yes, it is.' He joked. 'Wouldn't it be great if we could just be totally honest with the public when we do press conferences? It would cause uproar, wouldn't it?'

The speculation continued.

As the conversation wore on, Nobby sidled his way round to Steph. They went around the sliding screen partition, to put something on the jukebox, Nobby asked his regular question. 'Have you got your kit on today then, Steph?'

She smiled seductively. 'Have a feel.'

Nobby stroked her upper thigh; it was hard and shapely, and he felt the strand of lingerie and where stocking met bare thigh. That confirmed; yes indeed, she did have her 'kit' on. 'Steph, you're evil, do you know that?'

She caressed and squeezed his hard backside. 'Have you got your kit on?'

'Once a commando, always a commando.' He smiled. 'Why don't we sneak off? We can leave separately and meet back at my place.'

She placed her hand at the side of his stubble chin, her hard breasts rubbing at his chest. 'I've told you, Sergeant.' She exaggeratedly mouthed the words. 'No!'

'Let's go back in.' She said.

'Not yet.'

'Come on.'

'Steph, I can't.'

She looked down at his stomach and could see a thick penis head exposed above his belt line. 'Jesus Christ!'

*

Ash had made a mistake by coming to Ritzy's night club. Cynthia had come along but was surrounded by men, most of whom she seemed to know and was holding court, making them all perform for her attention. Worse than that Jim McIntyre had shown up! This was seriously cramping his style. In truth, if anything it was Ashley who was in the minority, being in his early thirties. Ritzy's was renowned for ladies of a more mature age attending for a 'good time'. It was affectionately known as 'grab-a-grannie' night. It was a little bit harsh, most of the women were in their forties and fifties. It was well known that the CID used the place and, well, everybody loves a policeman, don't they? It was a quarter to twelve and the dance floor was already crowded with women cavorting and gyrating to 'Toy Boy' by Sinitta, which was quite fitting.

After the scrum to get a bottle of beer, Ash and Jim took a position close to the bar to survey the scene. An array of women filed past them, some absolute dragons, some very nice and occasionally, a stunner. 'It's even more of a cattle market, than I remember, Ash.' Jim shouted above the music. Ash smiled and nodded. Normally, if Ash was with his mates, he would just take his position and wait. After a while, various groups of women would appear close-by, some were cop-groupies who he had 'known' before and were 'bankers', but not because they counted cash for a living. Others would be out-of-towners or hen nights, or even the odd group of work friends. Many of the women were married. So were many of the men. Ash was concerned that with

Jim as his wing man the 'gathering' around him would not take place.

'Shall we have a walk round, Jim?' Ash suggested. This was a euphemism for identifying some women they wanted to hit on.

'Aye, let's do it.' Jim said.

All around the large space was a mezzanine balcony where couples could go in search of privacy, and lechers to get a better view of potential prey. At Ritzy's it was usually unnecessary to have much of a plan of attack when chatting to ladies; the good thing about the place was the unpretentious and honest way most behaved. Unlike some night clubs, where the customers are too busy posing, Ritzy's clientele, generally were straighter to the point, and if one fancied the other it was usually only a matter of time before they were leaving to have sex somewhere. From the mezzanine it was evident that most of the people walked around the perimeter of the dance floor for some considerable time, looking for that knowing smile, or a hint of a chance. Ashley had locked on to a group of about ten women all together. They stopped. 'What do you think, Jim, are you game?'

'Aye, I'm game. Lad.'

The two approached the individuals whom they had decided to pull from the pack. They sauntered on to the dance floor with brilliant timing as the first smooch record began playing 'I Just Can't Stop Loving You,' by Michael Jackson and Siedah Garret. This meant that the other predators around the edge who were ready to strike, did not get chance to get to the women before Ash and Jim.

Ashley had chosen a stunner: long blonde hair, long eyelashes, long nails, long legs, and a long way from home.

As they danced, they took in the situation and surveyed each other's captures. Jim had got a woman in her early forties, leopard skin clinging dress, dangly earrings, a slight belly which fitted nicely under Jims fat gut. She sported a butterfly tattoo on her shoulder which made Ashley wince. It was unusual to see a woman with a tattoo and suggested a particular demographic. Jim was dancing at a bit of a distance from her. 'How d'ya get down here tonight then, love?'

He asked her.

'Taxi, why? Have you got a car? I don't live too far away, about twenty minutes.'

'An hour and a half round trip then.'

'No forty minutes, love.'

Jim shook his head. 'Twenty minutes there, twenty minutes back, 50 minutes talking about the weather.'

She cackled. 'Cheeky. I can tell you about the weather now if you like. To save a bit of time.'

'Okay.' Jim was intrigued.

She gave a knowing smile; she had been around this block before. 'It's hot but drizzling wet.'

They both laughed and Jim pulled her closer to him.

'I'm Jim, by the way.'

'Hello, I'm Sheila.'

Ashley was surprised by Jim's pulling powers, without giving it a thought that Jim had been doing this when Ash was still in nappies. Ash always chose the more attractive women. He had a host of ladies he could contact if he wanted some company, so an occasional refusal was of little consequence to him. Plus, he liked to keep his hand in, so to speak. He was fully aware that the beautiful women were often neglected by men without the balls to approach them. They were just the same as anyone else, but some men were intimidated by them, Ash wasn't. The only drawback was that the more attractive women usually wanted a couple of dates before dropping their knickers. It wasn't unknown for him to ring a lady friend, and arrange to meet her later, drop the women off and arrange a second meeting, and then go to the lady's house for guaranteed relief. It was quite a complicated rota system, of sorts. Quite who was playing who, in this scenario was not always clear, and Ashley sometimes felt a pang of jealousy when he saw one of his 'loose arrangement ladies' in a club with some other fella. He wasn't a stranger to being told he 'wanted his cake and eat it.' He had heard it so many times he was ready with his response. 'I prefer to eat out.'

'Are you a copper?' She asked him.

'What makes you ask that?'

'You look like one, that's all.'

'I don't know if that's a compliment or not?'

'It's a compliment.'

'I'm a copper.'

As the music faded into the next song, Ashley suggested to his woman that they go and have a drink and a sit-down. The attractive blonde went to sit down, looking like the cat that got the cream, while Ash walked to the bar which was three deep.

Suddenly he felt a tap on his shoulder, and he turned around sharply.

'Hello, Ashley.'

It was the nurse, Sharon.

'Hello, Sharon. Fancy seeing you here.'

'Fancy.'

'Are you on your own?' Various equations and possibilities started to flash into Ashley's mind.

'Sort of. I'm just with work colleagues. Are you on your own?'

'Again, sort of, I'm just having a chat with a young lady, though.'

'That's what you call it is it? A chat.'

'Well, you know how it is.'

'I do.'

Ashley was glancing at the barman who was still ignoring him. 'What are you doing later, if you are on your own then, Sharon?'

'I would need to get rid of...' She stopped speaking as her friend arrived next to her. 'Oh, Ashley can I introduce you, this is -'

Ashley beat her to it. 'Jonathon Stacey. We meet again.'

The two shook hands; Jonathon seemed a little embarrassed. 'Fancy seeing you here, detective.'

'Fancy.' Ashley said. Glancing at Sharon, who had a smirk on her face as she watched the two men joust and position.

'I take it you're not studying tonight then, Jonathon? In the library, I mean.'

'No, er, not tonight. You know how it is – the brain can only take so much.'

Ash could feel Sharon's hand rubbing gently against his thigh behind her back. 'Works "do", is it, Jonathon?'

'Something like that.'

'Is there a gang of you, then?'

'There was, but we seem to have lost them for now.' He turned to Sharon. 'Are you coming, Sharon?'

'Yes, OK.'

'Bye.' Ashley said, his voice a little higher than normal.

Jonathon took the lead, but Sharon turned and held her hand in a phone sign at the side of her head and mouth 'call me.'

*

The public toilets on slab square always stunk of urine, and any manner of foul stenches combined into a perfume that was hardly an aphrodisiac. Yet as the night wore on, various gay men could be seen pitted around these toilets. Hanging around. Watching, assessing, who was visiting the toilets. Sometimes, trying to catch the eye of a fellow loiterer, or someone known from a previous assignation. Homosexuality was not really accepted by the masses, if truth be known, and there were fewer opportunities for gay men to meet like-minded friends, or indeed to satisfy their needs. This drove them to the most unsavoury locations and put them in situations where there was a risk, both of physical violence against them, or of arrest by the police, for acts of lewdness, and homosexual acts in a public place. Attitudes to gay sex were still very superficial. Indeed, thousands of men a year were convicted for behaviour that would not have been a crime, had their partner been a woman.

David Seaton had seen the man with the walrus moustache, tight turned up jeans, and a skin-head haircut staring over at him. He looked a bit of a hard nut, and David was wary. He could be trying to bait him for a good kicking. There was little option, however. David nodded to him, and he received a nod in reply. This was not a couple who had much in common other than their sexual persuasion. David dropped a coin down and bent down to pick it up and looked over at the man. He nodded vigorously. David hurried down the steps into the toilet area and went into a cubicle. The walrus man followed him down, but there was someone at the urinal, so he stood next to him. Within a minute the toilet was empty. Walrus went to the cubicle with the door locked and tapped on it. David opened the door, and the man could see him bent over with his forearms on the top of the cistern. The frisson caused by the meeting had created enough excitement for him to take out his manhood and enter David. David did not make a noise as the walrus man thrust into him like the finalist in the World Disco dancing championship. Someone could come in at any time. The man reached around to feel David's erect penis and squeezed at his balls. David was pleasuring himself at the same time. It was all over very quickly, as they both orgasmed together. The man withdrew and scurried into the next cubicle to sort himself out with toilet tissue. It was all very perfunctory and sadly, quite sordid.

David sat on the toilet seat, wracked with guilt, but sexually assuaged. He was listening to the man next door to him. He would never know his name and he would never be in any sort of intimate relationship, other than a 'wham bam thank you man'. He felt he was destined to be lonely throughout his life. He missed Stuart. He missed the special relationship they shared. This was all that was left for a shy, inadequate, academic, out of the groove, gay man, with no outlet and no opportunity to meet someone he could be close to. A tear rolled down his cheek as he heard; 'Thank you, love. See you again.' from a gruff walrus moustachioed non-scene queen.

9

The double doors of Nottingham Police Station led into a foyer
that varied from shabby, to filthy, dependent on who had passed
through it that day. Shabby was about as good as it got. The
deserted counter was protected by a Perspex bubble, shielding a
telephone. A handwritten note pinned to the wood instructed:

WHEN COUNTER UNATTENDED PLEASE USE TELEPHONE.

The man spoke into the phone.

'I wish to speak to the Inspector in person, please.'

'Good morning.' A female. 'Which Inspector do you want to
see?'

'The duty Inspector. I wish to make a complaint about one of
your officers, and I won't be fobbed off.'

'I see. I doubt anyone will fob you off, sir. Can I take a name
please?'

'Prentice, Roy Prentice.'

'Will they know what it is about?'

'Hardly, I haven't told them, yet.'

'Take a seat, Mr Prentice. I'll see what I can do.'

'I'll stand, thank you.'

He paced around the foyer, rehearsing his speech. Fairly soon,
Bob Stanswick, the 'schoolboy inspector', as Nobby called him,

appeared, and ushered Roy upstairs to his office.

'Take a seat, Mr Prentice. Now, what can I do for you?'

Roy sat. 'I am afraid that one of your officers has been extremely rude, offensive and discourteous towards me, causing me great distress.'

'OK. That doesn't sound very good, now does it. Who is the officer in question?'

'Detective Cynthia Walker.'

'Really? This doesn't sound like Cynthia.'

'Here it comes the self-protection. All looking after each other's backs. I've been expecting it. Problem is Inspector, I have the whole episode on tape recorder.'

'Oh.'

'Yes. "Oh", indeed.' He wore a sickly grin on his face.

'What's happened then, Roy?'

'I am a key witness in the murder enquiry that is going on at the moment. They were supposed to be protecting me, or at least that's what I thought; but it turned out that they were just there supposedly investigating, and despite me falling over myself to be helpful, I was the subject of a real outburst of vitriol. It was shocking and totally uncalled for. I suspect she's got a chip on her shoulder, or something, I've never been so insulted in my life.'

Bob was taking notes as Roy went through it. 'So, what did Cynthia say to you?'

'It's all there on the tape.'

'Fine, but I'm just asking you in the first instance for the context. I will get the tape transcribed, don't worry.'

'Everything was fine, I couldn't have been more polite and helpful to them. I answered all their questions as well as I could, and then just as she was going out the door, she turned on me for no reason.'

'What did she say to you?'

'What *didn't* she say? She called me a "fucking idiot", pretentious, misguided, pathetic, you name it, she called me it.'

Bob was taken aback. 'That *is* shocking, I must say, I don't understand it, not from Cynthia. Not from any police officer, for that matter.'

'Well it's all there for you to listen to on the tape.' Prentice was really pleased with himself. He sat with his arms folded and a big grin on his face.

'OK, let me do just that, and I will be in touch.'

'I will expect some sort of response within a week, or I shall be in touch with my solicitor.'

'Fine, but you need to understand that these things take time. What is it you are hoping to achieve by the complaint? How would you want it resolving? Would some advice be sufficient, for example?'

'Advice! I hardly think so. This needs to go to the top! I mean do you think a person treating a member of the public, who is trying to help them should even be doing this type of job, because I don't!'

'OK. Let me make a start on it, and we will let you know what the process will be once I've sought some advice from the Police Complaints Department.

Once Roy Prentice had gone, Bob reached for the telephone and tapped out a number.

'Stark.'

'Hi Dave, it's Bob Stanswick.'

'Hi Bob, what's up?'

'Just a word on the QT.'

'What's that?'

'I've had Roy Prentice in the nick, just now.'

'Christ, that's all I need. What does he want?'

'He wants to make a complaint.'

'What, against me?'

'No, against Cynthia Walker.'

'You're joking!'

'I'm not. He says she's called him a "fucking idiot" and "pathetic" and all sorts. It's a tricky one.'

'He'll be lying, Bob.'

'You say that Dave, and I thought the same, until he produced a tape, he says he recorded it all.'

'Oh, poo.'

'Exactly.'

*

Stark took hold of Cynthia's arm as she headed along the corridor towards CID and dragged her into his office.

'A word in your shell-like.'

'What's the matter, sir?'

'That git Roy Prentice is the matter. He's made a complaint about you.'

'What? Seriously?' A thousand thoughts crashed into her mind. She had half been expecting this.

'Yes, seriously.'

'What is he saying I've done?' Cynthia was breathing a little heavier and she had a horrible feeling in the pit of her stomach.

'He is saying that you have been rude and offensive to him, and called him a load of names, things like "pathetic" and a "fucking idiot", apparently.'

Cynthia swallowed hard. 'Right.'

'It's awkward, with you being on your aide-to-CID, because the gaffers will hear about it.'

'But they know Roy Prentice, sir, everyone has heard of him, they'll take it for what it is.'

'And what's that Cynthia? Lies?'

'I may have been a little discourteous I suppose, off the record, but you should have heard what he said to me, making racist slurs.'

'Racist slurs?'

'Yes, calling me a choc ice.'

'That's good, well, it's not good, but you know what I mean, that will be on the tape as well, will it?'

'What tape?'

'He reckons he's got a tape recording of you insulting him.'

'The devious bastard! Sorry, sir, but he is.' Tears started to well in her eyes. She had not been in this situation before.

'It is pretty low, and devious.' Stark agreed.

'Yes, but it's worse than that, sir. I couldn't figure out what was going on. He was aggressive and insulting to us from the get-go, especially to me; abusing us, and making the racist comments and I called him out on it. He then got up and was suddenly being all nicey-nicey. I thought it might have been because I challenged him on the racism, that he changed tack, but I bet that is when he's turned the tape on. The scheming, rotten. . .'

'So, the tape will only have recorded your behaviours and not his. Hmm. Who was with you?'

'Steve Aston.'

'OK. Will he back you up, do you think?'

'He'd better do, it's the truth.'

'Forget the truth, Cynthia, that's got nothing to do with it. Did you make a full pocket-book entry about it, including his anti-police attitude, racism and his abuse, followed by the sudden change in his attitude?'

'Absolutely, I have sir. I knew he was up to something. Like an idiot, I didn't dream it would be this.'

'Does Steve Aston's pocket-book echo your own, Cynthia?'

'Yes, I made sure he put something in about it, because I just knew, I had a feeling about that guy, that's all. I've met his sort before.'

'Thankfully, I have got a bit of something in my book about his attitude from when I visited, way before you went; his anti-police attitude towards me, so it's a start. All I can say is to forget it for now, but when you get your official notices about the complaint, contact the Federation and make sure they represent you. Don't make a federal out of it, but if it goes as far as a tribunal, which I doubt, don't worry, I'll give evidence for you. All right?'

'Thanks, sir. I'm scared now. I've never had a complaint, believe it or not.'

'I believe it. Let me have a think about it. When people do this sort of thing there is always something they have missed, as they are too immersed in hatred to consider all eventualities.' Stark smiled. 'Just store it to one side out the way in your brain, don't let it distract your focus on getting through your aide ship. I've got high hopes for you. Don't let this no-mark spoil it for you.'

'I'll try.' She was chewing at her lip, her eyes full of tears.

'And by the way – this conversation never took place.'

'Of course. Thank you, sir.'

Cynthia ran out of Stark's office and across the corridor to the ladies' toilet. She ran into a cubicle and sat down, unable to stop the fountain of tears pouring from her. She sobbed. She was worried her career would be over before it had even begun. Her Mum had been so proud of her, and all those that called her a traitor would love it if their warnings turned out to be true. As she sat there, a dozen thoughts of doom crossed her mind, her panic rode over her in waves. This was going to cast a cloud over her whole aide ship. She kicked out at the cubicle door, rattling it on its hinges. 'Fuck you!'

She heard a knock on the cubicle door.

'Cynthia? Is that you, love? It's Steph.'

'Hi Steph.' She sniffed. How embarrassing, she thought.

'Are you OK?'

'Fine, why?'

'Because you are breaking your heart, and the cubicle door, by the looks of it, you daft sod, that's why. What's up?'

'Nothing, honestly, hormones probably.'

'Cynthia, open the door, please, so long as you've got your knickers on!'

'I'm fine, honestly!'

'Open the door, or I'll kick the thing in, myself!'

The door slowly opened. Cynthia's mascara was scarred down her cheeks.

'What's the matter? It's not Jim upsetting you, cos he's just a prat, and everyone is fully aware of the fact.'

'No, it's not him. I feel daft now.'

'No need to feel daft. What's up?'

'I've had a complaint from Roy Prentice who says I said some bad things and I did, because he was racist but he taped it, and the only bit he taped was me saying bad things, and not him saying all the racist stuff, and. . .'

'Woah! That's a big mouthful for a little girl.'

Cynthia laughed and dabbed at her tears with some toilet paper.

'I'm really worried, Steph.'

'Who was with you?'

'Steve, and he has put something in his pocket-book at the time, 'cos I asked him, and I have put something in mine. Mr Stark said he had put something in his, when Roy was rude before all of this happened.'

'Okay so that's good, then isn't it. Particularly Mr Stark's bit, well before the complaint came through. That will help, no end.'

'It's still shit.'

'I know, and I can, and will say to you, not to worry, but I know you will. I have had complaints which have chilled me to the bone, and nothing has come of it.'

'What if I get the sack?'

'You won't get the sack, as Nobby would say, "there's many a slip 'twixt cup and lip."'

'What?'

'I don't know either, Cynth, but it sounds good. The whole thing will be investigated, and Steve will back you up. Stark will back you up, too. It's early days. Stark won't take this, I would be glad he's on your side, if I were you.'

'I guess so.'

'All of us will back you up, Cynthia, if we can. Whatever is done is done. Just don't let that shit head, Prentice mess your head up.'

'I'll try not to.'

'Now, come here and give me a hug.'

They embraced and Steph moved a strand of hair from Cynthia's forehead. 'You look like shit. Get yourself sorted, and I'll put the kettle on.'

'Thanks, Steph.'

*

Weekdays weren't particularly busy for the leisure centre staff. The retired, the unemployed and women's groups being the main punters in the gym. Mark Winner was busy in the weights room. He was a narcissistic fellow, who strutted his muscular frame around the place as if he was a model on a catwalk. It wasn't a misplaced arrogance, in the sense that the frustrated housewives all fussed around him, plying for his attention. Fuelling his ego. His tracksuit bottoms were so tight you could tell what his religion was. He knew it of course. Most of the ladies wanted Mark Winner. In their imaginations they had already had him, whilst their husbands sweated and grunted on top of them, or when their other halves were at work, and they were alone.

Mark was surprised and puzzled to see the suited figures of Jim McIntyre and Charlie Carter gesticulating to him from behind the closed, glass double-doors. It was apparent they wanted to talk to him. Mark walked casually towards them, his movements like a cheetah about to break stride into a trot towards its prey. The women were all taking an interest in the men talking to 'their' Mark. Jim drew in his stomach as best he could, as Mark nodded and led them through to a tiny office on the second floor. He waited for them at the top of the stairs as the two aging detectives huffed and puffed up them. Mark had vaulted up, three at a time. He looked drawn, his features sunk in, cheekbones protruding. Jim and Charlie sat down. 'Ouch, you bugger!' Charlie exclaimed, as his ass hit the upholstery, sending the shockwaves shimmering up to his piles. 'Bloody knee.'
Jim was having a coughing fit, seemingly caused by the exertion of the stairs.

Mark stared blankly at the two detectives. England's finest. Mark would stand throughout, energetic and fidgety.

As usual, Charlie did most of the talking, saving Jim the bother.
'It's about the killings,' was all Charlie could manage.

'Oh, yes, those. I've been expecting you, to be honest. Not good.'

'You seem a bit casual about it, Mark.'

'No point having the screaming ab-dabs about it is there? Life goes on. A nasty business though.'

'It's just a bit of background we are hoping to get, Mark, just your take on things, and the group dynamic; that sort of thing.'

'My wife, Caroline, mentioned it, but I didn't go into too much detail about it. Funnily enough, I read about it only this morning, as there was an old newspaper left in the toilet. Which reminds me, I need to speak to the cleaners about that. According to the paper, the two murders are connected. Is that right?'

Jim chimed in. '*Probably* connected. D'you mean to tell us that you haven't read a paper or heard the news since it happened?'

'No. Believe it or not, I haven't. I find the news a bit depressing to be honest, and I am in a bit of a bubble here at the centre. Caroline's the same; she can't stand the news. After all, whatever the bad news is, there is nothing we can do about it, other than get all mopey, so I steer clear. Positive thinking, it's the new thing, haven't you heard?'

'I must have missed that memo.' Jim muttered.

Charlie noticed that Mark seemed to always answer a question with a question. 'As you know, we have been to see Caroline about this as well-'

'Have you? I didn't know.'

'Surely she has told you about it. I thought you said she mentioned it?'

'She mentioned the murders, but I don't remember her mentioning any visit.'

'Really? She's your wife, for Christ's sake. She must have mentioned that some detectives had visited. It's hardly an everyday occurrence is it, now?' Charlie said.

'Yes, she did mention it, thinking about it. Sorry. You've caught me at a bad time, to be honest, my mind's elsewhere today. Anyway, what can I do for you? And no. I didn't do it, before you ask!' He smiled. Charlie smiled back at him without broader expression, immovably.

'On that note, Mark, where were you on the times and dates in question? The Monday and Thursday?'

'Where was I? I don't know. Who can tell? I couldn't tell you what I was doing an hour ago. Live in the moment, I say.'

'Were you at work, at home, out, in? Where were you Mark? Have a think. It's fairly important.' Charlie wasn't going to be fobbed off so easily.

He laughed somewhat flippantly. 'I've honestly got no idea.' He shrugged. 'I'll have a think about it, honestly, I promise. I'll let you know if I remember.' He was grinning, inanely.

Jim looked grimly at Mark, 'No. You will think about it *now*. All right? Not tonight, or tomorrow, or next week, right now, my friend. We're talking about two deaths, just in case you had forgotten, *again*.'

'I'm thinking. I'm thinking!' His voice had raised an octave.

There was an embarrassing silence, punctuated by Jim's impatience. 'Bloody hell fire, man, it's not that long ago!'

He shook his head. 'Nah, sorry, but I can't think like that under pressure. If I could, I suppose I would be a cabinet minister, or a detective, or something, not working at a leisure centre.'

'Fair enough, let's leave that for now.' Charlie said. 'Tell us what you know about James Deely, Mark?'

Mark laughed again. 'Look, to be honest with you, I can't help you. James Deely was a solicitor, wasn't he? That's all I know about the dude. I don't see any of the college lot, anymore.'

'You don't see them anymore?' Jim asked.

'No, not really.'

'When did you stop going to the re-unions?'

'Oh, I go to them, yeah, but I'm not a fan. Most of the time, I don't bother going.'

'Most of the time?' Charlie said.

'OK, *sometimes* I don't bother going.'

'Not to support Caroline?'

'Huh. She's more than happy to go without me. There's no

doubt about that one.'

'Why do you say that, Mark?'

'No reason, I'm only kidding.'

Jim was getting more and more annoyed at his evasive responses. 'Can I suggest you *stop* kidding and give some clarity to your answers. We don't want to be misled now do we. We don't want you wasting police time, do we, Mark?'

'OK. Blimey. I'm trying to help, here, but it's not easy, I don't know much else.'

'OK, you can't tell us what you *don't* know, that's fine, we get that. It's when you hold back from telling us what you *do* know, that's when things start going a bit pear-shaped.' Jim let it hang for a while, before continuing. 'So, what about Stuart Millichip? What's the news with him?'

Mark was exasperated. 'You don't appear to be listening to me. *I don't know these people.*'

Jim wasn't having it. 'But you *do* know *of* them, because you went to college with them, didn't you?'

'Yes, I did.'

'So, tell us about them when they were at college, then.'

'What do you mean. What do you want to know exactly? I just don't get what you want from me.'

'Jeez. Are you taking the piss?' Jim asked.

'I don't know what you want to know. I'm not a bloody mind reader.'

'Let's go for gold, shall we? Tell us a reason why somebody might want to kill the two of them.'

'I've no idea. Look, I know I'm coming across as messing you about, I don't mean to. I don't really want to be involved. It's got nothing to do with me.'

'We will be the judge of that, Mark.' Jim said. 'And unfortunately, you are already involved, if only by association.'

'You would be better speaking to the others. Have you seen them?'

'Most, if not all. Why do you ask, Mark?'

'I guess they told you about Stuart trying it on, then. With me,

I mean, is that why you're here?'

'Maybe.' Charlie smiled at him, not having a clue what he was talking about, but happy to go with it.

'He had a feel of my backside, in a pub toilet, when we were all steaming, one night. Jonathon Stacey came in the loo while he did it. He made a big song and dance about it all, you know taking the piss. I'd be surprised if Jonathon hasn't told you about that.'

'So, in your view, was Stuart queer?' Jim asked.

'I don't know what he is, well he's not anything now is he, but you know what I mean.'

'Was he a full-bore queer or did he swing both ways?' Jim asked irreverently.

'Probably both ways. He certainly had the hots for Tracey Sewell. David Seaton told me that, one boozy night. In fact, I'm not a hundred percent certain on this, but I think Stu gave her one – something to do with seeing her at a party, or something. I think they were both stoned at the time, although it wouldn't take much with her, she had a fanny that would eat a lump of sugar, if you held it too close!'

They laughed, despite the vulgarity.

'Don't tell her I said that for God's sake. She'll kill me!'

There was a lull as Mark realised what he had said.

'In a manner of speaking.'

'So basically, when you were all at college, Stuart was interested in you *and* Tracey Sewell?' Charlie asked.

'You could say that I suppose. I'm relying on David Seaton's version of events though, with the Tracey story, so bear that in mind. He's a weird guy. He's weirder than all of us freaks put together, and that is saying something.'

'I thought you didn't know what they were like, nowadays?' Charlie asked.

'Assuming he's still the same. Let me finish.'

Charlie's face grew a little more sombre. 'Mark, I have to ask. When we did our checks, we noticed that you had two criminal convictions. Well. I say convictions, two cautions by senior officers-'

'Hang on that was a long time ago, I can't believe that they are still on record.'

'Well they are. What's the news with those?' Charlie asked.

'I was at college at the time; the kerb crawling was the zest of youth, excitement, something daring, that's all. I'd never been with a prostitute and it was a bit of fun. I still haven't – she turned out to be a policewoman undercover. Not that we, you know, did anything, obviously.'

'Oh dear. Who was with you?'

'No-one. When I say it was fun, I mean it was exciting for me, as a young man. Sometimes you need a change, don't you? And with Caroline following me around the college like a lap dog, all hours God sends. I needed a break. I wanted to try something; but not exactly be unfaithful emotionally, not to hurt her, you know.'

Charlie smiled. 'That's very considerate of you, Mark. Although, I'm not sure Caroline would see it that way.'

'No. I don't either. I'm not a pervert, or anything silly like that. It was years ago.'

'What about the other caution?' Jim asked.

'Oh, that was just a misunderstanding. Again, this happened a long time ago. Some tart in Nottingham just before Christmas. We'd all had a bit too much to drink and I grabbed hold of this bird and gave her a Christmas kiss. It was just a laugh; you must know what it's like in town before Christmas. It's one big party. But she got a monk on, the mardy cow, and reported it to the police as indecent assault! Bloody silly woman. Even the copper said it was ridiculous. Don't mention this to Caroline, for God's sake! She doesn't know about it, and I want to keep it that way if you don't mind.'

Charlie and Jim left the leisure centre still not convinced that they had got the whole picture from Mark Winner. He was so evasive. He wanted it all to go away, but of course it wouldn't.

'Is it snap time yet?' Charlie asked.

'Maybe. You hungry?'

Charlie still had the image of Mark Winner in his tracksuit bottoms in his head. 'I don't know why, but I've got an insatiable urge to eat a sausage roll!'

*

The concrete playground at the rear of Alderman Derbyshire Comprehensive school was deserted. Figures were still visible in the Science block as he braved the chill. A sharp breeze swept rivers of dust across its surface, which were overtaken by empty crisp packets and the odd cigarette end. It was almost four o'clock, and there wasn't a person in the place who was not aware of the time. Pupils, teachers, office staff; all were consumed by the time, their mood commensurate to the amount of sand that had poured the day away. It was all about the bell, just like the factory workers of the fifties, waiting for permission to live. David Seaton walked across the playground, carrying too many jotters in his outstretched arms. Holding them somewhat precariously and fighting the wind. He entered the double doors and onto the concourse area. His rubber soled shoes made little noise as he stumbled across the wooden floor and down the steps at the far end. It was as he got to the double doors of the woodwork room to his right that the bell went. He had another 40 feet before he got to the sanctuary of the staff room and he was caught in between the two exit doors. It was then that he heard a rumbling noise. It was the thunder of hundreds of pairs of feet running towards freedom, and he stood in their way. The tidal wave of children met him; loose jacket-zips scratching his hands, holdalls knocking the jotters askew and flailing arms invading his space. *'Walk don't run!'* he shouted to the ceiling, his squeaky voice lost in the hubbub and excitement of feral pupils. *'I am not King Canute, am I?'* He shouted, obtusely. Those spotting his full hands holding all the jotters, took advantage and pulled his tie out of his cardigan or ruffled his hair as they burst past. By the time the tide had subsided he stood in the reception area having kept the jotters in the large pile, but with his trouser pockets pulled out, his tie over his shoulder and his hair bedraggled. Only the odd stragglers intermittently appeared on the parquet flooring.

David was only twenty-six, but he looked ten years older in his cardigan with elbow patches, his brown tie, creased shirt and hush puppy 'comfortable' shoes. He was a confirmed bachelor and a complete introvert, so badly lacking in communication skills that he had become the focus of amusement and mockery to many of the pupils, which sadly was often imitated by some of the staff.

Once David had made the sanctuary of the staff room, and placed the jotters down, he collapsed into the battered leather armchair with great relief. He let out a sigh, seemingly oblivious to the other members of staff in various conversational groups around the spacious room. One of the PE teachers spotted David and shouted over to him.

'Are you off down the nightclub tonight then, David?'

David hunched his neck into his shoulders and smiled insipidly at the man. He giggled to himself but failed to answer. Another young teacher joined in the mockery. 'He doesn't waste any time down the nightclubs do you David?' David shook his red-face side to side. 'No, he prefers the gent's toilets, don't you, Davey boy?' There were some whoops and 'Wahey's'.

David spoke quietly. 'Now, hold on, that's not very fair, even though you are only teasing. . .'

'Woo! I'm teasing you, am I? I'm such a tease aren't I. David? I think David likes a bit of teasing, don't you?'

'Don't be vulgar, please. Or I will have to. . .'

'Have to what? Don't be silly, David. You couldn't fight your way out of a paper bag! You're as timid as a squeaky little teeny-weeny mouse.'

One of the teachers, Rebecca, shouted across the room.

'Yes, he's timid, and that's why you feel so brave. Pack it in Neil, you should hear yourself.'

'Sorry, miss.' He mocked.

'Yes, you act like a fucking twelve-year old, just behave and show some respect for people, will you?'

'Woo. Get her. I didn't know you liked a bit of Homo action. That's a shame for us real men.'

'*Real men,* don't make me laugh. Just grow up, you're making a tit of yourself.'

Neil was muttering to himself now. 'Can't even have a bit of banter, what's the world. . .' At that point the headmaster, a balding man with glasses, entered. The room fell quiet.

'Goodnight everyone. Thank you all for today. I'll be in my office for the next couple of hours if anyone wants me. David Seaton, where are you? Oh, You're there, would you hang fire for a moment? There are some policemen outside who wish to speak to you. I would think it's about your college friends. They're from the CID.'

David nodded. 'Oh dear. Righto.' He began chewing on his nails feverously.

'You can use the deputy head's office if you like. Do you want me to sit in with you? I know it's out of school time, but you are on our premises, if you want a bit of support.'

'I will be fine on my own, thank you, sir.' David's nasal way of speaking enforced the listener to strain to hear, sometimes.

'So, you're all right on your own then, are you?'

David nodded.

Once in the deputy's office, Cynthia Walker and Steve Aston stared across the desk at David Seaton with some disbelief. This man was teaching the adults of the future. A frightening prospect. David was nervy, and his hands appeared to be shaking as he toyed with the pencil in his hand.

Cynthia spoke first. 'We want to talk to you about the murders of your college friends, David. We called at your house earlier, but obviously you were at work, but anyway at least we've caught up with you now.'

'Yes, indeed.' He continued to fidget with the pencil.

'I understand you were close friends with Stuart Millichip?'

'Yes, we were close friends. You've obviously spoken to the others.'

'Yes, we have. Look, I'll be open from the start Mr Seaton-'

'David, please.' He smarmed an ingratiating smile.

'To tell the truth, your group of friends – including yourself – are as much under suspicion as anybody, if not more so.'

'I thought as much. Bertrand Russell said that "mystery is delightful, but unscientific, since it depends upon ignorance." Ignorance of all of us, I mean. You aren't suggesting that because Stuart and I were friends, years ago, that I am some sort of mass murderer, I take it?' He snorted a laugh.

Steve reassured him. 'Of course not. We would just like you to tell us what your relationship with Stuart was like, David, if you don't mind.'

'And if I do mind?'

'Well, er. . .'

'I'm jesting. We were very good friends, we...' David struggled to hold on to his emotions, tears began welling up in his eyes. 'I'm sorry this has all been a bit of a strain for me. I'm used to a quiet life.'

Cynthia put her arm on his forearm, which he slowly slid away without looking at her. She spoke. 'That's OK, David. Take your time, we're in no rush.' Steve continued with the conversation. 'Are you all right to continue?' he asked.

David produced an over-large white cotton handkerchief and blew hard on it. 'Yes, I'm fine now, thank you.'

Steve continued. 'David, whatever is said within these four walls is completely confidential and will go no further. I must ask you a somewhat delicate question. Are you homosexual?'

'Stuart was a sensitive soul, like me. A little too sensitive and a little bit out of the groove. An outsider to some extent, though latterly he developed a new persona almost, with his raucous biker friends. We were close, and Stuart and I shared a love of the night sky. We had a poem that we were fond of, as it touched the essence of our friendship. *"To have you near, is all I want. My rock. My muse. My love savant. And whilst the moon doth shine its light. Stay in my arms till death's respite."* It goes on but you get the premise.'

Cynthia smiled. 'That's beautiful, who is that by?'

'Who is it by? It's by me, my dear.'

'Oh, I see. That's sweet, David.'

'Thank you, I'm not sure it scans well, for the purist, but I like it. Things from the heart usually are special, don't you find?' he paused, seemingly lost in thought. 'Suffice it to say, I would prefer not to go into details, out of respect for Stuart's mother, but if you are asking if I loved Stuart, yes I did, very much, and I hope he did in return.'

'Didn't Stuart have relationships with women as well?'

'Not as far as I am aware. Why do you ask? Do you know something I don't?'

'Not at all, David, just asking. Were you close to James Deely?' Steve asked.

'No, I wasn't. I never liked him at college, and nothing changed thereafter!'

'Why did you dislike James Deely?'

'Simple. He was crass. No morals. No wonder he became a solicitor. I shouldn't speak ill of the dead but as Newton said: "Truth is ever to be found in simplicity, and not in the multiplicity and confusion of things." Not quite in this context of course, though the relevance remains.'

'What about his morals?'

'He was a womanizer, he had no understanding of love, just lust, the two are very different. He hurt people by his lascivious ways and I just think that is reckless and unforgiveable.'

'David, talking of which, it's come to our attention that you, well, you stare out of your window with a pair of binoculars at courting couples, late at night, on occasion.'

'Hah! I know where that has come from, the nosy old cow! Is there no sanity? Can you imagine me wanting to watch a courting couple? I mean, I ask you! I am an amateur astronomer; I love the night sky, as did, Stuart. Is nothing sacred to these people?'

'I did wonder. Why binoculars rather than a telescope, may I ask?'

'I hope she slips and breaks her neck, next time she sticks her nose in other people's business. Fat, pig ignorant, and a total waste of perfectly good oxygen. She and all those like her should be exterminated, removed from society for all the good she contributes. Seriously, what is the point of such ignoramuses?'

'Perhaps a little harsh.' Steve said.

'But true, as far as I am concerned.' David raised his eyebrows and stared at Steve, matter-of-factly.

'Going back to my original question, David. Why binoculars rather than a telescope?'

'Space. Hah. Space.' He shook his head and chuckled at his inadvertent joke. 'As in binoculars take up less space than a telescope, and actually you can often see more with binoculars. That's all. Nothing sinister. How sad.' He seemed lost in thought for a moment.

'Where were you on the nights in question?'

'It's true, you do actually ask that question? But why wouldn't you, of course.' David leaned his elbow patched arms onto the desk. 'The first one isn't a problem. I would be cycling to work. I set off from my house at eight o'clock on the dot every day, like clockwork, come hell or high water. And sometimes there is very high water, we are on the flood plain, you see.'

'Oh.' Steve shrugged. 'Just to clarify you are saying that is what you were doing on this *particular* Monday?'

'Yes, it is.'

'Did anybody see you?' Cynthia asked.

'No idea. Probably, I got to school for twenty to nine. Maybe you should ask my lovely neighbour?'

'Maybe.' Steve smiled. 'What about the Thursday night. Sorry if it seems insensitive of me to ask.'

David sighed. 'No, it's fine, I know you have to ask. I'm afraid I would be at home, feet up, with a glass of home brewed beer, watching *Prisoner Cell Block H*. Do you watch it at all?'

'No. I see enough cells at work.'

'Of course. Charming.'

'Were you alone?'

'Yes. Of course.'

Cynthia felt it a little sad that he added the 'of course.' She sought a little clarity on the situation. 'Can I ask. Were you and Stuart still seeing each other as close friends, or were you friendly but more distant?' It was the only way she could think of phrasing the question.

'Bless you. No, we were friends, but distant, and had been since we went our separate ways from college. Sadly, it is the way with life, enforced separations. We still socialised and we had a love, albeit a different love. It was quite sporadic, however. I saw him very recently actually.'

'When was that?'

'Only the day before...' He started to break down again and buried his face in the large handkerchief. 'He took me into Matlock on his motor bike. Typical Stuart. We often went out into Derbyshire on our little adventures.' He shook his head. 'What a waste of a young life.'

'Did you have time off work on Friday, then, David?'

'Yes, sometimes it works out that every few weeks I have a few free periods, so I took the afternoon off.'

'What time did you get back?'

'About nine o'clock. A little too late for me. I'm a home body. Stuart is. . .was, more of a butterfly, bless him.'

'What did you do in Matlock?'

'Walked the hills, held hands, took in the air and marvelled at the beauty of the countryside, just like everyone else does.'

Cynthia smiled at his innocence.

'Did Stuart come in for a coffee, or did he just drop you off?'

'He came in to check I was all right. He didn't stay above a couple of minutes and then he was gone... but not forgotten.' He broke into tears again.

Cynthia tried to soothe him. 'We've nearly finished, David. Did he mention any trouble or any concerns that he might have had?'

'Not a thing, dear. Not a thing.'

'David, thank you so much for your time. We will leave you in peace. We may need to speak again but thank you also for being so honest. Stuart would be proud, I'm sure.' Cynthia squeezed his hand as they left.

'That means a lot. Thank you.'

He wiped his hand on his trousers as she turned to leave.

As they got to the car park Steve asked Cynthia, 'What do you think?'

'I'm not sure he's capable of murdering two people in cold blood, but never say never.' Cynthia observed.

'He got a bit excited over old Mrs Roberts, that was a bit of a different side to him, don't you think?'

'He did, but hey.'

'He is a weirdo, though isn't he?' Steve said.

'No, he's not. He's a sensitive, educated, sweet and quite obviously, gay man. To call him weird is to be unkind in my view, and ignorant, Steve, you should know better than that. If you're different, you are weird. It's tribal shit.'

'OK. Let's agree he's not weird, but maybe not the norm, if that is less insulting.'

'Agreed.' Cynthia smiled, as they jokingly shook hands on the agreement.

*

Generally, there weren't many cars at Brickyard Cottages, at ten o'clock at night. There was no brickyard and no cottages, maybe years ago there was. The long track leading to the wasteland at the far end was occasionally used by local youths to swap stolen cars and do drug deals, as there was no street lighting, and it was lined with bushes obscuring the view from the main road. The main problem was that if the police came down the track you were caught like a rat in a trap; there was one way in, and one way out; it was risking a drive across the fields or leg it, neither put the odds in favour of the criminals. It was also a perfect venue as a lover's lane. There weren't many nights that there were one or two cars parked, with steamy windows along the long driveway.

PC Sam Dewer tried to always have a drive down at least once a shift when he was on evenings or nights. He was aware that the police were sometimes branded as voyeurs, because people don't realise that secluded spots are not only magnets for courting couples but for criminal activity also. On this occasion he had struck gold; there were a couple of cars parked up in the hedgerow, but to what end? Criminal or seminal? As he swung the police car round, the headlights exposed a lady's bare backside frolicking inside. Seminal. He did a full turn, and caught a glimpse of some rather attractive, pendulous breasts and a lady's face, which bobbed down with a look of abject terror as their gaze met. Sam noticed the other vehicle parked close by, looked empty. He parked up with the engine running, round the curve of the road, having made a note of both registration numbers. When he was out of sight, he killed the engine and his lights and sat in pitch darkness. He radioed the reg numbers in to the Control Room, and asked for a check on the Police National Computer.

It usually took a couple of minutes for a response. He took advantage of the darkness and gave his nose a good old pick, something he had been dying to do, but when you are in uniform there is always someone watching you.

The radio controller eventually gave his reply: 'NH to Papa Victor two nine.'

'Papa Victor two nine, go ahead over.'

'No reports on either vehicle. Not stolen. Do you require keeper details?'

He instinctively glanced in his mirror but there was only darkness. The frenzied putting on of clothes in the vehicle was not visible to him. 'Affirmative, over.'

'First one, Jonathon Stacey, 12 Stafford Villas, Hucknall. Over.'

'Received, over.'

'Second vehicle, Caroline Winner, 16 Rawson Street,

Nottingham.'

'Ten-four, much obliged. Papa Victor two nine.'

He reversed his patrol car twenty feet or so, until he got a view, and he smiled. He glanced back again at the frantic movements within the vehicle before resuming patrol. The names meant nothing to the patrolman, although her face did seem familiar. Perhaps it was wishful thinking. The poor woman looked as though she was going to die, of embarrassment.

10

'She gave me a smile I could feel in my hip pocket.'

Raymond Chandler

Stark and Ashley Stevens were outside the secretary's office of Nottingham Polytechnic. Stark sat on a pink designer chair, fashionable but spine destroying, his legs were crossed awkwardly, and he was rapping his fingers on his knee impatiently and running his fingers down the sharp crease in his trousers. Ashley stood with his hands in the trouser pockets of his expensive, double-breasted suit. He seemed puzzled as he peered at the display on the wall. 'What the bloody hell is this lot, supposed to be, boss?'

Stark got up and went over to stand at his side, relieved to get off the damned chair. He saw an array of drawings; strange angular lines and disturbing images contrasting with each other. Some of the pencil strokes were harsh and others more delicate. 'Let me see. I believe it comes under the auspice of art, young Ashley.'

'Art? Seriously?'

'Yes, this one here, look, you only see lines and paint daubing's, but I see a dystopian world, a world where pain and suffering is trapped under the Jack-boot of fascism.'

'Eh?'

'And this other one, I see silence. Can you imagine being able to capture silence in a painting? Yet, it is not a dormant silence, it is malevolent silence, seeking, probing.'

'Is it?'

'Oh, yes, Ashley, it is a tortuous silence, a silence that is mutating, building and swelling into a stifled scream that demands justice.'

'Incredible.' Ashley shrugged.

'The principle will see you now, gentlemen.' The middle-aged woman appeared suddenly and clip-clopped down the corridor towards them. 'I see you are admiring the art-work.'

Ashley spoke. 'I particularly like this one. It should be entitled "Rage imbued by silence". It has taken a lot of thought and soul searching to produce that.' He seemed pleased with himself.

The woman frowned. 'Oh, OK, they are my daughter's, she's only five, but I promised her I would put them up in the foyer, she was so excited, bless her. I'm, er, glad you like them?'

Stark was chuckling to himself as they followed her back from whence, she came. Ashley seemed deflated.

The receptionist knocked on the door briefly, as she entered, followed by the two detectives.

At one end of the spacious room stood an imposing desk, and at the other end were four chairs around a rectangular glass coffee-table. Rows of books lined the far wall, and there was an odd mixture of old and new furniture. The secretary-cum- receptionist brought in tea and biscuits, before retiring gracefully to her adjoining room.

The Principal, Amanda Bolton, had been at the college almost nineteen years. When Stark had telephoned her earlier, she had remembered the group of individuals well, but she had also researched them prior to the detective's arrival, to refresh her memory. Ever the professional. She was a classy lady. With her grey hair and half-spectacles, the Principle looked as though she was nearing retirement. She was slightly frazzled in her appearance, and gave the impression of being kindly and wise, her smile was broad which she displayed at the least excuse. Stark immediately warmed to her. Mrs Bolton sat with them around the coffee table on the low chairs.

'I didn't know how far you wanted me to go, Mr Stark.'

All the way, he thought.

'I've got everything I could possibly lay my hands on and I've spoken with their former teachers. I mean, where do you want me to start?'

Stark placed his hands together as if in prayer, putting them against his pursed lips.

'I'll tell you what you could do, if you don't mind, just go through each one very briefly, and describe them all in a couple or three sentences, just for starters? We can scrutinize the documentation at our leisure, but I'm interested in your observations, and those of the teachers who met them daily, when they were students here.'

'Any particular order, or as they come?'

'As they come, is fine.'

The Principal cleared her throat and looked at the first folder on her lap. 'Caroline Simpson, now Caroline Winner, I believe. Let me see, a clever, attractive girl, who competed with Tracey Oliver. Now Tracey Sewell, for attention, but never seemed quite to manage it. If my memory serves me correctly, she used to like Jonathon Stacey at the time. She was studying history and art. The girl next door type really, always polite and well turned out. Um, is that okay, or do you want a more detailed picture?'

'Let's keep it simple.' Stark said. 'If there is anything you feel you want to say about an individual that might help us, do so.'

'Very well. So that was Caroline. Rather appropriately next on the list is her now husband, Mark Winner. I always found Mark a rather bland character, not much personality. A very good sportsman, in fact an excellent sportsman. But that was his lot. What else? Not very good at other subjects. He certainly lacked communication skills, though don't misunderstand me, he never once caused a jot of trouble. Blink and you would miss him, that sort. I thought he may go on to be a physical education teacher, but you say he works at a leisure centre now, so maybe he has underachieved a little, which, in truth, does not overly surprise me.'

She sipped at her tea and threw Mark's file on the chair next to her. Stark was impressed with Amanda, her judgement of character was good, finely tuned after years of intermittent contact with students, whom she had to assess. There was also a grace to her, a finesse, and the scent of a rather appealing perfume.

'Next up is, Tracey Oliver, now Tracey Sewell, I understand. I think Tracey was a popular member of the college, very well known, yes, perhaps a bit of an attention seeker. This manifested itself by her flirtatiousness, even with the teachers, I understand. The male teachers were always concerned when they were in a room alone with her, it's a persistent problem, and was ever thus. What else? She would sometimes get rather intense and lacked a bigger picture view, quite narrow in her thinking. It was her world view and never anyone else's. She could be snappy, but many youngsters are, what with the soup of hormones floating around inside them. She was studying English Lit and Sociology. She always wore black, and short skirts, *very* short skirts.'

The two men smiled. Ashley was scribbling notes on a pad.

'Next, is Jonathon Stacey. An intelligent boy. He's done very well for himself. He was always a natural leader, people looked to him for decisions. He was liked, and well respected by the students and teachers alike. As a young man, he revelled in the attention of women. Rumour had it that he and Tracey had got it together, but there are always rumours, the college thrives on it, as do all large establishments.'

'Do you mean they had sex, when you say they got it together? Just for clarity.' Stark asked.

'That was the rumour; I wasn't in the room with them at the time you understand.'

The men laughed politely. Stark liked the way her politeness was punctuated with sharp observations and down-to-earth comments.

Mrs Bolton continued. 'I suppose that whilst we are on that thorny subject, I also heard from some of the form teachers, that James Deely had sex with both Tracey and Caroline. On *separate* occasions, of course; for clarity.' She smiled at Stark. She continued, 'It's amazing what gets back to teachers, Inspector.'

Stark smiled but was thoughtful, storing the different dynamics in the puzzle in his mind. 'I see Stuart Millichip, deceased, is next.' Stark observed.

'Yes, indeed. Such a waste. I had forgotten, but Stuart was a year below the others in age, yet he tended to tag along with them. He didn't really have too much to do with the lads, but the two girls seemed to take him under their wings a little bit, and he used to get along well with David Seaton. Stuart was an average student at best, who struggled to concentrate. Towards the end of his college days he became a bit of a loner, after the others had left. His grades seemed to suffer when the others went, and he underperformed. It was just him and his motor bike, really.'

'What did he study, as a matter of interest?' Stark asked.

'Let's see, yes, I thought so, Sciences; Physics and Maths. Tough subjects. I've mentioned David Seaton already. He was a good student, quite academic, quiet, broody almost. He had a studious temperament. I often wondered why he hung around with the crowd, putting up with the ribald comments of the likes of Jonathon Stacey and James Deely.'

'Did they give him a hard time, then?'

'A little bit, yes. He was an easy target in one sense, being studious and, dare I say, a little effeminate? He studied literature and the classics, which separated him from the herd, slightly. He tried to win approval from the lads by doing crazy stunts for them.'

'Really?' Stark was surprised, it didn't seem to fit. 'In what way?'

'I got the impression that he wanted to prove that he was just as much a man as they were, silly things, like them sending him in to shops to steal, or drink a whole bottle of vodka, all that type of nonsense.'

'Did the teasing have much of an effect on him?'

'I wouldn't know. Who can tell? Some people are suckers for that sort of thing and keep going back for more.'

Keith Wright

'What about Roy Prentice?'

Amanda laughed. 'Roy caused us quite a few problems.'

'You do surprise me,' Stark said caustically.

'I take it you've met him, then?'

'I have had that dubious pleasure, yes.'

'Well, Roy, as you will know, is rather politically motivated. He studied sociology and politics and was chairman of the Students Union at the college; hence the reference to the problems he caused us. He was very serious and cynical for one so young.'

'Were any of the others in the Student's Union?' Ashley asked.

'No, they weren't. That didn't stop Roy trying to recruit them, though. I think he just bored them to death with it. He's no fool mind you, and once he has a bee in his bonnet, he is like a dog with a bone.'

'Mixed metaphors from a college principal, Mrs Bolton.' Stark teased.

'Well, you know what I mean. Don't tell the kids.' She laughed warmly.

'I think we are getting there. James? James Deely. What sort of a guy was he?'

'Nice enough young man, another one who did well for himself. He was always driven, a bit of a go-getter, quite mercenary, money-oriented. He didn't get on particularly well with Jonathon Stacey, however.'

'Why was that, do you think?'

'I'm not a hundred percent sure. Perhaps a bit of rivalry between the two, stags locking horns, that sort of thing. I must admit that there seemed to be a bit more to it, than just that, but I'm surmising, I don't really know. James studied English remarkably well, I hasten to add. Good at debating. I'm afraid that is as much as I can tell you. All the papers are here. You're welcome to scrutinize them.'

Stark smiled. 'OK we'll do that. Thank you very much for your help, Mrs Bolton.'

'It's Miss Bolton, actually.'

'Sorry, well perhaps I'm not.'

'Call me Amanda, it makes life easier.'

'Thank you. Call me Dave.'

Ash felt like he was a spare prick at a wedding. '

'I don't suppose you can throw any further light on the mystery at all?'

'No, I've racked my brains trying to think. I'm worried that it is connected somehow to the college, as it is likely to mean adverse publicity. What is your view Inspector?'

'Personally, I think there is a connection between their college days, two dead in a few days and both from the same group of friends at college? I'm not a big one for coincidences.'

'With respect, I hope you are wrong.' She smiled warmly again. 'Obviously if there is anything I, or my staff, can do to help, please don't hesitate to ask. If there is a link, I would be intrigued to know what it is.'

'You and me both.' Stark laughed.

'It's all rather disconcerting. I must ask, am I right in assuming that there is no suggestion the college or students are in any jeopardy?'

'I doubt it. There is no evidence whatsoever, that is the case. Certainly not the college.'

'That's something at least. The education authority has got wind of it somehow, and asked me to play any connection down, but, if there is one, it is only right and proper that we help you find it.'

Stark thanked Amanda heartily as they shook hands and Stark couldn't help but notice that her hand seemed to dwell in his longer than the norm. Ashley took possession of the records. Somewhere amongst all of this was the link. What the hell was it? Something from the past had returned to haunt the present. He was convinced of it.

*

Mavis Enderby was seventy-two years old and a big lady, so it was difficult for her to get out of the car outside Nottingham

Police Station. After she had swivelled round on the passenger seat, she was helped by the care assistant, who took her arm and pulled her up after a 'one, two, three.' The carer stood holding her arm for a few seconds while she steadied herself. Mavis wore her best 'camel' coat, the carer wore combat trousers and a ring through her nose. Once inside the police station foyer she asked to speak to a police officer, and one eventually arrived clutching pen and paper.

Stark had collected his mail from the Control Room and was passing the foyer just as Mavis announced the reason for her visit. 'It's about the murders in the paper.'

Stark stopped abruptly and listened intently behind the door.

'Ronny' the carer chipped in. 'I'm Veronica Slater, and this is Mavis Enderby. I work at the care home on Beardall Street, and Mavis has been hounding us to bring her in, she has something she wants to tell you.' She turned to Mavis. 'Tell the policeman what you know then, Mavis.' Ronny winked at the policeman and gave him a knowing, albeit condescending, smile.

Ronnie was oblivious that this frail lady was made of much sterner stuff than she ever would be. She was a very intelligent lady and during the war had worked at Bletchley Park, as a code-breaker's assistant, briefly, having a degree in maths.

Mavis cleared her throat and began the speech she had been rehearsing in her mind most of the night. 'I've been reading about the murders in the *Evening Post* and I also read the Births, Deaths and Marriages. You do when you get to my age, you know. . .'

The policeman nodded at Ronny who was smiling to herself, looking at the floor. He was aware that the carer was trying to give him signals that this was all a load of nonsense and he was acknowledging that fact to her.

'Yes, go on love, I'm listening.' The officer said.

'Well, I've seen these entries in the personal column...' She rummaged in her bag and took out a purse. She had a little difficulty opening the clasp and the officer and Ronnie exchanged further glances. Mavis eventually produced three newspaper cuttings. 'Don't laugh, I know you think I'm a daft old bugger, but I think they could be something to do with the murders. The first message was put in just before the first murder took place, and the other messages were put in the day after both murders. See what you think.' She handed them to the officer, who started to read them. As he did, Stark's curiosity got the better of him, and he appeared in the doorway behind the counter.

'Oh, hello, sir.' The officer said.

'Hello, Steve. I couldn't help but overhear. Let's have a look.' He nodded to the two ladies observing proceedings and shook both their hands. 'I'm Detective Inspector Stark, I'm running the murder enquiry.' Mavis did a sort of curtsy, when she shook his hand.

The PC handed the clippings to Stark and he read them aloud in the order that he was given them:

Baby darling, I did not lie,
Others now must say goodbye.

Baby darling, you now know,
There are only two to go.

Baby darling, there were three,
Now there's only one to see.

Stark paused and quickly re-read them, 'Oh my God!'

'See?' Mavis said. 'Can you see what I mean, Inspector?'

'Absolutely. Thank you so much for bringing these to our attention. You have done the right thing, and amazing that you have seen the possible connection.'

Ronnie turned away from the gaze of the desk officer, both now feeling a little churlish.

'Thank you. I thought you ought to see them. They think you're daft these young uns.'

'Not at all. Do you want a job? I could use a new detective.'

Mavis laughed. 'Maybe forty years ago.'

'Have you got the dates when these were published? Actually, it doesn't matter; we can get them from the *Evening Post.*'

Ronny looked a little embarrassed about her overt scepticism, now that it was revealed that there may be some substance to Mavis' theory.

She took Mavis by the arm. 'So, if you don't need us for anything else, we'll get on our merry way then,' she said.

Stark was reading the messages to himself. He broke off. 'Yes, of course you can. This officer will just take your details, and thanks very much, this could be a great help. It really could.'

Stark ran up the stairs three at a time. As he passed the CID office, he shouted out, '*Nobby. Have you got a minute?*'

Nobby appeared, in the doorway of Stark's office.

'What's up, boss?'

'Have a read of these.'

'What is it?'

'Have a read.'

'OK.'

Nobby read them quickly. He shrugged. 'It could be something I suppose.'

'Oh, piss off, Nobby – it's our murderer. They were put in after the murders, the narrative matches the timing of the murders.'

'I guess so.'

'It's got to be. OK. Let me temper that, I *hope* it is. Get two of the lads to go down to the *Evening Post* and find out who put this lot in. It may just be as simple as that!'

Nobby disappeared and spoke to Steph and Jim, before returning to Stark's office. When he came back in, the two of them studied the clippings. 'Hold on a minute, there are eleven words to each message. I wonder if that tells us something?' Nobby observed.

Stark commented. 'Interesting spot, Nobby. I know what the last message tells us?'

'What?'

'There's going to be another murder!'

*

Steve Aston wiped the small rectangular copper slab, which was about eight inches long and used the petrol-based cleaner to get the printer's ink off. The Fingerprint Room was small, with a high table. In the corner was a sink, with a huge tub of Swarfega close by to help rid fingers and palms of the black sticky stuff. Fingerprint ink is difficult to get off sweaty hands.

Caroline Winner smiled at Steve as she stretched to pull her jacket over her shoulders clearly displaying that she was bra-less under her vest-top. Steve couldn't help but notice and his stare lingered longer than it perhaps should.

Caroline took hold of Steve's hand. 'I've never had my fingerprints taken before, but if I ever have them taken again, I want it to be by you.' She smiled.

Steve mumbled. 'Thanks. Erm do you want to witness their destruction once they have been checked, this is only for witness comparison, so it's your right to see it done.'

'Will you be there?'

'I don't know, probably not.'

'In that case, no.'

Steve placed the completed fingerprint form in front of her. 'Can you just sign here, please? Then you can go.'

'Anything you say, officer.'

Steve watched as she leaned over the table, throwing her hair back so that she could see where to sign. He showed her to the door and then promptly bounded up the stairs.

'Christ all-bleeding-mighty!'

Ashley glanced up. 'What are you looking so flummoxed about?'

'It's that Caroline Winner.'

'What about her?'

'I've just taken her fingerprints. God, she's fit, isn't she? I'm not kidding, as I'm taking them, she starts rubbing her left breast against my arm.'

'Are you sure it wasn't the other way around?' Ash said.

'No, she's a right hot-arse. She kept smiling at me. Looking right at me, as she was doing it.'

Cynthia was shaking her head. 'It's so bloody easy isn't it?'

'What do you mean?'

'Forget it, nothing.'

'Come on, what?'

'What I mean, is that she is playing you. It's easy for women to do this with you horny young bucks.'

'So, she didn't think I was sexy then? She said I was.' Steve seemed deflated.

Cynthia began giggling. She spoke. 'Oh, don't be upset, Steve, of course you are sexy,' She laughed. 'But my tip as a woman, and I know I'm just the aide, is to just be mindful that women, well, some women, will twist you round their little finger, if you let them. Don't take your eye off the ball if a woman starts flirting, that's all.'

'Sounds like she didn't take her eye off his balls.' Ash said.

'I give up.' Cynthia said.

'Anyway, her prints can now be compared with those in Deely's car. She said she had not been in it so let's see.'

'When are they doing the others? Ashley asked.

'They are doing them in batches.' Steve said.

'We might not need them if Steph can find out who has been posting these messages in the *Evening Post*.'

*

Stephanie Dawson and Jim McIntyre drew up alongside the historic Evening *Post* building. Jim parked immediately outside on double yellow lines.

'You can't leave it here, Jim. You'll get a ticket!'

'Bollocks to a ticket, we are the Queen's men, on Queen's business. We'll be fine.'

'No, we'll be *fined*!' Jim ignored her and opened the car door.

'OK. Please yourself.'

The two strolled over to the large front porchway and huge oak door, adorned by brass plaques, doorknob and letterbox. Once inside they approached the counter and spoke to a somewhat business-like young lady with swept-up black hair, and glasses on a chain around her neck. It was not every day that the CID called, on a murder investigation. Although she was not a journalist, she could smell a story, and she attempted to glean as much information as she possibly could.

'So, let me get this right,' she said, 'we have a serial killer on our hands and he's sending messages to the *Nottingham Evening Post*.'

Jim corrected her. '*Could be*, I said. Nothing definite has been found out. That's the reason we're here – to discover who arranged for the personal column entries to be put in.'

'Do you mind if I take notes about all this? It's terribly exciting.'

Steph was getting peeved. 'Are you a journalist, or a receptionist, or what, love?'

'I'm a receptionist, why do you ask?'

'Because we're here investigating a couple of murders, with the prospect of there being further attacks on people, and so I want you, and you personally, to take me to the Editor's office right now.'

'I can't do that. Why, what have I done?'

'Listen, you do exactly as I say, young lady. Where is the Editor's office?'

'It's on the top floor.'

'Come on, then. You'll understand why, when we get there.'

They headed towards the lift, with Jim following on in their wake.

Steph spoke briefly with the Editor's secretary and the three of them were shown in. Steph was in the zone, and Jim was hanging on to her coattails. Whenever she got something like this in her head, there was no stopping her. She had cursed herself for not going to the top straight-away, and Jim's ham-fisted approach needed rectifying pronto. The Editor, one Peter

Thrower, was surprised by the intrusion, but he eyed them, over his half-spectacles, and then beckoned them over towards his desk.

'Come in, make yourselves at home why don't you? Don't mind me.'

'I'm so sorry for the intrusion, but it's very important, and I hope you'll understand why I have had to do it this way. You see we are from the CID. . .' Jim closed the door behind them.

'I take it this can't wait?'

'No, it is urgent, I'm afraid. We're investigating the murder of James Deely and Stuart Millichip. You obviously know about them.'

'Yes, of course we have invested a lot of resource in covering the story. It's big news for the city. Front page, most nights.' Peter removed his spectacles as his interest grew.

'Well, we think that the murderer has been putting messages in your personal column.' She raised a warning hand. 'Although it's not definite yet.'

'Goodness me, that's a turn up for the books.' He clapped his hands together. He was beaming. 'I hope you're right; this is really going to raise the profile of the paper.'

'Fine, but we need to broker an agreement first.'

'OK, let's hear what you have in mind.'

'We need to look at who has been paying for the messages, it's as simple as that, however this needs to be kept secret. Any publicity could thwart the whole investigation.'

'Hmm.'

'We cannot have anyone knowing about this *until* the enquiry, or at least into this particular aspect, is completed'

'Why should I worry about your problems when I have a huge scoop of massive public interest, handed to me on a plate.' Peter was nothing if not succinct.

'You don't. You can do whatever you like. If, however, your publishing *against* our advice means that it delays catching the killer, and someone else gets killed, which is what the threat is, then your rivals and all the nationals will be able to point their fingers at you, with, I hasten to add, our full co-operation.'

'I see.'

'If you help us to keep a lid on it, however, you can then potentially claim all the wonders of the universe, as being the saviour of the citizens of Nottingham, and pour a huge dollop of cream on it as well, if you like.'

'Interesting.'

'Incidentally, this lady in reception needs to be sworn to secrecy, as well.'

'This is a conundrum. A nice conundrum to have, by the way.' Peter said.

Steph continued. 'You've a ready-made story here, that's not going anywhere.'

'Unless a rival gets wind of it, and we lose the impetus. We are going to look complete and utter chumps, if that happens.'

'No, we would destroy them, if that ever happened, but it won't get out. It's super-tight, and it won't take long to resolve, I wouldn't have thought.'

Peter stood and paced the room, before landing at the window and looking out at the city landscape. Jim was impressed with Steph's performance.

Steph continued to push. 'You know the problems that could arise if the paper obstructs the course of justice. You could be held in contempt of court at any subsequent trial of offenders.'

'You're right, of course.'

'It's a no brainer, be the heroes or the villains.'

He turned and strode towards Steph with his hand outstretched. 'Heroes it is, you have a deal.' They shook hands.

'Peter Thrower.'

'Stephanie Dawson, pleased to meet you.' She was smiling. 'This is my colleague Jim McIntyre.' They shook hands.

Peter spoke again. 'We'll need to review it every week, with your Detective Superintendent and Penny Staines in your press office.'

'Of course. They don't even know about it, yet, but all of that will be sorted out, no problem. We just need to secure the information post-haste.'

'Let's do it.'

They went out into the main office and watched as Peter spoke to a clerk. The lady went to a cabinet and obtained three envelopes, which she gave to Peter. There was further animated conversation and shaking of heads. Peter frowned.

He returned to the detectives.

'Who sent them, then?' Steph asked hopefully.

'I don't know, I'm afraid.'

'What d'ya mean you dinna know?' Jim said in broad Scottish; his default when riled.

'This is all we have. Three plain white envelopes, with the messages typed on paper inside. It was pushed through our front letterbox, with the correct amount of money, in cash. That's all we require. It is a personal column and people put all sorts of things in it, and they naturally want to remain anonymous.'

'Shit!' Jim said.

Steph was despondent too. 'OK, well, look. Let's stick to our agreement, there are all kinds of things we can do with the envelopes and notes, I suppose. It's just never, bloody straight forward.'

'No, it never is.' Peter agreed.

'Has the cash been banked?' She asked.

'I'm afraid so.'

'We'll take everything from you, for now, for forensic examination, if we may.'

'Of course.'

'And please, keep shtum.'

'As agreed,'

Steph took the envelopes in between her knuckles and popped them into a larger envelope off the desk next to her. The detectives turned to leave. Steph stopped in her tracks.

'Oh. I should ask. Do you have a cleaner?'

'Yes, of course. Why?'

'Does she clean the brass letter-box?'

'Oh, I'm with you, fingerprints. I'm afraid she does, first thing every morning. It's her pride and joy. It sparkles like a new pin, I'm afraid. Sorry.'

'Fair enough. I just thought I'd ask. I will get the relevant people to be in touch about what we discussed, OK?'

'Excellent. Good luck.'

'Thanks.'

As they walked away, Jim spoke out the corner of his mouth. 'I think you're in the wrong job, Steph.'

'We all are, Jim.'

*

Stark was smiling as he spoke to Derek Brook at Arnold Lodge children's home on the telephone. 'Keep it to yourself though, Derek, please, and I will collect it just as soon as I get the chance, OK?'

'No problem.'

'That's great, thank you Derek. Bye.'

Stark let out a self-satisfied sigh. He tapped out some numbers on the phone.

Detective Superintendent Wagstaff, was both pleased and concerned with the news about the personal column messages. Stark went through them with him again:

> *Baby darling, I did not lie,*
> *Others now must say goodbye.*

'So that was put in the day before Deely was killed.'

> *Baby darling, you now know,*
> *There are only two to go.*

'That was put in the evening of James Deely's murder *after* he'd been killed.'

> *Baby darling, there were three,*
> *Now there's only one to see.*

'This last one was put in the day *after* Stuart Millichip had his head squashed at the Fox and Grapes.'

Wagstaff gave his view. 'It's an important lead, and I think you are on to something, which is the good news. The bad news, of course, is that it suggests that one of the others is going to be killed. It's not best.'

'No, it's not best.' Stark repeated.

'There is no way we can give them all twenty-four-hour protection, David. The killer may not strike for months for all we know.'

'Or he may.' Stark said.

'Thanks for that, David.'

'I'm just saying that maybe we should consider doing something at least short term, and review it, say weekly.'

'The best way to stop it happening, of course, is to catch him.' There was a pause as the comment resonated with Stark.

'I suppose the other problem is that we would also be giving the killer twenty-four-hour protection.' Stark said.

'Which would also stop it happening, because he wouldn't be able to lose his alibi.'

'But would the protection be covert or overt?'

'That's a decision to be made, I suppose.' Wagstaff said.

'Well, if it is covert, it would cost hundreds of thousands of pounds. Twenty blokes and ten cars on all the potential victims. It would have to be Regional Crime Squad, and who is going to be investigating the rapes and kidnappings and armed robberies if they all come over to our job indefinitely?'

'I don't think they even have that amount of resource, David. The covert option is a non-starter. We could in theory put two cops with each one.'

'That is four cops per witness, on twelve-hour shifts, not including rest days, which if you factor in is probably about thirty cops.'

'Ouch.'

'Exactly'

'We could offer it to the witnesses, in a way that over-eggs how intrusive it will be, so that they refuse the encumbrance.' Wagstaff said.

'Naughty, but potentially nice.'

'It might be an option. Let me speak to the Chief about this one, but I know he's already over budget, we are supposed to be pulling our belts in, not going on a spending spree.'

'It's above my pay grade, thank God.' Stark said. 'In the meantime we can at least have Home Office Alarms installed at all the houses that offers some protection.'

'That's something, but there is only so many of those available. We will have to pull one or two out of other people's houses.'

'That's tricky, it's life and death. Can we borrow some from another force?'

'Good idea, David. Leave it with me and I will come back to you on it.'

'Thanks, boss. I've got a horrible feeling that our killer is on the warpath, though, he's been quiet a little while, and now we know he intends killing again, we must be due another.'

'In this instance, I hope you're wrong, although I fear you aren't. I have only one final request, David.'

'What's that, sir?'

'Can we catch him as soon as possible, please? Like, yesterday.'

11

'A man who moralizes is usually a hypocrite,
and a woman who moralizes is invariably plain.'

Oscar Wilde

The walls of the CID office were covered with pieces of paper, ranging from intelligence bulletins and teleprinter messages, to calendars depicting young women in various stages of nakedness. The more explicit were hidden behind cabinet doors, visible only when opened. A heavy cloud of smoke rose from Stark's cigar as he chuffed away. Cynthia stood briefly, as Detective Superintendent Wagstaff came in. Wagstaff waved her to sit down. It was still a thing for junior officers to stand when anyone above the rank of Sergeant entered a room.

'Morning team.' Wagstaff started.

'Morning sir,' came the replies.

Stark asked Cynthia to make tea, which was the job Steve Aston was most glad to pass on to Cynthia when she became the aide to CID.

Wagstaff addressed them as whole, informally. 'I take it we didn't get any success with the person posting the personal column messages, or I would have had a phone call at home and a body in the cell.'

Stark answered. 'No, sir. Whoever it is has merely pushed the letters through the letterbox with the appropriate amount of cash, but without leaving any details.' Stark began to feel a little strange. His chest was becoming tight and a sudden flop sweat broke out. Not again, he thought. This had not happened to him in such an informal setting before. Yes, there was a group around him, but it was only the lads.

'Wonderful. Have we submitted everything for fingerprinting?'

Stark wiped his forehead. 'Yes, and the letters were typed, so we'll need the relevant typewriter to compare them with, which of course we haven't got. It would be nice to think that there will be prints on the paper, but I'm not holding my breath, the killer has gone to a lot of trouble to cover their tracks.' Stark would lead the responses despite his growing unease.

'There will be an action for all the witnesses to allow searches at their houses for said typewriter, David, the SOU can do that, but in line with what you have just said, I will be surprised if they have it on display, but it's got to be done, you never know.'

'Absolutely, sir. The snag is that these people work in schools and offices and so it could be anywhere.' His breathing was becoming shortened, growing worse as he fought against it. A vicious circle, as his anxious state increased the calmer, he tried to make himself.

'Let's see if Forensics can come up with a make and model first.' Wagstaff said.

'That would help.'

'I've been wondering why the killer feels the need to publish his intent to the world.'

'You and me both, sir.' Stark said, leaning back and trying to appear calm even though his heart felt like it was going to burst out his chest. Was he going to have a heart attack? What the hell was this bullshit? 'Who does he want to read the messages, if anybody? Who is he communicating with?'

'I was hoping you might tell me that one, David. Anyone got any ideas?'

There was much shaking of heads and muttered, 'No, sir's'. Stark took the opportunity to run his hand through his wet hair as the focus moved away from him, briefly.

Stark wanted to think about the positives. 'We've got men doing observations on the Evening Post letterbox, and as far as

I can see that's all we can do for now, apart from hoping that Forensic turns something up and the analytical stuff.'

'That's necessary, of course, but from what I can see, the killer's next note is going to be after the next killing, which is a little inconvenient.'

'Just a tad, sir.' Stark said. 'Still, even if it was after, at least we would have them at that point rather than still struggling and another body, anyway.'

'Absolutely, I'm not arguing against doing it, it's just that it would be better if we can stop yet another bloody killing.'

'I know, sir.'

Stark sipped at his mug of tea as Wagstaff twiddled with his moustache.

'What analytical stuff are you doing, David?'

'We aren't doing it, but the wider team have been tasked to review all telephone numbers into the Evening Post ahead of the adverts going in.'

'Because. . .'

'Because whoever is sending them, has had to know the exact cost, for putting in such an advert, and that means that surely they have contacted the newspaper.' Stark explained.

'Fair enough. No CCTV I take it?'

'No, that would be too much to ask.'

There was a brief lull before Stark spoke again.

'Whilst there are these more direct approaches, I have been thinking about how we can understand the truth about the dynamic of the group. We only really know what they are prepared to tell us.'

'That's what I've been saying and that's why it is like pulling teeth.' Nobby chipped in.

'I think there are a few secrets that are being kept here, even if they are nothing to do with the murder, and it just clouds everything for us.' Stark said.

'We can't hypnotise them, boss! What are we to do, bug their houses?' Nobby asked.

'We wouldn't get the authority to bug people's own homes,

even under these circumstances, although, it might be worth a try.'

'I've never known it, sir. It's only terrorism, that will break that glass ceiling.'

'I will still enquire, but I fear you're right.' Wagstaff said.

'I have thought of a way where we can listen, without them knowing, however.' Stark's anxiety was easing slightly as Nobby spoke, and as he was focussed more on the dialogue than seeing himself in a sort of out-of-body experience.

'Eh? Listen to them, without them knowing, but not bug their houses; I've got to hear this one, boss.' Nobby was flummoxed.

'Today is James Deely's funeral, isn't it, now that the Coroner has finally released the body. So, all the college cadre will be there, chatting with each other at the wake, won't they?' Stark said.

'We are going around in circles, boss, because they won't talk if we are anywhere near them, sir.' Steph said.

'We *won't* be anywhere near them, Steph.'

'How can we hear what they are saying then?' Nobby asked.

'We aren't going to *hear* what they are saying; we are going to *see* what they are saying.'

It suddenly dawned on Nobby and a smile came to his face as it did Starks; they pointed at each other and said in unison; '*Sammy Trench!*'

*

Stark had fled to the toilet after the awkward engagement with Wagstaff and the team. He rinsed his face with cold water and wiped under his armpit with paper towelling. He would have to keep his jacket on, his shirt was stained. He was worried. Should he see a doctor? Should he declare it? Would it affect his position as a DI? These were questions he did not want to ask. He would be fine. It was probably just a middle-age thing?

He felt much better as he sat in the privacy of his office with an open window to cool him down. He picked up the telephone and dialled Sarah Deely's number from his diary.

He explained his intention to pay his respects at the funeral, which was standard procedure. 'As I have said Mrs Deely, I will be paying my respects as a representative of the police force. I won't stay too long. All I can do is thank you for all your help, despite this being such a trying time for you.'

There was a muffled reply. Stark spoke again. 'So, it's at the Green Gables public house at three o'clock. Thank you very much indeed, and if there is anything I can do, don't hesitate to ask. Goodbye.'

There was a knock on his office door. Stark beckoned Ashley to come in, followed by Sammy Trench.

'Thanks a lot, Ashley. We'll come in shortly, so tell the crew to wait in for a bit please.'

'Will do, boss.'

Sammy Trench stood there in an ill-fitting, cheap, light-blue suit. He was very thin. He looked unkempt and nervous, flicking back a lock of dark hair from his bespectacled face. Stark would have to put him at ease, the best he could.

Ashley went back to the CID office, and joined in the laughter. All the lads had watched him show Sammy Trench into Stark's office. Jim spoke first 'So that's the man who's going to solve out murders is it?'

Ashley giggled. 'I've seen it all, now. I knew things were desperate, but not that bad, surely? So much for Stark's ace informant!'

Even Cynthia seemed unsure. 'Who the hell is he?'

Charlie Carter was smiling knowingly. 'Give the boss some credit, lads.'

'Do you know who this guy is then, Charlie?' Ashley asked.

'I do, as does Nobby, we've been around long enough to see him in action, but I won't steal the boss's thunder. He can tell you about him. Never judge a book by its cover, you should all learn this valuable lesson.'

'He looks a daft bugger to me.' Ashley said.

Charlie continued. 'All I will say is that if he's used right, he'll be the best informant we could possibly use on a job like this.'

Ash was shaking his head in disbelief.

A few moments later, Stark entered the CID office with Sammy in tow. There was immediate silence, the atmosphere in the room tense with apprehension. Stark and Sammy sat down.

Stark was milking the moment: he was in no rush to make known his revelation.

Ashley whispered to Cynthia as Stark gave some background on Sammy. 'I can't believe we are that desperate, having this geezer involved.'

Sammy touched Stark's arm. 'I can't believe we are that desperate, having this geezer involved.' He said out loud.

The others turned to look at Ash and Cynthia at the back of the room, as he continued whispering. 'What is he a fucking mind-reader or something?' Ash whispered again.

Sammy spoke again. 'What is he, a fucking mind-reader or something?'

Everyone was laughing.

'Eh What's the fuck!' Ashley said.

'You are making a bit of a fool of yourself, Ashley.' Stark said. 'Sammy can't hear a word you are saying, but, and it's a big but, he is an expert lip-reader! Now, Sammy is a great friend to us on the CID, and he's kindly agreed to help us out this afternoon, at James Deely's funeral.'

Ashley looked chastened. 'Sorry, Sammy, I'm an idiot. I do apologise. Lesson learnt.'

'Good man, Ash,' Stark said. 'Sammy is going to observe all the college gang during today, and report back the conversations they think they are having in private.'

'Just for clarity, it's not evidence, boss.' Charlie said.

'No, of course, it is for intelligence purposes only. As we've been saying, they are all working to their own agendas, and telling us what they want us to hear. If they think we are not around, something may be let slip, particularly at such an emotionally charged event, as James' funeral.'

'This is brilliant!' Ashley had turned full circle.

'I told you.' Charlie said.

Stark continued. 'Very early on, I am going to make my excuses and leave, having officially paid respects on behalf of us all. And I'll leave Sammy in a good position to "listen" to what the college crowd are saying to each other.'

Cynthia looked thoughtful. 'It's great, sir, but surely Sammy can't remember all this stuff on his own?'

'He will be wearing a throat microphone under his shirt and tie, close to the larynx. He will merely repeat the conversation into the throat mike, which will be recording for posterity and we can disseminate it afterwards.'

'Won't he look a bit silly standing there talking to himself, though? They will think he is some nutter, and be wary of him, surely?' Cynthia said.

'He would stand out, if he was on his own, but we are taking an RCS undercover guy in as a stooge for him. He will be a bit like an extra in a film, in the background looking as if he is speaking to Sammy, but he isn't really, he is just mumbling.'

'Weird, but I love it!' Ashley said. 'I can't wait to hear the tape.'

'There are no guarantees here.' Stark said. 'But what have we got to lose?'

*

Nobby and Steph had been giggling like schoolchildren all the way to Mrs Millichip's house. They were getting on better than they ever had, and Nobby was beginning to feel he might have found a point of weakness in Steph's armour of celibacy.

The Millichip house was in Newstead, a former mining village with rows of terraced houses and an occasional corner shop giving a splash of colour to the drab, grey environment that lay in the awesome shadow of the towering pit headstocks, long since redundant. Nobby hammered on the door. Steph wondered if he could do anything quietly, and then a smile tickled her face. They could hear the wheezing and moaning of the approaching woman, slowly coming towards the door.

Mrs Millichip was in her early sixties and must have been at least eighteen stone. After a lifetime of smoking forty a day, her lungs strained to supply oxygen to her vast bulk. Despite her own untidy appearance, the house was clean. It was indicative of her entire life, she didn't care about herself, but she wanted as nice home for her children, as her meagre funds would allow. She made Steph and Nobby very welcome.

'Come in lass, I'll put the kettle on,' she said to Steph.

The living-room was compact. There was a television set, switched on in the corner, an ironing-board with a pile of clothes in the corner, two armchairs and a settee, well-worn at the ends of the arms. The adjacent kitchen was small. Mrs Millichip busied herself with the kettle and teapot.

'I suppose you've come about our Stuart?'

'Yes, we have love.' Nobby shouted back. 'We can chat when you've finished making the tea.' He hated having conversations in different rooms. Yet it never occurred to him to get up and go in the kitchen.

Mrs Millichip came into the living-room. 'It's all right, it won't be long, it's just mashing.' She leaned against the wall gasping for air. 'Oh dear.' She said to herself.

'Is there anything you can tell us about Stuart, that you think might help us understand why he was killed, Mrs Millichip?' Steph asked.

'Call me Milly. Millicent Millichip, thank you mother.' The two detectives laughed. 'There's quite a bit I could tell you, but I'm sure you know most of it already. You don't need me to tell you, lass.'

'I'm sorry, what exactly?'

'Listen, lovey, I call a spade a spade. I don't relish the fact that Stuart was a . . .you know. . .one of them queers, but you can't hide it from a mother – there's very little you can. It's only mothers that hide it from themselves, if it doesn't suit them.'

'Did he know that you knew about it?'

'All I said to him was; Stuart, lad, I know that you prefer men to women, but I shall stand by you as long as you don't bring trouble to the house.'

'And what did he say to that?'

'He didn't say a word. He just stared at the telly and the subject hasn't been mentioned from that day to this. I gathered he wanted it to be his secret, so if the neighbours were outside, when he went out, I would joke about him having girlfriends, that sort of thing. I don't know if it helped him, but I just wanted the lad to be happy, that's all. It couldn't have been easy for him.'

'I'm sure you did your best, and I'm sure he was grateful in his own way, Milly.' Steph smiled.

'I hope so, lass. He used to have girlfriends, mind, proper girlfriends when he was a bit younger, but, eh, I don't know how these things work.'

'Is there a Mr Millichip?'

'Not anymore, he had an accident when he was down the pit. The boys were only young.'

'You've seen some tragedy, then Milly.' Steph commented.

'Aye, still, never mind, eh.'

Nobby wondered if she knew Stuart had AIDS. It seemed unlikely. Mrs Millichip waddled back into the kitchen breathing heavily. She returned balancing cups and saucers on a tray.

'I don't know a lot about his friends, only one.'

'Who was that?'

'A lad called David. Shy retiring boy, a teacher, Stuart reckoned. He's queer as well, I should think.'

'Did Stuart tell you that this man was homosexual?'

'Not in so many words.'

'What do you mean?'

'They kept giving each other knowing looks, like a couple of daft teenagers at their parent's house for the first time.'

'So, Stuart was having an affair with this David then?' Nobby asked.

'You'd better ask David that question. Let's be right, you can't ask our Stuart, bless him.'

'Steph spoke, 'No we can't. You seem to be taking it very well, Milly.'

'What else do you want me to do, my love? Curl up into a little ball? Folks like us are no stranger to hard times, lass, and whatever life brings you, you have to stomach it, that's your lot, and you either sink or swim. I've got two other sons, to think about, who have been a big help.' She wagged a finger at Steph. 'Don't think I haven't spent nights crying my eyes out, because I have, if you must know. We just don't advertise the fact, where I'm from. People think I'm hard hearted, but I'm not, I just don't burden others, or act like I'm a bloody martyr.'

Steph considered herself told. 'How often did he see David?'

'Not too often. Once a week usually. Sundays mainly, I should think. They'd go out into the country, usually Matlock, around there, you know.'

'What about when Stuart was at college?'

'He seemed a bit freer in those days. He never brought anybody home, he would have been too embarrassed to bring his posh college friends back to our house, I should think. He used to mention a girl, thinking about it, a girl called Tracey – Tracey Oliver, that's it. That's why I was surprised that he was one of them funny buggers. He really liked that girl.'

'Tracey Oliver?' Nobby asked confused.

'Yes, that's it.'

'Maiden name, Nobby.' Steph said, rolling her eyes at him.

'Oh, yes.'

'Nobby was to the point: 'Do you think he had sexual relationships with women as well as men, then?'

'I reckon so, but then he just seemed to be interested in his motorbike. It's like he couldn't settle. A bit of a lost soul, was Stuart, but he's at peace now.'

*

From where they were parked, Jim McIntyre and Steve Aston could only just see the letterbox of the *Evening Post* offices.

The two detectives were squatting in the back of an old box van parked some fifty yards away. To a passer-by the van looked empty. It was Jim's turn to peer out of the hole. They had agreed to do half hour stints each. 'Why the hell can't Special Operations do this? It's not for us to do, this isn't. We're supposed to be detectives!'

'Stark said that we know the people involved, and are able to make judgement calls, it could be the key to the whole case.'

'Stark, this, Stark that – are you in love with the bloke or something?'

'Yes, that's it, Jim, I'm in love with him.'

'Hang on, someone's just put something in the box. Come on!'

The two men jumped out of the van and approached the gentleman, Jim produced his identification. 'We're from the CID. Can you please tell us what you have just put into that letterbox?'

The gent was in his seventies and wore a black duffel coat. 'Yes, officer, I can. It's an entry for the death's column. My sister passed away last week.'

Steve was taken aback. 'I'm sorry to hear that, and I'm afraid I cannot say why, but would you please be good enough to come with us and have a word with this security man.'

'Yes, if you say so. I can do that.'

'It will only take a minute.'

The three men walked back to the door. The security man, a boy of around twenty, had been instructed to open all letters that came through the letter box. He'd just finished opening the letter. as it was fiddly with the surgical gloves on. He took it out and noted that there was some money enclosed. He read the message out loud: 'Jean Bembrose. A loving and caring sister, who will be sadly missed. Love, your brother, Albert.'

'I'm very sorry to put you out, sir,' Steve said to Albert. 'Thanks very much for your help, and once again I'm sorry for your loss.'

'That's all right, young man. What's it all about then?'

'I'm sorry, we aren't allowed to say, for now. I'm sure all will be revealed to you through the press in due course, though.'

'Fair enough, sounds intriguing. Will my message to Jean still be in the paper?'

'Yes, of course, don't worry it will be in.'

'That'll do, then.' The old guy turned and walked off back the way he had come.

'Nosey old fart, what's it got to do with him?' Jim said.

'Jim, he's just been stopped by detectives, it's a big thing for him, particularly of his age group. It's only natural to want to know what it is all about.'

'He needs to mind his own business, if you ask me.'

'Nobody is asking you, Jim.'

The two clambered back into the van.

'I'm getting a bit pissed off to say the least.

'You don't say.'

'Well, this is ridiculous. I'm sick of chasing shadows.'

'But that's where the bad guys are, Jim.'

*

Nobby and Steph had stopped off at a pub for some lunch on the way back to the station. Nobby had ushered Steph into a quiet corner of the lounge. Inevitably the conversation came back round to his burning ambition – he and Steph getting together.

Nobby gave his version of events between the two of them. 'Nobody is saying we should get involved necessarily. I've already told you that. It's quite simple really. I think you are absolutely gorgeous and want to rip your knickers off with my teeth, and you're tempted to say yes, so what's stopping you?'

'It's not that I don't find you attractive, I do, but it's just, well, you know.'

'No. I don't know. You tell me.' He stroked her hand.

'You're my Detective Sergeant, my gaffer. It's an untenable situation, it could spoil everything.'

'Who has to know about it?'

'Look, Nobby, I'm thirty years-old. All the eligible men are ugly, or violent, and all the decent, attractive ones are married. I'm fed up with secret meetings. Why I can't go to this pub, or that restaurant, or to the pictures, without the fear of being seen by someone. And now more hiding in pub corners with you, in case we see someone from work. I don't think so.'

'I get it. I'm not saying we should do that. It may be that we go public at some stage. I just don't understand why we are living our lives because of what others think. Fuck them. We are grownups, if we want to sleep with each other, we don't need to do a survey of friends and family to see if it's OK, now do we? You get one shot at life, Christ, we know how fickle life is. One minute you are planning your life, the next someone is planning your funeral. Screw what everybody else thinks.'

'I'll give you one thing, Nobby, you are a tryer. You always were a good interviewer.'

'You know what I'm saying is true, though don't you, Steph?'

'Come on. Let's go.'

'Hang on a minute, I decide when we go.' Nobby said with a twinkle in his eye.

'Ooh, I like it when you are so masterful.' Steph smiled.

They waited a couple of seconds, until Nobby said. 'OK, let's go.'

They paid, and as they were walking to the rear car park, Nobby took Steph's hand and she felt a surge of excitement. At the car, they stopped and before either realized, they were kissing passionately, Steph yielding to Nobby's rock-hard body. His strong arms held her. He caressed her. She felt his excitement grow as their pelvises ground into each other, and she yearned to have him, on the bonnet of the car if necessary. His hand stroked her tiny waist and eased up to her firm breast; the nipple was erect. Steph couldn't help her own hands from roaming. She squeezed his hard buttocks and brought her hand round to the front and she could feel the outline of the shaft of his penis. The girth swelled as it throbbed in her hand. 'My God.' She gasped. 'Oh fuck!'

With all the will power she could muster, she pulled away, the two of them gasping, and their hearts racing. 'For God's sake Nobby, not here!'

*

Ashley was in the Incident Room leaning on the back two legs of his chair. Charlie Carter glanced over at him.

'Busy, Ash?'

'Oh, it's terrible. I'm going to have to ring a bird up, I think.'

'Lucky you. I'd hate the thought that the job might be getting in the way of your social life. You look absolutely knackered, by the way; another late night was it?'

'Half-three, and anyway this phone call is as much for the job as it is for me.'

'I believe you. Make sure you don't burn yourself out, kiddo.'

'I'll try not to, but what a way to go.'

Charlie grinned. 'Make your phone call.' Charlie continued checking through all the possible connections any of the suspects might have with a Ford Granada.

Ashley fished in his suit-jacket pocket for his diary and began thumbing through the pages. He eventually found Sharon's name. He would take a chance that she would be in nurses' quarters and not on duty. He tapped out the digits on the phone.

'Hello?'

'Hi, it's Ashley Stevens, the insurance salesman.'

Her voice rose a pitch. 'Oh hi. Hey, I was only talking about you this morning. How are you?'

'I'm good, what about yourself?'

'Fine thanks, when are we going out then?' she said cheekily.

'Wednesday?' Ash suggested.

'Great, I'm on mornings then. What time?'

'Let's say eight o'clock. I'll pick you up from the nurses' quarters. Number 23 isn't it?'

'That's right. Oh brilliant. I can't wait. I've got to decide what to wear, now.'

'Wear that short black dress with the low front that you had on before.'

'Yes, but. . .okay, whatever sir requires of me.'

'Good girl. Not at work today then, Sharon?'

'No, that's why I answered my phone, and am talking to you.'

'Smart arse. What shift are you on?'

'I'm off today, would you believe?'

'I don't know, some people don't want work, do they?' Ash smiled.

'No, they don't, and I'm one of them.' She laughed.

'So, you've not been stitching people up today, then?' Ash enquired.

'Funnily enough, I was going to ask you the same question.' She laughed and Ashley joined her.

'God, you're cynical. Funny, though.'

'It isn't that, I just know policemen.'

'You think you do. You'd have to be crazy to risk twenty grand a year, or, worse, prison, for that shit. We don't care that much, trust me.'

'I know, I'm only winding you up.'

There was a slight pause before Ashley spoke. 'It's a shame you were with someone else, the other night at Ritzy's.'

'Oh, Jonathon, I know. Sod's law. How do you know him?'

'Didn't he tell you?'

'No, he wouldn't say.'

'I just know him from going into the hospital, really, a bit like you.'

'Maybe *you* should go on a date with him.'

'Maybe I should. He seemed charming. I take it you aren't taking him on a second date, then Sharon?'

'We'll see. Probably not, cos he's pissed me off. He said he was going to ring, but he hasn't, sound familiar?'

'Ha ha.'

'To say he is a doctor, his vocabulary is pretty poor.'

'You what?'

'He didn't seem to know the meaning of the word "no".'

'I see. Mind you, I didn't know *you* did.'

'Cheeky sod! It's different with you, though.'

'Of course, it is. Anyway, I've got to go. I'll pick you up on Wednesday, yes?'

'Yes, see you then. Thanks for ringing. Bye.'

'Bye.'

*

Stark had taken a little detour and checked the car park of Arnold Lodge Children's Home. Roy Prentice's car wasn't in the car park. He was a bit concerned about the residents seeing him, but it was a risk he would have to take. He knocked on the door and Derek soon came to answer it.

'Hello, Inspector.'

'Hello, Derek, any joy?'

'Yes. I'll go and get it for you, I hid it, like you said.'

'Brilliant, thank you.'

Stark felt conspicuous standing at the doorway, but thankfully the usual tribe of kids who always showed an interest, were absent.

After a couple of minutes, Derek returned, holding a brown envelope with Stark's name emblazoned on it in thick black pen. Not very subtle.

'There you go. I think it's all present and correct; as requested.'

'Thank you, Derek, it's a shame we have to go to all these lengths, but when he starts messing about like he is, it forces your hand a bit, so whilst regrettable, it is necessary.'

'No, I understand perfectly well. I don't blame you at all.' Derek smiled.

'It's not something I want to be messing around with when I'm in the middle of a murder investigation, trust me.'

'I can imagine. There's no need for it.'

'All right, well, thanks again, Derek.'

'You're welcome.'

Stark turned and headed back to his car. He could feel the outline of the contents through the envelope. A smile came to his lips.

*

Jayne Warriner had worked in the Fingerprint Department at

Sherwood Lodge police headquarters for almost five years, ever since she had been twenty-one. It was after working a couple of years in the department that she had begun to need spectacles: the fine scrutiny of hundreds of documents and fingerprint forms had undoubtedly been the cause. Her long black hair swung over her white coat, as with great care she bent over the *Evening Post* personal column letters. They were on A4 paper and the message just typed in the centre. She checked that the documents were dry and there was no grease or other stains on them. In front of her was a small, shallow tray, slightly bigger than a piece of A4 paper, which contained the liquid chemical, ninhydrin, to about two millimetres deep. This was an operation she could do in her sleep, she had to force herself not to be too blasé about it each time. Using plastic forceps, Jayne picked up the first document and placed it in the chemical solution, ensuring that it was completely submerged. She fiddled with the papers using the forceps, moving it backwards and forwards. Allowing it to react with the chemicals which were slowly discolouring the paper. Thirty seconds later the document was sufficiently diffused. She removed it from the tray and placed it in a dehumidifying cabinet for three minutes, careful that the temperature did not exceed 80 degrees centigrade inside the cabinet itself. Once the three minutes were up, she took the document out and examined it carefully. The aminol acids had now fully soaked in and the entire document was a purple, pink colour. The chemical reacted with the sweat particles of a fingerprint and would show up the swirls and loops in purple. However, there were no fingerprints visible at all, nor any partial prints apart from a tiny trace where they had been handled in the corners but nothing that would be able to be identified. It was to be the same story for each of the pieces of paper and the envelopes. The person handling the document had worn gloves.

12

'Never murder a man who is committing suicide.'

President Woodrow Wilson

The family of James Deely were barely visible as they stumbled from the churchyard, towards the Green Gables public house across the road; grey silhouettes huddled together like a rugby scrum in the hazy mist of rain. Each one's private attempt at coping, at putting on a brave face, was wearing thin in this squalid, incessant drizzle. The weather matched the bleak graveside mood. Stark and Nobby were the last to turn away, the coffin already awash with rainwater mixed with the orange-brown clay, that peeled away from the sides of the newly dug grave. Stark had been to several such funerals as a representative of the force and he always felt a sense of alienation. He wasn't a family member, and he wasn't a friend, yet everyone knew who he was; an intruder, and worse, a reminder, of the most private of emotions – grief.

Stark spoke briefly with the uniformed officers at the church door who had recorded on pocket memo-cords the names of all those attending. He dismissed them, thanking them for their assistance, before crossing the road into the Green Gables.

As the two detectives entered the pub, the low noise level belied the attendance. It was a typical rural pub, with low ceilings and beams and yes, green gables. There must have been about 150 people crammed inside, all speaking in hushed whispers. It wouldn't be long before the level would rise, with intermittent laughter, from those least affected by the death of a young man in his prime. Stark was afraid that Sammy would not have a clear view, but a quick glance to the left revealed him apparently chatting away, facing the bar in an elevated position, with a full view of all those present, including, most importantly, the college cadre, who were milling in a group at the corner of the bar. Stark and Nobby kept to themselves, apart from a brief conversation with James' senior partner Alan Johnson, with whom Nobby had done the formal identification. Stark also went over to say hello to the college cadre and explained they wouldn't be stopping. Roy Prentice blanked him, of course. They had a pint of ale each, before bidding their farewells and giving their condolences to Mrs Deely. The atmosphere changed when they left. There was a definite wave of relief, as the policemen left the bar, everyone seeming to grow more relaxed. The noise of the chatter heightened.

Meanwhile, Sammy was having to work hard, reading lips. He spoke at an advanced rate of knots, each sentence beginning with the name of the speaker, and often with the person's movements tagged on, before or after the spoken word:

'*Tracey:* passing round sympathy card: "Come on, it'll be better from all of us. It doesn't matter if you've sent a separate one, it'll be from the gang. Come on Jonathon."'

'*Jonathon:* "Oh, all right then." Taking card, writing on it. "That's a nice thought, Tracey. Come on. Let's have a signature and personal message from you all."'

'*David:* "I thought the service was quite touching."'

'*Jonathon:* "It makes no difference, mate, we all end up as dust. It's only words, isn't it? He's probably better off out of it all, poor sod."'

'*Caroline:* "Oh, Jonathon, shut up will you, his wife might hear you. I thought it was a nice service as well, David. Ignore him, he's got no soul. Caroline keeps throwing her hair back and playing with it.'

'*Jonathon:* "Hark at Sister Mother Mary."'

'*Caroline:* kicking Jon's shin.'

'*Jonathon:* Talking. Can't see what he is saying, Tracey nodding.'

'*David:* "It's funny how life goes, isn't it? I mean, when we were at college, who would have dreamed that we would be standing at James's wake, with Stuart's yet to come." Hand to mouth; Caroline arm around shoulder. *David:* "I'm all right, I was thinking only last night about college. We had a great time, didn't we? Back then, I mean, before life began eroding us."'

'*Roy:* "You speak for yourself, David. Anyway, you only used to be a hanger on. In fact, I don't know what you're even doing here, because you and James were hardly the best of friends. Let's face it."'

'*David:* "Oh, and I suppose you and he were the best of friends, were you? And what about Jonathon? He and James hated each other!"'

'*Tracey:* "Keep your voices down, folks, for God's sake."'

'*Jonathon:* "Don't put words into my mouth, please, David."'

'*David:* "I don't need to. There's plenty there already, without me adding to them. We all know you like the sound of your own voice."'

'*Caroline:* "Come on. Bloody hell, guys, we're at a funeral. Let's not drag the past up. We were just kids. A lot of water has passed under the bridge since then."'

'*David:* "I'm just saying that I've as much right to be here, as anybody else. It was Jonathon, who accused James of nicking the fifty quid from the jacket, not me."'

'*Caroline:* "Here we go."'

'*Roy:* speaking, can't see what he is saying.'

'*Jonathon:* "He did nick it, Roy. It was in the locker room at college. I saw him walk away from it, and he knew I'd seen him."'

'*Tracey:* 'Just keep your voices down will you. It was bloody years ago, just move on guys, will you? I still can't believe all this is happening. It all seems crazy, to me."'

'*Caroline:* "It's just awful isn't it?"'

'*Roy:* "Of course, you had the hots for James, didn't you, Tracey?"'

'*Jonathon:* "Tracey had the hots for everybody, let's face it."'

'*Tracey:* hitting Jon on the shoulder; laughter.'

'*Tracey:* "I'll give the card to Sarah, later, when we go."'

'*Mark:* "If we hadn't met at college-"'

'*Roy:* "Then none of us would be here, blah, blah, well done, Mark. Your college education wasn't wasted after all, now was it?"'

'*Mark:* "Don't be such a smart arse all the time, Roy. Take a day off, will you."'

'*Roy:* "That's good, Mark, just off the cuff like that. Brilliant."'

'*Jonathon:* "I think that is one of the good things about us all having met, that Caroline and Mark got married. For Christ's sake, look at us all, bickering like kids in the playground again, trying to score points of each other."'

'*David:* "You're right, Jonathon. We should be thankful that we're all still here. My poor Stuart can't be, can he?" Hand to mouth again, looks upset.'

'*Jonathon:* speaking again, but I can't see what he is saying. "...and bloody Stuart!"'

'Tracey: "You really liked him, didn't you? I'm sorry, David. Come on, have another drink."'

'Roy: "Pathetic."'

'Mark: "I'll get them." Goes to bar to get served.'

'Jonathon: in Caroline's ear: "I'm going to fuck you so hard tomorrow." Both laugh.'

'Caroline: whispers back, "Not here, Jon, for God's sake. Half two, in The Unicorn, don't let me down this time."'

'Jonathon: "Don't bring a police car this time!"'

'Both laugh.'

'Mark: returning with drinks. Each of them taking a drink, Mark returning tray to bar. Returns. Caroline holding Mark's hand, kissing his cheek.'

'Caroline: "Thank you, darling, you're the best hubby in the world. I love you."'

'Mark: "I love you too, babe."'

'Jonathon: "Who's the murderer then? Anyone want to own up?"'

'Roy: "I can't see it being any one of us, really, I mean what possible motive is there?"'

'Tracey: "None apparently, but who's to know what private secrets, and meetings we have, eh, Caroline?"'

'Caroline: Doesn't like that comment. "No, they don't. Still, who else could want to kill James and Stu? It doesn't make sense. I mean, what's the point? And who's next? Or has it stopped?"'

'Tracey: "Does anybody know about the post-mortem reports? Have the police said anything, do we know?"'

'Roy: "Don't get into that. It's grotesque enough as it is. Spare us the gory details."'

'Tracey: "Has everybody had a police alarm fitted at their house?"'

'Jonathon: "Yes, well I say yes, I know I have. It's got a panic button thing with it, as well as an intruder alarm. I still don't bother setting it, it's all a bit intrusive."'

'Everybody nodding, yes.'

'Caroline: "Exactly, Jonathon, I think the police are bang out of order, suggesting that it's one of us."'

'Tracey: "I agree."'

'Jonathon: "That makes a change, Tracey agreeing with Caroline. My, things are looking up. It only took two dead, but we are getting there."'

'Tracey: "Don't be facetious, Jonathon, it doesn't suit you."'

'David: "There must be some link though, surely? Both James and Stuart in one week. That's strange, isn't it?"'

'Roy: saying something – can't make it out.'

'Mark: "Strange yes, but it's not impossible. Stu's death could quite easily have been an accident, couldn't it? Maybe the driver just panicked and drove off."'

'Tracey: "Could be, Mark, but didn't the police say they turned their lights off or covered their plates, or something?"'

'Mark: "The same still applies though; even if they had turned their lights off. I'm just saying, it could be a coincidence, that's all."'

'Jonathon: "Well, if it isn't a coincidence, and it's one of us, whoever it is, can you just stop now, please, for Christ's sake, stop it, quit, while you're ahead!'

'Silence. Nobody speaking. Silence. Still silence.'

'*Tracey:* "Perhaps it better if we don't talk about the killings, it just upsets everyone and brings the mood down."'

'*Caroline:* "You're right, Trace, how's your little girl? I've not heard you talk about her for ages."'

'*Tracey:* "Fine, thanks. You know, I can't help thinking what sort of people have we become? We all used to be much nicer, didn't we? Are we nice people to know? I'm not sure."'

'*David:* "I think it's only when we get together that we start chipping away at each other. As individuals we are all decent aren't, we? We are what we are, I guess."'

'*Mark:* "And we all know what you are, David."'

'*Caroline:* "This is exactly what we are talking about, Mark. It's not on, making comments like that, leave him alone."'

'*Roy:* "That's a typically ignorant comment, from someone with a moronic brain. I insist you withdraw it."'

'*Jonathon:* "Here we go again. Pistols at dawn. I don't fancy your chances much, Roy; Mark works out at the gym."'

'*Tracey:* "Is there really any point in us remaining here? What are we achieving, other than showing each other what idiots we are?"'

'*Caroline:* "I'm ready to go, now, Mark, come on."'

'Mark and Caroline going towards Sarah Deely, shaking hands with Sarah.'

'*Caroline:* "So sorry, we will keep in touch, and if there is anything we can do, you know where we are." Mark and Caroline Winner, are now leaving.'

'Jonathon and David, now approaching Sarah Deely, shaking hands.'

'*Jonathon:* "If there's anything I can do, please give me a call. I mean it."'

'*David:* "It's such a sad loss." Both David and Jonathon, leave.'

'Tracey and Roy, shaking hands with Sarah.'

'*Roy:* "I'm so sorry, Sarah. I'll miss our little chats. He was a good friend. I'll be in touch." Roy kisses Sarah and leaves'

'*Tracey:* "There's nothing I can add, but all of us will miss him. Goodbye, Sarah."'

'No handshake or kiss. Tracey leaving the pub.'

*

Sammy Trench, sat smiling at Stark across his desk. They both had a steaming mug of tea and broad smiles. 'So, all in all, everything went pretty well.' He said.

'Did you manage to get everything?' Stark asked.

'Nearly everything. There was the odd word or two, but to get this much with so many people talking is good. The problem can be when they over-talk, but they are a group who know each other well, so their cues are well practised and you don't have the jostling for verbal superiority, that you can get with strangers.' Sammy's appearance belied his knowledge of verbal communication. As the DC's in the office were to learn, the fact that Sammy looked as though he had been dragged through a hedge backwards, should not be a determining factor as to his abilities necessarily.

'At least they stayed together as a group.' Stark said thankfully.

'God, yes. If they had separated and mingled it would have been impossible, I would have picked one or two to read and it would have been a lottery as to whether we got anything of worth.'

Talking to Sammy you would have not been aware he was

deaf. He had been talking for a while before his deafness encroached, he perhaps seemed to be staring slightly more than normal, and obviously if he was not looking at you, you could not gain his attention. 'You've done a first-class job, Sammy, is there anything else you noticed or anything else you think I should be aware of?'

'Not really the tape should be self-explanatory.'

'Anything else I need to know?'

Sammy laughed. 'They're a funny bunch. They all seem to dislike each other in equal measure. I won't pass comment, other than to say that if they did anything, or moved anything, I did note it on the commentary, so don't assume they have done something if I haven't mentioned it. If I don't reference it: It hasn't happened.'

'OK. Got you, that's helpful, thanks. Now down to business: payment. How much do we owe you?'

'Two fifty, I think we said.'

'Blimey I'm in the wrong job. Two hundred and fifty pounds for three hours work.' Stark grinned.

'I know a guy who will do it for much less, it's just that he can't lip-read.'

Stark laughed. 'Point taken. You know I'm grateful, Sammy.'

'It will come in handy, trust me. When will you be listening to the tape?'

'I was going to quickly go through it and then study it over the next day or two.'

'That's fine. I only mention it, because Jonathon Stacey and Caroline winner have arranged to meet tomorrow afternoon at The Unicorn pub; for a bonking session, by the looks of it.'

'Have they really? That is a turn-up for the books. The Unicorn is at Gunthorpe Bridge.' Stark said.

'Just so you are aware about the meeting, that's all.'

'Maybe we ought to have a reception committee for them. I think we have been a bit too soft with this crowd.'

*

Dave Stark sat at the dinner table with his family around him for the first time in over a week. His suit jacket was off, his tie loose and his top button undone. His sleeves were rolled up, only two turns, the cuffs flared outwards. Carol sat opposite, wearing a baggy track-suit and a look of satisfaction. His sixteen-year-old daughter, Laura, sat at the end of the table and his fourteen-year-old son, Christopher at the other. Laura gave the appearance of being slightly older than her years, particularly when she was made-up. Her hair was a mousey brown and hung over her shoulders with just a hint of a wave. Dave thought the low-cut top she was wearing was a little too low-cut, but he let it slide. Christopher had black hair with a fringe; he was still a boy. Just the clinking of cutlery on plates disturbed the silence.

'So, what have you been up to all week?' Dave asked. If Dave didn't speak, there was little chance of anyone else starting a conversation.

'Nothing.' Laura said.

'Nothing.' Christopher said.

'OK.' He glanced at Carol who shrugged.

'You must have done something. What about school?' He scooped up some pasta, watching his children, as he chewed.

It was their turn to shrug.

Stark frowned. 'Hey, guys. Hello! It's me your father, we are trying to have a conversation, work with me guys.'

Laura was hostile: 'You wouldn't know what we have been up to, seeing as you have been missing without trace, for days.'

'I haven't been missing without trace at all, Laura. I've been at a place called work, earning money for my family, so that they have a roof over their heads, and food to eat. I don't have the luxury to mope around the house all day, now do I?'

Carol spoke. 'That's enough, Laura. You know your father would prefer to be at home if he could. Be fair, darling.'

Laura retaliated. 'No, he wouldn't, he loves it at work. You know it, and we know it. He just bloody sleeps here.'

Dave had heard enough. 'All right. Smart arse. There's only two people in this room allowed to swear, and you're not one of them. Now, let's all try to get along, shall we? You know, like a normal family, without any unpleasantness.'

'Huh, a normal family, what's one of those? You're an absent father. You and Mum might as well be divorced. I feel sorry for her.'

'Right, that's it, up to your room.' Stark said.

Christopher whinnied out a laugh.

'She's only just started her dinner, David,' Carol said.

'It's OK, Mum. I'd sooner go upstairs than be at the same table as a stranger.'

David's heart sank; it stung. He didn't respond. Laura thumped her feet down on every stair, as she flounced to her bedroom. Her outburst was followed by the slamming of the door, and a dull repetitive thud as she ratcheted up the latest music from the charts, which was now blaring down the stairs and shaking the house to its foundations. Carol stared at Dave. 'Wonderful. Welcome home, Dave.'

'Eh, don't have a go at me. She was out of order! At least we've solved what to get her for Christmas.'

'What?'

'Headphones.'

'Dave...'

'How long has she been swearing like that?'

'She hasn't. That's the first time.' Carol frowned.

Christopher chimed in. 'No, it's not, she's always swearing. You ought to hear her at school.'

'That's enough, Christopher. When we want your opinion, we'll ask for it, thank you.' Dave said.

'Charming! Just trying to help.'

'I know what you were just trying to do; stir it. That's what.'

The three continued their meal in silence. After a few minutes Christopher spoke again. 'Don't worry about Laura, Dad. She doesn't mean it, she's going through a funny time, she thinks she's a grown up.'

Dave smiled and put his hand on the boy's shoulder. 'Thank

you, son, I'm glad somebody understands. I'd love to see more of all of you, but sometimes, I just can't, and there is no escaping it. I don't get given a choice in the matter. So, we must pull together as a family, the best we can, or we will end up pulling ourselves apart. And that's no good, now, is it?'

Christopher smiled. 'I know, Dad, I understand.'

The meal over, Christopher vanished to play on his new computer. David and Carol smiled at each other, exasperated, 'I'm sorry, love.' Dave said. 'It's not the sort of evening I'd envisaged. When I've sorted this job out at work, I'll have some leave. We'll all go away for the weekend, I promise. Carol looked tired. 'Come on then, you can wash, I'll wipe.'

Later that evening, Dave knocked on Laura's bedroom door. 'Can I come in?' he enquired?

'Have you got a warrant?' She smiled.

Dave sat on Laura's bed, while she sat at her dressing table, combing her long hair. *'Oops upside your head'* by The Gap Band, was intruding his thought processes.

'Can you turn the music down a bit, please?'

'Sorry?'

'Can you turn the music down?'

'Oh, yes, sure.'

At last, he could hear himself think. 'Do you really think I want us to argue like this?' Stark asked.

'I don't know, I don't even know you. You're my dad and I don't even know you. Wow. That's tragic.'

'I think you are being a little bit melodramatic, don't you, Laura? It's just a busy time. You know what I do. I'm trying to catch the bad guys.'

'But why should the bad guys get you, and we don't. We want you. We deserve you, not them. That doesn't seem very fair at all to me.'

'I don't want that to be the case, but if you think about it, we *do* have time together, we have holidays and weekends and all that stuff. Life's not perfect, though, you know that.'

'Can't you get another job?' She continued brushing her hair.

'How can I? All I know is being a policeman.'

'I didn't mean that, I meant another type of job, in the police force, instead of, like, a superhero job, that you do now.'

Stark laughed. 'Superhero. Like what, though? If I went on a crime squad, or drug squad, I'd be here less, not more. That leaves me one option: to go back into uniform. Working weird shifts, doing admin, marching around the town, with shiny shoes, a peaked cap, and a silver tipped stick. Do you think that's me?'

'That would be funny, though, Dad.'

'I wouldn't be locking the bad guys up, anymore, it would be a thing of the past. I'd just be a supervisor. Do you think that sounds like your old Dad? Do you think I would be happy doing that?'

'But you'd probably see more of us, Dad, wouldn't you? So that part would make you happier, though, wouldn't it?'

'Maybe I would but I fear that doing something I disliked would make me grumpy.'

'You are now.'

'Ha ha. It would be good to see you more, but I worry that I'd be pretty miserable when I was with you, because I would be miserable at work.'

'No change there then.'

'Eh. What about you?'

'What do you mean, what about me?' she said.

'You're out with your boyfriend most nights, or your friends. And that's how it should be at your age. You're almost grown-up, Laura. You will be seeing less of me, probably. I still see you most weekends, unless there's a big job on.'

'Dad, there's always a big job on.'

'Do you really want me to stop what I'm doing, darling?'

Laura paused. She shook her head. 'I guess not. I just get a bit confused about stuff at times, Dad. I hate us falling out.'

'I know, it's all quite normal to feel like this, like everything, it will pass. I hate us falling out, too. Come here.' He put his arms around her, and they hugged.

'There is something else I've been meaning to talk to you about.'

'What's that?'

'Erm, it's a bit of an awkward one.'

'Dad, I know what periods are, I've been having them for the last three years.'

'No, not that, but a similar theme.'

'What, then?'

'The pill.'

'Dad!'

'We have to talk about it, Laura. You have your whole life in front of you. *You* need to decide when you have a baby, not some spotty faced youth.'

'How do you know we are even doing anything?'

'I hope you're not, but if you do something in the heat of the moment, at least you are okay.'

'For your information I am already on the pill.'

'What! You'd better not be, young lady.'

'Hold on, Dad, you have just been trying to persuade me to go on it.'

'I know, but when you said it like that out of the blue. It shocked me a bit. How long have you been on it?

'Just a couple of months, I'm not totally stupid you know.'

'Does Mum know about it?'

'She will, when you tell her in a bit.'

'Oh.' Dave seemed a little deflated. His baby was growing up and it rattled him a little.

'We aren't doing anything, if that's what you are worried about.' She said.

'Fine. It's no good me telling you to be a grown-up, if I tell you off for doing just that. I get it.'

'Exactly.' She smiled at her dad.

There was a pause as the cogs in Dave's brain whirred around. He eventually changed the subject.

'I tell you what, do you fancy coming to the pictures, all four of us?'

'Yes, sure – oh, I can't. I promised Terry I'd see him tonight.'

'Bloody, Terry.' They both laughed. Dave continued. 'I know how it feels, now.' Dave put his hand out towards Laura.

'Friends?'

She shook his hand.

'Friends.'

*

PC's Darrel Grant and Barry Croft were bored: it was one o'clock in the morning and it had been a quiet night on patrol. They were responsible for Uniform Two, or Panda Two, as it was known, the mobile response vehicle in the Bulwell area. They had been to a couple of domestics, a burglary and two fights at local hostelries, but for the last twenty minutes it had been dead. They were parked on Bulwell market Place; Darrel had the driver's window down and was smoking.

'Hang on a minute, what's this coming across the Market Place?'

Barry couldn't see. 'Where? Oh, I can see her now, I've got you.'

They watched the leggy blonde clip-clop across the Market in her high-heeled shoes and a mini-skirt which revealed the hint of stocking-top. The woman was obviously aware of the attention she was getting, since she exaggerated her wiggle and smiled over at the two uniformed officers.

'*Goodnight.*' Darrel shouted. The woman smiled and nodded, waving a hand displaying long painted fingernails.

This is not good for a red-blooded male.' Darrel commented to his friend.

'She wouldn't let you anywhere near her, if she had any sense. What's up with you, anyway?' Barry asked.

'You saw how she was – a little bit of chat and I'm sure we'd get along fine. But, no, I've got to look at your ugly mug all night.'

'Shut up and give us a kiss.' Barry pursed his lips.

'Bog off, you pervert.'

As their laughter diminished, Barry was the first to hear the unusual noise: two pips; then a pause, two more pips, then a pause, and so on, coming over their radio sets.

'That's a Home Office alarm sounding, Shush.'

The pips were interrupted by the Control Room operator.

'Panzer Two.' On nights there was often a bit of high-jinks and banter.

'Ja, Herr Oberleutnant. Mess your passage, over.'

'Home Office alarm sounding at 67 Brooklyn Drive, Bulwell, home address of Roy Prentice, potential target for murder.'

'Ten Four, travelling.' The mood in the car changed to something more serious. Darrel screeched the tyres as he pulled off the Market Place at great speed, flicking his cigarette onto the bricked square.

'Control to Panda Two.'

Barry answered, as he was being flung left and right in the speeding vehicle. 'Go ahead, over.' The adrenalin had started pumping.

'Panda One is travelling from Hucknall to back you up. I'm trying to get a dog man, but I think they're all tied up now, stand-by.'

'Ten Four, much obliged.'

Darrel was really thrashing the vehicle and as he screeched around the corner, on Highbury Vale, he veered slightly across the centre line and had to take drastic action when a vehicle appeared right in front of him.

'Fuck me. Darrel, let's get there in one piece, mate.'

'We will.'

The streetlights were a blur as he toed it along the stretch of road.

'Control to Panda Two.'

'Go ahead,'

'67 Brooklyn is a semi-detached house, with front and rear access, left onto Saxondale Drive, from Highbury Road, and third right after Brayton Crescent is Brooklyn.'

'Ten Four. E.T.A two minutes, over.'

Barry pointed at the red traffic lights ahead. 'Darrel, they're on red mate- *Darrel!*'

'Fuck the lights, there's somebody being murdered for all we know!' He ignored the red lights, moving into the centre of the road as he flashed through. 'There was a bit of green in there somewhere.'

He turned the car sharply into the left-hand turn, at Saxondale Road, dropped down the gears and into second and then pumped the accelerator to screech ahead.

Barry directed him. 'It's third on the right from here. First two should be Brayton Crescent. Right here, Darrel.'

The car careened into the street.

'That's 45, just a bit further down, mate. 55. There look – 67. There's a bloke outside. The car's tyres left a deposit of rubber on the tarmac as it squealed its objection to the point-blank stop. They ran from the car, Pete's hand on his truncheon pocket. They saw the figure silhouetted against the light of the door as they approached. Barry withdrew his truncheon, ready to cave in the head of any maniacal murderer.

'Good evening, or should I say good morning?' Roy Prentice's smiling countenance greeted them at the door. He was holding a stopwatch. 'I make it three minutes seventeen seconds. Not bad, but I could still have been murdered in that time!'

*

Johnathon Stacey was a risk taker, particularly where women were concerned. It was his one flaw. The killer had managed to get to his house ahead of him returning from his night out. The house had been in darkness, but his car was not on the drive. Break in and wait? No, just wait. The darkened alcove at the side of his house gave enough cover, and a sufficient view. Within minutes the headlights swung around the corner and up the drive. He seemed to be messing around in his car for ages, before emerging into the dark and strolling up to his door. He was humming an indiscernible tune. He looked like he had been drinking, and the killer watched Jonathon finally manage to locate the key in the lock at the umpteenth attempt. He turned all the lights on, illuminating the ground floor, as soon as he walked in, and he could now be seen easily from the outside.

He had clearly paid no attention to the police, telling him to be vigilant, and his front door remained unlocked. His assailant's fists clenched, tendons tight, as the hatred started to swell.

Jonathon had all the blinds and curtains open. He made a cup of coffee and flopped down on to the settee. He was tired, and a little tipsy, but not totally drunk. He was back early, really, for him, at least. The fright with the police car driving past the other day, had unsettled Caroline and that meant that the night ended abruptly. He would make it up to her tomorrow. He was a little edgy, as he had not completed the sex act with Caroline, and his balls knew it. Still, there was tomorrow. He had to decide whether to masturbate tonight, so that he wasn't too quick with her tomorrow, or just take the risk that he could hold it back. He couldn't be bothered right now, maybe when he went to bed. He used the remote to turn some music on and he sat, eyes closed, listening to the sounds of 'Freak' by Le Chic.

The killer approached carefully, trying to decide how best to approach it. Whether to wait or make the move now. Make the move, now. It was perfect. It didn't quite fit with the plan, but it could be made to work. He's on his own, the door is open, he's falling asleep. A little while longer and he would be there for the taking.

The murderer stretched around the window frame, slowly, to peer through the window; but in doing so knocked a small plant pot off the windowsill, and it crashed onto the floor. 'Fuck!' Standing there silently, listening, not daring to move. If necessary, he can be killed now.

A torch beam hit the killer's face. 'Oh, for God's sake! You nearly frightened the life out of me. Thank God it's you. What are you doing here?' Jonathon said. 'Is everything all right? You look terrible, you'd better come in.'

'I've been knocking, I think you were dozing.'

'I think I was. What's the matter? To what do I owe the

pleasure?'

Whiskey was always Jonathon's weak spot. That and women. Here was a chance to discuss such topics with an old friend. Maybe the party wasn't over after all.

He sat on the settee, sharing his whiskey, getting more and more inebriated. It was when he went to the toilet that the killer put the morphine tab in his glass. It was a worry at first, as it didn't seem to dissolve, put by stirring it and breaking it with fingers into a dust, it eventually broke down enough to go undetected. Jonathon was not in any fit state to detect anything now. His words were slurred. He had slid down the chair, so he was pretty much lying down, his shirt pulled out of his trousers. Whiskey didn't usually make him this drowsy. Everything was hazy and he couldn't keep his eyes open. His friend was speaking but he couldn't make out what the words were, he just sat there smiling, addled, semi-comatose. Then blackness. Nothingness. The killer tugged at his arm. There was no response. The killer swallowed hard, as a syringe was produced, this was the moment. This was the moment Jonathon would die. And it was just that he did so. Talking with him had made it a little bit more personal than was comfortable, but it had to be done. The promise had been made, and the killer would see it through. Now was not the time to get cold feet.

Jonathon stirred and mumbled something. This startled the killer who backed away momentarily. Was he sufficiently drugged to be finished off? He seemed to be a bit too frisky. What if he suddenly kicked off? Fuck it, the killer plunged the syringe in and pressed the solution into him. He scarcely moved.

13

'Whoever called it necking, was a poor judge of anatomy.'

Groucho Marx.

The bedroom was dark. Curtains drawn, the red digits of the radio alarm clock, being the only light visible. As it clicked onto 7:00, the radio burst into life; the disc jockey merrily projecting amiable noises to soothe the waking masses, followed by Level 42's *'Running With The Family.'*

Nobby grunted and wearily opened one eye towards the commotion. He reached over and turned it off. It had been a long night. His body ached, as he lay on his back, tanned and naked under the quilt. He felt to his left-hand side and sure enough there was a naked female there. Good, he hadn't dreamt it then. He spooned her. His arms reaching around to caress her breasts.

'Morning Sarge.' She said.

'Morning Constable.' Nobby said with a smile. 'How was it for you?'

'We're in so much trouble.'

'No, we aren't. Stop avoiding the question.'

She turned and gave him a peck on the lips. 'That's why I said we're in trouble. I think we ought to give this a go.'

'Yes!' He kissed her back. 'Me too. You're amazing, do you know that?'

She ran her hand through his bedraggled hair, scratching slightly at his scalp with her nails as she did. 'You aren't so bad yourself. We need to talk things through later, but unless I get to work, I am going to get a right bollocking off my Detective Sergeant, and he is a right miserable old scrote.'

'I've heard that.' Nobby said

Steph got out of the bed. She was naked.

'Wow.' Nobby said.

'Don't be daft, Nobby. Where is your shower?'

'Just through there, it's en-suite. You should know that you used it last night.'

'Oh yes, but my head was in a bit of a daze then, or have you forgotten?'

'No, I haven't forgotten, how could I?'

'I haven't woken up yet. And for some reason I feel like I've been hit by a tornado.'

'More like a freak storm. Although there was a heavy down pour, I seem to remember.'

'Ha, ha. I'll have to use your toothbrush, or do you use, *Steradent.*'

'Cheeky sod!'

He watched her beautiful body walk towards the shower and she sneaked a glance behind her as she entered to en-suite. He heard the shower turn on. He got out of the bed and put his underpants on, not feeling as confidant as Steph, in the cold light of day, so to speak. He punched the air as a wave of excitement ran through him. 'Yes!' he said quietly. He was smitten with this CID kitten.

*

Stark arrived at the station just before nine. Nobby greeted him in the corridor.

'What's up with you, Nobby? You look as if you've just run a marathon. Are you all right?'

'I'm fine, I just had a hard night, that's all.'

'Will you organize the troops today, Nobby? I want to listen to Sammy Trench's tape again. There's something niggling me about it.'

'OK boss. No problem. There's no joy with the Evening Post letterbox, by the way. We're are still doing the surveillance, of course.'

'Keep with it, as Brian Clough says, "It only takes a second to score a goal."

'That reminds me, I don't suppose I can have Saturday off, to go and give "the Reds" a shout, they're at home to Arsenal?'

'Sorry, Nobby. It seems unlikely, let's see how it develops.'

'Fair do's, I'll go and get the lad's sorted.'

'Cheers, Nob.'

Nobby disappeared into the CID office, as Stark went in to his own and closed the door behind him.

'You look knackered, Steph. Had a good night, have we?'

'God, yes, but it's none of your business, Sergeant.'

'You need a real man. You've not lived yet.'

'Are you volunteering, then.' Steph asked, playing along.

'As always, but I'm frightened I would spoil you for other men.' Nobby said.

Asley spoke up. 'Yes, he'd put you off for life, Steph!'

The team laughed.

The faint sound of laughter drifted into Stark's office. There was a knock on the door. 'Come in.'

Cynthia walked in with a mug of tea. 'Cuppa, sir.'

'Wonderful. Thanks Cynthia. You'll go far.'

She smiled and closed the door as she left.

He placed the cassette into the player and pressed the button; fast-forwarding and rewinding, to various parts of Sammy's recorded commentary, from the wake:

'Tracey, passing round the sympathy card to be signed. "Come on, it'll be better from all of us."'

Fast -forward.

'" He and James hated each other!" Jonathon: "Don't put words in my mouth, David, please."'

Fast forward.

'"...nick it, Roy. It was in the locker-room at college. I saw him walk away from it, and he knew I'd seen him."'

Fast forward.

'" ...give it to Sarah later..."'

Fast forward.

'Mark: "Yes, if we hadn't met at college – "'
Fast forward.

'"...fuck you so hard tomorrow."'

Rewind.

'" ...to get served" Jon, in Caroline's ear: "I'm going to fuck you so hard tomorrow."
Both laughed.
Caroline: "Not here, Jon, for God's sake. Half past two in The Unicorn, don't let me down this time."'

Fast forward.

'" ...killing has stopped?"'

Fast forward

'" ...about the postmortem? Have the police said anything?"
Roy: "Don't get..."'

Fast forward.

'" ...upsets everybody."
Caroline: "You're right, Trace, how's your little girl? I've not heard you talk about her for ages."
'Tracey: "Fine. You know, I can't help thinking what sort of people have we become..."'

Fast forward.

'" Mark, that's not on. Leave him alone."
Roy: "That's a typically ignorant comment."'

Fast forward.

'Sarah Deely. Both shaking hands.'

Fast forward.

'*Tracey:* "There's nothing I can add, but all of us will miss him. Goodbye, Sarah."

'No handshake or kiss. Tracey leaving the pub.'

Stark tapped the tape recorder. A cloud of smoke billowed from his cigar. He shook his head.

'Something isn't quite right, here. Something is missing. What the bloody hell is it?' He rewound the tape and pressed play again.

*

Stark welcomed the meeting with Roy Prentice. He needed a break from scrutinising that bloody tape recording. He felt he was a hair's breadth away from discovering the anomaly. He felt it was staring him in the face.

Roy sat on the orange settee. Dave Stark, and the uniformed Inspector Bob Stanswick, sat either side of him. The coffee table made Stark feel a little constricted, as he could not spread his legs out.

'Thanks for coming in Roy.' Bob was leading the conversation initially, as arranged with Stark.

'I hope it's important, I am a busy man. Is there a development?' Roy said.

'First of all, I must take issue with you, Roy.' Bob explained.

'Oh, yeah.'

'Yes. It has come to my attention that you intentionally activated a Home Office alarm, to test the response time of my officers.'

'That's true. What of it?'

'You don't do that Roy. My officers risked their own safety, to get to you as quickly as possible, not to mention the risk to other road users, and that risk was totally unnecessary.'

'How was it unnecessary?'

'Because you were not in danger.'

'It may have escaped your notice, Inspector Stanswick, but I am constantly in danger, until DI Stark here manages to catch whoever it is that is systematically killing my friends. I could be next on the list.'

'Roy, I am not debating this. It is not for you to "test" my officers. If it happens again, I will withdraw the alarm and the immediate response plan.'

'Will you, now.'

'Yes. I will. So, be warned.'

'This is just a bullying tactic, because I have complained about the policewoman who was abusive towards me, isn't it? What's happened with that? Nothing I suspect.'

Dave Stark took over the conversation.

'Have you had a chance to reconsider at all, Roy? The policewoman could lose her whole career, over something that was said, perhaps in the heat of the moment.'

'Why would I reconsider? She should have thought of that, when she started gobbing off at me.'

'You know she wasn't feeling well. Don't you ever have an off day, Roy?'

'Yes, but I couldn't care less. You people are expected to respect the public, regardless as to whether you are having an "off day", as you call it.'

'So, you still want to pursue it?'

'Look, if you have asked me to come here, to brow-beat me into withdrawing it, you are wasting your time.'

'Nobody is brow-beating you, Roy. So, let's just talk further about your complaint. I wanted to clarify some points. You said that the tape recording covered all the interaction, between the officers and yourself, is that right?'

'Duh! Yeah.'

'So, excuse my ignorance here, Roy, are you saying that the tape covers the whole time they were in the building, from walking in the door to leaving?'

'Yep.'

'How sure are you?'

'One hundred percent.'

'So, the tape you gave Inspector Stanswick, doesn't have greetings on it, such as them explaining why they are there, and so on.'

'Okay, if you want to get picky, but that is the only bit that is missing, it lasted a minute at the very most. The tape doesn't lie.'

'Couldn't it have been longer?'

'I know what you are trying to do here; the officers, well, that policewoman, was abusive, pretty much from the get -go.'

'The tape lasts 3 minutes 12 seconds.'

'OK'

'Who let the detectives in?'

'I did.'

And what happened then?'

'We went straight into the office and the conversation began.'

'No small talk?'

'No, just as the tape says. I've already explained all this.'

'What about afterwards?'

'I showed them the door, thank you very much.'

'So, they immediately left after the altercation?'

'Yes, I've already explained all this. What is it you don't understand? It's all recorded on tape.'

Stark reached into his briefcase and placed a videotape on to the coffee table in front of them. 'Do you know what that is, Roy?'

'It's a video tape.'

'Correct. It's actually a CCTV tape from the care home, which shows the detectives arriving and leaving.'

'Is that one of those new security cameras that watch the

outside of the house.'

'Yes, the government have been trialling them, at some of their buildings, like kiddies homes, but you obviously don't know that.'

Roy swallowed hard and shifted in his seat. He was starting to see what was happening. 'I didn't know that, no. OK. So what?' His heartbeat started to increase.

'Guess what?'

'What?'

'The time between the detectives arriving and leaving, is 12 minutes 42 seconds. Not 3 minutes 12 seconds, as you have said. You've been lying to us, Roy, haven't you?'

'This is ridiculous, maybe they were, erm, waiting about.'

'But they weren't Roy, were they? You've already told us you met them at the door, and went straight into the office and then immediately showed them out after the altercation.'

He did not reply, he merely stared at the tape on the table.

'And as you have said to us already, Roy, the tape doesn't lie.'

Bob Stanswick was stifling a smile as he spoke. 'So, what this means, is that we won't be pursuing your complaint any further.'

'I knew this would be a stitch up.'

'It's no stitch up, Roy, that's your department.' Stark said.

Bob continued. 'You do have the right to an appeal. However, I should warn you, that if you do appeal, then you will have to suffer any consequences that come from lying to us, and wasting our time; investigating something that you have tried to deceive us about.'

Roy stood up. 'Don't bother. Leave it. Just carry on abusing members of the public and treating us all like dirt.'

He headed to the door and stopped to give a final comment, but all he could muster was. 'Good day!'

The door slammed behind him.

The two Inspectors were grinning. Dave extended a hand and Bob shook it. 'Good work, Dave.'

'Rather kind of you to say, Bob, thank you.'

*

The Unicorn public house at Gunthorpe was in a lovely setting. On the banks of the Trent, with outside tables and waiters and a rustic setting, ideal for a romantic meeting or a nice lunch time break for businessmen and reps. It was off the beaten track and tended to be busier at weekends and bank holidays rather than in the working week.

Nobby and Charlie sat at a table at the back of the pub, the lunch-time rush having dissipated, and the demographic was returning from business types, to families and couples. It had been standing room only, for some considerable time, but now there was a number of vacant tables in the mid-afternoon lull.

Charlie glanced at the huge railway station clock situated behind the bar. 'Twenty-five past two.' He said, breaking the silence.

'They should be here any minute.' Nobby observed as he tapped his fingers on the hard wood table.

'What do you want to do Nobby, take them back to the nick or what?'

'No, we'll get them a drink and have a chat. A grown-up chat, if you like. It's time they had a bit of a reality check. If they want we can have the chat at home, and see what Mr Winner's view of proceedings are.'

Charlie shrugged out a laugh. 'We wouldn't really do that, though?'

'God, no, but they don't know that do they? I think stark is right that we have been a bit too courteous with this lot. We need to start holding the mirror up. Exposing them for who and what they are, and giving them a bit more motivation to tell us the bloody truth, for once.'

'They've been taking liberties, haven't they?'

'I think some of them have.'

The two fell quiet again. Nobby toyed with his pint, the outside of the glass sticky to the touch. After a couple of minutes, Charlie spoke.

'Are you all right, Nobby?'

'Yes, never been better, why?'

'You just don't seem your normal self, that's all.'

'I'm fine. I'm a bit loved up at the mo...'

'Hang on, sorry, Nobby there's Caroline Winner.'

'Aha! She's on her own, we'll wait for Jonathon Stacey to get here, before we make ourselves known. Let's just keep tabs on her for now.'

Caroline was wearing a burgundy three-quarter-length overcoat, black stockings, high heeled court shoes, black gloves and black handbag. It didn't look like she was going for a stroll through the rural countryside or along the towpath at the side of the Trent. She kept checking herself out in the mirrored wall behind the bar, throwing her hair back and running her hands through it. Ten minutes became fifteen; there was still no sign of Jonathon. Caroline was becoming impatient. She glanced furtively at her watch, feeling self-conscious in doing so. Jonathon had never stood her up before. An unwelcome shiver rippled down her back, and she suddenly felt alone and a bit silly. Everyone must realise she had been stood up. How embarrassing. Could he be waiting outside, perhaps? She started to walk towards the door. Charlie and Nobby got up to follow her out. As she got to the door Nobby shouted.

'Caroline!'

She turned, and the horror on her face illustrated the level of surprise the detective's shout had caused her. She recognised Charlie from his visit to her house, with Jim, and she had been aware of Nobby from the wake. The two men walked over to her as she stood frozen to the spot, just outside the door. Her mind was invaded by a thousand thoughts. Her heart thumping, as she tried to play it cool. 'Hello there. Fancy seeing you here. I just popped in for a drink, like you do.'

'Hello Caroline.' Nobby said.

'It's no coincidence, Caroline. We know why you're here.'

A wasp's nest crashed inside her stomach, and her face

dropped.

Nobby offered a thin smile. 'Let's talk about this inside, shall we?'

'Um, I'd love to, but unfortunately, I've got an appointment, maybe some other time?' She started to turn away.

Nobby caught her arm. 'Caroline, don't make this any more difficult than it already is.'

Her eyes began to fill with tears. 'I don't know what you mean, Mr Clarke.'

'I think you do Caroline. Where's Jonathon?'

Her shoulders dropped and she sighed. 'How the hell did you know?'

'Let's go back inside and have a chat, shall we?'

The three returned to the bar. The smell of cooking hitting them, and the clinking of glasses from behind the bar, seemed to be magnified above the low backdrop of voices.

'What do you want to drink, Caroline?' Charlie asked.

Her mouth was dry, but she managed to mumble: 'G and T please, no ice.'

Nobby ushered Caroline to a table in the corner. There was an old wooden bench, as well as chairs, with a thin length of cushion along it. Nobby thought he had better occupy the bench with the thin cushion, for the sake of Charlie's posterior.

Caroline was worried. 'What is this all about? How did you know about me and Jonathon?'

Nobby took the lead. 'I can't really tell you, Caroline, but suffice it to say, we know. Where is he?'

'I don't know. He's never let me down before. Could he have seen you perhaps? Have you frightened him off?'

'No chance.'

'That worries me then.'

'You should have told us about this Caroline. It's important that people are truthful when they are in the midst of a murder enquiry.'

'I wanted to, honestly, but I was scared. I didn't know what you would think.' She flicked her hair off her forehead.

'Caroline, we are detectives, we know how the world works, it's not our first rodeo. Everybody is having sex with everybody else, well, not quite, but you know what I mean. The important thing is that you are one hundred percent honest with us from now on. If we feel you aren't, we will then have to speak to others to check things out. And by others, I mean Mark, also. Otherwise there is no reason why we should need to discuss this with anyone but Jonathon; as it stands at least.'

Charlie arrived with the drinks.

Caroline took hers and sipped gratefully.

'Please don't tell Mark, he'll go berserk.'

'Are you sure he doesn't know already?' Nobby said as he lit a cigarette.

'Positive. I assure you, if he knew, I would be in the Queens Medical Centre, I shouldn't wonder, as an in-patient.'

'Is he violent, then?'

'He's never hit me, but he is quick to temper. He's really strong, well, you've seen him – he's solid muscle.'

'Does anybody else know about the affair?'

'No, I certainly haven't told anyone about it, and I'm fairly sure Jonathon hasn't said anything. I wonder why he isn't here. I'm worried, to be honest. Will you be able to check he's okay?'

'Sure, if that's what you want.'

'Unless something has happened with his work, at the hospital, but I would have thought he would have rung the pub and left a message.'

'We'll check he's okay. He'll be fine. But this is the sort of hypocrisy I am talking about, Caroline. You want us to help and do this and do that when the shit hits the fan, yet you are delaying us and messing up our enquiry by not being candid with us. It's not a game, Caroline. It's a bloody murder enquiry.'

'I'm sorry. I get it.'

'Well, our patience is wearing a bit thin, and it's not just you. I will be straight with you, but it's a two-way street.'

'Thank you. I know.'

'Are you seeing anyone else, other than Jonathon?'

She laughed. 'No, what do you take me for? As you know, Jonathon and I have known each other for a long time, and our relationship is a bit more than a fumble behind the bike sheds.'

'Are you thinking of leaving, Mark, then?'

'Maybe. The problem is, Jonathon is a bit more of a...what can I say?'

'Open relationship guy?'

'I suppose. I know he sees other women, and that's OK. Or rather it was OK, but recently it's hurt me more than it used to.'

'Is Mark seeing anyone else.'

'Not as far as I know. I hear rumours about his little group of housewives and him banging one of them in the equipment store, but to be honest, I couldn't care less. I'm not sure I love him anymore. I'm not sure I care. It's all a bit of a mess really.' Tears began to appear in her eyes, and she stared at the table. It was the first time she had said this out loud and the acceptance was painful.

'How, and when did your affair with Jonathon start?'

'Well, we had a fling at college, of course, but then I saw Jonathon about two years ago in a pub. At Harvey's bar. Do you know it?'

'I know it. It's more of a pub/club, it opens late doesn't it? So, everybody goes over there for late drinks.'

'That's it. At West Bridgford. I was with a girlfriend, it was her birthday, and there he was. He was drunk. We had a bit of a kiss and a cuddle. He lives life to the full, does Jonathon, he's not your typical Doctor.'

'Oh, I don't know, medical students are the worst of the lot for partying.' Nobby said.

'I don't know, is that right?'

'I think it is.'

'Anyway, I had his number because of the re-union stuff we do; so, one particularly bad day, when I was feeling particularly low, I gave him a call, and that was it. I think we ended up in bed on the first day, and it's been brilliant ever since.' She threw her hair back and raised her chin, her eyes glistening.

'OK.'

'My Mark's an attractive guy, but he pays more attention to himself than me, I know it's wrong, but there was no intimacy between us, not just the sex; but holding hands, cuddling, that sort of thing. We were like flat mates. I was lonely, I suppose. I know it's no excuse, but you said to be honest and I am being.'

'So, are you in love with Jonathon?'

'I am. I think Jonathon is with me, maybe he's in lust, more than love. We nearly got caught the other night. A policeman stopped near us and checked the cars. It was so embarrassing.'

Nobby glanced at Charlie. 'When was this?'

'The other night, it was at Brickyard cottages. I just thought: "I'm getting too old for this, I'm not a teenager anymore". Jonathon was pissed off because he was sexually frustrated, in the moment, you know. It was horrible.'

'Did the cop speak to you?'

'No, nothing like that, but his headlights shone in the car and he parked up in front, to let *us* know, that *he* knew what was happening, I suppose.'

'We'll have to enquire about that.'

'I thought that was how you knew about us?'

'No. Does it bother you that Jonathon might still be seeing other women?'

'In one sense it does.'

'That'll be a yes, then.'

'No, not necessarily.'

'Caroline.'

'No, it does bother me, of course, but in another way, it keeps the relationship alive. I'm probably not explaining this very well, but because I feel that I'm competing, we keep making an effort with each other. I know it sounds ridiculous, but I know what I mean.'

'No, I get what you are saying, Caroline. Why haven't you left Mark?'

'I keep asking myself that question. I just don't have the guts to do it at the moment. Plus, I'll be honest, it is security. Jonathon isn't exactly the settling down type yet.'

'Yet?'

'You know we women love a challenge, we always think we can change men, don't we? I suppose I'm reasonably happy with how things are, but I know something must give eventually. Maybe this is it.'

'Maybe.'

'Listen, I am really worried about Jonathon. I've got a bad feeling about it, especially considering recent events. The only thing I can think of, is that he has seen you waiting for us.'

'He hasn't seen us, Caroline.' Charlie was confident.

'Do you mind if I try to contact him? He's never let me down in two years – well he has, but he always got a message to me, I am getting concerned, to be honest.'

Nobby glanced at Charlie. 'I think you had better ring Stark up, Charlie. Use the bar phone. Put him in the picture, but I think a visit to Jonathon's house might be appropriate. If you can't get hold of Stark, get a couple of the lads to go around, with my compliments.'

'OK. Sarge.'

Charlie stood. 'Ouch, you bugger!' He rubbed his knee.

*

Stark put the phone down and walked out of his office, across the corridor, and into the general CID office. Cynthia and Ashley Stevens were in there.

'Cynthia, can I have a word, please?' Stark asked.

'Yes, sir.'

'Ash, hang fire in here, will you? I want you and Cynthia to do a little job for me in a minute.'

'Of, course, boss, no problem. Do you want me in your office, as well?'

'No, just Cynthia, we won't be long.'

Cynthia followed her DI into his office.

'Close the door, please, Cynthia.'

'Am I in trouble, sir?'

'Why does everyone always think that? No, quite the reverse actually.'

'OK, sounds interesting.

'I saw Roy Prentice earlier.'

'Oh.'

'Don't worry, I've been doing a bit of work on your little problem, and he has now dropped the complaint.'

'Oh, brilliant! Thank you, sir, that's terrific news. I've been worried sick about it.'

'I know you have.'

'What made him change his mind? If you don't mind me asking?'

'Well, it was obvious from what you'd said, that he only taped a short section of your conversation, even though he was insistent that it was the whole lot. I just got the CCTV from the care home and it showed he was lying.'

'That's brilliant.'

'Hardly brilliant, Cynthia, but I'm glad to be able to put it to bed for you.'

'I'm so grateful. Thank you. I owe you one, sir.'

'Don't be silly. Now I want you and Ash to do a little job for me.'

'What's that?'

'Charlie and Nobby are up at The Unicorn pub, and whilst Caroline Winner has turned up for their little assignation, Jonathon Stacey hasn't. Will the two of you nip around to Stacey's house and just check he's OK?'

'Yes, of course. If he is in, do you want us to talk to him about Caroline?'

'Um. Yes, OK, do that.'

Cynthia stood up; she was still smiling from the news. 'Thanks again, sir, you're the best.'

'You're welcome, and you're right of course.' He smiled.

Cynthia explained the situation to Ash and before long he was carefully parking his Porsche in the road leading to Jonathon Staceys' home address.

Cynthia spoke. 'I've got a funny feeling about this, Ash.'

'It'll be nothing, it's fine. He's probably got another tart on the go. He's a bit of a lad, is our Jonathon.'

They got out of the car, and Cynthia stared up at the house. It looked as though nobody was in. The downstairs curtains were drawn, although the upstairs ones were not. 'Have we checked he's not just been called in to work?'

'No, but they will want a physical visit to close the action anyway, so we might as well just come and check it out for ourselves. You've got to be so careful marking actions off, Cynthia, they can be a minefield.'

The two of them strolled up the slight incline of the driveway towards the front door. Ash knocked. No reply. He hammered, harder this time. Not a sound, no sign of movement.

'I tell you; he'll have another woman on the go. He's got a police alarm, there's been no activation, no sign of any attack.'

'You can't say that, Ash. We can't see if there is any sign of an attack; the curtains are drawn. I'm not so sure. I'm getting bad vibes.' Cynthia said.

Ashley used his car keys to tap stridently on the frosted glass panel. Nothing. He stepped back and stared up at the bedrooms. He looked through the letterbox, seeing nothing other than the hallway and a couple of letters on the floor. He shouted through it.

'Jonathon, it's the police. Are you there?'

Deadly silence.

'Are there any other addresses we could check for him?' Cynthia asked.

'Only his mother's, and the Incident Team have contacted her already, apparently, and she hasn't seen him for a week or more, which isn't unusual, according to her. As you say, he could be anywhere.'

Ashley looked at his watch; almost four o'clock. He stared at the houses along the row. 'Come on, let's knock on a few doors.'

They split up. Almost inevitably, the houses to either side, were empty. Ashley finally got some success at the house next door-but-one. It was answered by a woman in her early thirties, whose dark hair was tied back with a piece of cloth, no doubt to save her having to style it.

'Hello, love. I'm from the CID. We want to speak to Jonathon Stacey, next door-but-one, do you know him?'

'Yes, he should be in. Isn't he answering?' The woman fended off a small child, who appeared around her legs, as she spoke to the detective.

'No, he isn't. That's why I've had to pester you, I'm afraid. I take it you haven't seen him go out then?'

'No, I've not seen him for a few days actually, but then again he does disappear every now and then.' The woman stepped outside the house enabling her little boy to run down the drive. 'Oi, come here!' She chased the lad on to the path and caught him before turning to look at Jonathon's house. 'His curtains are drawn. That's strange.'

'Is it strange? I know a lot of single men don't always bother too much with things like drawing the curtains.'

'It's rare that Jonathon hasn't opened his curtains.' She said somewhat dramatically. 'I've never seen them like that in all the time I've been here, it's weird that the upstairs curtains are open, as well.'

'You don't happen to know which room he sleeps in do you?'

'I think it's the front, that's where the main bedroom is, we had a look, when it was up for sale. Nosy neighbours, and all that.' She laughed, joined by Ashley. Her face drew a concerned expression on it. 'Do you think he's all right? He was telling me about a couple of his mates being murdered. You're getting me worried, now.' She put her hand to her mouth.

'I'm pretty sure he's OK, but do you know any other places he might be, friends, girlfriends?'

'He's got plenty of those, but he laughs about the fact that he always brings them back to his place, so that he doesn't have to get up and leave, and he can "throw them out, when he's had enough of them." He's a bit of a playboy, our Jonathon is, you know.'

'So, I understand. Has anybody been to the house at all?'

'Not as far as I am aware, but they could have been. I was only joking about being a nosey neighbour, you know.'

'I know. When did you last see him?'

'Like I say. A couple of days ago, I guess.'

Ashley eventually got around to asking the obvious question, pointing down towards Jonathon's drive. 'Is that his Ford Sierra?'

'Oh my God, yes, it is.'

'OK. Thanks for your help.'

'I'm frightened.'

'No need to be.' Ash smiled disarmingly. 'He could have been picked up by a friend, or gone for a walk, or something.'

'And pigs might fly. That's not Jonathon's style.'

'Anyway. Thanks a lot.'

Ash re-joined Cynthia who had returned and waited for him by the CID car. 'I'm thinking of a forced entry.' Ash said.

'Why, what's she said?'

'Well, the state of the house, the curtains, missing an appointment with Caroline and that's his car, the silver Ford Sierra.'

'We do have a common-law power of entry, to save life and property.'

Ash laughed. 'I do know, Cynthia.'

'Sorry, just thinking out loud really.'

'I know.'

Ashley pulled his radio from the clip on his belt. 'DC Stevens to control.'

'Go ahead, Over.'

'Re: Action…Standby.'

He spoke to Cynthia. 'Have you got the action sheet, Cynth?'

She unravelled it from her pocket and quickly handed it to Ash.

'Re: action 873, myself and DC Walker, are going to force an entry at the property, downstairs curtains drawn, car in drive, concerned neighbour's etcetera.'

'Standby, please.'

'Stark's phone will be ringing now.' He said to Cynthia smiling.

'Good luck with that. He's stopped answering it since he met Roy prentice!' She said.

Ash laughed.

'Control to DC Stevens.'

'Oh, here we go. "Go ahead."'

'The DI is not answering his phone, but if you are comfortable that it is to protect life and property, the Sergeant says it is fine.'

'Ten-Four, I'll give you an update shortly.'

He clipped the radio back on his belt and opened the CID car door, he leaned in, and re-appeared clutching his wooden truncheon. They walked back to the door. Ash checked there was no key in the lock; there wasn't, thankfully it was a Yale lock.

'Stand back, Cynthia.' She obliged.

Ash struck the frosted glass panel at the side of the lock, initially cracking it, and then smashing through with a couple of more blows. He used the end of the truncheon to knock out remaining shards, adding a few more scars and indentations to the shaft. He reached through and opened the lock. The door swung open. The two walked in. 'I'll check upstairs.' And off he went.

Cynthia was nervous. She'd done this type of thing a few times over the years, when in uniform. It was a regular occurrence. Usually it was when elderly people hadn't been seen for a time, and milk bottles or newspapers, or both, were building up on the doorstep.

It isn't necessarily the thought of the sight of the body, that made her apprehensive. It's the unknown. It is opening each door and not knowing what is behind it. A decayed body? A suicide? A murder? It wasn't long before Cynthia had her answer. She stepped into the living room and immediately halted. She froze, rooted to the floor, by the sight that greeted her. Then the smell hit her. A fusty, foul smell of decay. She put her hand over her nose and mouth to try to stifle the funk. After a couple of seconds, she shouted.

'Ashley!'

'What?'

'I think you'd better come in here. In the living room.'

Ashley quickly bounded down the stairs and joined her. 'Oh shit!'

Jonathon Stacey was lying on the settee, his eyes fixed wide and staring, blind to the incredulous expressions on Ashley and Cynthia's faces.

Ash grabbed his radio off his belt. 'DC Stevens to control.'

'Go ahead.'

'Yes, update on the forced entry: it's a one oblique one. Can you notify DI Stark, urgently please?'

'Ten four – is it suspicious?'

'Very.'

14

'For three days after death, hair and fingernails
continue to grow, but phone calls taper off.'

Johnny Carson.

Stark was careful to wear gloves, as he picked up the ripped piece of card at the side of the body on the settee. He read the message that was scrawled on it in black pen:

I'm so terribly sorry about everything you have gone through. I wish I could turn the clock back.

Jonathon Stacey.

'Suicide, sir?' Ashley asked.

'That's what it seems. A scribbled note, no sign of a disturbance, doors and windows locked.'

'So, is Jonathon our killer?'

'That would be convenient wouldn't it?'

Stark peered at Stacey. He was supine on the settee, fully dressed, his shirt unbuttoned at the neck, both sleeves rolled up, tie loosely hanging. His left arm dangled outwards; a pinprick of blood apparent at the vein. A syringe lay behind him on the settee. On the coffee table was a cheap Biro and a glass of whiskey. Stark spoke aloud as thoughts popped into his head. 'Preserve that whiskey for forensic tests, Ash.'

He picked up the pen from the table, and requested a pad, which Ashley promptly produced. Stark wrote out the same message on to the pad and scrutinized it, comparing it with the scribbled note. He beckoned Ashley. 'Is it me, Ashley, or is this Biro medium tip, and the suicide note fine tip?'

Ashley compared the two. 'I'm no expert, sir, but I think you could be right. Obviously, Forensics will clear that up, but it does look different to me. I think you're right, boss.

'Seize every pen in the house.' He raised a cautionary hand to the young detective. 'Not yet, Ashley! When Scenes of Crime have finished.'

Stark looked around the room. 'Cynthia, are those Stacey's work notes, at the side of the chair? Look.'

Cynthia put gloves on, and gingerly picked up the notes, and handed them to Stark. Again, he looked at the notes, and at Jonathon's confirmed handwriting. It matched. Jonathon had written the note. 'It looks like it's his handwriting, all right. Ashley, as well as pens, I want you to find whatever it is that this piece of card is ripped from.'

'OK, sir.'

Stark shook his head. 'Is Wagstaff coming over, do we know?'

'He's on his way, sir.' Cynthia said. 'He was at a meeting at headquarters.'

'Who with?'

'The head honcho, Detective Chief Superintendent Davies, sir.'

'Brilliant. So, he knows already. This is going to cause so much shit, it's not true.'

'Why will it, sir?' Ash asked. 'All it is, is a suicide and an admission of guilt for two murders. I thought you'd be pleased. This suicide is the end of the line for the investigation, with a bit of luck, surely.'

'Is it bollocks, Ashley. It's another murder, man. It's bloody obvious it stinks. He's not committed suicide – look at the note. Signed "Jonathon Stacey". How many suicides have you been to, Ashley?'

'About four or five.'

'And how many of them signed the suicide note with their full bloody name written as a full, formal signature? We know who it's from, for Christ's sake. Why now, for the first time do we have a suicide with a formerly signed note. Why? Because it stinks, matey boy. It's a reasonable attempt, to make us think it's suicide, that's all.'

'But how can you inject somebody in the perfect position without a struggle?'

'I don't know. Perhaps he thought it was a happy drug, or he was asleep, or drunk; comatose, or perhaps there's something in that glass of whiskey. It can be done – it can be done, fairly bloody easily. Let's face it, it's not difficult to kill a man. It's the evasion of capture that is the tricky bit.'

'I suppose you're right, sir. I'm a bit confused about the note, though. If you are right, the shit has really hit the fan, and the press will have a field day.' Ashley observed candidly.

'And guess which direction shit travels?'

'erm.'

'Downhill.'

Ashley laughed.

'Ash, will you make a note for the pathologist to do a blood/ liquor test at the PM?'

'Yep.'

Stark went outside and re-examined all potential points of entry. The only forced entry had been caused by DC Stevens. Ashley insisted that the house had been totally secure when they arrived, otherwise they wouldn't have had to force entry themselves. Stark insisted it be checked again.

Scenes of Crime were finishing up their examination. Stark passed the time smoking his cigars outside, and away from the house. Wagstaff arrived and was briefed, he bore news that Detective Chief Superintendent Davies had requested the pleasure of their attendance at Sherwood Lodge later on. Intermittently Stark instructed Scenes of Crime to do various activities or answered various queries from them: 'Yes, take that.' 'No, leave that where it is. Just film it. And so on.'

As soon as they had finished, Stark and Wagstaff went inside to have a nosey around. There was still a lingering smell emanating from the decomposing Jonathon Stacey, who bore mute witness to the detectives roaming around his house.

'Ash, open some more windows, mate. It fucking stinks in here.'

'Alright, boss.'

It was always a bit weird when there was a dead person in the room with you. Stark often felt compelled periodically to check to see if it had moved. Stark opened drawers and units upstairs and down, still with his blue rubber surgical gloves on. It was while he was in the kitchen that he made his discovery. He opened a cupboard door, and inside was an ornate whiskey glass, in amongst the wineglasses. He felt along the carved ridges in the pattern on the glass and felt the heaviness of it. He looked over at a circular table next to the armchair, opposite Mr Death, where the decanter had stood, prior to Scenes of Crime removing it. Around the perimeter were eight glasses, all identical to the one in the cupboard, and the one which had been on the coffee table in front of Jonathon Stacey. There were two vacant spaces.

'Ashley! Stop Scenes of Crime, quickly!' He shouted.

Within a minute, Detective Sergeant Stuart Bradshaw, still in his white overalls, came back inside, smiling.

'Stuart, will you fingerprint me this glass please?' Stark asked. 'The killer put this in here, I'm sure of it.'

Stuart unpacked his metal case and removed a soft haired brush and a pot of aluminium dust. He dusted the glass carefully.

'Sorry, nothing, sir. You can see for yourself.'

Stark nodded. 'Take it for Forensics, will you, please, Stuart?'

Ashley, standing outside the house, poked his head through the kitchen window, that he had opened, to get rid of the funk of death. 'The undertakers are here, sir.'

'OK, we've finished in here. Who is it?'

'Smiths, and they're handing out complimentary pens. Do you want one, sir?' Ashley produced the inscribed plastic pen.

Stark laughed. 'No, thanks. And for Christ's sake don't mix that up with the ones you've taken from here!'

'Don't worry. Scenes of Crime have got those.' He

disappeared briefly, before being followed back in by the three undertakers. The younger of the three winked at Stark, as he entered, before inserting a piece of chewing gum into his mouth. Then they expertly manhandled Jonathon into a bag, and onto the trolley. As the young man zipped up the bag, he tapped the deceased's nose with his index finger.

'And no snoring!'

*

Stark sat at his desk, in his office, resting his chin on his hand. His door was open, and he was becoming increasingly infuriated at the conversation he could hear from the CID office. Jim McIntyre was pontificating again.

'I still don't see what Stark's problem is; now he's got a bloke who killed himself, and pretty much confessed to the killings. The killings will stop now, which we know from the text of the *Evening Post* personal column messages. One to go, or something like that. Wasn't it? Two detected murders and a suicide by the killer sound a lot better to me, than three undetected murders!'

'How can you say that, Jim?' Cynthia asked, clearly irritated. 'It's obvious even to me as the aide that here's been foul play. What are you suggesting – a cover up?'

'Cover up. Jeez. Don't be so bloody dramatic. I'm not suggesting that; I'm just asking where the actual hard evidence is that he hasn't killed himself?'

'We don't just deal with watertight evidence, do we? We look at circumstantial evidence, don't forget.'

'Christ. Two minutes out of training school. What court takes circumstantial evidence then, Cynthia? Come on if you've got all the answers, let's hear it.'

Cynthia stuck to her argument. 'Look at it from this angle, then. Where's the evidence that he *did* kill the other two? And if it is him, the *Evening Post* letter must be wrong, because there's no third killing!'

Stark smiled to himself, as he listened; Cynthia was turning out to be something of an asset.

'Look, I've been in this job a damned sight longer than you have, Cynthia.'

'So, what? So has Stark, and Charlie here, for that matter. It still doesn't give you the monopoly on an opinion and logical thought, does it?'

'Long words don't make you right, either.'

'What are you talking about long words?'

'I'm just saying, you've got a lot to learn, kid.'

Charlie interrupted. 'Yes, she has, but not necessarily off you, Jim.'

Stark grinned, but his forehead furrowed into a frown. If only it was as Jim had said. Still, there is only one truth; it's just tough shit. He knew the Headquarters' top corridor would hit the roof, and they would be looking for someone on whom they could pin the gilded badge of blame upon. He fingered his lapel.

*

Detective Chief Superintendent Davies was only a couple of years older than Stark, though with a few more grey hairs. He was a clean-cut man, well groomed, and he wore tailored, but old-fashioned suits. Despite his rank, his office was not overly large, crammed in between his 'worker-bee' subordinates, and the Force Intelligence Bureau at Sherwood Lodge headquarters. To the run-of-the-mill detectives he was God. They never saw the man, only his signature, on various memo's, that filtered through the internal mail system.

This man *was* the CID. Any decisions made at the highest level, he was instrumental in, if not the instigator. He had the ear of The Chief Constable – 'which I keep in a drawer' was one of his regular 'jokes'. John Davies had worked his way up the hard way, it was nigh on impossible to be a senior CID Officer without doing so. There was no drafting in somebody senior from uniform, thank heavens. It wasn't a role you could bullshit your way through. You had to know your stuff. Horses for courses.

Davies was undisputedly a highly intelligent individual, but he was very rank conscious which was unusual for CID. He was quite diminutive in stature, so maybe that was it. Stark could remember as a DC, Davies, then a Detective Inspector, tore him a new arsehole, screaming at him like a banshee, merely because Stark had referred to his, then senior, Detective Sergeant, by his first name. 'He has been promoted by the Crown of this country, and he will be referred to as Sergeant by the likes of you. Now get out until you have some common decency and an understanding of the rank structure of the police force.'

'But sir...'

'Are you deaf as well as daft? I've told you, *get out.*'

Since then Stark had disliked the man intensely. He considered his pettiness, a weakness, in his character, and was averse to the way he used his rank, rather than thrashing things out man-to-man. Davies was not, however a man to be crossed, so he tried to keep his contempt to himself, when in his company. The threat of wearing a tall pointy hat was never far away, when on the CID.

Stark and Wagstaff stood outside Davies' office like two naughty schoolboys. The secretary informed them that he would see them now.

He tapped on the door.

'Enter!'

Stark looked skywards. Keep calm; just keep your big mouth shut, Stark told himself. The two walked in. Davies was scribbling at his desk and failed to acknowledge their presence. Stark coughed. Without looking up at them, Davies pointed a finger, indicating they should sit down, which they did. After what seemed an age, Davies spoke; it was sharp and to the point. His piercing eyes flashed between Stark and Wagstaff.

'Mr Stark, you are Acting Detective Chief Inspector. Mr Wagstaff you are a substantive Detective Superintendent. Why aren't you fulfilling those roles adequately?'

Stark glanced at Wagstaff, incredulously. Wagstaff spoke. 'Well, we are – what...?'

'I'm sorry Mr Wagstaff, you perhaps didn't hear me correctly. I said, why aren't you fulfilling your obligations?'

Wagstaff was starting to sweat already. Stark could see Wagstaff was babbling so he answered the question for them. 'I take it you are referring to the murder investigation, sir.'

'Yes, I am, of course.'

'We are making progress, sir, and in recent days, we have had a series of significant developments.'

'I take it you are referring to the fact that another poor sod, a bloody doctor, no less, has been murdered while you stand idly by?'

'I wouldn't say we were standing idly by.'

'Oh, wouldn't you. I'm not interested in what you say. A typical example came from one of your peers, Detective Inspector Mole, he was saying he has been trying to help you, but you are more interested in cups of coffee, and piss-ups in the station bar.'

It was Stark's turn to start sweating at the mere mention of that odious prick, Lee Mole. 'So, you are not interested in what I say, sir, being the person actually dealing with the case, but you are with that prat, Lee Mole, who knows nothing about it, or anything else, for that matter!'

Wagstaff whispered. 'David!'

Chief Superintendent Davies continued. 'I presume he's making it up, then, that he saw you in the bar only the other night?'

'No, but.'

'No, but. No, but what, exactly? I'm interested in results gentlemen, and I don't see any. You have failed, haven't you? Three fucking dead! Three! It's a bloody massacre! You have failed me, you have let the department down, let yourselves down and most importantly let the public down. I don't like failures, Mr Wagstaff, there is no place for them in my CID.'

Wagstaff was speechless. Davies turned to Stark. 'Anything else you want to say?'

'Only that old army saying, "that it is easier to offer advice from the trenches than to test its merit at the point of attack."'

'How dare you!'

'I'm talking about Mole, sir, not you, of course.'

'I should bloody hope so. Are arrests imminent? Or is that just wishful thinking on my part?'

'Our job is to see if there are connections between the college friends and the killings...'

'Oh, for Christ's sake, David, of course there is a connection! A blind man could see that. What the hell are you doing about it?'

'We are fairly certain that the last death, is not a suicide, and probably murder...'

'Probably murder. Jesus Christ!'

'...so that leaves the remaining college group as suspects-'

'Well, with a bit of luck, soon there will only be one left, and that will make things easier for you.'

'If you have read the reports, sir, you will know that the *Evening Post* personal column entries indicate that this will be the last killing.'

'Don't even think about patronizing me, DI Stark, because trust me, you will be the loser.'

'I'm not patronizing you.'

'"If I have read the reports". Who the hell do you think you are! Other than a bloody incompetent, it seems to me.'

'With respect, sir, I am not incompetent. We are open to suggestions, if there is something we have missed.'

'Don't get fucking smart. You have three days to sort it. I want to see every single action you've done, and yes, smart arse, you may well find a few suggestions coming your way, along with a P45. So, piss off out, and do the job you are being paid to do.'

Wagstaff and Stark left. Stark was fuming. He knew he shouldn't have said what he did, but he was incensed by Lee Mole sticking the knife in again. It was getting beyond a joke. At least his daughter, Laura would be pleased if he got the boot.

*

Nobby had to shout down the telephone to Stark. He was struggling to be heard above the drone of the numerous trepans, cutting off the tops of heads, in the Post Mortem room, next door to him.

'We've just finished, Dave.'

'What's the crack, then Nobby?'

'Pretty much what we already knew. Syringe mark to left arm. It looks as though he died through an overdose of drugs.'

'What sort of drugs? I don't suppose we know yet?'

'No. The stomach contents have gone to Toxicology, for analysis. The Pathologist has given me a bit of a steer though.'

'Who was the pathologist, Hargreaves?'

'Yes.'

'He's usually pretty helpful, what did he say?'

'He reckons it could be a morphine overdose, off the record, like.'

'Morphine?'

'That's right. Not the easiest of drugs to get your hands on.'

Stark pondered the news. 'Well, he did work at a hospital. Would he have any lying around the house, I wonder.'

'I asked Hargreaves that. He says he most certainly shouldn't, it's a controlled drug. Of course, that doesn't mean he didn't have. Anything is possible.'

'Still, the killer would have had to know that.'

'Unless the killer had their own supply.' Nobby mused.

'How could any of the others get hold of Morphine?'

'God, knows.'

'OK, we'll talk about it later, it's a bad line, Nobby. Anything else of relevance?'

'No, that's it.'

'Did he have AIDS?' Stark asked.

'No, definitely not.'

'OK, as I say, let's discuss it later, Nobby. Are you coming straight back?'

'I suppose, but I could do with a shower. I stink of death, it's bedlam here. It's like an abattoir. It's on my clothes and everything.'

'All right, nip home, have a shower, and change your clothes and I'll see you at the station.'

'Great, thanks. How did you get on, with Davies?'

'Absolutely wonderful. I wouldn't hear a bad word said about the man.'

Nobby laughed. 'See you, later.'

*

Stephanie typed out the final warrant, as instructed by Stark. He had also suggested that it would take her beyond normal court hours, to finish, and so would have to visit the magistrate at home. It always seemed easier to obtain a warrant from the magistrate's house, than from the formal court setting, hence Stark's advice. The typewriter was a modern Olivetti, an electric one. Only Steph could use such a contraption, all the others used the manual one, where you had to hit the keys with such force that after an hour's typewriting you were grimacing with pain. The beauty of the electric typewriter was that there were always fresh ribbons in them, which sent the ink to the page as the metal indenter intended. The manual ones usually meant swivelling the cartridges around to find a piece of ink on the ribbon without a hole in it.

The DI was happy with the application criterion: Section 8 of the Police and Criminal evidence Act 1984: A serious arrestable offence had been committed, and they had reasonable suspicion that there was evidence at any one of the college friends' houses, that could be of evidential use to the investigation. A good firm application, and some harsh facts about the killing should sway it.

Steph completed the 'persons or articles to look for' column:

- Knife believed used in murder of James Deely.

- Vehicle or documents of vehicle, believed used in murder of Stuart Millichip.

- Typewriter or paraphernalia associated with letters to the personal column of the *Evening Post*.

- Morphine, or container, or syringes or ancillary paraphernalia.

- Pens or card relevant to 'suicide' note of Jonathon Stacey.

She scratched at her head. After last night's session with Nobby, she was exhausted – she'd had little sleep. She couldn't think of anything else, so she merely added:

- Anything likely to be of evidential value regarding any of the murders of James Deely, Stuart Millichip or Jonathon Stacey.

The difficult bit had been the phone call to the Clerk of the Court. She always did this from notes, before typing it up in case it was refused, and she wasted her time. The Clerks were the ones you had to get past. If you could not sell it to them, they would not forward the application on, with it being out of hours. Many arguments had taken place over the phone about such matters. In this instance, she outlined the murders first to set the scene and the severity of the case. Thereafter it was pretty much plain sailing.

She looked at the clock in the office. Timing was everything. The magistrate she had been designated was somebody called Godfrey Minter, and the address was only a ten-minute drive away.

With the new roadworks on Hucknall Road, and a trilby hatted driver insisting on driving at twenty-five miles an hour, the ten-minute drive became twenty. Eventually Steph wove her way up the garden path, which was where she was hoping to lead the magistrate, taking care not to step on the beautiful lawn, or flower beds. The house itself was quite large, a four-bedroomed structure with ivy creeping up the walls, probably built in the 1930's. Steph found it eerie, as darkness built up the shadows around the approach. As she neared the door, a security light flicked on, illuminating the whole garden. It made her jump and she instinctively put her hand on her chest, to emphasise the point. The door was opened by Mr Minter J.P. himself. He was in dinner-jacket and bowtie, and he removed his silver-framed spectacles to smile disarmingly at Steph, as he let her in.

'Hello, I've been expecting you, of course. The clerk has explained a lot over the phone, but do come in.'

Steph could smell pipe tobacco on his breath as he spoke. She followed him into his study, which was spacious and had a whole wall crammed with books on various subjects from Psychology, to Home cooking recipes. 'Please, sit down, officer.' Steph sat at the coffee table, clutching the cardboard file that contained her papers.

'You look very smart, sir,' She offered. 'I hope I'm not interrupting anything?'

'No, not at all. I'm having a dinner party tonight, it's my turn. Members of the judiciary and other JP's have it every quarter, and for some reason they insist on keeping this damned tradition of dressing up. Bunch of fuddy-duddies really. I can see how it worked in a mansion house, in the eighteenth century, but we all feel a bit silly in a four-bed detached. Never mind. It takes all sorts, doesn't it?'

'It does.'

'Sorry if you thought I'd dressed for your attendance.' He said with a twinkle in his eye.

'I naturally thought you had, sir, so I feel a little disappointed it is for someone else.'

'If I'd known what an attractive officer was attending, I would definitely have made the effort.'

Randy old sod. Steph thought. 'Why, thank you, sir.'

Mr Minter continued. 'I'm afraid I don't entertain as much as I used to, since my wife died. I get a woman in now, and it's all a bit too much trouble, if truth be told. Just to sit around a table, with a bunch of self-important people trying to solve the problems of the world. Would you care for a drink, at all?'

'No, but thank you, anyway.'

'What about a Martini? I know perhaps you shouldn't, but I

won't tell, if you won't.' he smiled.

'Really, no thank you.'

His worship went to his desk drawer and got out a small leather pouch and pipe. 'It's my only sin, nowadays.' He sat down opposite her and lit the pipe with some aplomb. 'So, what can I do for you, young lady?' he asked, smoke billowing out of his mouth, as he spoke.

Stephanie explained the situation, and he nodded intermittently. Because of the gravity of the situation, he quickly signed on the dotted line. He didn't even ask her to swear on the bible, which was the usual protocol. Maybe he just forgot. Steph was relieved. As he showed her out, he smiled warmly. 'Well, good luck with it all. Do let me know how you get on, won't you?'

'Yes, of course. I hope you enjoy your dinner party. I shall think of you, when I tuck into my cheese and onion sandwiches later, sir.'

'I can always set another place?' The two laughed and bade their farewells.

Steph clip-clopped down the path and felt his eyes watching her. She put a bit of a wiggle on for him. She liked old-school gentlemen.

15

'I think of my wife, and I think of Lot,
and I think of the lucky break he got.'

William Cole.

Steve Aston paced the white-walled corridors of the Forensic Science Laboratory in Birmingham. Various people passed by, eyeing him suspiciously as a fresh face. The laboratory was a large room which had wall to ceiling windows and the scientists could be seen working inside. He peered through the glass window at them, at the large microscopes, indeterminate machinery, and masses of documents scattered around. The lights in the room were dazzling, but necessary for the minute attention to detail required by the examiners. It was this laboratory which dealt with handwriting analysis and typewriter comparison. When he had handed the *Evening Post* messages over to the receiver at the front desk, he had insisted that he wait for some sort of result. It was a vicarious insistence from Stark. The analyst had only been in the sealed room for an hour when she came out: a plain girl, with short black hair, in a bob, with misshapen teeth and glasses. Her dress was old-fashioned, a sort of woollen material with different shades of brown making an abstract pattern. It looked like her Mother's from the 1970's. She wore a wooden locket on a leather thong with a matching leather bracelet. All very ethnic. He guessed that, like himself, she was a vegetarian. She inexplicably took off her spectacles to speak.

'It's an Olympia portable typewriter. I can't seem to get any more details now, other than it looks like it's an old machine. I'd have preferred to have had a look before the ninhydrin test had been performed.'

Steve smiled. 'That's Ok, we don't expect miracles. I understand it being stained with a purple solution would be a hindrance, but a fingerprint would have been crucial to us, obviously. That's why we ninned it first. Is there anything else you can tell us about it?'

'Not really. I could hazard a guess that it was typed fairly quickly, maybe someone who had been trained, but that's my feel by the lightness of the ink on the paper. As I said to you, we need a typewriter to compare it with, to be able to say whether it was definitely that individual one.'

'That's OK. You've been helpful. It gives us a great start. We know what we are looking for, at least. Every little helps, as they say.'

This was Steve's idea of flirting. The lab technician was oblivious, of course.

'Glad to be of service. Send us some typewriters to compare the letters with, and we'll let you know one way or the other, very quickly.'

'Right, thanks very much. I think that's brilliant.' Steve stood there looking at the young woman. She looked puzzled.

'Right, well, is there something else you want?'

This, of course, was his cue to say 'Yes, your telephone number.' But of course, it never entered Steve's head. Settling instead for an awkward, thumbs up, and 'No, I've got everything, thanks.' And turning away to walk back towards reception.

He approached the receptionist. 'Can I use your telephone, please?'

*

Mark Winner answered the door to DC Ashley Stevens and Cynthia Walker. He was in tracksuit bottoms and a T shirt. Instinctively, Ashley placed his foot in the crook of the door to prevent it being closed. He explained the situation. 'Hello, Mark, we have a warrant to search your house. Don't worry about it; you're not the only ones this is happening to. All the group are being seen today. Unfortunately, someone else has been killed.'

Mark was puzzled. 'Hold on a minute. You've had a look around the house before, so what's the point in doing it again?'

'Because, as I've just said, there's been another murder.'

'I don't think it would be unreasonable to object, bearing in mind it's already been done.'

'I wouldn't advise saying no, Mark, but if you did, we would have to come in by force, which isn't likely to be in anyone's interest, I wouldn't have thought. I do understand you being narked about it, but it won't take too long.'

'What do you mean, you can come in anyway?'

'The warrant gives us the power to enter by force if necessary, so it's obviously better if we have your co-operation and prevent a scene.' Ashley was fully aware that Mark and all the group were suspects, and with the history between Jonathon and Caroline, he was not going away simply because Mark had the hump about it. He also thought it strange that he had not enquired about who had been killed, and all he seemed bothered about was the search.

'In that case, you'd better come in, although it's not really convenient.'

'I'm afraid it never is, Mark, but thank you for your co-operation.'

As they assembled in the hallway, Caroline came downstairs, in a dressing gown, obviously alarmed. 'He's dead, isn't he?'

'I'm afraid so, Caroline. Yes.'

Caroline collapsed on to the stairs, heaving sobs wracked her body. 'I knew it, I knew it.' She was thumping at the stairs with her clenched fist.

'What the bloody hell is going on? Who's dead? How does Caroline know?' There was anger in his voice.

'It's Jonathon Stacey. We think he's been murdered,' Ashley said.

'You *think* he's been murdered? Well has he, or hasn't he?'

'Yes, he has.' Ashley said solemnly.

Caroline looked up, tears streaming down her face. 'How was he killed?' she howled.

'A drug overdose, Caroline.' Cynthia said, walking over to her. She couldn't just stand and watch such distress, she wanted to try to console her.

'What's the matter with *you*?' Mark spoke unsympathetically to his wife, his agitation growing. 'You weren't like this when the others were killed, so what the hell's going on!'

'Just shut up, you...you...you heartless sod.' She continued to weep, despite Cynthia holding her hand, as they sat on the stairs.

Mark turned to Ashley and asked him. 'How does Caroline know about it?'

'I think you'd better ask her that one, Mark.'

'Caroline, I won't ask you again – what is going on?' Mark demanded. 'How do you know about it, and why are you in bits about it, for Christ' sake!'

Cynthia tried to placate him. 'There is no need to raise your voice, Mark, you know they have always been close friends. All of this has been a great strain. Let's just, all calm down, and go in the living room.'

'Don't tell me what to do in my own home.' He was pointing a finger at Cynthia and walked towards them. 'She's been a *fucking whore!*'

Ashley took hold of his arm. 'Oi! Just calm down, Mark. Or you're going to end up getting nicked. I mean it.'

Mark ripped his arm away from Ashley's grasp.

'*I will not calm down, until this whore starts giving me some answers! Have you been making a fool of me?*'

Caroline continued to sob. She couldn't make eye contact with him. 'You know what the answers are, you just won't accept them! I am not a whore.' She looked at him through her smudged mascara and screamed at Mark. '*Here's your fucking answer. I've been seeing Jonathon! Happy now? I loved him, and now he's dead. Happy?*' She put her head into the crook of her arm and cried.

Mark gritted his teeth, his anger spilling over; all rational thought gone. He drew back his fist, aiming for Caroline's head. He lashed out, but missed, and struck Cynthia on the shoulder, causing her to cry out.

Mark was aware of travelling backwards. Ashley had him by the throat, and Mark's journey through the air, ended abruptly, as he crashed against the wall. Mark was strong and fit, but he'd never been in a physical fight with a man. Ashley, poseur or not, had been involved in many, throughout his police career. He knew all the moves, headlocks, wrist locks, restraint holds, but he preferred the less formal, neck strangulation! Mark clawed at Ashley's hand to try to get a release. It was futile, and his eyes widened, as his attempts to draw in air, were failing.

'Mark, calm the fuck down! If you don't pack it in, you are going to get hurt! Are you listening?'

Mark was gurgling and couldn't speak. He nodded.

'When I release you in a couple of seconds, you had better behave yourself. I know this is a shock to you, but violence will only get you a prison cell. Agreed?'

He nodded again. He was going limp. Ashley gave him a bit of an extra squeeze for good measure, before releasing him, and then adjusting his sleeves and cufflinks. He straightened his tie and checked he hadn't creased his suit too badly. Mark fell to his knees and gasped for air. Eventually, he had taken in enough oxygen to speak, his voice rasping. 'You...you can't come in my house and assault me!'

'That's right. I suppose you think it's OK to assault my colleague here, while trying to kick the shit out of your wife? What do you expect me to do, buy popcorn?'

'She's been unfaithful.' He was getting tearful.

'So, it seems, but this ain't going to help your cause, now is it?' Ash turned to Cynthia. 'Do you want him nicking? Are you hurt?'

'No. I'm fine, leave it as it is. If he behaves.' Cynthia helped the sobbing Caroline into the living room. She started to calm down a little, and sat in an armchair, staring blankly at the carpet. Ashley and Mark followed them in. There was a lull, as everyone tried to process what was happening.

Ashley broke the silence. 'Look, the pair of you have a lot of sorting out to do, so the sooner we've finished here, the sooner you can start talking to each other.'

'There is nothing to sort out. As soon as you leave, Caroline will be out the door.' Mark said.

She didn't react.

Ashley explained the procedure to them. 'We will search the house, and any outhouses you have, and cars. If you kick off again, Mark, you will be arrested. I guarantee it. No second chances. Do you understand?'

He looked at the floor. 'Yes.'

'Good. Obviously, the search includes the two of you, so firstly we shall have to ask you to empty your pockets.' The two complied in silence. No pens were evident.

Ashley gave Mark the blue copy of the warrant, before beginning the search. Cynthia went upstairs, taking the sniffling Caroline with her, to avoid any further aggravation, and to mitigate any malicious allegations of theft, and the like. Ashley stayed downstairs with Mark. The two detectives searched every drawer, every cupboard, every crevice, every nook and cranny. It was over an hour and a half later, that they left empty-handed. Caroline had opted to stay in the house, despite an offer to leave with them. As soon as the door closed, the shouting started inside. Ashley made a mental note for a patrol car to check on them, in a short while, to make sure Caroline was all right.

'How are you?' Ashley asked his partner.

'Fine, he didn't catch me full on, I doubt there's even a mark.'

'That's good, I'm glad, let's hope he doesn't complain about the throating. Maybe, I should have nicked him. It just gets in the way of the murder enquiry, I guess.'

'You did ask me, and I said there was no need. I'm fine with it.' Cynthia put her hand on Ashley's forearm. 'I'm grateful for the intervention, it would have been much worse if you weren't there.' They reached the car.

'You're welcome. What did you make of Caroline's reaction? Do you think she was being a bit melodramatic?'

'Not really. It seemed genuine. Why do you?'

'I don't know. The wailing and shouting seemed a bit OTT, that's all. One thing we have learned is that Mark wasn't aware of her seeing Jonathon, if we are thinking about motive.'

'Yes. I think it was a genuine shock to him, so we ought to feed that back to the team, asking the question, why would he kill Jonathon, if he didn't know about the affair?'

*

Darkness shrouded the back of David Seaton's flat, where the straggly dead grass and lack of plants displayed his lacklustre gardening ability. There was a group of children playing at the front of the house. They could only have been ten or eleven years old, but the four-letter words they shouted at each other were indicative of the society they were forced to grow up in. The arrival of the suited strangers had caused some interest and they stood at the fence of Seaton's garden, standing on tiptoes, craning their necks to see what was happening. Nobby was aware of a large woman downstairs peeping out through the blinds at her window. He swung the sledgehammer back with some relish, at which point David Seaton answered the door, causing Nobby to stagger backwards slightly, still holding the sledgehammer above his shoulder. Seaton was aghast, and his mouth dropped open. 'What the-'

'Hello,' Nobby said cheerfully, allowing the heavy hammer to drop to the floor. 'We've been knocking for ages.'

'You were going to smash my door off with that, weren't you?'

'That was the general idea, yes.' Nobby said, smiling, the sledgehammer now resting at his side.

'Why?'

'We have a warrant here, David, to search your house, and without an answer, we enter by force. We've been knocking about five minutes. You didn't answer.'

'I thought it was the local kids messing around again. They're forever causing trouble and picking on me.'

'Anyway, thankfully, we've avoided a bit of damage.' Nobby said. 'Let's make a start, the sooner we start, the sooner we finish.'

'You're not coming in here, I'm afraid.'

Nobby glanced at Jim. 'Ah. Oh dear. You see, David, the problem is we've got the full weight of the law behind us...' He gave David his copy of the warrant. '...and unfortunately, whether you want us to come in or not; come in, is exactly what we will be doing, Mr Seaton.'

'Well, I'm terribly sorry and all that, but I'm afraid, I have no choice but to be resolute on this one, and it is just not convenient for you to come in right now. You're welcome to come back tomorrow.'

Nobby and Jim laughed. 'Oh, OK then, I mean if it's not convenient, give me a call when it is, and we'll drop by.'

Seaton sighed. 'OK, thank you.' He started to close the door. Nobby stepped inside, brushing the protesting Seaton out of the way, as if he wasn't there. 'Out the way, David.'

Seaton wasn't going to give in. What had been a minor irritant to Nobby, suddenly took on a different slant, when Seaton ran into the kitchen, produced a carving knife and yelled at the two men, raising the stakes considerably.

'Get out! Do you hear me, get the fucking hell out! I won't be bullied anymore. Do you hear me! Get out.'

Jim took a step behind his Detective Sergeant. This is a man with something to hide, thought Nobby. He pointed a finger at Seaton. 'Put that bloody thing down, you daft bugger. What's the matter with you? You've got nothing to worry about, have you? What's the problem?'

Seaton stammered his reply, the need to answer a question taking the edge off his aggression. 'I've got nothing to hide. I am just fed up with everything. My Stuart is dead. I've got nobody, now. And you march in here...' tears were welling up in his eyes as he spoke.

'Put it down, David. Let's have a chat. You're going to get hurt, mate.' Nobby spoke reasonably and calmly, an air of sympathy evident in his suggestion. He held out a hand for Seaton to give him the knife. David hesitated. Within a second Nobby grabbed his arm and twisted it down and then backwards forcing David to yelp and drop the knife as Nobby took him down to the ground with ease. Jim picked the knife up and put it in an exhibits bag for now, out of harms way.

Nobby got up off one knee and left David on the kitchen lino amongst the grease that had accumulated there. His head resting against the cooker. Nobby placed a comforting arm on his shoulder and grabbed his arm.

'Come on, get up, David. You're fine.'

David was pulled up, and he staggered sobbing into the living room. He sat on the arm of the settee; his head in his hands as he sobbed. Nobby glanced at Jim, who stifled a grin at the unlikely scene. 'It's all right, David. I know you're upset. Calm down. There's nothing to worry about. You're just getting out of your depth, my friend. You don't pull a knife on police officers, now do you?' He patted Seaton's back awkwardly, and he eventually started to regain his composure. Jim was stifling a giggle.

'I'm sorry. I'm just desperate. I don't know what to do, anymore. I can't go on living like this. It's wretched, truly wretched.'

'I'm sure it's all a bit much, but everything changes, David. This won't last forever, now will it. Things will get back to normal.'

He sniffed. 'I suppose.'

'I'll leave you two lovers to it.' Jim said. 'I've got a flat to search.'

Jim began to search the house, Seaton, still sniffling, followed him around like a lost sheep. When Nobby started to search as well, Seaton flitted between the two, protesting lamely, insistent that there was nothing to find, that it was an outrage. It was obvious to Nobby that this was the behaviour of someone who was hiding something. Nobby threw off a sheet, covering something on a table. It was a portable Olympia typewriter. The Detective Sergeant looked over at Seaton, who returned the stare. Nothing was said.

Jim opened a door. 'What's in here?'

'Nothing. It's just the airing cupboard, that's already been checked. Come on, I'm sorry I was misbehaving just now. Let me make you a nice cup of tea.'

Jim turned away from the cupboard. 'That's rather nice, thank you. Two sugars, David, please.'

David went into the kitchen, Jim following him, aware of the array of sharp implements in there, should David suddenly decide to throw a wobbler again.

Nobby moved over to the airing cupboard. Searching a house was a bit like 'hunt the thimble' only instead of clues as to whether you are 'hot' or 'cold', the closeness to discovery is commensurate to the amount of protesting the occupant does. He could feel heat on his face as he peered in, coming from the boiler. It was arid and dusty in there. He took out his mini-torch and shone it behind the copper cylinder. He could see a battered cardboard box jammed behind the pipes, and with some effort removed it. The contents were a revelation. Nobby removed several homosexual magazines; depicting men in various stages of full buggery and oral sex. He took out a scrapbook and opened it. Inside were newspaper cuttings of the coverage by the media of both James Deely's murder, and that of Stuart Millichip. More importantly, there were cuttings of the personal column message to 'baby darling', at the *Evening Post.*

'Bloody hell.' Nobby said. Also, in amongst the goodies, were letters that Stuart Millichip had sent to David, outlining explicit sexual favours they had performed together, in return for David giving Stuart money, to fuel his drug habit.

Seaton's heart sank, as he entered the room with the teas, Jim in tow, and saw Nobby rifling the box. Nobby looked up at him. 'Now I see why you didn't want us to search the place.'

Seaton put the mugs down. 'It's not what it looks like, honestly. I was having an affair with Stuart, fair enough. Surely that's not a crime?'

Nobby was sceptical. 'Not if it's in private, David, but what about these?' He displayed the scrapbook, with the newspaper articles and the cuttings of the personal column messages.

'I have an interest in the murder cases, don't I?'

'But what about the personal column messages? How do you know about these?'

'It was obvious they were connected, for heaven's sake!'

'If that is the case, why didn't you tell us about them?'

Seaton was rattled. 'You obviously knew about them, didn't you?'

'Yes, but you didn't *know* that we did, now did you?'

'Look, this is all a big misunderstanding. I'm sorry I didn't tell you about them, OK?'

'I think we had better have a chat back at the station, David.'

'No, please. Why there? We're OK here, aren't we?'

'I'm afraid not, David. You'd better come with us, eh?'

Seaton stepped backwards. 'Am I under arrest?',

'I haven't decided yet. What about the typewriter?'

'That's an old thing that's been around for years and I haven't used it for years either, for that matter.'

'Let's get to the nick and sort all of this out.'

'I'm not coming there. I couldn't bear to be locked up. I'd die.' He began breathing heavily and gasping for air.

'You leave me no option, David. I am arresting you on suspicion of murder.'

He cautioned him about his right to silence. Jim took hold of Seaton, and bustled him out of the flat, handcuffing him at the same time. Seaton was hyper ventilating as they walked him to the car. The portly neighbour, Mrs Roberts, came out her house. 'It's long overdue, the bloody pervert.' The children joined in the haranguing. 'Boo.', 'Pervert' and 'Homo', they shouted, as David ran the gauntlet.

Nobby had taken possession of the incriminating cardboard box. Other officers would have to return and complete the search. Seaton was silent. He was in a state of shock. He had been a fool.

*

Stark had listened to the tape for the umpteenth time. He would listen to a section and then stare, semi-comatose at the bland walls of his office. His mind kept being invaded by the memory of the altercation he had with John Davies, and the nastiness that lee Mole kept displaying towards him. What was his problem? What was Stark going to do about it? He tried to let the intrusive thoughts develop and then dismiss them from his mind. He was starting to get focus. He had separated Sammy's commentary; listening to the conversation the college friends were having at the wake, and then separately focusing on their actions and behaviours; picturing it in his mind. Realization dawned slowly, but it came.

He could hardly tap out Sarah Deely's telephone number; he was shaking with excitement, praying that she would be in, and respond to the call. Mercifully, within moments. Stark heard the somewhat despondent voice of Sarah. There was one main question he needed to ask her. His enthusiasm grew as he drew his conversation with Mrs Deely, to a close. '...so you definitely didn't get it then?'

'No, I was a bit surprised, to be honest. I only looked at them an hour ago, and when there wasn't one from them, I was a little disappointed, to say the least.'

'You're sure, you haven't misplaced it?'

'Positive.'

'Thank you very much, Sarah. I'll leave you in peace, now. You've been very helpful. Thanks again.' He put down the telephone, and pressed rewind on Sammy Trench's tape. Once more, he played the end bit. He nodded to himself. It was finally all coming together. 'It was staring me in the face all the time.' He now knew who it was. All he needed to do was confirm why. He had his suspicions, and the next call would tell him. He thumbed through his diary and found the number of the Coroner's office. He was smiling as he tapped out the digits; he had it sussed. After being put through to the third person in the office, he finally had a result.

'So, what does it say as cause of death?'

'Pneumonia, facilitated by acquired immune deficiency syndrome.'

'I knew it! Thank you very much.' He slammed the phone down and leaned back in his chair. He punched the air. 'Yes!'

It had turned out to be Stuart Millichip who had had the disease, but the killer couldn't have known that, only that it was one of the three.

'Screw you Detective Chief Superintendent frigging Davies!'

16

'I don't believe in an afterlife, although I
am bringing a change of underwear.'

Woody Allen

It wasn't a busy time in the custody suite at Nottingham Police Station; in fact, there was only a juvenile in the Detention Room at the time that David Seaton arrived. There were three female cells and twelve male cells to choose from. The uniformed sergeant – the 'Custody Officer' – was in his early thirties, with bright ginger hair. He stood behind an elevated desk, which was on a sort of stage, an array of clipboards were visible behind him; for safe keeping of all documents relating to all prisoners in each individual cell. To his right was a Perspex board with categories for each prisoner: name, custody number, time arrived at station, time detention would be reviewed by a senior officer, officer dealing with that prisoner, and any remarks.

The officer scribbled on to the custody sheet all details of David Seaton. He instructed him to take off his belt, take out his shoelaces and empty his pockets. Jim McIntyre donned disposable gloves and frisked him carefully to ensure there were no offending articles secreted anywhere. Jim finished what Seaton felt to be the degradation and then completed Seaton's ignominy by writing in large red letters in the remarks box of the Perspex 'runners and riders' board. 'CAUTION – SUSPECTED AIDS!'

Seaton was handed a piece of paper outlining his rights: To have someone informed of his detention; to consult a solicitor or legal representative: to read the Codes of Practice.

Seaton quickly gave his intimation. 'I want the lot!'

Nobby had been itching to get to a phone since they had brought Seaton in. He used the telephone in the privacy of the adjacent sergeant's office. After what seemed a long time, Stark answered.

'Stark.'

Nobby was excited and garbled down the phone. 'Hello, boss, it's Nobby. I've arrested David Seaton! Before you say anything, I didn't have any choice, he refused to come. But guess what? We've found a whole box of goodies hidden behind some pipes in his airing cupboard. There were gay porno mags, love letters from Stuart Milichip, indicating that Seaton was paying for sex off him, but more importantly, there were newspaper clippings about the murders and cuttings of the personal column letters to the Evening Post! As you know, we haven't released that to the public, and the piece de resistance was a portable Olympia typewriter hidden under a sheet on a table. I wasn't going to nick him at first, but he threw a right wobbler, picked up a knife and all sorts, so I couldn't very well leave him there. I had to nick him. What do you reckon? It looks as though we've finally got our man.'

'Bloody hell, Nobby. Take a breath, will you? That's very well done, mate; you are absolutely right to nick him, of course.'

'Thanks, boss. Shall I see you in the cell block, for the interview?'

'No, you and Jim crack on. I've got a little visit to make.'

'Eh? A little visit? But this is our man. This is the killer. What do you mean you've got a little visit to make? Surely we need to focus on Seaton?'

'You concentrate on him for now, Nobby, but I'm confident I know who the killer is, and I'm afraid it isn't Seaton.'

'You're joking?'

'Sorry mate. Have a chat with him about his relationship with Stuart, and about the various stuff you've seized. He had a motive perhaps to kill Stuart, but who is the person in the group who had the motive to kill all three?'

'Yes, who? So, who is it?'

'I need to make my little visit, first, Nobby, I just need to check something out first. Once I've confirmed it, Seaton can be released. See you later.' The line clicked off. Nobby still held the handset to his ear, mouth open, disbelief spreading across his features.

'Well, bugger me!'

*

Gary Sewell peeped through the net curtains at the stern-faced visitors. They saw his concerned face at the corner of the window and he reluctantly let them in. DI Stark and DPW Dawson removed their coats, and remained in the hall, despite Gary's invitation to go into the living room.

'Is Tracey in?' Stark asked.

Gary appeared to have a lead weight around his neck, but he still tried to be chirpy for appearance's sake. 'No. She's been out most of the day, Mr Stark. Can I be of help?'

Stark handed Gary the warrant and scrutinized his reaction to it. He decided to overemphasize the significance of it. 'I think you're aware that the magistrates don't give these out willy nilly, Gary...' Stark prevented Gary's response with a raised palm. '... Let me finish. All I will say is that you're not in trouble for keeping the secret to yourself, but it has to stop now, doesn't it?'

Gary paused momentarily, his eyes widened, and he swallowed deeply, his mouth dry with anguish. 'Yes,' he said.

'Now, are you sure Tracey isn't in the house?'

'Yes, I'm sure. She's not here, honestly. God knows where she is.'

Stark nodded to Steph, who briefly checked all the rooms and possible hiding places before the search proper, which would take place after they'd had a little chat with Gary. Stark stared out of the living room window, hands in pockets, silhouetted against the low-level winter sun shining into the room. He didn't speak for a while. After a short time, Steph came into the room with a sympathetic smile on her face. He quietly sat down. Stark turned and faced Gary, who bit into his fingernails, sitting cross-legged on the soft chair. "Softly, softly, catchee monkey" thought Stark. 'I suppose it's all a bit of a relief to you, Gary? Now that it's over.'

Gary bowed his head. 'Yes, I suppose it is.'

Stark continued, conscious that he must choose his words carefully, to keep Gary in an acquiescent frame of mind and not switch into him being more defensive.

'How long have you known, Gary?'

'I think almost from the first one, since James. Well, let's say I had an incline that it could be our Tracey.'

Steph sat quietly, she knew when to keep her mouth shut, Stark was doing the business.

'Did you discuss it with her, Gary?'

'Not at first. I mean how do you accuse your own wife of murder. I didn't want to believe it myself. I didn't want to hear those words, myself. Maybe I was in denial, or just stunned into what became a zombie like existence, just trying to get through each day, not allowing myself to go there in my mind. Hoping it might all go away.'

'It must have been really hard for you. But did you ever get to the place where you spoke with her about it?'

'Eventually, I dropped hints, told her that the killer would be caught soon unless he stopped, things like that.'

Steph realized that Gary had passed the Rubicon, so she felt comfortable enough to stand up, and speak briefly and quietly to Stark and to Gary. 'I'll make a start with the search and leave you in peace. Is there anything here I should know about Gary?'

'Um, not to my knowledge, but I wouldn't know for definite.'

'That's fine, I'll have a look around.' She smiled warmly and touched Gary's arm, as she left the room.

While Steph went upstairs to begin her search, Stark continued his 'chat'.

'Did she come home bloodstained from the killing of James

Deely?'

'No.'

'Didn't you see the stained clothing at all?'

'No.'

'Has she lost the clothing since then?'

'Don't get me wrong, maybe her clothing was blood-stained I'm just saying I didn't see it. Inspector.'

'So is the clothing in the house?'

'No, when I was doing my own bit of investigation, I tried to find the clothing to look for myself, but she has got rid of it. A pair of jeans, a brown coloured top and a thick black woolly jumper is missing. If I'm right.'

'She was obviously out of the house at the time of the Deely killing. Was she out of the house for both of the others?'

'Yes she was, of course.'

Stark shook his head as he sat down on the settee. He sighed. 'Why didn't you tell us about it, Gary? We could have prevented two murders, or at least Jonathon's death! You could have rung in, anonymously even.'

Gary's eyes welled up with tears. His sigh was jagged as he fought back his emotions. 'The last couple of years have been hell for us, Inspector. I mean desperation and depression to the depths of blackness. We didn't think we would ever recover from that place. We even talked about killing ourselves together. We got the knife ready and everything. It hit Tracey particularly hard, obviously. To lose our little daughter. Our precious little girl.' He broke down, crying. 'It drove her to murder, for God's sake. But to betray her, and tell you about it, to betray our little girl, and send her Mummy to prison for loving our little girl with all her heart. I couldn't bring myself to do it. I wanted to. I just couldn't do it. I'm sorry.'

'You could have saved at least one life, Gary.' He paused. Recriminations were not going to help anyone. 'I can't imagine the hell it must have been for you both. Would you say she is mentally ill?'

'Of course. We both must be. We've been desperate, manic,

we've even fought physically with each other, in our madness. No-one knows unless you've been through it. She's killed people, of course she's unbalanced, but she's all I've got.'

They both fell quiet. After a moment Gary continued. 'I'd say she has had a complete breakdown. I wouldn't make excuses for her, don't get me wrong, but what has happened; Sally I mean; has taken its toll on our sanity. Nothing makes any sense and all the normal boundaries don't exist anymore. I can't really explain it.'

'I understand, Gary. I get it.' He paused momentarily. 'So where is the evidence, other than you knowing about it, and her absence at the relevant time? What is here in the house?'

'Like I said, Inspector, the clothes have gone, but honestly I don't know that anything else is here. She's mad, but not stupid; I doubt there is anything here. I couldn't say for certain.'

Steph appeared in the doorway. 'I'm afraid that's not strictly true, Gary. Did you bring that bit of card, boss?'

Stark produced the piece of card that was supposedly Jonathon Stacey's 'suicide' note. It was sealed in a see-though plastic bag. Steph melodramatically produced a 'With deepest Sympathy' card from behind her back. 'Look what I've rescued from the wheelie bin!' Part of the card was soggy and dirty but it was otherwise intact, apart from the one section which had been torn off, and fitted the piece Stark had produced. Jonathon's suicide note was his condolence written into the college group card which Tracey *did not* give to Sarah Deely at the end of the wake.

It was Tracey's failure to give the sympathy card to Sarah, as highlighted on Sammy Trench's commentary, that had eventually alerted Stark to the possibility of Tracey being the killer. A few telephone calls literally fitted the pieces in the jigsaw together, relatively quickly. Steph was beaming, her need for discretion diminishing. She took hold of the piece of card and placed it against the sympathy card. Despite the sealed bag it was apparent that it fitted perfectly, this would be verified forensically, of course.

'The final piece of the jigsaw, so to speak.' Stark said to Gary.

He nodded. 'Will I be in trouble?'

'We'll see. It may be that the prosecution uses you to give evidence, instead of being a co-accused, as they won't admit your evidence if you are also charged. It's a tricky with the subsequent murders happening. It's too early to say, but we will get your account and take it from there. If you co-operate, you've got a chance. That's all I'll say.'

'I get it. I am genuinely sorry.' He looked despondent.

'I know.'

Stark radioed for others to come to the house to continue the search and speak further with Gary. He also put those doing observations at the *Evening Post* offices on high alert. He had a hunch where Tracey might be, and he wanted to get to her, before she knew they were on to her. It was time for the whole sorry affair to be ended. It was time for Tracey to see the inside of a cell.

*

'I keep asking, sir; where the hell are we going?' Steph was driving.

'Just humour me, Steph, turn left here.' Stark said.

'The cemetery?'

'Just do as I ask, Steph. Bear with me.'

The local graveyard was a huge complex, with a mini-road system of its own. The main 'ring road' had ornate streetlamps, generously spaced out along the way, some dedicated to loved ones, long since gone to the hereafter. Numerous tributary paths fanned out from the main thoroughfare, branching out to the thousands of graves, shadowy in the light given off by the headlamps of the detective's car.

Stark instructed Steph to drive slowly around the main drive, while he stared out into the diminishing light of the cemetery. Dusk was playing tricks with his eyes; shadows of graves and trees gave off the appearance of being people. Occasionally he would hit the jackpot and see a mourner, and be able to focus on an individual, mainly elderly people, in the murky glow. A mist was starting to descend, adding to the already eerie atmosphere that graveyards always engender.

'*There look!*'

Steph jumped at Stark's unexpected shout. 'Christ, sir! You frightened me to bloody death!'

'Sorry Steph.' He laughed as he pointed over to the right-hand side. Steph pulled over and as she craned her neck, she could see the huddled figure of Tracey Sewell, sitting about fifty yards away, on a small perimeter wall.

Tracey had her arms folded and was rocking gently backwards and forwards, a large shopping bag by her side. Her damp hair straggled over her face, which appeared strained, grimacing and creased with anxiety. Her coat was open over a thin T-shirt and miniskirt that barely covered her midriff. She did not appear to notice their arrival.

Stark opened the car door, as did Steph. He touched her arm. 'Wait here, there's no need for us both to go.'

'Are you sure, boss?'

'Yes, in this case, three might just be a crowd. Keep us in view though, but I'll do this alone.'

'OK, you're the boss.'

Stark got quietly out of the car and Steph, somewhat reluctantly obeyed his instructions. She took the added precaution of requesting a back-up vehicle to remain in a nearby street, outside the cemetery. Tracey might be a woman, but she had managed to kill three men with ingenuity and guile. Steph did not want there to be a fourth.

Stark walked slowly towards the hunched figure. He felt calm, yet alert. He pulled the collar of his overcoat up, to shield him from the chilly air, worsened by the slight wind sweeping across the bleak surroundings. As Stark drew closer, Tracey stopped rocking, but she did not look up to acknowledge his presence. He sat down on the wall next to her, just arms-length away. He didn't want her to feel threatened. He didn't speak. He peered at the gravestone opposite them, where he could just make out the inscription in the gloom.

Sally Anne Sewell, born 25th January 1984
Taken from us 4th August 1987
Beloved daughter of Tracey and Gary
Too young to go, happy in Heaven

After a short time, Stark said. 'Hi, Tracey.'

She didn't answer.

'How long have you been here? You must be freezing; do you want my coat?'

Tracey remained silent. Stark could hear the distant hum of the CID car engine.

'The grave is beautiful, Tracey. I'm sorry, love.' They sat a while longer, neither speaking, Tracey intermittently sniffing and wiping her nose with a handkerchief.

She spoke in a whisper, her voice sounded hoarse, it was too quiet for Stark to make out what she said.

'Sorry, Tracey?'

She cleared her throat. 'I said, I wondered how long it would take you.'

'You must have known this day would come, Tracey.'

'Oh, yes, I knew all right. It doesn't make things easier though, does it?'

'No.' Stark agreed. There was more silence. Stark blew into his hands to relieve the encroaching numbness.

'You should have brought some gloves. You obviously aren't practised at sitting by graves.'

'Thankfully not. You're right.' There was another pause, before Stark spoke again. 'I think I know why, Tracey, but all three of them?'

'We were so happy, Gary and me. For once, we had something, you know. Something money can't buy, something, *somebody* who was mine, that had been created out of love. God, I was happy. We did all those crazy stupid things couples do. Gary did the nursery up. I bought clothes – neutral colours. I didn't care what sex it was, but I knew, secretly, I knew it was a girl.' She clenched her fists and screamed: *'I should have known what would happen. I should have fucking known!'* Her voice tailed off. She whispered, 'Sorry Sally. I don't want to wake you up. Sorry, baby darling.' Stark grimaced at the sadness of her mania. She seemed distant, disturbed.

Stark warned her. 'You don't have to tell me all this. I can tell a court what you are saying, Tracey, love.' It was a sort of caution. It didn't seem appropriate to do the formal one. Who knew if it would suffice?

'I'll tell a court myself. The truth needs to be told. Just give me a few more minutes here, please.'

'Sure, there's no rush.'

They both fell silent for a little while.

'As soon as I heard that first cry, I knew it was a girl. Sally Anne Sewell. I had the name in my head for months. It wasn't easy. God knows it wasn't the paradise I had envisaged. Jesus! It was tough.' She laughed. *'What a fucking joke that was!'* She closed her eyes tightly. 'Sorry...' She addressed the grave, not Stark. She sighed. 'I should have known when she had her first cold. Every kid has them, no problem, we coped. It was all good. Just another thing. It seemed to go away for a little while, and she got a bit better, but then another, and another, and more and more illnesses. Each time, it seemed to take her longer to recover. We ended up in A & E that many times, but I sensed it was more than just colds. Something more sinister. You know what the Doctor said?'

'No.'

'He just laughed. Cocky bastard. "They all go through it" he said. Prat. I had to kick up a stink, until the Registrar came to see me. He examined Sally at my insistence. He examined her, looked down her throat and all that shit. His face changed, when he saw the inflammation at the back of her mouth and gums, yellow and swollen. Foul it was. Poor mite. I had to wait in a side room for more than two hours. Then he came poncing back in.' She rubbed her nose with the sleeve of her coat. 'Had I considered an AIDS test, he said, and one for Sally too? Well. I just went berserk. I shouted and screamed at the mere suggestion. What did he think I was? A whore? A druggy? He just stood there with his puny little arms folded. They brought a nurse in with tea, all very cosy. They were whispering, and then he came smarming over in his white coat. He asked me everything, and I mean everything. Personal things, you know. About me and Gary. It was obvious I wasn't a druggy, and I had only had sex with three people before I married Gary...'

'James Deely, Stuart Millichip and Jonathon Stacey.' Stark said sombrely.

'Gary was the obvious choice. He'd been with a few women before me, but when all the test came back, he was negative, and I was HIV positive! Me! My world fell away. My soul peeled away in that moment. It was me! I had given my baby, my poor baby darling, I had given her AIDS!' Tracey covered her face in her hands and sobbed. She groaned and wailed, her heart breaking. She jumped up, startling him.

'Don't come near me. Don't touch me!' She had a wild look in her eye and was smiling in a strange way, that wasn't a smile, but contorted grief.

Steph, looking on attentively, pulled at the door handle of the car, and opened it slightly, ready to intervene if necessary.

Tracey put her face close to Stark's. *'You see I'm dirty. I'm unclean. Infected, a fucking leper!'*

'OK sit down, love. You are just someone with an illness, you aren't a leper. No one thinks that.'

She sat down again, as suddenly as she got up; all her energy seemingly sapped from her, by the outburst.

She let out a whimper. Then shrugged out a laugh. 'Sally had got full-blown AIDS, the poor little baby. What did she know about anything? She was innocent. But that was it you see. It wasn't *me* who had given it her.' She shook her head, her teeth gritted. 'It was *them*; one of those dirty *bastards!*'

She again wiped her seeping nose across her sleeve. She was

staring straight ahead, remembering the awful moments that had led to this encounter with DI Stark. 'I made a decision there and then. No drama. It was calm, it was calculated, it was just a decision, that's all. It *would* happen and it did. I was determined to punish him. Determined to get him. I didn't know which one it was, of course, so it would have to be all of them. Then I would be sure. You see I promised, Sally, didn't I darling?'

Stark shifted in his seat. It was cold and getting darker; the mist thickening, adding to the gloom of the whole wretched scenario.

'I know what you're thinking. I'm as much to blame. Why let them do it without a condom?'

'I'm genuinely not thinking that, far from it.' Stark said.

'Who'd heard of AIDS a few years ago? We thought it was just a gay thing. None of us straight people knew much about it, when we were at college. I was on the pill. I thought I was safe. Everyone does it. It wasn't me. I couldn't have known. You understand, don't you?'

'Yes. Of course, it wasn't your fault, Tracey, how could you possibly know? Don't be silly.'

'Not you. Sally. She hears me, don't you darling? I stayed with her every single hour till the end. We talked it through. She and I. Planned it all, and then the nurse left the drug trolley, to take a phone call, and that was when I got the morphine. Dead easy. It was a sign, don't you see? God saying that it was all right. It was the right thing to do.'

Stark was worried that Tracey might be reluctant to repeat this in custody, once she'd got it off her chest. Maybe it was all academic, she was clearly unhinged, maybe she would be sectioned and detained indefinitely? Still, he couldn't assume that. 'Come on Tracey, let's get back into the warmth.'

'Sally died on the 4th August. 11.56pm. I knew she was going. I was helpless. I just cuddled her, and I felt her go. I felt her soul leave her body. I felt her life pass through my hands, and she turned into a little china doll. People don't believe me, but it's true. I kissed her little cold nose. I died that night too. I didn't want to live, anyway. What did I want to live for? But why should *they*? Why should *they* live? They had killed an innocent child. My innocent child. You tell me why they should live? Come on. Tell me.'

'I wouldn't dream of it. I can't begin to imagine it, Tracey.'

'You're right. You can't. Hate is just as strong as love, you know. It takes over you, and lives inside you, telling you what you must do.' The vacant expression swept over her face again. 'Must do it.'

'How come Gary hadn't got AIDS?' Stark asked.

'This is it; you see, we don't understand it. Even you don't understand it. Blokes only get it from a woman if they have a cut in the wrong place, when having sex, it could then transfer. That's nothing to do with this anyway. I killed James. I killed him with a hatred you wouldn't believe, ripping through his throat was ecstasy to me, the bastard. And Stuart, he was even easier, I just used one of the compound cars from work. They are always getting vandalised, so no-one thought anything of it. In fact, I think it was you, no another detective, DS Clarke? Who was at my house when I got a phone call from work about "the bloody kids again" causing damage.'

'Of course.'

'Who was it? Jonathon?' She asked.

'Who, what?'

'Who was the one with AIDS?'

Stark hesitated but told her anyway. 'Stuart.'

'Bastard! Gay bastard!' Murdering, arse fucking, bastard!'

'Tracey, come on, love. It's over. You need some help.' He stood up.

'Just give me a minute, please. I need to say goodbye to Sally.'

'No more than a minute.' He walked a few yards away, and sat on a bench, keeping his eyes on her. He watched as she hugged the head stone and kissed it.

He sighed.

Steph could see Stark standing a few feet away from Tracey as she clawed at the headstone. 'Come on, boss. Bloody hell, what are you playing about at?'

'Goodbye, my darling, see you soon.' She said, kissing the marble stone. She reached into her shopping bag. Stark saw a flash of steel. 'What the hell?' He stood rooted to the spot.

Tracey held the knife in front of her. She was trembling.

'What are you doing Tracey?' Stark said calmly, despite his heart beating ten to the dozen. 'Come on, love, put that down. It's over, darling.'

'Don't you *darling* me.'

She put the knife to her wrists.

Steph had kicked off her shoes as she exited the car and the grass was squelching beneath her feet as she ran in an arc to approach Tracey from behind.

Stark could see Steph approaching Tracey at a fair pace in his peripheral vision but forced himself not to look and give Tracey a clue what was happening.

'Tracey. Wait!' He said.

'Why? It's over. I want to be with Sal-'

She didn't finish the word as Steph charged into the back of her. She had never done a rugby tackle before, but she seen them on telly, so she knew the basics. She hit Tracey with considerable force and her face crashed into the gravel path and the knife went flying. Stark joined the mess of arms and legs rolling about on the floor. He ripped the handcuffs from the belt at the small of his back.

He quickly got them on Tracey.

Her eyes were wide as she gasped for air with the weight of the two officers on her. She was dazed from the impact.

'Now it's over, Tracey.' Stark said.

He lifted her to her feet, the cuffs on her hands behind her back.

'Are you all right, Steph?' Stark asked, trying to catch his breath.

'No, I'm bloody not; I've laddered my tights!'

*

Stark lit up a cigar, as he stood with Steph outside the cell block. The air was a bit chilly around her legs as she had now disposed of the torn stockings. Nobby wouldn't be pleased. It had been a tiring day and quite traumatic to say the least.

'All's well that ends well, boss.'

'I guess so. I'm glad we got the basic confession down on tape. I know it was a pain, but just a quick interview to capture her version, puts my mind at ease.'

'Definitely. I couldn't agree more. I wouldn't have slept unless we got her to repeat what she told you at the grave side.'

'We can do a more detailed one tomorrow. Wagstaff and Davies are appeased at least. I just need to think about what I am going to do about that shithead Lee Mole. He's getting fucking dangerous. It's no longer a joke. I'd love to know what his problem is.'

'Just jealousy, sir. We've got to be careful that we don't get drawn into it and become like him. We need to rise above it.'

'You're probably right, but I just want to chin the prat.'

'So, do I!' She laughed, as did Stark.

'He wouldn't stand a chance from what I've seen in the last couple of hours!'

Steph laughed.

Stark puffed on his cigar.

'The whole thing is pretty tragic isn't it? With Tracey, I mean.' Steph said.

'Of course, it is. I think we need to get her assessed for her mental state. She is clearly unhinged, poor sod. Whether it's enough to make her unfit to plea, is a matter for the experts. We will see.'

'It, kind of, doesn't matter, I suppose.' Steph said.

'No, not really, but I want Gary Sewell nicking. Now we have a confession from her. If he had done the right thing, Jonathon at least, would still be alive, regardless of the circumstances. Now there is enough evidence for Tracey, without having to use him as a witness, he can be a co-accused for withholding information. He needs to get what is coming to him.'

'I'm glad about that. I don't know about you, boss, but I could do with a drink. Problem is, there is word of an indecent assault coming in, or possible rape in Bulwell. They are checking it out.'

'Screw that, let night crime deal with it. We'll pick it up in the morning if it's legit. Let them get the full story first. Where are the lads, do we know?'

'They're at the Horse and Groom, at Linby.'

'Let's go and join them, I owe them a pint for all their hard work.'

'That reminds me, sir. Nobby left a message in the cell block asking if it's OK to let David Seaton go?'

Stark laughed. 'Shit. I forgot about him. I suppose it would be rude not to. Pint first, though.'

Stark put his arm around Steph as they walked to the car and she reciprocated.

*

The following day was busy. Sorting all the paperwork out, the press, and the senior officers suddenly re-associating themselves with the case, now it had been a success. Stark sat in his office and saw the headlines of the first edition of the *Evening Post*:

'*Evening Post catch killer*'.

Stark smiled to himself. He picked up the telephone.

'Amanda Bolton.'

'Hello, Amanda, It's Dave Stark, the DI from Nottingham CID.'

'I know who Dave Stark is.' There was a smile in her voice. She spoke so eloquently. He could imagine her at her desk.

'I promised I would let you know if we got anywhere with the murder investigation.'

'I can see from the Evening Post that they have solved it for you.'

He laughed. 'Absolutely. That's the press for you. Anyway, I guess you know the details. Tracey Sewell is in custody and has admitted her involvement in all three murders.'

'Excellent. Well, done, Inspector.'

'Erm, thanks.'

'Might it be an idea to meet up for lunch just to go through the finer details?' Amanda suggested.

'OK, when do you have in mind?'

'I thought tomorrow, if you are able.'

Stark hesitated slightly. 'OK fine, I'll pick you up from the college at around one o'clock.'

'Sounds perfect. See you then.'

The phone went dead. Stark smiled, but this turned into a frown. It was all perfectly innocent, wasn't it? Just business, that's all.

THE END

Follow the author on Twitter *@Keithwwright.*

Visit his web-page: *Keithwrightauthor.co.uk*

If you enjoyed this novel the author would appreciate a brief *review or star rating* on Amazon or Goodreads.

Printed in Great Britain
by Amazon

43979260R00169